Edwardson, Åke.

EDW

Room no. 10

DUE DATE   25.99

ALSO BY ÅKE EDWARDSON

THE CHIEF INSPECTOR ERIK WINTER NOVELS:

Sail of Stone

The Shadow Woman

Death Angels

Frozen Tracks

Never End

Sun and Shadow

Room No. 10

Åke Edwardson

TRANSLATED BY RACHEL WILLSON-BROYLES

Simon & Schuster

New York   London   Toronto   Sydney   New Delhi

Simon & Schuster
1230 Avenue of the Americas
New York, NY 10020

Copyright © 2005 by Åke Edwardson
English language translation copyright © 2013 by Rachel Willson-Broyles
and Åke Edwardson
Originally published in Swedish in 2005 by Norstedts Förlag as *Rum Nummer 10*

First Simon & Schuster hardcover edition March 2013

SIMON & SCHUSTER and colophon are registered trademarks of Simon &
Schuster, Inc.

For information about special discounts for bulk purchases, please contact
Simon & Schuster Special Sales at 1-866-506-1949 or business@simonandschuster.com.

The Simon & Schuster Speakers Bureau can bring authors to your live event.
For more information or to book an event contact the Simon & Schuster Speakers
Bureau at 1-866-248-3049 or visit our website at www.simonspeakers.com.

Designed by Akasha Archer

Manufactured in the United States of America

10   9   8   7   6   5   4   3   2   1

Library of Congress Cataloging-in-Publication Data
Edwardson, Åke.
  [Rum Nummer 10. English]
  Room no. 10 /Åke Edwardson; translated by Rachel Willson-Broyles.—1st Simon &
Schuster hardcover edition
     p. cm.
1. Winter, Erik (Fictitious character)—Fiction. 2. Detectives—Sweden—Fiction.
3. Murder—Investigation—Fiction. 4. Sweden—Fiction. I. Willson-Broyles, Rachel.
II. Title.
  PT9876.15.D93R8613 2013
  839.73'74—dc23 2012022527

ISBN: 978-1-4516-0852-6
ISBN: 978-1-4516-0855-7 (ebook)

To my father, Karl-Erik

Warm thanks to Chief Inspector Torbjörn Åhgren, who read the whole manuscript and had valuable opinions, and equally warm thanks to Chief Inspector Lars Björklund for his help through the years.

Room No. 10

I

The woman's right eye was blinking. One, two, three, four times. Chief Inspector Erik Winter closed his eyes. When he opened them again he saw that the blinking continued, like a spastic movement, like something alive. Winter could see the August light reflected in the woman's eye. The sun sent a ray through the open window. Winter could hear the morning traffic down on the street; a car passed, a streetcar clattered in the distance, a seabird screeched. He heard steps, a woman's heels against the cobblestones. She was walking quickly; she had someplace to go.

Winter looked at the woman again, and at the floor under her. It was made of wood. The ray of sunlight carved its way through the floor like fire. It continued through the wall, into the next room, maybe through all the rooms on this floor.

The woman's eyelids trembled a few more times. Take away those damn electrodes now. We know now. He moved his eyes away from her. He saw the curtains in the window billow from a slight breeze. It brought with it the scents of the city as well as the sounds. The smell of gas, the oil perfume. The salty scent of sea, he could smell it. He thought suddenly of the sea, and of the line of the horizon, and of what lay beyond. Of journeys, he thought of journeys. Someone said something in the room, but Winter didn't hear. He was still thinking of journeys, and of how he would have to go off on a journey through this woman's life. A journey backward. He looked around in the room again. This room.

The desk clerk had been on an errand to the room; it was still unclear why.

He had rushed up to her.

He had called from there, on his cell phone.

The county communications center had sent an ambulance and a patrol car to the hotel. The police car had driven the wrong way on a one-way street. All the streets were one-way in the old neighborhoods south of Central Station.

The two detectives, a man and a woman, had been shown to the room on the third floor by a woman who looked very frightened. The desk clerk had been waiting outside. The door had been open. The police saw the body on the floor. The desk clerk had explained in a thin voice what he'd seen. His gaze had searched its way into the room, as though it belonged there. One of the police officers, the watch commander, the woman, had quickly gone into the room and knelt next to the body, which lay in an unnatural position on the floor.

The noose was still pulled tight around her throat. There was an overturned chair a meter from her head. There was no life in her face or in the ruptured eyes. The commander felt for a pulse that didn't exist. She looked up and saw the beam that crossed the ceiling. It looked strange, medieval. The whole room looked medieval, like something from another world, or from a film. The room was neat, aside from the overturned chair. She could hear the ambulance howling through the open window now; first from far off and then loudly and brutally as it slowed down on the street. But it was a meaningless sound.

She looked at the woman's face again; her open eyes. She looked at the rope, at the chair. At the beams up there. It was a long way up.

"Call forensics," she said to her colleague.

The forensics team had come. Winter had come. The medical examiner had come.

Now the examiner was taking away the two electrodes she had stuck next to the woman's right eye. There was nothing she could fix here anymore, but she could try to determine how long the woman had been dead. The closer she was to the moment of death, the stronger the contractions of her muscles. The moment of death, Winter thought. It's a strange phrase. That is a strange method.

The medical examiner looked at Winter. Her name was Pia Eriksson Fröberg. They had been working together for nearly ten years, but to Winter it sometimes felt as if it had been twice as long. That might be a result of the crimes, or of something else.

"Six to eight hours," said Fröberg.

Winter nodded. He looked at his watch. It was quarter to eleven. The woman had died in the early morning, or late at night if one preferred. It had been dark outside.

He looked around the room. The three forensics technicians were working with the chair, with the beam, with the floor around the woman, with the few other pieces of furniture that were in the room, with everything that might yield clues. If there were any. No, not if. A perpetrator always leaves something behind. Always. If we don't believe that, we might as well pack up and head out into the sunshine.

The flash from the camera caused the room to take on a different light at uneven intervals, as though the sun outside also wanted to be a part of the action in here.

If there is a perpetrator. He looked up at the beam. He looked at the woman on the floor again. He looked at the overturned chair. One of the technicians was working with the surface, the surface for sitting. Or for standing. He looked up at Winter and shook his head.

Winter looked at the woman's right hand. It was painted white, bright white, snow white. The paint was dry; it extended halfway up to her elbow. It looked like a grotesque glove. White paint. There was a can on the floor, on a sheet of newspaper, as though the most important thing in this room was to protect the floor. More important than life.

There was a paintbrush on the sheet of newspaper. The paint had run out a little bit, over a photograph that depicted a city in a foreign country. Winter recognized the silhouette of a mosque. He could smell the paint when he stood nearby, when he knelt.

There was a sheet of paper on the room's only table.

•   •   •

The letter was handwritten and barely ten lines long. Maybe she'd
written it somewhere else. There were no pads of paper, no pens in
the hotel room. Room number ten. The numbers were made of gilded
brass; they hung from the door on a nail. The third floor of four. Inside, a scent lingered after the window had been closed. It was sweet,
but that word has many implications.

Winter picked up the copy of the letter from his desk and studied
the handwriting again. He couldn't tell whether her hand had shaken
as she wrote her last words, and he hadn't yet been able to compare
them with other words, with other writing by her. They had sent
everything to SKL, the national forensics lab—the letter and other
things the woman had evidently written.

I love you both and I will always love you no matter what happens
to me and you'll always be with me wherever I go and if I've made you
angry at me I want to ask for your forgiveness and I know that you'll
forgive me no matter what happens to me and no matter what happens to you and I know that we will meet again.

That's where she had put the first period. Then she had written
the next lines and then it had happened. No matter what happens
to me. It was repeated two times in the letter to her parents, written
with what Winter thought was a steady hand, even if the technicians
thought they saw tremors under a microscope.

The hand that she'd used to write the letter that Winter held in his
own hand. He looked at it. He couldn't see it shaking, but he knew
that it could be. He was still human, after all. Her white hand. A perfect painting. Or a hand made of plaster. Something that no longer
belonged to her. That might as well be removed. That's what he had
thought of. He wondered why. Had someone else thought the same
thing?

Her name was Paula Ney and she was twenty-nine years old and
in two days she would have turned thirty, on September 1. The first
day of fall in Sweden. She had her own apartment, but she hadn't

been living there the past two weeks because the landlord was reno-
vating and the workmen went from apartment to apartment and
then back again; one hour here, one hour there, and the renovation
was going to take a very long time. She had moved back to her parents' house.

Early yesterday evening she went to the movies with a friend and
after the show they each had a glass of red wine at a bar in the vicinity of the theater and then they parted at Grönsakstorget. From there,
Paula would take the streetcar, she had said, and that's where the
traces of her stopped until she was discovered in the room at Hotel
Revy the next morning, one and a half kilometers east of Grönsakstorget. There was no streetcar that passed Revy. It was a strange name.

The hotel was also strange, as though it had been left behind from a
worse time. Or a better one, according to some. It was in the dense
neighborhood south of Central Station, in one of the buildings that
had survived the demolitions of the sixties. Five blocks had survived,
as though this particular part of the city had been in the shadows
when the city planners had studied the map, maybe during a picnic in
Trädgårdsföreningen just across the canal.

Revy had been there for a long time, and before that a restaurant
had been there. It was gone now. And the hotel stood completely in
the shadow of the Sheraton on Drottningtorget. There was some sort
of symbolism in that.

Revy had also had a reputation for being a brothel. It was probably its proximity to Central Station and the great turnover of guests
of both sexes. Most of that was over now; the rumors and the reality.
Winter knew that the trafficking team took a look at the place sometimes, but not even the whores and the johns were at home in the
past. Maybe the owner had been charged with pimping one time too
many. God knows who stayed there now. Hardly anyone. The room
they had found Paula Ney in had been empty for three weeks. Before
that, an unemployed actor from Skövde had stayed there for four
nights. He had come to the city to audition for a television series but

hadn't gotten the role. Just a small role, he had said on the phone with Winter's colleague Fredrik Halders: I was going to play dead.

Winter heard a knock and looked up. Before he had time to say anything, the door opened and Chief Inspector Bertil Ringmar, third in rank in the homicide unit, stepped in through the door and closed it behind him and walked quickly through the room and sat down on the chair in front of Winter's desk.

"Please come in," said Winter.

"It's just me," said Ringmar, pushing the chair closer. It scraped against the floor. He looked at Winter. "I went up to Öberg."

Torsten Öberg was a chief inspector, like Winter and Ringmar, and he was the deputy chief of the forensics unit on the floor above the homicide unit.

"And?"

"He was working on someth—"

The telephone on Winter's desk rang and interrupted Ringmar in the middle of his sentence. Winter lifted the receiver.

"Erik Winter here."

He listened without saying anything else, hung up, stood.

"Speak of the devil. Öberg wants to see us."

"It's hard to hang someone else," said Öberg. He was leaning against one of the workbenches in the laboratory. "Especially if the victim is fighting for his life." He gestured toward the objects on the counter. "But it's difficult even without resistance. Bodies are heavy." He looked at Winter. "That goes for young women, too."

"Did she fight?" Winter asked.

"Not in the least."

"What happened?"

"That's your job, Erik."

"Come on, Torsten. You had something for us."

"She never stood on that chair," said Öberg. "From what we can tell, no one has ever stood on it." He rubbed the bridge of his nose.

"Did the desk clerk say that he jumped up and grabbed hold of the end of the rope?"

Winter nodded.

"He never climbed up on the chair?"

"No. It tipped over when the body fell."

"She has a wound on her shoulder," said Öberg. "She could have gotten it then."

Winter nodded again. He had spoken with Fröberg.

"The desk clerk, his name was Bergström, Bergström got hold of the end and pulled down as hard as he could and the knot came loose."

"Sounds like he knew what he was doing," said Öberg.

But he hadn't had any idea, he had said to Winter during the first short interrogation in a small, nasty-smelling room behind the lobby. He had only acted. Instinctively, he had said. Instinctively. He wanted to save lives.

He hadn't recognized the woman, not then, not later. She hadn't checked in; she wasn't a guest there.

He had seen the letter, the sheet of paper. The suicide note—he had realized what it was the second before he took action. Someone who was tired of life. He had seen the chair standing under her, but also the end of the rope, and he had thrown himself forward and up.

"That chair has been carefully cleaned," said Öberg.

"What do you mean by that?" Winter asked.

"If she wanted to hang herself, first she would have had to climb up on the chair and tie the rope around the beam," said Öberg. "But she didn't stand on that chair. And if she did, someone wiped it off afterward. And it wasn't her."

"We understand that," said Ringmar.

"It's a smooth surface," Öberg continued. "She was barefoot."

"Her shoes were by the door," said Ringmar.

"She was barefoot when we got there," said Öberg. "She died barefoot."

"No clues on the chair," Winter said, mostly to himself.

"As you gentlemen know, the lack of clues is as interesting as clues themselves," Öberg said.

Winter could see that Öberg was proud, or something like that. He had something to tell them.

"There are no fingerprints on the rope, but I forewarned you of that, didn't I?"

"Yes," Winter answered, "and I'm not unfamiliar with nylon rope."

The rope was blue, an obscene blue color that recalled neon. The rough surface seldom captured any prints from fingers. It was hardly even possible to tell whether someone had been wearing gloves.

But there were other clues. Winter had seen the technicians working in room ten. They carefully swabbed the rope for traces of saliva, strands of hair, sweat. It was very difficult not to leave some trace of DNA behind.

A person who wore gloves might have spit on the glove.

Brushed back his hair.

But it wasn't impossible to go free. Winter tried to keep a cool head these days, when the DNA dream of solving and resolving every crime could be a pipe dream, a daydream.

He knew that Öberg had sent all the tests to SKL.

"Gert found something more," said Öberg, and there was a flash in one of his eyes. "Inside the knot of the noose."

"We're listening," said Winter.

"Blood. Not much, but enough."

"Good," said Ringmar. "Very good."

"One of the tiniest flecks I've seen," said Öberg. "Gert loosened the knot, and because he is a thorough man, he took a thorough look."

"I didn't see any blood in that room," said Winter.

"None of us saw any blood," said Öberg. "And above all, not on the woman." He turned to Winter. "Has Pia found any small cuts on her body?"

"No. At least not yet."

"So if the rope isn't Paula Ney's . . ." Ringmar said.

". . . then it's someone else's," Öberg supplied, and his eye flashed again.

"I talked to Paula's parents an hour ago," Ringmar said; he moved his chair back half a meter, and the sound was louder now. They were back in Winter's office. Winter felt a warmth, like the beginning of a fever. Ringmar moved his chair again; it scraped again.

"Can't you lift up the chair?" Winter said.

"But I'm sitting in it!"

"What did they say? The parents?"

"She hadn't seemed different on the last night, or the afternoon. Or the week before. Just irritated at the workmen, or the landlord. That's what they said, anyway. The parents. Or the mom, rather. I spoke to her mom. Elisabeth."

Winter had also spoken to her, yesterday afternoon. He had spoken with her husband, Paula's father. Mario. He had come to Sweden at a very young age and found work at SKF, the ball bearing factory. Many Italians had found work there.

Mario Ney, Paula Ney. Her purse had been on the bed in the hotel room. Until now, Öberg and his colleagues had not found out whether anyone had gone through the contents in the purse. There was a wallet with a debit card and some cash. No driver's license, but a gym membership card from Friskis & Svettis. Other little things.

And a pocket with four photographs, the kind that are taken in photo booths. They looked recent.

Everything in that bag indicated that it belonged to Paula Ney, and that it was Paula Ney who had been hanged in the dark hotel room that only let in a thin streak of sun at a time.

"When would Paula have moved back to the apartment?" Winter asked.

"Sometime in the future, as she put it."

"Did she say that? Did her parents say that she said that?"

"It was the dad who said it, I guess. I asked the mom."

Winter held up the letter, a copy of the letter. The words were the same as in the original. Those ten lines. Above them: "To Mario and Elisabeth."

"Why did she write this? And why to her parents?"

"She didn't have a husband," said Ringmar.

"Answer the first question first," said Winter.

"I don't have an answer."

"Was she forced to?"

"Absolutely."

"Do we know that she wrote this letter after she disappeared, or whatever we should call it? After she left her friend at Grönsakstorget?"

"No. But we're assuming it."

"We're linking the letter to the murder," said Winter. "But maybe it's about something else."

"What would that be?"

They were into one of their routines, methods, questions and answers, and questions again in a stream of consciousness that might move forward or backward, any direction at all, as long as it didn't stand still.

"Maybe she needed to get something off her chest," said Winter. "She couldn't say it face-to-face. Face-to-faces. Something had happened. She wanted to explain herself, or find reconciliation. Or just contact them. She wanted to leave home, for a little while. She didn't want to be with her parents."

"That's wishful thinking," said Ringmar.

"Sorry?"

"The alternative is just too horrible."

Winter didn't answer. Ringmar was right, of course. He had tried to see the scene in front of him because it was part of his work, and he had closed his eyes when he saw it: Paula in front of a piece of paper, someone behind her, above her. A pen in her hand. Write. Write!

"Are those her words?" Ringmar asked.

"Was she taking dictation?" Winter asked.

"Or was she allowed to write what she wanted?"

"I think so," Winter said, reading the first sentences again.

"Why?" Ringmar asked.

"It's too personal."

"Maybe it's the murderer's personality."

"You mean that it's his message to the parents?"

Ringmar shrugged.

"I don't think so," said Winter. "They're her words."

"Her last words," Ringmar said.

"If more letters don't show up."

"Oh, hell."

"What does she mean by saying she wants to ask forgiveness?" Winter said, reading the words again.

"What she writes," said Ringmar. "That she wants to ask forgiveness if she made her parents angry."

"Is that the first thing a person thinks of in a letter like this? Would she think of that?"

"Would a person think at all?" said Ringmar. "She knows that she's in a bad situation. She's ordered to write a suicide note." Ringmar fidgeted in his chair again but didn't move it. "Yes. It's possible that thoughts of guilt would pop up then. Same with thoughts of reconciliation."

"Was there any guilt? I mean, real guilt?"

"Not according to her parents. Nothing that was . . . well, anything more than the usual between parents and children. There's no old feud, or whatever you'd call it."

"Although we don't know that," said Winter.

Ringmar didn't answer. He got up and walked over to the window and looked out through the slits in the blinds. He could see the wind in the black treetops in front of Fattighusån. There was a weak light over the houses on the other side of the canal; it was something other than the clear glimmer of a high summer night.

"Have you ever been involved in something like this before, Erik?" Ringmar said without turning around. "A letter from . . . the other side."

"The other side?"

"Come on, Erik," Ringmar said, turning around, "the poor girl knows she's going to be murdered and she writes a letter about love and reconciliation and forgiveness, and then we get a call from that damn flea-ridden hotel and all we can do is go there and find out what happened."

"You're not the only one who's frustrated here, Bertil."

"So—have you ever been involved with something like this before? A suicide note like this one?"

"No."

"Written by a hand that is then painted? Painted white? As though it were . . . separate from the body?"

"No, no."

"What the hell is going on, Erik?"

Winter got up without answering. He felt a sharp pain in his neck and across one shoulder blade. He had sat deep in concentration over the letter for too long and had forgotten to move his forty-five-year-old body, and that didn't work anymore; he could no longer handle sitting still for very long. But he was still alive. He had his hands in front of him. He could lift them and massage his neck. He did so, lowered his hands, and walked over to Ringmar, who was still standing at the window. Winter opened it a few centimeters. He could smell the scents of the evening; there was a sort of freshness to them.

Ringmar was furious. He was professional and furious, and that was a good combination. It invigorated the imagination, urged it on. A police officer without an imagination was a poor hunter, mediocre at best. Police officers who managed to turn everything off when they stepped out of the police station and went home. Perhaps it was good for them, but it wasn't good for their work; an officer with no imagination could turn it all off after working hours—and then wonder why he never got results. Many were like that, Winter had thought many times during his career at the CID; there were plenty of barely competent second-raters who couldn't think farther than to the top of the hill. In that way, they were related to psychopaths, lacking the ability to think past their own noses: is there anything on the other side of the hill? Nah, I can't see anything there, so there can't be anything there. I think I'll pass this car.

"I don't know if it's a message to us," Winter said. "The hand. The white hand."

"What was it about her hand?" said Ringmar.

"What do you mean?"

"Is there some . . . history surrounding her hand? Why did he paint her hand with that damn enamel paint?"

The paint came from Beckers; it was called Syntem, and it was an antique white semigloss enamel paint for indoor carpentry, furniture, walls, and iron surfaces. All of this could be read on the liter can that stood in room ten. It was the technicians' job to establish that the paint had also been used on a human body. There was no reason to doubt it, but they had to be certain. One thing was already certain: Paula Ney had never touched the paintbrush that lay next to the can, which was nearly full. The paint that had been used had been used to paint Paula's hand. Then the shaft of the paintbrush had been carefully wiped off.

"Nothing . . . abnormal about her hand, according to her parents," Winter said.

Good God. Her parents hadn't seen her hand yet. Fröberg and Öberg weren't done with it. Winter had had to keep it from her parents and simultaneously tell them about it, ask questions about it. What a fucking job this is.

"I have all the family photos in my office," Ringmar said.

"We won't find anything there," Winter said.

Ringmar didn't answer.

"What was he going to do with it, then?" said Ringmar. "The hand?"

"You make it sound like he was carrying it with him."

"Well, doesn't it feel like that?"

"I don't know, Bertil."

"There is some reason for this. That bastard wants to say something to us. He wants to tell us something." Ringmar flung one hand into the air. "About himself." He looked at Winter. "Or about her." He looked out through the window. Winter followed his gaze. There was only darkness out there. "Or about both of them."

"They knew each other?" Winter said.

"Yes."

"They had planned to meet at an out-of-the-way hotel? And to be on the safe side they didn't bother to announce their arrival in the lobby?"

"Yes."

"And we believe this?"

"No."

"But she knew the murderer?"

"I think so, Erik."

Winter didn't answer.

"I have been in this damn line of work ten years longer than you, Erik, I've seen almost everything, but I'm having trouble putting this together."

"We'll put it together," said Winter.

"Naturally," said Ringmar, but he didn't smile.

"Speaking of before," said Winter. "When I was really green, it was my first year as a detective, I think, I worked on something that involved Hotel Revy."

"This is definitely not the first time that place has been involved in an investigation," said Ringmar. "You know that as well as I do."

"Yes . . . but the case . . . or whatever I should call it, was special."

Winter contemplated the night outside, a dim darkness and a dim light, as though nothing could make up its mind out there now that summer was nearly over and autumn was slowly sliding up out of the earth with the mist.

"It was a missing person," said Winter. "I remember it now."

"At Hotel Revy?"

"It was a woman," said Winter. "I don't remember her name right now. But she disappeared from her home. Was going to run some errand. She was married, I think. And as I recall she had checked in at Hotel Revy the night before she disappeared."

"Disappeared? Disappeared to where?"

Winter didn't answer. He sank down into his thoughts, into his memory, as the darkness out there sank over roof ridges and streets and parks and harbors and hotels.

"What happened to her?" Ringmar asked. "I guess I've investigated too many missing persons; they run together."

"I don't know," Winter said, staring at Ringmar's face. "No one knows. I don't think she was ever found. No."

Winter had been twenty-seven and a green detective, and the late summer had been greener than usual because it had rained more than usual all summer. Winter had moved through the city every day without a thought of vacation, but he had thought of the future, this future, the future of a detective; he had cut his legal studies short before they really even started in order to become a police officer, but after his training and one year in uniform and six months in plain-clothes he still wasn't sure if he wanted to devote his life to penetrating the underworld. There was so much aboveground that was so much brighter. Even when it rained. In his six months or so on the force he had seen things that normal people never see, even if they live for a hundred years. That was how he thought: normal people. The people who lived aboveground. He lived there, too, sometimes; he came and went, crawled up and crawled down again, but he knew that his life would never be "normal." We have our own world down here, we police officers, along with our thieves and murderers and rapists. We understand. We understand one another.

He had begun to understand what understanding involved. When he did, it became easier. I'm becoming like them, he thought. The murderers.

I'm becoming more and more like them because they can never become like me.

He realized that he had to think in irregular patterns to find answers to mysteries. It was easier then. It was also more difficult then.
He could feel himself changing as he became better and better at his
job, at the way he thought. When he had found the answers to the
mysteries, or parts of the answers, he said that he had an active imagination and that was all there was to it. But it wasn't just imagination.
He had thought like *them*, gone into the darkness like *them*. He didn't
have a life of his own for long periods of his life; the more clever he
became, the more difficult it was to live "normally." He was alone. He
was like a rocky point of land. He didn't keep track of the time of day.
He didn't keep track of anything more than his mystery. He tended
to the mystery, tucked it in, watered it; when it came to the mystery
he was a perfectionist, compulsive in his care. His documents lay in
straight lines on his desk. At home, his clothes lay in messy piles on
the way from the bedroom to the bathroom. He had neat civilian
police clothes because he didn't see any virtue in being a slob, but sure
as hell, he was a slob beneath a lovely shell. He tried to cook real food
but gave up in the middle of it. He opened a bottle of malt whiskey
instead, when hardly anyone knew what malt whiskey was; that put
Winter ahead of the game in the normal world, and he tried to drink
the whiskey as slowly as possible and listen to the atonal jazz that no
one else could stand. Whiskey and jazz, that was his method, when
night fell, and so did everything else out there, and he sat in the half
darkness with his plots, his mystery, and soon enough with a laptop
that dispersed a cold light.

After a few years in the unit he realized that he had found himself
because he had slowly lost what had been himself, and he thought
that it was nice; it was liberation from normalcy.

Ellen Börge had been liberated from normalcy. Or had liberated
herself. She had gone out to buy a magazine and never come back. It
really had happened, reality imitated fiction: Ellen had really gone out
to buy a magazine, a so-called women's magazine. Winter had guessed
at first that it was *Femina* because there was a small pile of *Femina*

magazines on the coffee table, and no other magazines. Her husband, Christer, had no idea. *Femina*, huh? Well, I have no idea. She didn't say.

She had never arrived at the ICA store nearby where she usually bought her magazines, and everything else, too. They were lucky in the sense that the two clerks who had been working that afternoon recognized Ellen Börge and they said they would probably have remembered if she had been there.

Christer Börge had waited for five hours before he called the police. First he was transferred to local district station three, as it had been called then, and after twenty-four hours without Ellen the investigative unit was called in; more specifically the security forces that worked with missing persons reports. Greenhorn Erik Winter had gotten the case; wet-behind-the-ears Winter. He suspected foul play because it was his job to suspect foul play; it was also his nature to suspect foul play, and he had sat in front of the coffee table with *Femina* on it and asked questions about the twenty-nine-year-old Ellen of her thirty-one-year-old husband. The trio were all about the same age, but Winter felt like an outsider; he hadn't met Ellen, and Christer hadn't rejoiced when Winter arrived. Christer had been nervous, but Winter didn't understand what kind of nervousness it was. That kind of understanding of people required years of being an interrogator. It wasn't something that could be taught at the police academy. All you could do was wait for years, or wait them out, ask your questions again and again, read faces, listen to the words and simultaneously try to understand their implications. Winter had known even then, at the beginning of time, in 1987, that scholars of literature talked about subtext, and that was a good word for police interrogations, too: there could be a gulf between what was said and what was meant.

"You waited five hours before you called the police," he had said to Börge. This was no question.

"Yeah, so what?"

Börge had shifted on the sofa across from him. Winter had been sitting in an easy chair, some kind of white plush; he had thought that the furniture seemed too . . . adult for people of his same age, the whole home seemed . . . established, lived in, as though by a couple in late middle age, but here he didn't trust his own judgment; his own apartment was two rooms with a bed and a table and some kind of easy chair, and in a direct interrogation he wouldn't have been able to account for what kind of furniture he had, and what its purpose was.

But Börge would be able to account for everything in his home, a complete contents list down to the number of napkins in the second kitchen drawer from the top. Winter had been sure of it. Börge had looked like someone who had to have total control if the world were to retain its normalcy. His wife looked about the same in a photograph that stood on the coffee table, a conservative face, a hairstyle that didn't take any chances, a gaze that was somewhere else. But Ellen had had beautiful features, neat and regular, in that photo. It was a face that could be nearly sensational in a different context, with a different hairstyle, and Winter had thought, while sitting in the chair, that perhaps Ellen Börge hadn't been so happy with her husband. Too much control. Maybe children had been planned in their timetable, but not for a couple of years, when the moon was in the correct position, when the tide had gone out, when finances permitted it. Winter didn't have any thoughts of children himself, but on the other hand he didn't have a woman to share such thoughts with.

Maybe Ellen hadn't been able to stand it.

Five hours. Then her husband had called the police. If Christer was who he seemed to be, he ought to have called immediately. Demanded his rights. Demanded a massive effort. Demanded his wife back.

Winter had wondered.

"Weren't you worried? Five hours can be a long time when you're waiting for someone."

"Would you have done anything if I'd called earlier, huh?" Börge's voice had suddenly become more clear, almost shrill. "Wouldn't you just have said that we had to wait and see?"

"Have you called before?" Winter asked. "Has Ellen disappeared before?"

"Uh . . . no. I just mean that you have to wait. You know, that's what you read. The police wait and see, right?"

"It depends," said Winter, who was suddenly the one answering questions. This was difficult; interrogations were very difficult. "It's impossible to generalize."

"Sometimes . . . she would take a walk," Börge said, though Winter hadn't asked a follow-up question. "She would be gone for a few hours without saying anything. Like, ahead of time, I mean."

"Five hours?"

"No, never. Two, maybe; three on rare occasions."

"Why?"

"What do you mean why?"

Börge was sitting still on his sofa now, as though he had begun to calm down when he looked back on what had been.

"Why was she gone for hours without saying anything ahead of time?"

"I said a few."

"Did you ask her?"

"What would I ask?" Börge stroked the plush, as though he were petting a dog, a cat. "She was just taking a walk, after all."

"And this time she went out to buy a magazine. Maybe *Femina*."

"If you say so."

"That's the only magazine here," Winter said, grabbing the pile in front of him and reading the month of publication on the top issue. "You're sure that she said that she was going to buy a magazine?"

"Yes."

"Did she subscribe to any others?"

"What? No . . . she used to . . . but now I guess it was . . . single copies or whatever it's called."

"When did she stop subscribing?"

He could check everything like that, but he wanted to ask anyway. They could be important questions. Often you didn't know until afterward.

"Well . . ." Börge said, looking at the little pile on the table. "I don't really remember. A few months ago, I think."

"Does she read any other magazines or journals?"

"Well, we have the daily paper of course, *GP*. And other than that it's just those." He pointed at the pile that Winter was still holding in his hand. "You're welcome to look in the closets, but I've only seen that one."

"She had it already," Winter said.

"What?"

Winter held up the two top magazines.

"She had the August issue, and the September one."

"September? But it's not September yet."

"They come out a bit before the new month starts, I would guess." Winter read the cover again. "It says here: September 1987."

"Maybe it wasn't that magazine," Börge said. "I mean, the one she talked about going out to buy."

Winter didn't say anything. He waited. He knew that it was good to wait sometimes. That was the hardest thing, the hardest part of the art of interrogation.

Thirty seconds went by. He could see the silence causing Börge to think he had said something that Winter didn't like, or had become suspicious of, and that he ought to say something now that made the atmosphere around the coffee table a little better, a little lighter, maybe.

He suddenly got up and walked over to the bookcase, which mostly resembled a very large cabinet along the wall, a glass case, with space for china, knickknacks, books, a few photographs in frames. Winter had seen Ellen's face.

Börge was still standing in front of the books, as though he were looking for a particular title. He turned around.

"We had argued a little bit."

"When?"

"Before . . . when she went out."

"What were you arguing about?"

"Children."

"Children?"

"Well . . . she wanted to have children but I thought it was early. Too early."

Winter said nothing to the thirty-one-year-old in front of him, mostly because he himself didn't have anything to say about children because "early" in his case was just the beginning, just a preface. A family of his own lay eons in the future. Not even *his* imagination could see over that hill.

"You were fighting about it?"

"Like I said. But it wasn't so bad."

"What do you mean by that?"

"It wasn't really a fight. It was just that she was . . . talking about it."

"And you didn't want to talk about it?"

Börge didn't answer.

"Had you argued about it before?"

"Yes . . ."

"Did these arguments end with her going out? Without saying when she would come back?"

Börge nodded. Winter wanted an answer in words. He repeated the question.

"Yes," Börge answered.

"Is that the reason she went out this time?"

"Well . . . we weren't really arguing. And, you know, she was going to go out and buy a magazine." Börge's eyes fell to the magazine that Winter had lifted from the pile, the magazine she was going to go buy but already owned.

"Was that always the reason that she left?" Winter followed Börge's gaze. "Arguments about when you would have children?"

"Eh . . . I can't remember," Börge said. "But she always came back." He looked straight at Winter now, sought his eyes. "She always came back."

But this time she didn't come back.

She never came back.

"I remember now," Winter said. "She never came home. Ellen. Her name was Ellen. Ellen Börge."

They were still standing at the window. The late August evening was as dark as in November. Winter thought of a magazine cover with "September" printed under the magazine's name.

September came and went through the years, but Ellen Börge didn't collect magazines in a pile anymore; not on that coffee table, anyway.

"I remember, too," Ringmar said. He gave a weak smile in the glow from outside. "And I remember you. I think that was your first case, or one of the first."

"First case, first failure."

"In a long line," Ringmar said.

Winter nodded.

"But all jokes aside," Ringmar said, "that's a missing-person case that we didn't solve, but we never found out whether there was foul play behind it."

"We haven't even solved whether it was a crime that we would then solve," Winter said.

"Does it mean something to you?" Ringmar said. "Something in particular? Her disappearance? Ellen's?"

"I don't know." Winter suddenly felt damn tired, as though the years from then to now had come staggering in a single line and lay down on top of him, all at once. "But there was something about it . . . about Ellen . . . that made it hard to let go of."

"It's worse at first," said Ringmar. "When you're green."

"No."

Winter stroked his chin. He felt and heard the rasp of his stubble. It had begun to turn gray a few years ago. It wasn't his age. It was genetics, pure normalcy. He wasn't that old yet.

"I've thought about it occasionally," he continued. "Throughout the years. That there was something there. Something I could have done. Something I could have seen. It was there, in front of me. I should have seen it. If I had seen it I would have gotten farther."

"Farther where?"

"Farther toward . . . Ellen."

"You talk about it like it was a crime," said Ringmar. "That she was the victim of a crime."

Winter threw out his arms, toward Ringmar and the night.

"But we have a completely real and obvious crime in front of us," Ringmar said.

"Mm-hmm." Winter shook his head. He felt something rattling suddenly in there, a loose screw or something. "I suddenly feel tired. Now I can't even remember how we got on the topic of Ellen Börge."

"Hotel Revy," Ringmar said. "She had also checked into the city's coziest lodgings."

"But Paula Ney never checked in," said Winter.

"No," Ringmar said. "And she never checked out either."

2

Had Paula Ney really written the letter to her parents, Mario and Elisabeth, herself? The handwriting looked like hers, and at present they were assuming that Paula had written the letter, but closer analysis would settle the matter. Closer analysis of everything they'd found at the scene was under way, but Winter couldn't just sit in his office and wait for others to do all the preliminary work, or the background work. The analyses would arrive when they arrived. From the very start, he had to think about four big questions that always had to be asked, immediately: What happened, exactly? Why did it happen, and why in that particular way? Who could have carried out the murder in that way? In which case, what are the reasons behind it?

Winter was standing in the hotel room at Revy. The living city moved outside, mumbling behind the drawn curtains. He walked over to the window and pulled aside the curtains, which were like drapes, and the light over the city blinded him and the sound suddenly became louder, as though someone had turned up the volume by way of a central dial in city hall.

Just a few more days until September, and the warmth that had remained at the Tropic of Cancer all summer, and never reached up here, had suddenly been pushed north. The sun was on its way down to Capricorn now, but the warmth itself was heavy and compact over Scandinavia. Rusty grills came into use, fires burned in yards in the black evenings, it smelled like soot in the humid darkness and Winter thought of other countries, down there between Cancer and Capricorn. The tropics. One day he would be on his way there, Thiruvananthapuram, Kochi, Madurai, Georgetown, Singapore, Padang, Surabaya.

There were no shadows in the tropics. A person cast no shadow; it ran straight down through your body and disappeared under the soles of your feet.

He blinked in the surprising light that came through the window-pane and turned in toward the room again and waited for the contours to become sharp.

The room shimmered with gold. Red gold. If he squinted, he couldn't see the stains on the walls. Some of them belonged to the wallpaper; some had come later.

He took a few steps back toward the bed, which stood beside the far long wall. He moved his eyes to the door. There was a pattern on it, like a flower. It looked as though someone had thrown a glass of dark wine at the door. Wine? Why did I think of wine? It looks like ink. It's as black as the writing in Paula's letter. The suicide note.

Most everything in there looked like before, when they had come here for the first time. The silence hung there like a reminder, or a memory. Like one of the pictures on the wall, the biggest one. There were no traces left that he could see now. No stains of that kind. The red in here was the red gold as fake as the room, the hotel, the neighborhood, sometimes the whole damn city. But it was quiet in here now, as though the cordon also kept out all the sounds of the city.

But it was related; everything was connected in a way that he couldn't see yet, like when you look at a pile of puzzle pieces and know that all those pieces fit together, but you don't yet know how.

The awful message in the letter was part of a larger message. He knew the words by heart now, her words. They were about love, a great love. Or only about the opposite. Had she been drugged? Was he dictating? What do you write for your last words? Did she know that they were her last words? No. Yes.

He let the question and the answers go and concentrated on the room. What happened in here, exactly? Paula had come here but they didn't know whether she had done so alone, as though she were preparing for a meeting. The man down at reception hadn't noticed anything, and maybe it wasn't his job to notice anything. She hadn't checked in, and no one remembered her standing alone at the reception desk. If she had stood there. People came and went here, women, men, women, men. Seldom any children. There was no playroom here. There were no sounds of children, and Winter didn't think there ever had been. There were no such memories here.

The murderer had come here. Paula Ney had written her words on hotel stationery. There was stationery, like the remains of a better time. Remains. What a hell of a word that was. Had the murderer known that there was stationery in the room? Or was the letter a sudden decision, a random whim? Paula hadn't left this room after she'd come in the door. Winter felt certain of this. After a few hours she had written a letter. He looked around again. Why this room? Why this hotel? Room ten. He thought suddenly of Ellen Börge. She had stayed here for one night. Which room had she stayed in? It must be in her file, such as it was. Winter could see it in front of him. It was down in the archives, a file that hadn't been digitized because the contents dealt with a crime that happened before 1995. Then came modern times. The documents about Ellen Börge were stamped "No investigative results. PI suspended," and it had been many years since Winter had held the papers in his hands. If it even said anything about a preliminary investigation.

Technically, there hadn't been any preliminary investigation. He didn't remember all the details of the text. Suddenly he wanted to know, as quickly as possible, and he took his cell phone out of the pocket of his linen shirt.

Janne Möllerström, the registrar, answered.

"The documents from Ellen Börge's disappearance," Winter said. "I mentioned the case to you yesterday."

Ellen had disappeared long before Möllerström came to the unit. Winter had given him a brief description of the events.

"My short-term memory still works," Möllerström said now.

"A day? You call that short-term?"

"Ha-ha."

"Have you found the documents?"

"Yes. A missing-person case documented for posterity."

"It's no normal missing-person case."

"In which case you'll have to settle for paper, from the beginning."

Möllerström was a big fan of computerized archives.

"Have you had time to bring up the archive file?"

"Actually, the answer is yes," Möllerström said. "Feel free to ask how I had time to do it."

"How did you have time to do it?"

"No idea."

"One detail," Winter said, staring straight at the wall above the bed. It was bare, without pictures. The pattern of the wallpaper ran together at this short distance. "Can you find out which room Ellen Börge had at Hotel Revy?" Winter tried to make out the pattern of the wallpaper anyway. "I'm standing in the Ney room now."

Winter looked over at the window. The light was still bright out there. He felt a vague sense of recognition, an uneasy feeling, like the beginnings of feeling nauseous. There was something about the facade of the building on the other side of the street. The copper roofs.

"Should be somewhere at the beginning," he said into the telephone.

"If it's there at all."

"I was there myself, damn it."

"Well, in that case."

"Call me as soon as you find it."

Winter hung up and stood there with the phone in his hand. The sun swept over the green copper roofs on the other side of the street. It wasn't more than twenty or thirty meters over there. There was a sudden flash in through the window, like from a powerful spotlight, as the weathervane on the roof to the left turned in a sudden breeze and was hit by the sun.

Winter knew that it was a rooster, a red comb.

He had stood here before, in a different time, another life. A younger, more uncertain, more open one. Unfinished, more unfinished than now.

The sense of unease moved in his stomach again, like a reminder of something.

He felt his hand tremble the second before the phone rang.

"Room number ten," Möllerström said. "It was on page two."

"Yes."

"You don't seem surprised."

"I just recognized something." He watched the rooster revolve in a quarter turn and the spotlight went out. "But thanks for the quick answer, Janne."

Winter hung up and remained standing in the middle of the room.

A coincidence?

Of course.

How many rooms did this stinking flea nest have?

More than anyone knew.

Was room ten reserved for solitary women without escorts? Escort services had otherwise been Revy's specialty. He had been back here a few times during his career. Prostitution, narcotics, assaults. Revy was like an old punch-drunk boxer who always got up at the last second. The building had been allowed to remain when the rest of Nordstan and the surrounding neighborhoods were torn down by the wrecking balls. Was it for nostalgic reasons? Was it the blind sunspot on the map in Trädgårdsföreningen? Had the city planners been old customers here? In two cases they were, a city architect and a former municipal commissioner. Social Democrat. They tore down everything else, the beautiful and the ugly indiscriminately, but Revy was allowed to remain. The city architect allowed construction on lots that the municipal commissioner had had demolished. Maybe they arranged it at the bordello, two old gangsters. Winter saw the Social Democrat around town now and then; he walked with a cane now and presumably still thought with his dick. He had a lot on his conscience. He always seemed to be in a good mood.

Revy had remained until now, until Paula Ney's death. Had stood here during Ellen Börge's disappearance. Room ten. Had other things happened here? He would have to put Möllerström on it. Keyword: room ten. Good God. And a dig through the dusty archives. Without archives, electronic or otherwise, they might as well quit, give up. Everything that happened now was related to the past, directly or indirectly. It was never like in the tropics. The past cast long shadows here, at Winter's latitude.

There were shadows that moved in room ten. The bed didn't really look the same now as when he had come in; nor did the table or the easy chair; nor the pattern on the walls and floor. A reproduction of a work of art hung on the wall next to the window. It was the worst place for a picture; there was almost no light there. It was a portrait of a woman with dark features. Gauguin. Winter had seen the original at a museum in Rome, a work on loan. Gauguin, he thought with his dick, too. Winter had quite recently read a biography of him. He chose the tropics, lived there, died there. Syphilis. Winter took his notebook out of the back pocket of his linen trousers and wrote: Check pictures all rooms. He didn't know why right now. It wasn't necessary to know. He knew that there were more questions than answers; there were a hundred questions for every answer. It would change; there would be more answers, but the questions would continue to be in the hundreds, thousands; and if the answers became more plentiful than the questions, it still wouldn't be a given that they'd come closer to solving the mystery. Solving. Dissolving. Resolving. There were several words for something that almost always remained unclear, unfinished.

He moved around the room. Paula Ney hadn't checked out. She had been murdered. She had died here. She had died because someone hated. Was that the case? Naturally. How could anyone hate so much? She had written about love and then she'd died. The nature of the violence was such that it must have been personal. It wasn't apparent in this room; there were no traces on the walls and floor. You murder the one you love. Or: The violence had increased to such a degree of impersonality that it had become . . . personal. Did they know each other, the murderer and Paula? No. Yes. No. Yes. He saw the shadows

moving again, becoming longer. The afternoon traffic seemed to increase in density down on the street. He could hear it suddenly, as
though the blockade had been broken. He heard a shout, honking
from a car, a sudden ambulance over to the west, and, in the background, a dull buzzing from the whole city. A seabird started up when
the sound of the ambulance cut off. And now: the sound of steps in
a new pocket of silence. A woman's steps. Paula must have heard all
of those sounds; heard life outside, the city's . . . normalcy. What had
she thought of? Did she know that she would never again get to move
around among all of those wonderful sounds? Yes. No. Yes.

"No," said the man behind the desk, "I don't remember there being
anyone with her. I don't remember her."

He had an indeterminate appearance, which had been shaped during several decades. Maybe he was the same man as when young Winter stood here asking about Ellen Börge. No. It wasn't him. Winter
would have known. But he looked as though he had been here then,
as though he had always been here. Some people had that sort of appearance; they appeared to be part of their surroundings.

Winter asked an impossible question. He wanted to ask it. Maybe
it wasn't impossible, maybe it was the best thing he could ask right
now.

"Do you remember a young woman who checked in here in 1987?
Her name was Ellen Börge."

"Sorry?"

"She disappeared the next day."

The man looked at Winter as though he were looking at someone
who'd drunk his way through lunch.

"We were here asking about her. I was here."

"I don't remember," said the desk clerk.

"She stayed in the same room," Winter continued.

"The same as who?"

"Ney. Paula Ney."

"In 1987?" The man looked around, as though there were a witness standing somewhere who could confirm that the inspector in front of him was drunk, or crazy. They got all sorts here. "Eighty-seven? At the moment I don't remember anything from the eighties at all."

"You don't seem to remember any of last week at all."

The man didn't answer. He had already answered. He didn't remember the woman checking in, and that was that. People came and went through the lobby all the time, and as far as he knew, they were all guests of the hotel. Someone had had a key to room ten, but he didn't remember giving it to her.

"Do you have many regular customers?" Winter asked.

The man looked even more perplexed, behind his attitude. Winter realized why. He had phrased the question wrong.

"Regular male customers."

"Some businessmen," the man said, and smiled.

"Any you recognize?"

"I don't usually recognize people."

The man yawned. It was a big yawn. It was very demonstrative.

"Is there something wrong with your eyes?"

Winter had raised his voice.

"What? No . . ."

The man's jaw had become stuck, half-open in the middle of another yawn.

"I haven't done anything wrong, have I?!" he said after a few seconds. "You don't need to get angry."

"There's been a murder here and you pretend that you're a blind, deaf idiot. Get it together, for God's sake!"

The man looked around again. There were still no witnesses in the lobby; no one behind the sooty cretonne that drooped at the base of the stairs, no one halfway up or down the stairs, no one behind a half-open door that led to God knows where, no one behind the palm in the pot over by the entrance. Winter suddenly thought of the tropics again; it was the palm and the fan that was rotating on the ceiling above them, and the humid warmth in there. The late summer had become tropical in the last few days. He felt the sweat through his shirt. And the lobby of Hotel Revy reminded him of a colonial hotel, or the set of one. It was the movie version of the tropics. But this movie was for real.

"So," said Winter, taking out his notebook.

Detective Inspector Fredrik Halders declined coffee. No one in this apartment wanted any damn coffee anyway. He understood how they felt. The couple in front of him was trying to get through one day at a time, and coffee and buns were of no help with that. Nor was liquor. Halders had tried liquor when his ex-wife, the mother of his children, was killed by a drunk driver. He hadn't started drinking right away. It began months after Margareta was murdered. Halders had felt the shock slowly letting go and the hate streaming into him, and he had drunk to keep the hate at bay, to make himself immobile, so that he wouldn't carry out an execution of the murderer or slash his murder weapon to bits. Halders knew where the fucking car was, in front of the house that was waiting to be set aflame.

He had drunk his way out of the depression, and afterward he was ashamed. Not because he hadn't carried out his plans for the drunk driver, but because he had used liquor as an anesthetic. Liquor had been an active accomplice in the murder. He ought to become a tee-totaler, and he practically was one now. There was still time to be flexible; it was still too soon for AA, he wasn't there yet. He drank coffee, liter after liter. But not at this particular moment.

Perhaps Mario and Elisabeth Ney were thinking of hate, or maybe they couldn't think at all. But Halders had asked about enemies of theirs, of Paula's. Who could have so much hate?

"Everyone liked Paula," said Elisabeth.

It was one of the great clichés of language, but not for her. Elisabeth looked as though it was true for her. Halders found himself on the other end. Not everyone liked him. It was better now; he could actually count his friends on the fingers of one hand, but before, for many years, all it took was one extended middle finger. His own.

"How was her job?"

"What do you mean, Chief Inspector?" She spoke in a monotonous voice. Her husband, Mario, didn't speak at all.

"Detective. But please, don't worry about titles." Halders had thought of himself as chief for several years, but that was also behind him now. He was not boss material. He couldn't even compromise with himself.

"Her coworkers," he continued.

"I . . . never heard anything."

"Heard what?"

"That she had any enemies at work."

"Did she like it there?"

"I never heard otherwise," Elisabeth said.

"Did she like the work itself?"

"She never said otherwise."

No enemies, no conflicts, no concern about her work. That was unique, he thought. Or else it was quite simply the case that she never said anything about anything at all.

He looked at the portrait of Paula. It was standing in the middle of the kitchen table. Elisabeth had placed it there when they sat down. Paula would be there during the conversation. It was about her.

The photographer had captured her in a black-and-white picture for eternity in the middle of the start of a smile, or maybe at the end. Halders had never understood portrait photographers' obsession with smiles. Children who were scared into smiling by toys. Adults who were supposed to think of something pleasant. Say "cheese." For Halders, it might as well be "shiiit." Smiles. Did people become more beautiful clad in a demanded smile? Did the future become more beautiful?

Paula Ney was beautiful, in a conservative way. She didn't take any risks with her hairstyle. Her gaze was somewhere else, maybe on the wall above the photographer's head, maybe far beyond the wall. Paula Ney had beautiful, regular features in that photograph; it was a face that wasn't transformed by the unfinished smile, and Halders thought, as he sat on the hard kitchen chair, that perhaps Paula Ney hadn't been so happy.

"How many years did she work at Telia?"

Halders had turned to Mario Ney, but Elisabeth answered:

"Nine years. But of course it wasn't called Telia before."

"One year after secondary school . . ." said Halders. "What did she do that year?"

"Nothing . . . in particular," Elisabeth said.

"School? Job?"

"She traveled."

"Traveled? Where did she travel?"

"Nowhere . . . in particular."

Everywhere is particular, Halders thought. Especially if you choose to travel there.

"In Sweden? Abroad?" He leaned forward over the kitchen table. The tablecloth was yellow and blue. "It's important that you remember. Everything can be important in a preliminary investigation. A trip can be—"

"We don't really know," Mario interrupted. This was the first thing he had said; he hadn't even said anything when they greeted each other in the hall. He didn't look directly at Halders; his gaze was directed upward, toward the kitchen wall, maybe far beyond it. "She didn't say very much."

"She was nineteen years old and she traveled away for a year and she didn't say where she was?" Halders asked. "Weren't you worried?"

For his part, he would have called the police if Magda did that. Some other police.

"It . . . wasn't a whole year," Elisabeth said in her hesitant way. "And she sent us a few postcards. We knew that she was out traveling, of course." Elisabeth looked at Mario. "We waved good-bye to her at the station."

"Where was she on her way to then?"

"She had a ticket to Copenhagen."

"Is that where she went?"

Mario shrugged slightly.

"Where did she send the first postcard from?"

"Milan."

Halders tried to catch Mario's eyes, but they slid away, up again. The man had been born in Italy. He looked like someone who came from a different part of Europe, or the world. A darker appearance, eyes, chin. His hair was nearly gone, a grayish-black crown around his ears. Halders's hair was completely gone; what hadn't fallen out on its own he had shaved off.

"Did she want to search for her roots?"

"Her roots are here," said Mario. His tone was unexpectedly hard.

No Bella Italia for him, Halders thought.

"But she went to Italy," he said.

"She went to other countries," said Elisabeth.

"Do you still have her postcards?"

"Does it really matter?" said Mario.

"As I said before," said Halders. "Everything can matter."

Mario got up. "I'll see if I can find them."

He wanted to get away. Halders could see that his hands were trembling; maybe the rest of his body was, too. He kept his face turned away.

"Your husband doesn't seem to be homesick for the old country," Halders said when Mario had left the kitchen.

"Maybe he left for a reason," Elisabeth said.

"What happened?"

She shrugged slightly, exactly the same way as her husband had. She had learned it from him, or he had from her. But it looked like a movement from a country far to the south.

"Was he forced to leave?" Halders asked.

"He hasn't mentioned anything about that."

Good God. Did anyone say anything about anything in this family?

"Did he come to Sweden alone?"

She nodded.

"From where?"

"From Sicily."

"Sicily? That's a big island. What part?"

"I don't actually know." She looked Halders in the eye. "I realize that it sounds strange, but it's actually true. Mario has never wanted to talk about it." She turned her gaze away. "And I . . . don't understand what this has to do . . . with this."

"Has Mario seen his family? Since he left?" Halders continued. "His family from Sicily?"

"No."

"He's never gone back?"

"No."

"None of you?"

"I don't understand."

"That's not where Paula was headed?"

"Wouldn't she have said so if she were?" said Elisabeth.

I'm not so sure of that, Halders thought. But what did she know about Sicily? All she had to bring to her father's island was her name, and perhaps Ney was a common name.

"Did Paula speak Italian?"

"Not then," Elisabeth answered.

"Now *I* don't understand," said Halders.

"She learned it . . . a little later. A little of the language."

"After that trip?"

Elisabeth nodded.

"After Milan?"

Elisabeth nodded again.

"Did she travel back?" Halders asked.

"I don't actually know," Elisabeth said, looking straight at Halders again, and he believed her. Or he thought that he believed her.

"She didn't have a traveling companion?"

"No."

"Never during that time?"

"If she did, she didn't say anything about it."

"What was she like when she came home? Had she changed?"

Elisabeth didn't answer. When Halders had come here, he hadn't been thinking of travel. Now his questions were leading him around the Mediterranean. Maybe it was completely wrong, a meaningless field trip.

"Was she happy? Sad? Exhilarated?"

"She was the same as usual," the mother said.

She turned her head abruptly, as though toward a sound out in the courtyard. Suddenly Halders saw the similarity. There was something about the light. He hadn't seen it before. There was something about her profile. Halders moved his eyes back and forth between the woman in the photograph and the woman who was sitting in front of him. At that angle she was a dead ringer for her daughter; he hadn't seen it right away. Dead ringer. What a hell of a phrase.

"What does that mean?" he asked. "That she was the same as usual?"

Maybe Elisabeth had planned to answer. She had turned her head back. But Mario had come back into the kitchen and walked up to them quickly and placed several postcards on the table.

"This was all I could find. I think she took some home with her, too."

Home. Halders had been in Paula's apartment. The renovations were nearly finished, one and a half rooms wallpapered and painted. It had been a strange experience. Walking around in an apartment that was in the process of getting a new face, and a different smell, while at the same time the person who had lived there no longer existed. He couldn't remember having been in the same situation before. There was something repulsive about it. An affront to life.

Halders had seen cupboards and shelves and a freestanding chest of drawers, all half-covered with transparent plastic; it looked like mist, as though someone were breathing under the plastic cover. In one corner, Öberg's technicians had lifted the plastic and begun to move her belongings. That, too, felt like some kind of affront.

Maybe they would find a ten-year-old postcard. Would that help them? Yes. No. No.

3

The group gathered in the conference room. It had been renovated twice during Winter's time in the unit, but now that was over. There would be no more polishing in these corridors that were clad in a kind of brick that suggested another time. There would be no more renovation. The money for such things was gone. The bricks outside his office would fall to the floor in time.

He could see the remains of the sunrise over Ullevi, the soccer stadium. The sun rose reluctantly over his part of the world. A pointless job. Winter cold would come no matter what. The sun was on its way to the equator, where it belonged. This time of year was dominated by one big sunset, and then darkness. Arctic night, only a few months away. The long johns would itch at first, but you always got used to it.

"Damn, it's warm," said Ringmar, who had just come into the room and sat down, and he wiped the layer of sweat from his forehead.

"Stop that," Halders said.

"Sorry?" Ringmar said, his hand still on his forehead.

"I hate it when northerners start whining about the sun as soon as it comes out."

"I just said it was warm," Ringmar said.

"You said *damn,* it's warm," Halders pointed out against the haze of heat. "Isn't that a negative comment?"

"Says the great optimist in the police force," Ringmar said, and wiped his forehead again.

"Carpe diem," Halders said, smiling.

"Mea culpa," said Ringmar, "mea maxima culpa."

"Can someone translate?" said Lars Bergenhem, still the youngest detective in the group.

"Didn't you do the classics option?" Ringmar asked.

"Classics what?"

"The classics option at the police academy," Halders said. "Think first, act later. It's gone now. Swept away."

"Carpe diem I understand," said Bergenhem, "but the other part?"

"My fault, I'm to blame," said Ringmar.

Winter drank the last of the coffee in his mug. At least the coffee was cold in the warm room. He cleared his throat. The warm-up talk between Halders and Ringmar and Bergenhem grew quiet.

"The floor is open for debate," he said, "but unfortunately the police can no longer afford translators."

Aneta Djanali laughed very abruptly. It was the first sound from her in the conference room this morning. She had spoken with Halders earlier in the morning, and with Fredrik's children, Hannes and Magda, but she was happy to stay out of the warm-up. She was already warm. This evening they would go out to the cliffs of Saltholmen and take the last dip of the summer. They had been saying this for a whole week already. But the sun went down behind Asperö like a blood orange every evening, and that meant it would come back the next morning.

"There is a big split between Paula and her parents," Halders said. "Was."

Winter nodded.

"No one's saying anything, or has said anything, and that always makes me suspicious."

Winter nodded again.

"I think she left home that night planning not to return," Halders said.

"Without a suitcase?" Ringmar leaned over the table. "Her purse was of the minimalist type."

"She had an apartment, didn't she?" Halders looked around the room, around the table. Bergenhem nodded encouragingly. "She had a key, didn't she? It was evening; the painters had gone home for the day. She could have gone home to her apartment and packed a suitcase and met that friend whateverhernameis and gone on from there."

"To Hotel Revy?" Ringmar said.

"I don't know if she really planned to go there in particular."

"The friend's name is Nina Lorrinder," Winter said. "She didn't mention any suitcase."

"Did we ask about one, then?" Halders said.

"No," said Bergenhem. "I didn't ask her about it."

"That's what happens when you don't do the classics option," Halders said.

"So that was the first thing you would have asked her about?" Bergenhem said. He began to look angry. That was the expression Halders was waiting for.

"Quit it," Winter said. "She's alive. We can ask her now."

"I'll call right away," Bergenhem said, getting up.

"Good idea!" Halders said.

"Stop it, Fredrik," Djanali said.

"There was something awfully strange about her parents," Halders said, unmoved, without turning his head toward Djanali.

"They just lost their only child," Ringmar said.

"It was the silence at their place," said Halders, as though he hadn't heard Ringmar. "In ten cases out of nine, everyone wants to talk after such a hellish trauma. People can't talk enough. Cry enough. But there were no tears at the Neys'."

"They're still in shock," said Ringmar.

"No," Halders said, and his face was transformed. "Believe me, Bertil, I have . . . experience. There is no shock in the first few days. Only hate."

The room became quiet. Everyone could hear the coffee machine take one of its last sighs. Ringmar wiped his forehead again. Winter could hear the traffic outside. Djanali could hear the air conditioner, like sad whispers all along the low ceiling.

Bergenhem came back.

"No suitcase," he said.

"She could have put it in the coat check. Movie theaters have those sometimes," said Halders.

"They met outside. She only had her purse."

"She could have been inside and left her suitcase."

"They left there together, went to the pub. The bar. No suitcase."

"And you asked about all of that?" Halders said.

Bergenhem nodded.

"She could have gone ahead to the pub and checked the suitcase there," Halders said.

"No."

"You asked about that, too?"

"She, Nina, said that she was the one who suggested they go there. Paula had suggested another place."

"Then we'll have to look there," said Halders.

"They open at four o'clock," said Bergenhem.

"You checked already?"

Bergenhem nodded again.

"Well done, kid. You do have an imagination."

"But all we have is an imaginary suitcase," said Winter.

"Can someone translate?" Halders said, and looked around the room.

"She also could have gone to Central Station," said Djanali. "If she had a suitcase and if she had planned to leave for good and if she didn't want to carry the suitcase around."

"There was no key in her purse," Bergenhem said. "I mean, to one of those storage boxes. Storage lockers."

"The murderer might have taken the key," said Ringmar. "It might have been a temptation too great to resist."

"Or else it's lying someplace else," said Djanali.

"Maybe the locker is still locked," said Bergenhem, "with the suitcase still inside."

"That's what I wanted to get at," said Djanali.

"So we have two things to do," Halders said, "check again in

Paula's apartment and determine whether she packed a bag. And find out where it is."

"And if we manage to find it?" said Djanali. "Then that means that she was planning to leave. That maybe her parents didn't know. But that might be all it means."

"It could also mean that she was planning to go away with someone else," said Halders. "There might have been tickets in her purse."

"Soon there will be lots of imaginary things we're missing in that purse," said Ringmar. "Why not steal the whole purse? That's nothing for a murderer. Probably a precautionary measure."

"It might mean that there was nothing in her purse that he wanted to have," said Winter.

"So my talk about an imaginary suitcase is just . . ." Halders began.

"Imaginary," Bergenhem filled in.

"It's worth a follow-up," Winter said. "Do a check in her apartment, Fredrik."

Meanwhile, Djanali was reading Paula Ney's last letter. They assumed it was her last letter. She read aloud: " 'If I've made you angry at me I want to ask for your forgiveness.' " She looked up. "Is that something a person wants to write as a final message?"

"Maybe she didn't think it was a final message," Ringmar said.

"But if she did think so. If she thought she was going to die. Is that the moment when someone who is condemned to death asks for forgiveness?"

No one around the worn table commented on Djanali's words. A thin ray of sunlight suddenly shot through the window and split the table in two: Bergenhem and Halders on one side, Winter and Ringmar and Djanali on the other. It was like a boundary, but there were no boundaries between them. We have been together for a long time, Winter thought, keeping his eyes on the sun boundary. Even Bergenhem is starting to get wrinkles.

"She was Catholic, wasn't she?" Halders said. "Maybe she was asking for forgiveness for her sins."

"No," Winter said, "Paula wasn't Catholic."

"What sins?" Bergenhem asked, leaning forward, toward Halders.

"I mean figuratively. Like a routine thing, or whatever. A confession."

"Paula was confessing, you mean?" Djanali asked.

"I don't know. Maybe that's the wrong word."

"Maybe someone was prepared to forgive her for her sins," Ringmar said.

"Like who?" Halders said.

"The murderer."

"The murderer became her confessor?" Bergenhem said.

"He let her write the letter."

"Or forced her to," said Halders.

"Dictated," Bergenhem said.

"No," Winter said, "I don't think so."

"But it might indicate that there's some big, and old, clash between Paula and her parents," Halders said.

"When isn't there?" Djanali said. "Between children and parents?"

"I said *big* clash," Halders said.

"We'll have to check it out," said Ringmar.

"It won't be easy," Halders said. "It's not like we can hear both sides."

"There are more than two sides," said Bergenhem.

"Look at that," Halders said, turning to Bergenhem, "first Latin and then philosophy. Have you been taking night classes this summer, Lars?"

"I don't need to do that to understand that we can talk to people other than her parents about her relationship with her parents," Bergenhem said.

"Did you make a note of that, Erik?" Halders said, turning to Winter.

"Let's get to work," Winter said, and got up.

Winter was working at the telephone. He called the desk clerk at Revy; it was the same man. No, he hadn't seen any suitcase. He hadn't found any suitcase. Why would he have? Winter thought as he hung up. He didn't see anything else, didn't hear anything or say anything.

The phone rang.

"Looks like someone rummaged around a little through her clothes and shoes," Halders said.

He sounded far away.

"Oh?"

"Might be her, might be someone else, might have been a hundred years ago. But I don't think so."

"Why not?" Winter asked.

"There's no suitcase here. No backpack either, or anything you could carry your clothes in."

"Have you checked in the attic? In the basement?"

"Of course," Halders answered. "I've taken my night classes."

"At her parents' house, then?"

"I just called."

"She must have had something to carry things in when she moved home," Winter said, "during the renovation."

"I thought that far, too," said Halders. "And guess what: the parents can't find it either. They say that she had a Samsonite that was pretty new, black, but it's not at the Neys' house now."

"Good, Fredrik."

"God knows. I've been thinking here in this haunted apartment. It looks like one big fucking shrouded corpse in here. White, plastic, some kind of antiseptic smell from the paint and the thinner. It's not fun to be here, Erik. It's too white here."

"I understand what you mean, Fredrik."

Halders didn't say anything. Winter could hear a rushing sound through the telephone. Perhaps Halders had opened the window in Paula's white apartment; maybe it was the wind out there in the gray heights of Guldheden.

"You said that you'd been thinking?" Winter said after a moment.

"What? Well, I don't know about thinking . . . but maybe all this is just a dead end. The suitcase, I mean. Maybe it doesn't have anything to do with the murder. That someone took it. The murderer. She just had a bad fucking stroke of luck on her way to Central Station. Met someone. And then it went to hell."

"You think she was on her way to Central Station? In the evening, after having a glass of wine with her friend?"

They had tried to establish Paula's final hours. Final hours of freedom, as Winter had thought of it. But so far they hadn't spoken to anyone who had seen her, noticed her, recognized her. As usual, the big city was the place for the anonymous; it always gave shelter, for the worse, sometimes for the better, offered insecurity, security. There was a great and strangely obvious paradox built into the big city: the more people, the greater the loneliness. Out in the boonies, no one could keep to himself; everyone within a hundred kilometers of primeval forest heard everything, saw everything, noticed everything, recognized everything.

"Enough thinking," Halders answered. "Now it's time to find out."

Halders hung up. He looked around, at the protective plastic, at the half-finished painting of the walls, as though everything was final and at the same time a continuation that had been stopped only temporarily. The apartment was a condo, nothing exclusive, not junk, even if none of that mattered anymore because all apartments were wildly expensive; this two-roomer up on the top of Guldheden would go for about half a million kronor, maybe more, not to mention the monthly fee. When had she bought it? Had anyone asked yet? In any case, Halders hadn't found out yet. How many years had she lived here? Did the parents buy it? Someone else? I'll have to keep reading, Halders thought. Keep asking.

Outside, the trees swayed in the wind; elms, lindens, maples, twenty-five-meter-high crowns, hundred-year-old giants that would still be standing here when he was gone, too, along with all the others who had sat around the coffee table this morning; the whole gang would be gone from this earthly paradise, some earlier, some later, and all that green halfway up in the sky would keep on swaying in the sweet summertime. He had started thinking about existence during the last few years, had become an existentialist because it was only a matter of time in this line of work. He worked in the middle of the end of existence, the premature end. It was hard work, delicate work, and he sometimes wondered why God and the minister of justice had given it to the police in particular.

He shook off his thoughts, or whatever they were, and went into the bedroom for the second time.

There was something he hadn't seen when he was in there the first time. Something he had expected to find but without knowing what it was. It often happened that way—he knew that he was missing something, but not what. It might be in a room, on a person, at a discovery site, at a crime scene. What wasn't there could be more interesting than what he could see or hold. The picture wasn't complete if he didn't figure out what was missing.

What had he missed in this room a little bit ago, before he spoke to Winter? It was something you usually see in a room, especially in a bedroom. A bed? No, the bed was still there, still with its plastic canopy. A bureau? No.

Halders had stood in hundreds of bedrooms during his career as an investigator. He had investigated. He had registered. He had studied details; tried to think of the problem in a different situation, a different life.

What was it that was always in a room like this one? Something personal, even intimate. Something that the person who inhabited the room saw at night, in the morning; as the last thing, the first. It was usually hanging on a wall. Or it was on a nightstand. Nothing was hanging on the wall here. Right now, that was because the walls were daubed with primer. There was nothing on the little table next to the bed. There could have been; the plastic canopy protected everything in there.

There were no photographs in the room, not of Paula, not of anyone else. There were no photographs in frames anywhere in the apartment. It was as though loneliness was amplified in there and became emptier, more blank.

They had found some photo envelopes with regular prints, everyday pictures, but things like that always gave an impersonal impression; they were momentary scenes from momentary instants, things you could take or leave.

It was different with ones that were put in frames. That was somehow more for posterity. It was . . . intimate.

He hadn't found any photographs like that in any of the boxes or on any of the shelves where things had temporarily been placed during the renovation.

He would have to ask her parents about that; Halders picked up his notebook and wrote. They would have to help identify all the faces in the prints anyway. Maybe nothing was framed. Maybe that wasn't Paula Ney's style.

What was her style?

Halders left the bedroom and stood in what he called the living room, which was a damn strange name; it was probably left over from the time when there was a parlor in people's houses, cold and closed up, that was used only when people came to call—which might have been never—and wasn't for living in. The room just stood there, like some sort of permanent lodger. At least, that's how it had been in Halders's childhood home; no one came to call and the door to the parlor was never opened; the table silver was never taken out of its chest. As a boy, Halders would sometimes stand outside its door and try to see the things in there through the milky glass. Everything was blurry, there were mostly fluid contours, as though he were nearsighted and wasn't wearing his glasses, but still he wanted to know what was in there, what it might look like when it was sharp and clear. As though he could somehow find out why no one lived in there.

Suddenly he couldn't remember if he had ever been in the parlor of his childhood. He ought to remember that. And later, while he was still a child, his parents got divorced and everyone went in different directions and the parlor became a memory, blurry from the start, but never blurrier with time. The opposite happened, as though the image became clearer with time for the very reason that it had been so hard to see back then.

Her style; Halders had been thinking of Paula's style. Her style was not being murdered. The murder proved that no one could escape. Soon, as they learned more about her life, her previous life, maybe that image would also change, become clear, or become dark as it became more and more obvious.

"How did we get on the topic of storage lockers?" Ringmar said.

They had decided to take a walk in the park, to the Shell station and back. It wasn't much of a park. The station was bigger than the park.

"Aneta pointed us toward Central Station," said Winter. "And of course there could be a suitcase down there." He looked up, as though he was determining the time with the help of the sun. His black glasses suddenly shimmered with gold. "I called and asked for the guy who's responsible for the lockers."

"And?"

"They were going to find him."

Ringmar nodded.

Winter followed the path of the sun again. He looked at his own watch.

Suddenly he realized that they were about to make a mistake.

"They have security cameras down there now, don't they, Bertil? I mean, twenty-four hours a day?"

"I think so."

"When do they erase those pictures from the hard disk?"

"After seventy-two hours," said Rolf Bengtsson, branch manager of Speed Services AB, which had taken over the storage lockers from Swedish Railways. "Sometimes sooner."

Winter had driven down to Central Station. It took five minutes, including parking illegally in the taxi zone. He walked into the building quickly. The locker area in there had recently been rebuilt, just like everything else. He had to ask the way. The lockers were now in the underworld of Central Station. The stairs down were steep. Winter heard the elevator swish behind him. He made note of the security cameras on the ceiling. They were convincing decoys.

"I have a card of those photo-booth pictures I have to show you later," Winter said as they walked down the stairs.

"Why?"

"Is it possible to tell when someone took their picture in a booth? What time the pictures were taken?"

"No."

"Okay, but can you determine which booth the pictures were taken in?"

"Yes. We can do that; we know our machines' idiosyncrasies."

"Good," Winter said.

The area down there was bathed in a green color that the contractor had perhaps thought restful. Maybe calming, therapeutic. It was green everywhere, like in a tropical forest. People came and went in the restful light. Maybe it was too restful, too sloping for them to be able to see anything useful in the pictures. If there was anything to see that they wanted to see.

"But the time depends on the level of activity in here," Bengtsson continued. "The camera doesn't start until someone moves."

Seventy-two hours, Winter thought. They might get lucky, or have made a big mistake. Or else it didn't mean anything.

"Every corner in here is caught by the camera," Bengtsson said. "No one gets away."

"If there's any image left," said Winter.

"Sometimes there can be film left from five days back. Like I said, it depends on the level of activity in here."

"Isn't it still possible to get it back anyway?" said Winter. "Even if the disk has been erased?"

"I'm an expert in photo booths and storage lockers," Bengtsson said, "not in computers. But I know that your computer experts at the police station have tried and failed." He smiled. "Call me Roffe, by the way."

The level of activity by the lockers had been so low that there were still images from four and a half days back. Winter felt a rush of warmth for the counter mechanism. It made certain that they would likely be able to see whether Paula Ney had put a suitcase into a locker. And if she, or someone else, had taken it out during the last few days. The victim. The murderer.

Roffe Bengtsson showed Winter into the control and storage room inside the small office to the left of the stairs. Two people were work-ing there, on cleaning, storage, reception, monitoring. They were a younger man and a younger woman. They had a lot to do. People were coming and going out there. There were lots of people upstairs; it was the day's peak time.

The woman introduced herself as Helén and shook his hand. She nodded toward the display to the right, on the wall.

"Have you been here before?" she asked.

"No, not since it was redone," Winter said, and he walked over to the flat display. It looked like a board, divided into six squares. An installation. In the squares, people moved with strangely jerky mo-tions, and not only because they were heaving suitcases up and down out there. Everyone in the images looked like cases for an orthopedist. Winter knew that was the price the viewer paid for digitization.

"How many cameras do you have?" he asked.

"Eight." She nodded toward the display. "The other two are run-ning, too, of course. One of them is filming people on their way up the stairs. That one's what we call our secret camera."

"Good," Winter said, studying the pictures in real time. "The de-coys look good, by the way."

"One of them was stolen last week," she said, smiling.

"Where are the cameras?"

"In the sprinklers and the fire alarms."

"I did think there were a lot of those."

"You can never be too careful," she said, smiling again.

Winter sat in front of the display and studied the films from the evening of Paula's disappearance. Just for a first look. They would get copies from the hard drive down here and run everything in magnification on their own monitors up at the police station. Or take the whole computer from here. It had happened before.

He concentrated on women at first. He saw women in summer clothes opening lockers, closing lockers, locking them, unlocking them, walking back and forth in the strangely jerky resolution on the display. It was like a silent film, but these pictures were in color, surprisingly sharp, but at the same time it was as though they were coated by the green tint that overshadowed everything down there. Shadows fell over the far corners of a few of the aisles; it wasn't as easy to see what was happening over there, who was doing what.

But Winter saw a man starting to undress in one of the corners, which seemed to be a dead end.

"There's no decoy over there," Helén said, nodding toward the display. "People think they can do whatever they want over there."

Winter looked at the man. He was completely naked now, and he looked around, as though to find more clothes to take off. His face was partly in shadow. His dick swung in time as he moved back and forth.

"What happened with that guy?" Winter asked.

"Your colleagues came and got him."

Winter read the display. Mr. Naked had stripped at twenty-eight minutes past eight the evening before Paula disappeared. But at that time she had been at the movie.

"When they took him away he shouted something about how it was unseasonably warm."

"He was right about that," Winter said, studying the squares again. He would need compound eyes for this. He concentrated on the women again. There weren't many of them. And somehow, oddly, the cameras didn't show faces straight on. Maybe this was out of respect for people's integrity. An absurd adjustment that could only happen in this country, he thought: monitor but don't reveal anything; ascertain whether someone was in a particular place but protect personal integrity. Criminal integrity.

"It's hard to see any faces," he said.

"The secret camera above the stairs is best for that," Helén answered. "That's where we get all the faces." She pointed toward the green room. Winter could see the stair railings. "They pull off their masks halfway up the stairs."

4

They took the computer to the police station. Ringmar and Djanali were waiting in a larger conference room, with a larger monitor. Other colleagues were waiting in other rooms.

"Does everyone have a clear idea of what she looks like?" Winter had said.

"What she looks like in the pictures they got, at least," Ringmar had said. He had held up a few photos of Paula. "But it's a different matter on worthless videotape."

"Should we try to be a little bit positive?" Djanali had said.

"It's not worthless," Winter had said.

They had been positive, all the police in the room. There were a few guesses, but nothing definite.

Winter was sitting in his room and looking at the guesses now. The women in late-summer clothes. He knew how Paula had been dressed that last night, but it didn't have to mean anything.

First they would try to find Paula in the shimmery green images.

Then they would look for someone who might be retrieving a suitcase from the same locker it had been put in.

Winter had six possibilities in front of him, six possible Paulas. He looked at the images over and over again, six-seven-eight-nine-ten times. All of these women were lifting a suitcase that looked like Paula's, a black Samsonite. Some had trouble lifting them. Others just heaved the suitcase in, no matter the height.

He compared them with the photographs they had of the twenty-nine-year-old woman. Almost thirty-year-old. She hadn't really reached that age when some people suddenly feel old.

They had a span of a few hours when she could have left the suit-case, as long as she hadn't done it days earlier. But if it had happened the evening she disappeared, earlier that evening, or rather during the afternoon, then any of the six anonymous profiles in the images could have been Paula's. The magnification hadn't given him the guidance he'd hoped for. There was something about the light, and the colors underground. The way in which people held their heads.

Winter called the prosecutor for a decision on a search warrant.

They identified the numbers of the six lockers with Roffe Bengts-son's help.

They opened the lockers right on the spot.

There were orderly luggage tags on the outside; in some cases on the inside.

They could quickly identify all the owners.

None of them was Paula Ney.

Once again Winter left Bengtsson's office, which was hidden behind rows upon rows of lockers. It looked as though the whole world had something to store. As though the whole city were on a journey. There's no place like elsewhere. Or maybe they hadn't had any choice in the matter. Winter knew that more people than anyone would guess were evicted from their homes and moved their belongings to Central Station. They had to get everything into a few plastic bags, maybe a suitcase.

He heard Bengtsson behind him.

"How many lockers do you have?"

"Three hundred and ninety-four," Bengtsson said, and looked around, as though to count through them again.

"And how many of them would fit a suitcase of the size we're look-ing for?"

Bengtsson laughed. It echoed through the room. A woman ten meters away turned around and gave them a sharp look.

"You know how there are world records for how many people

would fit in a Volkswagen bug?" Bengtsson said, following the woman with his eyes as she left the room. She walked quickly, as though she had just been subjected to an insult. "Back when they existed, I mean. The old kind." Bengtsson gestured with his hand. "That's what it's like here. It's crazy how much crap people can cram into a storage locker. They try to break records every day."

Winter nodded. As though to confirm what Bengtsson had said, a family came into the room dragging trunks that would each require its own truck, if not a cargo plane. The group came to a halt in the middle of the shining floor and the man began to look for open lockers.

Bengtsson laughed again. The man looked up and smiled. He was of Indian origin. He turned back to the lockers again.

"That one will have to rent thirty lockers and also cut the suitcases into five parts," Bengtsson said. "Maybe there are engine blocks in them. Some foreigners try to carry home cars in construction kits."

"I want you to open all the lockers down here," Winter said as he watched the man out there return to his family and fling out his arms.

Ringmar had bought a shrimp sandwich that looked like it had been lying in a locker for seven days. Winter told him this before he had time to stop himself.

"Why seven?" Ringmar asked, wiping mayonnaise from his upper lip.

"That's when the time runs out," Winter said. "There's a counter mechanism for up to seven days, and when it's counted down and no one has collected his things from the locker, Bengtsson opens it and checks it out."

Ringmar looked at his shrimp sandwich.

"So he found this?"

They were sitting at one of the new cafés in Central Station. Bengtsson had called for help, locker-opening help. The search warrant was still in effect.

"Where is he?" Ringmar asked, setting down the sandwich on the plate, placing his napkin over it, and looking around.

"I was just kidding, Bertil," Winter said, looking at the plate. "I'm sorry. The sandwich looks wonderful. So fresh. You don't need to hide it."

"Then you can eat the rest," Ringmar said, pushing the plate over.

"I don't have much of an appetite right now."

"I did have one," Ringmar said. "You pulled me away from my lunch on the town."

"I'm sorry, Bertil, it was just something Bengtsson said."

"Are you blaming him now? He's not even here." Ringmar looked around again. "Where is he?"

"Coming soon. But what he said was that pretty often they have to open lockers because of food smells. Or whatever they call it."

Ringmar got up and grabbed the plate with his half a shrimp sandwich and carried it over to the cart of dishes.

"I'll buy you a new one," Winter said when Ringmar had returned.

"Not here."

"It's even worse than it sounds," Winter said. "The food comes from someone's pantry. When people are evicted they take what they can with them and lock it in here. Some photographs. Some knick-knacks. Some clothes. Food from the fridge." He flung one hand out. "It's their living room and kitchen all in one."

"Room number three hundred," said Ringmar. "Or number ten."

"Soon we'll get to see what it looks like for ourselves."

Winter had asked Bengtsson whether he had ever checked all the boxes at the same time before. Almost, Bengtsson had answered; one time when a horrible smell was driving all living things out of Central Station. They finally found food that some poor evicted bastard had brought from his fridge. The owner never came back. Maybe he, or she, had jumped in front of a train. That was common. The tracks were nearby, after all.

"What does he do with all the things that people never retrieve?" Ringmar asked, drinking the last of his café latte. There was no regular coffee here. "And I'm not talking about rotten cheese."

"Keeps most of it for a few months," Winter answered. "If there's space. If no one calls, he gives the things to the Salvation Army. Which then gives some of it away to the homeless."

"So you could say that it's a cycle," Ringmar said.

He knew that many of Bengtsson's customers were vagrants. Many died with the key in their pocket, or disappeared in other ways. Some actually left on a train.

"He empties ten or fifteen deserted lockers every day," Winter said. "Here he comes, by the way."

Halders couldn't find any postcards in Paula Ney's apartment. Not from ten years ago. Not from any year at all. Apparently no one thought about her, not even with the hasty thoughts that fit on a post-card, or else they had also been removed from the apartment, along with the photographs.

The bag, he thought, the suitcase. She never traveled away, but the suitcase has to be somewhere. I don't think it's been emptied. Some-one has saved it for some special reason.

A painted right hand. What the hell kind of sick shit was that? Never seen such a thing. Can't have to do with identification. Birth-marks. We don't need that. Is there a photo of the hand in the suitcase now? Why am I thinking like this? Is the white hand on its way some-where? Why did that bastard need her hand? A hand collector? Good God. Halders walked over to the window and looked out. These thoughts. What a job. Occupying your intellect with thoughts about painted dead hands. Dead people. He could have been a nuclear physicist, a disc jockey, a hockey coach. Could have watched the sun go down over the city without wondering what kind of shit it would bring up the next morning.

Now it was on its way down again, farther and farther down, and gone. At the end of October next year he would take Aneta and the kids to Cyprus; they had already planned on it. It was still warm there in October, and a bit into November, too; he knew this because he had done winter battalion exercises down there in the eighties. An MP with a severe crew cut who still had his hair. Now he had a severely bald head. That was better; he wouldn't scratch someone if he head-butted him. But he didn't head-butt anyone, not even the car-borne drunk murderer. Cyprus. He would show them Cyprus for the first time. He hadn't been back, himself. But it was still there. He didn't think Larnaca had changed too damn much. He knew that Fig Tree Bay had. There had been nothing there then, only a bay they went to in an old piece-of-shit bus, a shed that sold drinks. Aiya Napa, not much then. A tired fishing village, hungover UN soldiers, Nissi Beach. A few dips in the salt water, a siesta in the shade of the palm grove near the entrance, two beers at the Pelican Bar and you were ready for everything again.

October. This one, or the next. Would they have caught Paula Ney's murderer by then? He looked out through the window; it was the same view that Paula had seen for the past few years. In October, the trees on that hill would be as good as bare. There wouldn't be much color left in this city. And that would just be the beginning of winter hell. It would be time to leave it. To travel. Traveling. This case was about traveling, in a way they didn't yet understand. He turned around. It wasn't just the suitcase.

Halders's cell phone rang. The sound was muffled in the half-finished apartment. He thought of it as half.

"What are you doing?" said Djanali.

"Thinking about Cyprus, actually."

"During working hours?"

"Don't tell anyone."

"Maybe she was on her way to the sunshine," said Djanali.

"Or anywhere."

"Are you still in the apartment?"

"Yes."

"Found anything?"

"No. Nothing personal."

"We don't know much about Paula Ney's personal life," said Djanali.

"Surprisingly little."

"She doesn't seem to have had any friends at work. Not that I met, anyway."

"Not so easy with headphones over your ears day after day," said Halders.

"She was working on other things, at least just now."

"What, exactly?"

"Well . . ."

"Thanks. Can't be more precise than that."

"It was services. Upgrading services for the customers."

"Oh, shit. I thought it was all about degrading customers," Halders said, turning in toward the room, the living room. The parlor. "Ex-customers."

"That's a bit retrograde of you," said Djanali.

"Yes, I can understand that."

"But anyway, she didn't have headphones over her ears."

"We'll have to have a good talk with her service-upgrading friends," said Halders. "Anything else new?"

"Winter is in the process of emptying all the lockers at Central Station."

"My thanks." Halders took a few steps into the room. He wasn't completely passé yet; they still listened to him. He saw the branches moving grandly outside the window. The crown of the tree was very green.

"There are almost four hundred of them, you know," said Djanali.

"Then they need help."

Paula Ney had owned a black Samsonite and that's what they could look for. They had gotten its approximate measurements from Paula's parents. It wasn't one of the largest models. It was one of the older ones.

Bengtsson was opening lockers with the help of two part-time employees of Speed Services AB and six police officers.

"What are you actually looking for?" Bengtsson had asked as they began.

"Just a suitcase," Winter had answered.

"What's in it, then?"

"Clothes, photos, maybe tickets. That's what we're going to check."

"Mm-hmm," Bengtsson had mumbled, looking as though he didn't believe what Winter said.

There were a lot of suitcases.

"Lots of suitcases here," said Halders, who had joined them.

They tried to work as quickly as possible. It felt like an impossible task; it was an impossible task. What are you actually looking for? Winter thought. It isn't just a suitcase.

It was lucky that the peak vacation time was over now, and travel had died down. A third of the lockers were empty. Some contained all the goods of a household, a home in a box. There was a garden gnome in one of the largest lockers. The gnome looked at Winter when he opened the locker.

After an hour's work, Bengtsson called out from over by the west end. Winter looked up and saw him take a few steps backward.

Winter ran through the aisle.

Bengtsson turned to him with a strange expression on his face.

"It doesn't smell," he said. "Shouldn't it smell?"

Winter bent down; the locker was low to the ground. It took a few seconds for his eyes to adjust to the darkness.

He saw a hand. It was wrapped in a transparent plastic bag. The bag was held closed by a rubber band that looked colorless. The hand was white as snow.

It was locker number 110.

There wasn't any smell in there.

The hand looked like plaster.

It was plaster. It lay on a table under Central Station. The cold light made it even more naked. As though it were alive. It had been caught in an open handshake, or at rest. The fingers were hardly separate.

"What the hell is this?" said Halders.

"A plaster hand," said Winter. "A perfect casting."

"Of Paula's hand?" said Halders.

"We don't know yet," said Ringmar.

Halders looked down at the hand. "It's not large." He looked up. "Her hand was just as white."

"Do you find a lot of these?" Halders asked, turning toward Bengtsson, who was standing a few steps beyond the table.

"This is the first time," said Bengtsson, who still appeared to be in some sort of shock. "I've seen plaster cats, and frogs . . . but not this."

"A perfect casting," Ringmar repeated. "If it is a casting."

"The hand was at rest when it was made," said Winter.

"It was probably dead," said Halders.

"There's some sort of scar on the upper side," said Winter, "a line."

He looked down at the hand. He bent down, bent closer. It was a horrible object. It shimmered green now among the green lockers and the green walls, a shade that made people feel nauseated. He was no longer certain that it was so perfect. It looked more like it had been cast from a standard form. Maybe it had even been purchased in some strange shop.

But the important thing wasn't what it looked like. It was what it was, what it meant. Symbolized, one could say. Winter was convinced that this hand had something to do with the case. With Paula. It was the murderer's greeting to them.

A wave. He wanted them to see him.

He knew that they would.

The murderer knew that they would *see* him soon.

See him on a shimmery green videotape.

Maybe he would wave. Make some signal that they would understand.

They would understand that he knew.

Winter felt the old familiar chill in his body. It appeared in certain cases, the most difficult ones. There could be years between times. It was a feeling that was related to dread.

Look at me! the murderer screamed.

Look what I did!

This is *me*!

"Someone carried the hand here and locked it in," said Ringmar.

"Time to watch TV again," said Halders.

Winter suddenly thought of ancient statues. They were missing limbs, heads. They were often only a torso, a snow-white torso. He had seen hundreds on his trips to southern Europe.

This was the opposite. A limb with no torso, a lone hand. Did that mean anything here? A statue was a dead thing that depicted the living.

Winter turned to Bengtsson.

"The timer had started to count down the second day," he said. "Someone locked this locker hardly forty hours ago. Should still be on the hard disk, right?"

Bengtsson nodded.

According to the display, the locker had been locked at 12:17 a.m., almost exactly thirty-nine hours ago.

The videotape showed a back and not much more.

They stood in front of the display in the bare room inside the office. The back was visible at the far end of the corridor. The image was as sharp as it could get, but that wasn't much help now.

They could see only a back, a long coat, the back of a wide-brimmed hat. It wasn't possible to determine how large the person was. They would have to measure against the height of the lockers.

"There's our man," said Halders.

Winter ran the sequence again. It lasted for fifty seconds. During that time, the Back had time to put coins in the slot, put something in, close it, turn the key. They could follow what he was doing from his movements.

"That bastard has gloves," said Ringmar.

"Good," said Halders. "Who has time to check fingerprints on ten thousand five-krona coins?"

They ran the tape again.

"Look how he moves," said Ringmar. "Not even a half profile. It's just his back the whole time."

"A long coat in the middle of summer," said Halders. "He was certainly dressed for a spot in the limelight."

"He knows exactly where the cameras are," Winter said, turning toward Bengtsson again. "Or is it luck?"

"Run it again," said Bengtsson.

They ran it again. Winter felt an excitement, and an even greater frustration. They might have the murderer right there. He really was here in this city; at least he had been recently. He stood there in the image, walked there in the image with the jerky movements of the digital resolution.

Winter could reach out his hand and touch him.

And he knew that Winter could do this, knew that Winter would see this. Why did he do it? It was a risk, after all. He was exposing himself. He was protected by his clothing and the way he placed his body, but still his clothing and his placement were visible. A body always revealed something about its owner. Height. The manner of walking, of moving the parts of the body, even when it was affected by technology.

The Back extended his hand. Winter saw the movement now, from the back. He extended the hand with . . . the hand.

"He's avoiding the cameras in his face, from the front," said Bengtsson.

"It can't be luck," said Ringmar.

"Then he knows this place better than I do," said Bengtsson.

"Is that possible?" Ringmar asked.

"No."

"Then he's studied the room and the lockers carefully," said Halders, "ahead of time."

"Or else he's a former employee," said Ringmar. "He knows where the cameras are."

"No," Bengtsson said again, "it's just me and a couple of old extras here. And they don't have backs like that." He looked at Ringmar. "And I don't either."

"Maybe he's in other tapes," said Winter. "If he walks around and checks the angles."

"Those would probably be erased," said Halders.

"There are a few days. We have a few days."

"This may have been planned far ahead of time," said Ringmar. "He might have been here months ago."

Winter didn't answer.

The figure disappeared from the display.

"He never took the stairs!" Winter said.

"The secret camera," Ringmar said.

"What do you mean by that?" Halders asked.

"If he had taken the stairs, we would have gotten him straight in the face," Ringmar explained.

"Do you see the light under the stairs?" Winter said.

He ran the sequence again. It was like a light turned on for a few seconds.

"He took the elevator!" Winter said.

"Isn't there a camera in it?" Halders asked.

"No," Bengtsson answered. "But there is outside it."

"Not from what we've seen," said Ringmar.

"It should work," said Bengtsson. "It's worked before."

"Don't you check things like that?" Halders asked.

"Of course."

"Let's do it, then," said Halders.

They found the sequence. But all they saw was a bit of a coat that was hidden by the elevator door.

"He must have climbed on the wall," said Bengtsson.

"Is it the same coat?" said Ringmar.

"Yes" Winter said, turning to Bengtsson. "How often do you clean down here?"

"Sorry?"

"How often do you mop the floor down here?"

Winter could see a bit of the floor out there, smooth stone tiles, even these shimmering green.

"I'm not the one who cleans," Bengtsson answered. "I'll have to ask Helén." He went out to the office and came back after thirty seconds. "At least four or five times a day, she says."

"Shit," said Winter, "but we'll try." He turned to Bergenhem, who had just come back after checking the fire alarm above the elevator. "Make sure to cordon that locker off. And call Öberg."

"What does this hand *mean*?" said Halders. "It does mean something, right? He means something with it. He knew that we would find this plaster shit sooner or later."

"He didn't know when," said Winter.

"Okay, maybe he thought it would be later, but he *knew,* and he knew about the surveillance, and he took the risk of leaving . . . the message."

"Maybe it's not a message," said Ringmar.

"What is it, then?" Halders asked.

"It's exactly what it looks like. Storing an object. Someone wanted to store it in the locker."

"In the same locker he retrieved Paula's suitcase from?"

"We don't know anything about that," said Winter. "We don't know if she even left it here. We don't even know if it's relevant to this case. She could have given it away, sold it, stored it somewhere else entirely."

"Well, we have to check the tapes again," Halders said, "the scenes where locker number 110 plays the lead role."

Winter nodded.

"And check who was here just after midnight the day before yesterday." He turned to Bengtsson. "Were you here?"

"Yes. Here in the office." Bengtsson looked around, and then out through the closed door, as though he was only now realizing that he had been only ten or twenty meters from a possible murderer.

"We close at twelve thirty," he continued, "and open at four thirty in the morning."

"Were there any people out there then?" Halders asked.

"When?"

"Twelve thirty at night. Around midnight."

"At least one," Bengtsson said, nodding toward the flickering monitor.

"Did you see anyone else?"

"Yeah . . . there were probably some other people out there. Out in the station, that is. Some poor souls who wanted to stay warm as long as they could."

"No one by the lockers?"

"When I closed up down here it was empty."

"Should we watch a movie again, then?" said Halders.

5

There!" Halders flew up and pointed with his whole hand. "That's her suitcase!"

Winter saw a black Samsonite. Ringmar saw it, and Bengtsson. Winter saw a woman he didn't recognize, and the open locker, number 110. The woman set the suitcase inside and locked up and walked away without looking around. He had seen part of her face; her clothing in the late summer. No long coat, no hat. Her hair was very light on the screen, white or blond. She was wearing dark glasses that largely ruined any chance of identification.

"She isn't worried about the cameras," said Ringmar.

"Maybe she doesn't know about them," said Winter. "Or doesn't care."

"Do we know her?" said Halders.

"So it's not Nina Lorrinder, the friend?" Ringmar asked. "You're the only one who's met Lorrinder, Fredrik."

"It's not her; I can tell through the sunglasses," said Halders. "Lorrinder is prettier. And above all, younger."

"What time is it?" Ringmar said.

He was thinking of the time he saw on the screen. What was happening there had happened four days ago.

"Five thirty," said Bengtsson. "In the afternoon."

"When did Paula meet her friend?" Ringmar asked. "For that trip to the movies?"

"Six fifteen outside Biopalatset," said Winter. "The movie began at six thirty."

"She would have had time to deposit the suitcase herself and then go to the theater," Ringmar said.

"But she didn't, did she?" Halders said. "That's not her, is it?"

"Run the tape again," Winter said.

He saw an unfamiliar woman place an unfamiliar suitcase in a familiar locker.

"It could be a regular citizen, and any Samsonite at all," Ringmar said, pointing at the monitor. "After a few hours she retrieved the suitcase again and someone else used the locker, and someone else, and so on."

Winter looked at Bengtsson.

"It's not possible," Bengtsson said, "we'd see it. That shady bastard had to pay a three-day surcharge to open the locker." He nodded toward the screen. The woman in the picture was leaving for the fourth time. Winter thought of the making of movies, of retakes. They still hadn't gotten it right.

"Number 110," Bengtsson clarified.

"So it's one hundred percent that the Back took out the same suitcase that the blond woman put in?" Halders asked.

Bengtsson nodded.

"Who is she?" Ringmar said.

They had two people who were connected to the murder of Paula Ney. One clear, one unclear, like a shadow, but both unknown. Sending a picture of the woman to the media would be pointless; they would get tens of thousands of witnesses who had seen a blond woman in sunglasses. It would be essentially the same as sending out a picture of a man's back.

"There's something . . . crafty about this," Ringmar said. "On both of these characters' parts."

They had returned to the cafeteria. The waitress was already treating them as regulars. She smiled several times. We're not getting away from here, Winter thought. Look at her. The case begins and ends here. If it does end. He didn't want to think of any sort of symbolism; he did that too readily and such things could lead anywhere, often in the wrong direction. It seldom led forward. He pushed away thoughts of someone sitting at a train station, never getting to see their train come up on the monitor. Sitting there for hours, days. A harsh fate. But not as harsh as death. The waitress smiled at him as she placed his cappuccino on the table. He had seen that they had whiskey at the bar, half a meter's worth of bottles. The waitress was blond, like the woman on the monitor.

"Take the blond," Ringmar said. "She trots in with her nose in the air but with sunglasses on its tip. It's a disguise. She knows she's being observed, or will be. Maybe she's wearing a wig, for that matter." He sipped his latte. It tasted like milk and nothing else, and he suddenly missed the horrible coffee from the machine up at high command. It was Halders who called it "high command," because their unit was on the floor above the floor below. "But she doesn't care. It's crafty some-how . . . there's something arrogant about it. She choo—"

"Why would she care?" Halders interrupted. "She wasn't commit-ting any crime. Just leaving a friend's suitcase. Paula was going to get it later."

"Is that what you think?"

"No."

"She's leaving someone else's suitcase," Ringmar continued. "It might be her own, but we're assuming that it's someone else's be-cause she didn't retrieve it herself. Why? Why drag a suitcase there? It looked pretty heavy when she lifted it in. Was it because Paula Ney asked her to? Or was the suitcase stolen? Why keep it at Central Sta-tion? Why wait several days to pick it up?" He nodded over toward the departure hall. "I mean, when the Back picked it up."

"Well, there is one thing that indicates that this woman is involved in Paula's murder, somehow," Winter said.

"What's that?" Halders said.

"She hasn't contacted us," Winter said.

They were still sitting at Central Station. They couldn't move. We can think here, Winter thought, there's something about this place. If we leave, our imaginations will disappear. We have other people who are good at working with photos. But this is the thinking booth. This is high command. I don't like my office anyway. I'm not going back.

The café had no windows facing the train tracks, but he could see out through some sort of arcade that had arisen at the same time as the other renovations. He could tell that the sun had gone down now, outside. Electric lights were blazing all over the station. The light wasn't noticeable until the sun went behind a cloud or went down. The columns cast faint shadows over the white walls. Everything looked like plaster.

"We're going to find her," said Halders.

"If she's alive," said Ringmar.

"Why wouldn't she be alive?" said Halders.

Ringmar shrugged slightly. His gesture said that Paula Ney was dead and that other people might be dead, too.

"If she's alive—and not being kept prisoner—she has to be involved," Winter said.

"Like our friend with the long coat," Ringmar said.

"He's not my friend," Halders said. "I don't like that bastard, no matter what he's done or hasn't done."

"He's done a hand," Winter said.

"I can hardly contain myself until I find out why," Halders said.

"Don't contain yourself, Fredrik," Ringmar said. "Why start now?"

Aneta Djanali called as Winter was on his way to the car. The north annex of the station was a wall of sharp metal and glass that had a mirror effect in the sunshine. There were no columns, just swinging doors that swung back and forth as travelers went back and forth. Buses drove in and buses drove away. As he was on his way to the car it struck him that he hadn't traveled by bus for many years, not even to the annual chief inspector conference somewhere in a coastal town in Bohuslän. He always drove.

"They're tight as clams at the hotel," Djanali said.

"They probably think they have a reason to be."

"I know you mean the suspicions of prostitution. But this is a murder investigation."

"Doesn't matter," Winter said.

"Not because they have a reputation to protect, but still."

"The hotel protects its customers," Winter said. "The johns, and God knows who else."

"I haven't gotten the names of all the guests," Djanali said. "I don't think I have, anyway. It's not easy, you could say."

"I understand."

There was a scratching sound in Winter's earpieces, as though they had switched to another frequency.

"But you're not surprised, are you?" Djanali said.

"What?"

"About the people who are guests in the beds at Revy. Or who have been before."

"No," Winter answered. "Not anymore."

"They're probably going to close down, by the way."

"They are?"

"The clerk I talked to said so. He didn't know anything more. But there was something going on."

There had been a time Winter could be amazed by anything. Amazed, aghast, afraid. Astonished. There was so much he didn't know then. Once he learned, it helped him with his work, soon enough, but he didn't feel that he became any richer because of it, or more whole as a person. All the darkness he encountered made him long for sunshine, lots of sunshine. He felt that he became a more solitary person the more experience he got. He couldn't hang his thoughts on a hook inside the door when he left his office. He couldn't leave the police station and forget everything when the doors swung closed behind him. He knew he had colleagues who forgot everything when the evening came; not many, but enough to make it harder for him and others who took their work seriously. At first he had thought that he took this job far too seriously. But how else could he take it? And his solitude was a condition of this. He had never had a large group of friends. Some women, a few men. A childhood friend or two. He had never had anything against solitude. He didn't feel lonely. If the alternative was to sit with people and talk his way through the evenings, he preferred his own company. He could talk to himself if he wanted to hear a voice in the evening. He had done so once in a while. He could call someone. He didn't need to be alone with himself if he didn't want to be. He found his own method. It presumed a silence that existed only in his apartment, not at the department.

He lived up in Guldheden then, in a rental apartment between Guldhedens School and Doktor Fries Torg. The building was tall and he could see a long way, over the river, the hills, the lakes to the east, the highways that had been built around the city, thirty years too late, but which simultaneously encircled some sort of innocence that had existed in this city where he'd grown up and remained. He could stand on the rickety balcony on the seventh floor and watch the wide net of roads twine themselves around the old roads that led out; he thought of them more as roads out rather than roads in; the highway down there was built meter by meter, and a remnant of the innocence would stay inside the roads as it had done inside the old city walls. Outside the roads: wilderness. Or maybe it was the other way around. All the statistics, every one of the available facts, indicated that the city had become a worse place to live during the nearly twenty years he had been a police officer here. More dangerous, more unpredictable, like an ax to the skull on a mild spring evening. Twenty years, half a working life. If I can stay for another twenty years, there will be only wilderness; the jungle has taken over but there are no beautiful palm trees.

He had several thoughts like that. He didn't mean to think like that, but he knew what it was: his method. Or the preliminary phase. In the beginning of a case he wasn't much use. His world was meaningless and he was the one who had made it so. When he was gone for good, there would only be a thicker crime registry, a larger hard disk. He became smaller with each year, more replaceable. And so on, and so on.

He got up and walked out onto the balcony and lit a thin cigar and contemplated the copper roofs on the other side of Vasaplatsen. The obelisk down in the park was a finger to the sky. The sound of the streetcars was muffled on its way up to his balcony; the light was clearer down there, like slow-motion flashes as cars and streetcars slowly started moving or slowed down.

Some time on the balcony. It was one of the better times, especially now, and especially in the evening, in the seam between August and September, when the air around him had a simplicity and a particular blond and blue brightness that made everything more transparent than ever. Up here there were scents that lingered from the height of summer and blended with something spicier, more humid. The autumn had a more humid scent, the summer a drier one. This summer had been neither. And suddenly it was over.

He went into the room and poured a whiskey from the carafe that stood among other carafes and bottles on a corner table. He knew which brands were in the carafes, but friends who came to visit might want to test their knowledge of malt whiskey. He had friends, new friends. That was one thing that had changed. Angela had probably helped with that, and Elsa; because some of the new parents continued to get together even when they weren't so new anymore. And then came Lilly, and everything started over again, possibly without as many new parents.

Angela.

He looked at the clock. Either she'll call in the next five minutes or I will. He lifted the glass to his mouth. The phone rang as he felt the first sip of the day burn its way down through his throat and chest and stomach.

"High command," he said.

"What if it hadn't been me," she said.

"High command is where I hang my hat."

"You don't have a hat."

"It's a figure of speech."

"It's an Anglicism. Besides, it's 'home.' 'Home is where I hang my hat.'"

"This is home," Winter said, looking around.

"How is it at home, then?" Angela said.

"Lonely. How is it there?"

"Pretty warm. But it rained yesterday. People danced in the street. The last time it rained here in August was in 1923, it seems."

"The year of my birth," he joked, taking a few drops of whiskey in his mouth. It had a scent of burned peat and five-degree-Celsius Atlantic water. Tasted like wild herbs from northern Europe. It was a continent away from Costa del Sol. Angela and the girls were still staying with Siv, his little chain-smoking mom. He had come home ten days ago with a deep sunburn and a mild hangover from Mother's very dry martinis. But she had reduced the drinking during the past few years. Maybe it was related to Elsa's birth. Maybe she wanted to live a little longer. A life on the sunny coast took its toll, among golf courses and galleries and shopping malls and bored tax evaders who tried to escape existence even during the early-afternoon cocktail parties.

Angela liked Siv. She had even gotten her to start swimming in the salt water, after only a few decades on the Mediterranean. They had found a good beach past Estepona. There were also small coves closer to Puerto Banús if you looked. Elsa and Lilly went swimming, laughed; Elsa ran in and out of the umbrellas' shade, becoming dark as chocolate.

There was suddenly life in the chalk-white house up in Nueva Andalucía, laughing, children's tears, clatters and rumbles from the kitchen, and no longer just from the blender, which had long been Siv's favorite appliance. Elsa played under the palm tree in the yard; one-year-old Lilly was learning how to walk. Angela was sometimes tired of their apartment at Vasaplatsen. She sometimes said so. They had a plot of land by the sea, south of Billdal. Something was holding him back, back in the heart of the city. The apartment was large. Children like to play in large apartments. That's what he told Angela. Maybe she agreed. But the balcony was no yard. The plot by the sea could give them room for a summer house, for a start.

"Are you feeling old again, Erik?" he heard her voice. There was a buzzing through the line, as though he could hear the cicadas all the way up here.

"I was thinking about those first years," he said.

"The twenties?"

"When I started this damn job."

"So it's that bad tonight?"

He gave a brief explanation of Paula Ney's fate.

"So that's what you came home to."

"I should have stayed."

"Well, that's what I said."

"But who would support the growing family?"

"I would, of course."

"You haven't talked more with the people at the clinic in Marbella, have you?"

"No, not yet."

"Are you planning to?" he asked.

"I would earn more than you and me combined, Erik."

"I hope you're joking."

"Not about the salary."

"I could stop working. We would still be okay."

"That's what I'm saying."

"I mean that there's money apart from the job at the clinic."

"I know that, too."

"So in other words, you don't need to take it."

"I probably don't want to anyway. But six months or so down here . . . the girls are at the right age; we don't need to think about schools . . . a winter in the sun . . . well . . ."

"What would I do, then?"

"Be with the girls, of course."

It sounded so simple. And so obvious.

That was because it *was* simple and obvious.

He looked at the clock, as though to see when winter would begin. Suddenly he had made up his mind.

"It's a good idea," he said. "It's just a matter of a leave of absence."

"Why not retirement?"

"I'm not joking now, Angela."

"Do you mean it?"

"It's a good idea. I just realized it now. I'm serious."

He was serious; he felt serious. The liquor wasn't affecting him; not yet.

"I'll talk to Birgersson tomorrow. I can take a leave of absence starting December first."

She didn't answer.

"It's by the book. It's more than two months until December."

"Your . . . case, then? This murder?"

It will be solved by then, he thought. It has to be.

"We'll find substitutes to run the primary investigation," he answered. "It will work. We could do it even now, just in case."

She didn't say anything.

"Has the job at the clinic gone to someone else?" he asked.

Winter himself could tell how anxious his voice sounded. Suddenly he wanted to wander in the sun this winter, more than anything. Ice cream with the girls down at the harbor. A trip to Málaga, a glass of cava among the casks and the sawdust at Antigua Casa de Guardia, Picasso's old haunt. More ice cream for the girls. A swim. Grilled sea bass. Various tapas in sunset after sunset.

"Angela?" She must be able to hear the anxiety in his voice. "Did you say no? Did the job go to someone else?"

"I've only spoken with them once, Erik. And it was almost only in passing. At least on my part."

"Call them right away and make an appointment for an interview."

"Things are moving quickly," she said. "But . . . where will we live, for example? In that case. We can't live with Siv the whole time."

"Forget that for now! It will all work itself out."

Now their roles had changed. She was hesitating. He had made up his mind. But she had never made up her mind. It was an idea, an impulse, something different. A nice memory, maybe. You only live once. And Elsa would quickly learn to order for him. *Un fino, por favor.*

"Okay, I'll call," she said. "But it's too late tonight."

"Spanish clinics open early in the morning."

"I know, Erik."

He sensed her smile.

"Now I want to talk to Elsa," he said. "And Lilly."

"Lilly fell asleep hours ago. Here's Elsa."

And she told him about her day. The words came in clumps; there was no space between them.

He didn't tell her about his day.

He dreamed about a woman who was waving at him with one hand. She held the other hidden behind her back. She had no face. There was nothing. Where her face should have been there was only a white surface; it was dull. She waved for the second time. He turned around to see whether someone was standing behind him, but he was alone. Behind him was only a white surface, a wall that didn't end. Someone said the word "love." It couldn't be her, because she didn't have a mouth. It couldn't be him because he knew that he hadn't said anything. Here it was again: love. It was like a breeze. Now he could see the breeze; it was red, it rushed down over the wall and made the wall red. The woman stood there the entire time with her arm moving, a dress that was clutched by the breeze. Everything turned red, white, red, white. He heard something again but it was a voice without words, or words that he couldn't understand, a different language that he'd never heard. He didn't know what he was doing there. There was nothing he could do. He couldn't help the woman who was swept away with the wind. He couldn't move. The wind picked up; the sound of something being struck, wind, strike, wind. He heard a name. It wasn't Paula's name, not Angela's or Elsa's or Lilly's.

Winter woke up naked. His first thought was of the white wall that had turned red. He couldn't see it in the darkness. He was freezing.

He heard the sound of something being struck, and wind, and realized that he had fallen asleep with the window open and the wind had come up out there and the window had come loose and now it was striking the window frame with perfect regularity. It sounded like a cry.

He heaved himself up and placed his feet on the sheet, which had ended up on the floor. He looked at the clock. When he had turned out the light a few hours ago, it had been a warm and humid night, early night. He had had trouble falling asleep and had pulled the thin comforter out of the duvet cover. Now the weather had changed, with a wind from the north. From tropical to temperate, or northerly. He shivered again and pulled on his linen pants and walked through the darkness out into the kitchen and took a bottle of sparkling water from the fridge and drank. It was still black night outside the window, toward the courtyard. It had recently been like day at this time, only a few weeks ago. There was always the same surprise. The darkness couldn't wait. It couldn't contain itself. Just a few more months and it would be night at three in the afternoon. Welcome to Scandinavia.

He put down the bottle. He remembered the name he had heard in the dream. Ellen. A woman's voice had shouted it, straight through the wind. Ellen. He had seen Paula but heard Ellen's name. He hadn't seen Paula's face, but it must have been her. She had hidden her hand.

They were connected. Ellen and Paula were connected.

No.

He remembered what he'd said to Bertil the other day, when they were talking about the case of Ellen Börge: There was something there. Something I could have done. Something I could have seen. It was there, in front of me. I should have seen it.

What was it he should have seen? Did it have to do with Paula Ney's case? Why had he started to think about Ellen Börge when Paula Ney's death came into his life?

It was the room.

The hotel, he thought. Revy, they have it in common. And the room, and their age, twenty-nine years old.

But I'm not the same.

Winter freed himself from the sink counter; it felt as though he had become fastened to it.

He went into the living room and sat down on the sofa. Everything was still dark.

Where is Ellen?

Was she wearing sunglasses?

No, quit it now, Winter.

What did Paula's hand mean? What was it for? Did the fingers point anywhere? Were they supposed to understand it? Go in the right direction?

No.

Yes.

No.

6

A much younger Erik Winter stepped in through the door and nodded at the guard behind the glass. The man smiled, as though they shared a secret joke.

Winter looked at the elevator doors. They gleamed with a dull sheen that threw his mirror image back like a silhouette. You could be anyone.

In the elevator he thought: This is like my first trip.

The doors opened into the hall and he walked out. He could see the lawn of Gamla Ullevi, the old stadium, through the window. It was green like in a painting. He walked across the hall and pressed the combination to the tempting corridor inside. It was the first time. He could tell it was a special day. The door didn't open. He pressed the combination again, but nothing happened. It wasn't the wrong code, as long as they hadn't changed it since yesterday afternoon. He pressed it a third time.

"You must be lost, kid."

He turned around. The man was smiling, but it wasn't a friendly smile. Winter didn't recognize him. He was dressed in civilian clothes, like Winter. But "civilian" was a definition with a wide scope. Maybe Winter looked like a snob. The other man definitely looked like a thug. Winter recognized most faces at the police station, but not this one. It wasn't a pleasant face. It could scare people, and not always in the right way. The chin was square and the ears were smaller than they should be. The eyes had a particular shine that Winter suspected was there a little too often. He had a smile that wasn't calming. That face belonged on the other side of the law, on page one or two or three in the crime registry. It belonged to a new client.

Or a new crime-buster.

"Identification, please," said the crew-cut thug, extending his hand and smiling his strange smile again.

"Listen here . . ."

"Identification! We don't want every Tom, Dick, and Harry scraping on the door of the CID."

"I work here," Winter said, backing up a step as his aggressive colleague took a step closer. He was a colleague. Winter recognized the scent of yesterday's liquor in the thug's morning-fresh breath. There were a few small ruptures in his eyes. He wasn't in a joyful morning mood. Winter wasn't either. He was starting to become annoyed by this act.

"We haven't ordered any shoe or window polishing today," his colleague said, smiling his smile again and shoving Winter in the shoulder. Winter landed one where it hurts most.

"I have never seen the like!"

Winter was staring straight into a different face, more wrinkled than the other one, but with clearer eyes. The face was close. Winter sensed a vague but definite scent of tobacco. It came from the man's clothes and was blended with a fresh smell from the cigarette he was holding in his hand. The smoke suddenly stung Winter's eyes. He blinked to avoid tears. That wouldn't look good.

"What the *hell* are you two doing?!"

The older man turned toward the younger one, who was sitting beside Winter, the guy with the smile, and pressed his face close to him. There was no smile on the older face. The smile had disappeared from the younger one.

"Do we have to send you out on the street where you belong again, Halders?!"

"He started it."

"Shut *up*!" the older man yelled; he kept his face where it was, and Winter could see the man's spit fall like drizzle across Halders's face. So his name was Halders. He must be new to the unit; not quite as new as Winter but almost. Winter knew that this yelling and spitting and chain-smoking man was Sture Birgersson, the chief inspector and the boss of the CID. A problem solver with an imagination. That was how he solved problems. But this problem had made him dangerously red in the face. His blood pressure didn't know where it should go; it looked as though the blood was racing around his body, desperately searching for a way out.

"Are you sitting there *blaming someone else*, you fucking cowardly shit?!"

He pulled his face away from Halders and threw a hard look at Winter. Winter saw that Birgersson's eyes were yellow, clear and yellow. This was the first time he was working under him. The first day, first hour, first minutes. A brilliant start.

"And what are we going to do with this mannequin?"

Halders sneered.

"I said *shut up!*" Birgersson yelled, without looking at Halders. His face came close to Winter's again. "I guess you misunderstood the job, huh? Have you seen too many American cop movies? *Miami Vice,* or whatever the hell they're called? Snobby fags in Armani suits who can beat up anyone they like? Is that what you think this job is all about?"

Winter opened his mouth, but Birgersson yelled "*Shut up!*" before he had time to say anything.

"I put in my vote for you, kid."

Birgersson stared into Winter's eyes. Birgersson's eyes resembled a lunar landscape. He also seemed about as far away as the moon, even though he was so close that Winter could smell the cigarette stink from his mouth. The smoke from the cigarette in Birgersson's hand rose and stung in Winter's eyes again, and he had to strain not to blink. Blinking would be a sign of weakness. If he blinked even once, he would be thrown out of this corridor and this department on his head, and he would never again get to solve a case dressed in an Armani suit. It would be the uniform again for him, night patrols in the red-light district around Pustervik again, presumably in the company of Halders. Death would be preferable.

"*Voted* for you, you little shit," Birgersson said, jerking his face back and sitting with a heavy crash in his office chair. It was a miracle that it didn't break. "I even had to *raise my voice*," Birgersson continued, as though this was something unusual for him to do. "There were people who raised objections about you, and I had to bet my honor that you were ready for the job!" He abruptly turned to Halders. "And then this!"

Halders had the sense to keep quiet.

"If Bertil hadn't come out of the hall at that moment, who the fuck knows how this would have ended!"

"Presumably with the police commissioner," said the fourth man in the room. He hadn't said anything earlier. He was Bertil Ringmar and he was a detective in the unit. He was ripe for the title of chief inspector, overripe; but it was hard always to be in Birgersson's shadow, hard to step out of it. Winter had exchanged a few words with Ringmar now and then during the past year, and he thought that he was a decent guy. He was about ten years older than Winter. Winter had looked forward to working with him, learning from him.

Now he might have ruined that forever.

At the same time, he would do it again. Ruin it again. Bash Halders for the satisfaction of seeing that damn smile smooth out into something else. Maybe he *wasn't* ready for this job.

"Not just with the boss," Birgersson said. "That would be the manageable part. I'm talking about Sahlgrenska Hospital, probably the emergency room, and then the papers of course, and the TV, and court, and the appeal, and the government, and the whole fucking UN!"

There were giant plants in pots in every corner of the café. It was like a jungle, like a reminder that it was possible to go on a long journey. Winter might get all the time he needed soon. It depended on how mature he was in the near future.

They had left the police station as quickly as they could. No one felt like drinking coffee twenty meters from Birgersson's office.

Halders made a face as he sat down.

"Does it hurt?" Winter asked.

"What?" said Halders.

"I'm really looking forward to working with you," said Winter.

"Don't be so sure," said Halders. "The old man has changed his mind before."

Old man Birgersson had run out of voice and cigarettes and thrown them out with a warning. Ringmar had been sent off with the two rascals.

"And I don't think I have time to babysit at work," Halders continued.

"I don't plan to sit," said Winter.

"What do you plan to do, then?" Halders said, smiling his smile.

This has to end, Winter thought. If it takes years, this has to end for good. He's got the upper hand. Should I ask him to give me a good punch to the gut so we're even?

Ringmar cleared his throat.

"What Birgersson was trying to say in his, uh . . . subtle way is that this isn't a schoolyard or a playpen."

"What does subtle mean?" Halders said.

"Sensitive," said Winter.

"I knew that you knew it," said Halders, smiling.

"Sensitive like you," said Winter.

Halders's smile remained.

"Does anyone here actually understand what I just said?" said Ringmar.

August had been greener than usual because it had rained more than usual this summer. It was still raining as Winter stood outside Hotel Revy. It was four o'clock in the afternoon and the light had disappeared, sucked up into a sky that was low and gray, a winter sky already, in early September.

He looked up at the third floor, a row of windows out toward the street—three windows, and the one in the middle belonged to room number ten. No one had climbed out of that window in the middle of the night; he knew that much.

Not Ellen Börge. Not anyone else.

The dimness in the lobby was the same as outside. The dimness was intensified by the plants. Winter thought of the café where he and Ringmar and Halders had sat a week or so ago. He thought of southern lands again. There was a strange smell in the lobby. Maybe that was it.

He was alone in there. Music was coming from somewhere, maybe from a radio. The music told him nothing. It sounded like no one was listening. The music stopped and he could hear the rain against the awning over the entrance. There were holes in it; a raindrop had landed on his cheek as he walked up the steps.

The hotel seemed closed, deserted. But a hotel was never closed, especially not this one.

He walked up to the desk and looked around. The music had started again, a low hum. Maybe it was a vacuum cleaner. The sound seemed to come from above. Maybe it was a maid in room ten. Winter had been up there; a technician had been there but there was nothing to investigate. Ellen had stayed there for one night, or almost a night, and had been gone with the first morning light. That was last night. No one had seen her leave Revy, not even the desk clerk. She had paid when she checked in; that was the policy of the establishment. Winter understood why. Most of the guests stayed here for only an hour, half an hour. He wondered why Ellen had chosen a place like this. Maybe that was exactly why. No one said anything, heard anything. Revy was a good choice for a person who wanted to run away. A few hours of contemplation, if that was possible here, maybe rest, hardly sleep, and then away with the morning train, or the bus, south, east, north. To the west there was only sea; in that case it would have to be ships, ferries. They didn't know which direction she'd gone, if she'd gone. Up to now, no travel agent had sold her any tickets.

The desk clerk showed up behind the reception desk. He stepped out through a doorway that had been in shadow, like everything else in there. There was no door, only a curtain. He yawned, like after a siesta. Maybe it was a difficult job to be a hotel clerk, especially here.

He was a clerk who was responsible for room keys, and it was probably difficult to get uninterrupted sleep here at night.

The man yawned again, without trying to hide it. He was about Winter's age, not yet thirty. He was wearing a jacket, like Winter, but the difference was that this guy also used his as pajamas.

"Hard day?" Winter asked. "Or night."

"Uh . . . what?"

The clerk scratched his head. His hair was long in back, short over his ears. He could be Elvis. An ice-hockey-playing Elvis.

"I was here yesterday," Winter said.

"Oh?"

"The missing person. Ellen Börge." Winter held out his identification. The clerk studied it with eyes that seemed nearsighted.

"You weren't here yesterday," Winter said. "Your colleague said that you would be here now. You were the one who checked her in."

"Who?"

He hadn't really woken up yet. Maybe he never really woke up.

"Ellen Börge. You checked her in at eleven thirty."

"Mm-hmm."

"You remember it?"

"I'm not stupid."

"No one said you were stupid."

Not yet, Winter thought. But you're a cocky bastard. This isn't the first time you've run across the police. The police are here all the time. You're tired of them. Of us.

"Your colleague showed us the guest register. Her name was there. Can you get it out again?"

"I remember her," the clerk said without moving. "Börge. I checked the name when she'd gone up to her room. It's like a guy's name for a girl, isn't it?"

"Do you usually check people's names when they check in?"

"Uh . . . no. But . . . she came alone."

"And she didn't look like a whore? Is that what you mean?"

The clerk looked down at the desk without answering, as though he was suddenly taking the shame of the hotel upon himself. He looked up. "She didn't have a bag either, only a purse." He waved a few fingers toward the desk. "She set it down when she was writing. And when she left I thought of that, how she didn't have a suitcase."

"Describe her purse," Winter said.

"Oh . . . black."

"Black? Is that all you remember?"

"Yes . . . and small. A strap. The way ladies' purses look. I can't tell them apart."

He looked over toward the stairs, as though he would see Ellen there. "She looked like she was, like, on her way somewhere. I remember thinking that. This place is close to Central Station, you know, and we have lots of customers who take the first room they find before they move on. Travelers. I'm, like, used to recognizing people who are on their way somewhere."

"And she looked like she was on her way somewhere?"

"I thought so."

"And she did get away."

"So I hear."

"Sometime during the night, or the early morning."

"That's what they say."

"Don't you believe it?"

"I don't believe anything. I don't *know* anything. I wasn't here. Got off at twelve."

"Your colleague didn't notice anything."

"I know. I can imagine."

"What do you mean?"

"He never notices anything. He sleeps." The clerk smiled. "He hands out keys in his sleep."

Winter believed him. He had gotten the same impression. This joker was sleepy, but the other one was worse.

"How did she seem?"

"What?"

"Ellen Börge. When she checked in. You were watching her, after all. You noticed her. What was she like? Did she seem nervous? Was she tense? Was she looking around? Anything?"

"She seemed calm, I thought."

"It was raining. Was she dry?"

"I don't really get what you mean."

"It was pouring rain out there. Did she have an umbrella? Was she like a drowned rat? Did it seem like she was seeking shelter from the rain?"

"Well . . . I didn't see any umbrella. And she was wet, especially her hair." He passed his hand over his mullet haircut. "Well . . . maybe she was in here to rescue herself from the rain. But it's a long way from that to checking in here, isn't it?"

Winter didn't answer. Ellen had left home in sunshine, hardly a cloud in the sky. Christer Börge couldn't say exactly what clothes she'd had on when she left, but it was "something light." No coat; he claimed that everything was still hanging up. The umbrellas, two of them, were still standing in a prim umbrella stand. Yes, Winter had thought, why would she take an umbrella with her when the sun was shining.

Seven and a half hours later, she had checked in here, come in from the rain.

"Describe her clothing," Winter said.

"Can you describe her clothing again?" Winter said to Christer Börge.

"Is that really necessary?"

"Please describe her clothing," Winter repeated.

Börge told him about her clothes.

"I really did try to do my best," he said when he was finished.

"But you're not certain?"

Börge shrugged.

"Who can describe his wife's clothes in detail? Later on? Can you?"

"I'm not married."

"You get what I mean, right?"

Winter nodded.

"But she probably didn't have a jacket. It was a warm day, or night. Or afternoon, I don't know what to call it."

Winter nodded again, though there wasn't anything to nod at. Börge was still standing still in front of him, as he had been doing since Winter stepped into the hall. Börge didn't want him here, and Winter understood.

"Can we sit down for a bit?"

"Why?"

Winter didn't have to answer this, and he didn't. He nodded toward the room. It was illuminated by an intense evening light. The sun was going down in red and gold, September colors.

Börge turned around and went into the living room, and Winter followed him. They sat down. There was a sudden scent, as though from the light outside, like spices Winter didn't know the name of and might never taste. The door to the balcony was wide open. There was no wind. The room, and the balcony, gave an impression of elegance when the light fell in on them from the clear day. But the furniture was as plushy as when he had been here a day and a half or so ago. Maybe it would remain so. He wondered whether Börge would still be living here after a year, half a year. Whether Ellen would come back here. Winter thought that she would live happily ever after somewhere else. She would make contact from there. Christer would continue in unhappiness, or happiness. Maybe he was hiding his anxiety behind a mask of distaste. He was a stranger to Winter, like most people. Winter worked with strangers, some of them alive.

"Hotel Revy," Winter said.

"Never heard of the place," Börge said. "I've told you that."

"That's where she stayed."

"Stayed? Stayed? It was only a couple of hours. She didn't have a bag. I don't call that staying."

"What would you call it, then?" Winter asked.

Börge didn't answer.

"Why that particular hotel?" Winter said.

"Why a hotel?" said Börge.

"That's what I'm asking myself. And you."

Börge said something that Winter didn't catch.

"Sorry? What did you say?"

"She had no reason," Börge said in a low voice. There was something about his voice that Winter didn't recognize from before, a different tone.

"What do you mean by that?"

"What I'm saying." Börge looked Winter in the eye. "She had no reason to stay at that place, not even for a few hours. Or to go anywhere at all. She must have gotten sick. Her home was here." He looked around, at the home. "She belonged here." He looked at Winter again. "This was where she belonged."

The guy sounds like he'll never get to see her come home again, Winter thought. And at that moment, right there on the soft sofa, as the sun was suddenly hidden behind a cloud and everything became dim, dim like in the lobby of Hotel Revy, Winter believed that Christer and Ellen had seen each other for the last time.

7

The awning over the steps out front was blue now. There was no wind and no rain. The steps were dry. There were vertical cracks from the bottom up. A system of rivers without a delta.

Winter went up the stairs. He saw the cracks between the steps, and the weeds that were on their way up from the underworld. The third world, he thought. It goes quickly once it's started to go backward. An equalization occurs. It goes to hell on both sides of the equator.

It was dim in the lobby, and the darkness was intensified by the bright light outside. The sky was wide open out there, as though it were trying to move the horizons. It had a lighter shade of blue, as though it had been scrubbed by the summer rain.

He was alone in the lobby. Music was coming from somewhere, maybe from a radio. The music told him nothing. It sounded as though no one was listening.

He walked up to the desk and looked around. The music had started again, a low hum. He remembered. Almost twenty years had gone by, but everything was the same. His sense of déjà vu was not déjà vu. It was real. Nothing really happens in twenty years, he thought; everything just repeats itself.

The desk clerk showed up behind the reception desk. He stepped out through a doorway that had been in shadow, like everything else in there. There was no door, only a curtain.

Winter recognized him immediately.

The clerk recognized Winter immediately. Winter could see it in his eyes. They gleamed for a tenth of a second, like a flashlight, through the lobby.

The clerk didn't say anything, but his eyes made their way over to the stairs, up them, through the corridor, up to room ten. The room was still cordoned off. The whole floor was cordoned off.

This man must have had a few days off. Winter hadn't run into him during this investigation. But Winter wasn't the one who interrogated the hotel attendants, not yet. Not until now. What was his name? Winter had forgotten. He had read it and forgotten it, strangely enough. This guy's name was in Paula's file, like all the employees of Revy. That meant that his name was in two files with twenty years between them. He didn't look twenty years older. His hairstyle was different. Time moved more slowly in here, in the dimness. Out there in the light, beyond the awning, everything aged faster. But the clerk had recognized Winter. Salko. His name was Salko. Richard Salko.

"It's been a while," said Salko.

"So you recognize me?"

"Just like you recognize me."

"The years have sure been kind to us," Winter said.

"Probably depends on what you started with," said Salko, "in the beginning. What you had from the beginning."

Salko's eyes slid off toward the stairs again, and back.

"Horrible thing," he said. "How could it happen?"

Winter didn't say anything.

"I wasn't here," said Salko. "I was sick."

"I know."

"So I have nothing to say."

"What kind of illness was it?"

"Migraine. It can last for a few days. A week, every once in a while."

Winter nodded.

"I have medicine. I go to a doctor."

"I believe you," Winter said.

"When it . . . that happened, I was lying at home."

Winter held up a photograph.

"Seen her before?"

Salko studied Paula's face.

"That's not the same picture as in the newspaper."

"No."

"She hardly looks the same."

"That's why I'm showing you this one."

"No," said Salko, shaking his head. "I haven't seen her before."

"She hasn't been here?"

"Not that I know of."

"None of your colleagues recognize her either."

Salko shrugged.

"Yet she chose this hotel," Winter said.

"Did she?"

"What do you mean?"

"Was she the one who chose it?"

Winter didn't answer.

Salko shrugged again.

"She checked herself in, if you can put it like that."

"She went up to the room, number ten," Winter said. "As far as we know, she never left the room. She didn't have a key. No one saw her come or go. She stayed there during the night. She had a visitor. We don't know when. No one here saw any visitor."

"It's a hotel," Salko said. "People come and go." He threw out his hand toward the lobby. "You can see for yourself. It's so damn dark in here that you can hardly see your hand in front of your face."

"Why is that?" Winter asked.

"Ask the owners."

They would. But it wasn't a crime to skimp on electricity. And anonymity was part of this place. Electricity didn't go very well with anonymity.

"I hear you're going to close," Winter said.

"Who told you that?"

"Is it just a rumor?"

"Don't ask me."

"You don't know anything about it?"

"There are so many rumors," Salko said. "This place has been about to shut down for twenty years."

"You must have a precarious job situation," Winter said.

Salko didn't smile. "Maybe this time it's true. The rumors might be true." He looked straight across the desk at Winter. "I suggest you ask the owner."

Winter nodded. He noticed that Salko moved his gaze. He heard a sound behind him and turned around. The door was swinging, but he didn't see anyone. He hadn't heard anyone walk through the lobby. He turned back to Salko.

"Who was that?"

"Sorry?"

"Who was that, who went out through the doors?"

"I didn't see anyone."

"But the doors were moving."

"Must be the wind."

"There is no wind."

"I didn't see anyone, I said."

Winter could tell that he was lying. That was something you learned in twenty years. Seeing lies, that was his inheritance.

"We've talked to the maid and she didn't notice anything. I mean, the day before, or the few days before. Also, she didn't clean the room the last two days."

Salko shrugged for the third time.

"It was empty. What's the point?"

"Don't you do . . . well, an inspection? Go through the rooms every day? Or night?"

"No."

"Aren't the rooms cleaned every day? At least if someone is staying there?"

"It's up to the guest. There's a sign you can hang up."

"No cleaning, please?"

"Do not disturb."

"That's not the same thing," said Winter. "I can't understand how a hotel can not give a damn about cleaning."

Salko noticed the shift of nuance in Winter's voice. If he had been planning to shrug, he stopped himself.

"You realize what that could mean?" said Winter. "Do you realize?"

Nina Lorrinder was half a head taller than Aneta Djanali.

She had also been half a head taller than Paula Ney.

It was quarter past five and the pub on Västra Hamngatan had opened. It was called the Bishops Arms and was the closest you could get to London in Gothenburg. Djanali had been there before, one relatively recent evening, along with Halders. After half an hour Ringmar and Winter had shown up. Winter had ordered a pint of the recently arrived fresh ale for everyone. It was the first time for Djanali, and the last. She could get a cheaper drink with the same taste and scent by wringing out a dishrag.

"Ahhhh," Winter had said when he'd taken a drink. "One more?"

But now there wasn't one more. There wasn't any ale at all. Djanali and Lorrinder were drinking tea.

Lorrinder and Paula Ney had each had a glass of white wine. They had sat at this table. It was the only one in the place that was empty, as though word had gotten out.

Djanali had asked Lorrinder whether they should sit there, and she had nodded. This is macabre, Djanali thought. Maybe it will help her remember.

"How long did you sit here?"

"Haven't I already answered that?" Lorrinder asked, but without a hostile tone.

"We often ask the same question several times."

Sometimes because we're stupid, Djanali thought, and sometimes because we get different answers each time.

Lorrinder lifted her cup without taking a drink. She set it down again. She looked over at the door, as though Paula would step in. She moved her gaze to Djanali, as though Paula were sitting there.

She began to cry.

The cup trembled in her hand.

"Let's go someplace else," said Djanali.

At a French café far south on the street, Djanali repeated the question.

"About an hour."

"What time was it when you said good-bye?"

"About ten."

"Was that outside the pub?"

"I followed her up to Grönsakstorget. She was going to take a streetcar from there. The number one." Lorrinder jumped as a streetcar clattered by outside. The door was open to the street. It was a warm evening, an Indian summer evening. "But you know that."

"Did you wait until she got on?"

"No."

"Why not?"

"My own streetcar showed up. The three."

"Why didn't you get on at the stop at Domkyrkan?"

"Oh . . . I guess we wanted to walk a little."

"So you got on the three while Paula waited for the one?"

"Yes." Lorrinder looked very pale in the light inside the café. The light in there was a pale mix of electricity and autumn sun.

"Was that wrong of me?"

Djanali saw the tears in her eyes.

"Should I have stayed?" Lorrinder rubbed her eyes. When she took her hand away, her eyes had a film of tears. She sniffled. "I've been thinking about it. Almost all the time. If I hadn't left, maybe it wouldn't have happened." She looked at Djanali with her transparent eyes. "Do you understand? If only I had stayed."

"You can't blame yourself for any of this," said Djanali.

"How could I have known? How could anyone have known?"

Djanali lifted her cup and drank her new tea. Right now, she was wishing for a glass of wine, or a whiskey. Lorrinder looked like she could use a whiskey. They could go to a bar in a little bit. It could be her treat. She had forced herself into Lorrinder's sorrow.

"None of us could have known," said Djanali.

"How could it happen?" Lorrinder looked at Djanali as though she could give her an answer. "Why?"

"That's what we're trying to find out."

"Can you?" Lorrinder threw out a hand. It was like a reflex. "How can you find an answer to something like this?"

How should she answer? There were thousands of answers, but maybe none of them was the right one. There were thousands of questions.

"Among other things, by talking to everyone she knew," Djanali answered at last. "What we're doing now. You and I."

"She didn't know that many people," said Lorrinder.

Djanali didn't say anything, waited.

"She wasn't exactly the . . . how should I put it . . . the superficial type." Lorrinder made that motion again, as though it went along with her voice. "Paula mostly wanted to withdraw a bit. Do you know what I mean? She didn't want to be in big groups of people. She didn't want to be the center of attention, or anything."

"What did she want to do, then? What did she want to do most of all?"

"I . . . don't know."

"Didn't you ever talk about it?"

Lorrinder didn't answer at first. Djanali let her think; it looked like she was thinking.

"She wanted to be someplace else," Lorrinder said at last.

"Where did she want to go?"

"Where? Where did she want to go? If you mean a place or something, a country, she never said."

"But you know she wanted to get away?"

"Yes . . . it's hard to explain . . . it was like she *was* somewhere else sometimes. She wasn't *here*. Do you know what I mean? She was here but at the same time she was somewhere else, where she most wanted to be."

"And she never talked about this place? Where she most wanted to be?"

"I don't even know if it was a place," Lorrinder said. "I don't even know if she knew, herself."

A young woman came into the café from the white street outside. She looked around for a table. There were several free. She saved the table closest to the wall with her long scarf and went back out and held the door open for a young man who pushed a stroller in and put it beside the saved table next to the window. A two-year-old child was sleeping in the stroller. The man sat down and took off his dark glasses. He blinked a few times in the weaker light inside the room.

"Did she talk about anyone else?" Djanali asked, leaning over the table. "Was there a man in Paula's life? Or a woman, for that matter."

Lorrinder gave a start.

"That is one of the questions that has to be asked," said Djanali. "It's part of the routine, or whatever it's called."

"Do you call it routine?" Lorrinder said, looking straight at Djanali. "How can you call it routine?"

"It's not a good word. I'm with you there."

"Do you do this kind of thing every day? Are people mur . . . murdered every day?"

"No, no."

"What a job," said Lorrinder.

Djanali didn't answer.

Lorrinder turned her gaze toward the table over by the wall where the woman was coming back with a tray. She placed it on the table. The man spread it out. The woman sat down. The child was sleeping.

"She wasn't a lesbian, if that's what you're thinking," Lorrinder said, her gaze still on the young family. "And I'm not, either."

"I'm not thinking anything," said Djanali. "Right now I'm not allowed to be thinking anything at all."

"That's part of the routine, right?"

Lorrinder had looked back. Djanali tried to find a smile in her face, somewhere, but there was no smile.

"Are you tired of this now?" Djanali asked. "Should we stop?"

"There was a guy," said Lorrinder.

She looked at the couple again. The child had woken up and the mom was lifting it up right now. It looked like a boy. The coverall was blue. The mom gave him a kiss. The dad poured water into a glass.

"Did Paula have a boyfriend?" Djanali asked.

"Not now." Lorrinder returned her gaze again. "Not that I know of, anyway. But there was probably someone a while ago."

"Who?"

"I don't know."

"You didn't meet him?"

"No."

"How do you know about him, then?"

"Paula said something."

"What did she say?"

"She didn't *say* that she had a boyfriend. It was like, that wasn't *her* . . . to even tell me wouldn't have been her. But it was like I knew. Do you know what I mean? The kind of things you notice. As a friend. There's something that's suddenly a little different. We didn't see each other as much as before, for example. She did something else on the weekends sometimes, when usually we would have seen each other. She went somewhere."

"Went somewhere?"

"Yeah, for example."

"Is it just an example? Or did she really go somewhere? That you know of?"

"Do you mean abroad, or what?"

"I mean anywhere."

"I don't actually know. But I know that I tried to reach her a few times one week and she didn't seem to be home."

"When was that?"

"It was . . . a few months ago. Three, maybe." Lorrinder made that motion with her arm again, like a vague spasm. "Does that mean something?"

"I don't know," said Djanali. "You never know. But I want you to try to remember when this was, as precisely as possible."

"I'll try."

"Was it unusual?" Djanali asked. "For Paula to travel out of the city?"

"Well, I don't know that she did. That time. But from what I know of her, I guess it was . . . unusual."

"You never talked about it."

"No. It didn't really come up."

"You never went on a trip together?"

"Abroad?"

"Anywhere."

"No. As long as you don't mean on the streetcar."

"Not right now," said Djanali.

"We stayed here, in the city. But on the other hand we didn't get together very often. It wasn't even every week."

"How did you meet?" Djanali asked.

Lorrinder nodded over toward the window. Djanali followed her gaze, past the young family. Djanali saw the street outside, a streetcar passing, people walking by. The facade of Domkyrkan, the cathedral.

"We met at church," Lorrinder said, nodding toward the window again.

"Church?" said Djanali. "Do you mean at Domkyrkan over there?"

"Yes."

"Tell me."

"There's not much to tell. I went there sometimes . . . just to sit a little and . . . and think. An evening service or two. Well . . ." Her eyes were still on the church. The facade was nearly hidden behind the branches around the church square. "I still go there sometimes." She moved her eyes to Djanali. "It feels safe, somehow. Oh, I don't know how to explain it."

"It makes you feel good," said Djanali.

"Yes."

"And so you met Paula there."

"Yes."

"How did it happen?"

It almost looked as though Lorrinder was smiling. "Well, maybe a church isn't a place you meet new friends. And I guess it was more like outside. I guess we had noticed each other a few times, and then I guess we decided to go out for coffee afterward. I guess that's what happened, one time. I don't really remember, actually."

"When was this?" Djanali asked.

"When we went out for coffee?"

"When you talked to each other for the first time."

"Well . . . it was probably a few years ago."

"Was Paula alone?"

"Yes."

"Always?"

Lorrinder nodded. Djanali could see in her eyes that she had been alone, too. That she was alone. You don't go to church with a big group. The sense of community you were looking for might be there. Djanali turned her gaze toward the window again. The branches swayed around the church, like a circle.

The little boy at the table had taken off his coverall. He was wearing a T-shirt that had something on it that Djanali couldn't read from where she was sitting. He squirmed around on his dad's lap, back and forth, here, there, as though he wanted to get away, out into the sunshine again. The dad stood up and lifted him toward the ceiling and he laughed. The laughter sounded loud inside the café, bright and clear, like the day outside. It had been like night in here, Djanali thought. The boy changed that, for a little bit.

"Did she ever talk about Italy?" Djanali asked.

Lorrinder had also been watching the gymnastics over at the table.

Djanali had seen the small smile on her face. It had been hard not to smile. She had smiled, too.

"Italy? No. Why do you ask?"

"She didn't talk about her dad? That he came from Italy? Sicily? Or that she'd been there?"

"She'd been to Sicily?"

"We don't know. It's possible."

"When?"

"Ten years ago."

"No. She never said anything about that."

"Did she talk about her dad?"

"That he was from there, you mean?"

"In general."

"Oh . . . she probably did once or twice. But it wasn't really anything specific."

Lorrinder's gaze was outside again, by the church. Djanali couldn't remember that she herself had ever looked at Domkyrkan for such a long time.

"What kind of relationship did Paula have with her father?"

"I assume it was okay."

"Just okay?"

"Why are you asking me this?"

"We always try to find out about the relationships in the family."

That was no good. It was awkwardly put. Everything like this was very difficult.

"The routine, you mean?"

"Did she see her parents often?"

"I don't actually know."

"Did she talk about them often?"

"Haven't I answered that?"

"Did she talk about her mom?"

"I guess she did. Sometimes."

"But you didn't notice any signs that they might have a . . . that there could be some problems?"

"Problems?"

"Between them. Between the parents. Or between Paula and one of her parents."

Lorrinder shook her head.

. . . if I've made you angry at me I want to ask for your forgiveness . . .

Paula's last words in writing. It was about guilt, and about forgiveness. Djanali felt herself shudder every time she read Paula's letter to her parents; it was more than a shudder, it was like a cold wind overtaking a warm day.

8

Winter walked from room to room, opening windows. The apartment was warm, warmer than it had been in months, and the dust in it had turned into air. There was a word for it: stuffy. It would be hours before any cool air would come in from outside; the evenings were also the warmest they'd been in months, but he opened the windows anyway. At least there was a bit of a breeze. The late afternoon had a scent. The Indian summer contained a few autumn smells, and that was enough to mask a little of the exhaust perfume that rose from the traffic. Not that he had a problem with it. He had smelled it his entire adult life; he moved through it every day and if it became annoying, he lit a Corps.

He lit a Corps now. It was the most expensive cigar in Europe, but it was an old habit. It tasted good. It was hygienic. The smoker had to peel the protective wrapper off the long, thin cigars himself. Winter had had to special-order Corps from Brussels for several years, because apparently he was the only person in the city of Gothenburg who smoked that brand. That gave it an exclusivity that it didn't really deserve.

He stood on the balcony and inhaled smoke, blew out, let the scent of the cigar blend with the other smells. An SUV down there was circling around, on the hunt for a parking spot, or two, really. Winter could see blond hair in the front seat. A woman was looking for a spot. She stuck her head out through the rolled-down window. The Chrysler looked like a tank. Tractor wheels. Just what a family needs, he thought. Just what this city needs. SUVs.

The telephone rang inside. He placed the half-smoked cigar in the ashtray on the balcony table and went in to answer it.

"I took my chances that you were home," she said.

"I came home fifteen minutes ago."

"Were you smoking on the balcony when I called?"

"No."

"You're lying."

"Yes."

"Are the plants in our apartment still alive?"

"I let oxygen in for them first thing."

"Is it hot?"

"Record highs."

"Then there's no difference between here and there."

"It smells like fall here," he said. "Early in the morning, and late in the evening."

"I miss it."

"It will be even stronger when you come home."

"Speaking of which, I went to the clinic," Angela said.

"And?"

"Yup."

"Starting when?"

"December first. Until May first, maybe."

"Maybe?"

"On their end, it's open, Erik. They suggested a year. But we don't want that, do we?"

"No."

"The question is, what *do* we want? Is this such a good idea?"

"Yes."

"Is that all you can say?"

"I've already indicated my enthusiasm, Angela. It is a good idea. December to May in a mild climate, it's a damn good idea. It's the period when Gothenburg is a damn awful idea."

"But you've always been such a local patriot."

"Not when it comes to Gothenburg in the winter."

"I guess I agree with you."

"When you're as old as I am, you'll agree even more, Angela. It goes straight into your bones. The wind, the rain. It gets worse every year."

"So this is only about the weather?"

No. It wasn't only about the weather. It was also about life. He needed more than a month of vacation to put some distance between his work and his life. These had been tough years, long years. Now his life was also his work, and it was a life he had chosen, work he had chosen. He sacrificed too much, he knew that. He was a public servant, but it was no service he was doing for himself and his family. It was *him,* but it was too much of his life. He would always be like that, even if and when he came back after half a year in a different country. He wouldn't change completely. But maybe it would help him, make everything a degree milder. He was curious, curious about how he would be then. How he would think. Maybe he would think even more clearly. Maybe he would think more poorly, more obtusely. No. Maybe his imagination would be different. He thought that it would be deeper, and wider. He would be able to see farther.

"It's about a lot more than that," he answered. "You know that, Angela."

"I know," she said.

"So what do you say? You're the one who has to work."

"I'll work no matter what."

"So what do you say? You've been to the clinic."

"So can you take time off, Erik?"

"You're answering a question with a question. Of course I can take time off. I've already had a chat with Birgersson."

"He didn't throw you out?"

"Birgersson is starting to become soft. It's his last year. He's become like the father he never was."

"What does that mean?"

"He's started taking care of us."

"So that means he's letting you take time off for half a year?"

"He had thought of suggesting it himself, he said."

"And you believe that?"

Winter did, actually. If it had been a few years ago, his pride would have stood in the way of this insight. But recently, his pride had stayed away. He had noticed a weariness he'd never felt before come sneaking up on him. It wasn't his family, the small children. Or they were part of it, of course, but it was *him,* his way of lighting a fire under himself in his work. Nights without much sleep. The late nights at the laptop, when it was quiet and he could try to think.

"Can you really leave in the middle of it like that, Erik? You've never been able to do that before. That's what's been—" she said, but she interrupted herself.

"I know," he said.

"So how will it be this time? If I sign the contract and start at the clinic on the first of December, you have to be down there, too. Siv could maybe handle a few days alone with the children, but not a week."

"Mm-hmm."

"Her emphysema isn't getting any better, you could say."

"Hasn't she quit smoking?"

"Don't act dumber than you are, Erik. That's the problem with you smokers. You act dumber than you are. And you're all dense from the start, anyway."

"I never pull any smoke down into my lungs."

"Like I said. Dumber than you actually are."

He had quit. Then he had started again. Birgersson had quit and that's how it had stayed. Winter admired Birgersson for that; he had chain-smoked unfiltered cigarettes as an adult and quit before he would die. But he had pulled the smoke down into his lungs. Maybe that made him softer now.

"But you're working on the murder of a woman," Angela continued. "Aren't you leading the investigation? Shouldn't someone else take over right away?"

He had told her, of course. She had read Siv's day-old *Göteborgs-Posten* every day. A person who had done that long enough didn't miss much. He had given a few statements himself.

He hadn't given any details. Not to the readers. Not to Angela.

She was assuming the case wouldn't be solved before he left.

September. October. November. Three months, almost.

He suddenly thought of Ellen Börge. He suddenly saw her face in front of him. Eighteen years. They didn't know any more now than they had eighteen years ago. Two hundred and sixteen months. But you're working on the murder of a woman, Angela had said. Which murder? Which woman? He couldn't let it go, let Ellen go. Her face popped up in his head when he saw Paula. He knew that he was also working on the murder of Ellen, that maybe he always had been, and that it had contributed to the weight of his work and commitment. His failure. The weight of his failure. His mistake. He had made a mistake back then. If he could just figure out what it was. If only he could figure it out, and remember. Before he left it. Before he got the sun in his face.

"We're going to solve it," he answered after the short silence between Vasastan and Nueva Andalucía.

"Are you as sure as you sound?"

"No. Yes."

"Oh, God."

"But we're doing what we decided, right?"

"But what are we *doing*, then, Erik? In four days the girls and I are coming home and we have to have made our decision. In two days, actually. They want a decision by then."

"We've already decided," he answered.

Eighteen years earlier, the sun was going down faster than ever. He was cold. His jacket was still up in his office. A few hours ago it had been almost seventy degrees, but in the twilight it was autumnal September again.

He crossed Drottningtorget. A newspaper from today or yesterday blew past, on its way to the canal. He could see a *B* and an *S* from a headline that was impossible to read. The paper blew away, as though it had a meeting with a reader.

He went into Central Station. There was noise from the loud-speakers, a voice that was impossible to understand. There must be a school somewhere for people who are going to speak over loudspeakers, he thought, a school of unclarity. Bus drivers, streetcar drivers, announcers at train stations. Honing their pronunciation until it was impossible to make it out, redo the homework if a single bastard understood a thing.

He turned to the left and could feel the swelling in his ankle. There was a considerable bruise there. He was limping slightly.

Halders had thrown himself on top of him when they were playing soccer at Heden late yesterday afternoon. Soccer was the physical training of the season. And Halders couldn't forget. It had been a month since Winter had hardly brushed Halders outside the department door, but Halders did not forget easily. He had stomped Winter with his cleats and then looked as innocent as an Italian defender. What was his name, the bone splitter on the Italian national team . . . Gentile. Claudio Gentile, the man who left invalids in his wake in the grass. Innocent expressions after horrible crimes. A fitting name: the nice one, the generous one. Yes, he lavished his skill on them, just like Halders did. Halders was lavish with his charm, a very lovely man in all ways.

"Did you twist your ankle?" Halders had asked.

Winter had stood up, but he had trouble putting weight on his leg. He noticed Ringmar shaking his head.

"Are we even now?" Winter had asked.

"I don't know what you're talking about," Halders had said.

Winter thought of Halders's expressionless face as he passed the storage lockers. Would he be able to cooperate with him in the future? Was Halders familiar with that expression, "cooperate"?

He had to swerve out of the way of a large extended family who tramped out of the locker area with backpacks that were heads taller than they were. All of them had the same clothes, the same faces. The loudspeaker blared again and the family began to run. The train was going to start rolling, to Kiruna, Constantinople, Kraków.

Maybe Ellen Börge was on her way. Or else she wasn't on her way anywhere anymore.

He went in through the doors to the little information room, the smallest room in the station, boxed off for the thousands of people who were looking for information about their travels. Maybe there was a logic to it, but Winter had never understood it. He himself had had to stand in line for hours before train trips to find out something he needed to know in order to be able to stand in the next line and buy the ticket itself. It was pure Italy, corporate fascism, and when he thought the time had come, he would buy his first Mercedes and stop standing in line.

He walked up to the counter, and the line stared at him as he passed.

"We happen to be in a line here," someone said.

How nice for you, he didn't say. Only Halders could have said that.

The clerk behind the counter recognized him and nodded. She pointed toward the door behind her with a hand that was holding a city map. In front of her stood a man with dark glasses and a leather vest. He mumbled something Winter couldn't hear.

In the room, a woman was leaning over a desk full of papers. She looked up when Winter came in. Behind her he could see lots of notes attached to a bulletin board. They were in several layers. Maybe there was a logic to that, too. The room was very small, without windows.

Winter introduced himself and showed his ID. The woman might have been ten years older than he was. She looked at his ID and then at him with an expression like she didn't really believe this. He had seen that reaction before. He looked too young. But that problem would go away.

"Well, please sit down," said the woman.

Winter tried to sit on the chair in front of the desk, but it didn't work; there was no room. And his foot hurt. It throbbed harder when he sat down.

"Thanks, I'll stand."

"You're here about a passenger?"

Winter took a photograph out of his breast pocket and handed it over. She looked at Ellen Börge's face as she had just looked at Winter's face. She looked up at him.

"And the idea is that we might recognize her here?" She looked at Ellen's face again. "But she looks like lots of other people."

Winter didn't answer. He let her look at the photograph again.

"Well, I don't recognize her, anyway. So the idea is that she might have been here?"

The idea, he didn't know what the idea was. The only thing he wanted to know was whether Ellen Börge had been to the station. Whether anyone had seen her. If she had been here there was hope, at least that she might be alive. If she had been here, they didn't have to abandon all hope. Ye who enter here. He thought of a church, a cross, a grave.

"Is that the idea?" the woman repeated.

He had the urge to answer yes.

"We're just trying to find out whether she left from here," he said. "She's missing. We're looking for her."

"Well, I don't recognize her, anyway," the woman repeated. "When did she disappear?"

Winter told her the approximate date.

"But she could have been here later, of course," he added.

"She stayed hidden at first, and then she started traveling?" the woman asked.

Winter shrugged.

"So what can I do?"

"Show the photo to your colleagues."

"There are only three of us."

"Show it to them. We've given copies to everyone who works at the station."

"That must have been quick," she said, making a face. "There doesn't seem to be anyone else who works here. Everyone comes to us." She waved a hand at the door behind Winter. "You saw the lines, I'm sure? Everyone comes here."

"Maybe she did, too," Winter said, nodding at the photograph, which the woman was still holding in her hand.

He was sitting in the perfect apartment again. Nothing had been moved in it; maybe nothing had ever been moved there. Christer Börge was sitting across from him. His clothes were the same. The balcony door was open out onto the afternoon. The room smelled like sun and fall, and something Winter didn't recognize. But he recognized Börge's face. The man had looked disappointed when he opened the door. He knew that Winter was coming, but he looked as though he had been waiting for someone else. Winter thought he understood. Börge was living on hope. Maybe that was all he was living on. He looked thin, more slender than when Winter had met him the first time. That wasn't long ago. For Börge it must have felt like seasons, several Indian summers in a row.

"You have to have some clue," Börge said.

"To be honest, we don't," Winter said.

"Why wouldn't you be honest?" Börge said, but Winter couldn't tell whether there was a smile on his face, or the shadow of a smile. "Isn't the idea that police officers are supposed to be honest?"

The idea again. It was haunting him today. That was probably the idea. As though everything were preordained. Everything is repeated. Maybe I'll be sitting here again in twenty years. Maybe Ellen and Christer will have four kids. Maybe she never will have come back. Maybe I'll have kids, a family. Is that possible? No. Yes. No.

"So people can just disappear?" Börge said. "What the hell kind of society is this that people just disappear?" He didn't raise his voice. That was strange. Börge was using words that demanded a raised voice, but his tone was the same as if he were asking Winter to please pass the cream. "It's just like in . . . like in . . ." he continued, but he didn't seem to come up with what he should say.

Uruguay, Winter thought, Argentina. Chile.

"It's best if you don't come here anymore," Börge said. "I don't understand why you can't ask your questions over the phone, if you have any." He looked at Winter. "Questions, that is." He didn't smile this time, either.

"How was Ellen feeling the day before she disappeared?"

"You've asked that before." Börge pointed toward the notebook that Winter was holding in one hand. He hadn't written anything in it yet. "Check in there and you'll see that you've asked that before."

No smile, just like a normal remark. Börge moved around on the sofa the entire time, small movements that resembled tics but were probably general anxiety. Maybe I look the same, Winter thought.

"Sometimes you think of the same thing more than once. We're working on this together. We just want to know what happened to Ellen."

"Yes, yes, yeah," Börge said.

He suddenly got up and walked across the floor and closed the balcony door.

"It's starting to get cold," he said, with his face turned out toward the street.

"How did Ellen feel?" Winter asked.

Börge turned around. Winter saw the roofs of buildings in the background, and suddenly the sun slid out from behind a small cloud and Börge's face became a silhouette as the sun shone straight in from the short distance to the other side of the street. He turned his face, as though toward the sun, and Winter could see his silhouette in profile. He would remember that for a long time afterward.

Börge walked back and sat down. Winter got the sun in his face and shielded his eyes with his hand.

"Should I draw the drapes?" Börge asked.

"No, no. It's going away now."

The sun slid behind a cloud again and in a few minutes it would be gone for the day.

"You were asking something," Börge said.

"Ellen. Was there anything in parti—"

"Oh yes. How she was feeling. I think she felt fine. The days just before? Well, you don't really feel the same all the time. One day it's this and another day it's that, right? Isn't that what it's like for every-one? Isn't that what it's like for you? That's what it's like for me."

"Was she uneasy? Restless?"

"No more than . . . usual."

"What do you mean?"

"We've talked about that, too. The thing about kids. Stuff like that."

"Has she ever talked about going away?" Winter asked.

Börge didn't answer.

"Going away for a while. Alone."

"Not without a suitcase," Börge said, but he wasn't smiling this time either.

"And you've never been to Hotel Revy?"

"I didn't even know the place existed," Börge said.

"But Ellen knew."

"You've got the wrong person."

"No."

"Ellen would never have stayed at that place. Never." He looked at Winter again. The sun was gone for good now. The room had sud-denly become dark. This place needed electric lights. Winter could hardly make out the features of Börge's face. On the other hand, they didn't change. His face never seemed to change.

"People look like each other," Börge continued. "Many people look more or less the same. Every country has its distinctive features. Here we're blond and blue-eyed. To a foreigner, everyone can look alike. In Africa, for example, it's the same. An African at a hotel in darkest Africa doesn't see any difference between this European check-ing in and that one. It's the same in China."

"They recognized her at the hotel," Winter said.

"What does that mean? A desk clerk who was hungover? Or half-asleep? I don't think much of that. You shouldn't either." He leaned forward. Winter could see his expressionless face. There was no agita-tion in it. "Haven't you considered that she might never have been there?"

"Yes."

"Well, then."

Börge leaned back.

"What do you think, then?" Winter asked.

"About what?"

"About where Ellen is?"

Börge didn't answer.

"About what might have happened to her?"

Börge didn't answer now, either. He turned his head again, as though someone had suddenly shouted from down on the street. The sky on the other side of the roofs was very blue. Winter suddenly longed to go out there, out into the blue.

"I love her," Börge said. He turned back to Winter again. "And she loves me."

9

We will meet again. Winter read the words for the hundredth time. We will meet again. He could see the tremors of the hand that had written the words, now that the technicians had said that they were there.

We will meet again.

He saw the hand that lay on the table, a cast of the hand that had written those words from hell. If you chose to see it that way. Maybe there wasn't much choice. Paula hadn't had much choice.

"A bird flew past the window a little bit ago and soon I will be like the bird. Think of me when you see a bird, any bird at all. I'm thinking of you, now and forever."

"It makes you want to cry," Ringmar said, looking up from the copy of the letter he held in his hand.

"So cry."

"I'm trying. I'm really trying."

"Her last words," Winter said.

"Did she write what she wanted to, herself?" Ringmar said.

Winter didn't answer. He had just seen a bird fly past the window. It could be any bird at all. He wasn't good at birds.

"Erik? What do you say? Are those her own words?"

"Who could know that? Besides her, and the murderer?"

"The bird. Is it a symbol?"

"Her parents couldn't interpret it if it was," said Winter. "Can you?"

"Escape," said Winter. "Escape, freedom."

"Beyond her reach," said Ringmar. "What was beyond her reach."

"Maybe not."

"What do you mean?"

"She was going to be like the bird, she wrote." Winter looked up. He had been staring down at nothing on the top of the desk. "It was going to be her escape. And freedom."

"She wasn't the one who decided," Ringmar said.

Winter didn't answer. He looked out through the window, but no more birds flew by. It was a gray day out there. A light rain was falling, fall had begun, the season was here to stay.

"She hadn't chosen to sit in this damn room and write about freedom. And love. That wasn't what she chose."

"Maybe it became what she chose," Winter said.

"The rope against her throat? She didn't have a choice?"

"That's how it was at first," Winter said. "Soon enough she was just as certain."

"Just as certain? Just as certain as the murderer?"

Winter didn't answer. These were horrifying thoughts. That's what he dealt with. Horrifying thoughts.

"He convinced her that she had to die? Your time is over, Paula. Write a letter to confirm it."

Winter still didn't answer.

"She became as certain as he was?"

"Keep going," Winter said.

"He managed to convince her that she would feel better dead?"

"Feel better?" Winter said. "Did she feel bad?"

"Let's assume she did. She wasn't satisfied with her life. She wanted to get away. She wanted to do something else. She wanted to escape. She wanted another kind of freedom. She wanted to *become* someone else."

"Say that again," Winter said.

"Let's assu—"

"No, the last part," Winter said.

"She wanted to become someone else," Ringmar said.

"Yes. That's what this is about. She was going to become someone else. He would make her into someone else."

"For God's sake, Erik."

"She was going to get to escape, get away. He helped her."

"Who did she become, then?" Ringmar said. "Who was she going to become?"

"Part of him," Winter said. He repeated it: "A part of him."

Ringmar didn't say anything. He was thinking about Winter's words. He knew that it was part of their routine; words could mean a lot, or nothing, and he hoped that this last part wouldn't mean anything at all. That Winter was wrong. If he was at all right, it could mean that they had just begun.

"Who is he?" Ringmar said. "A preacher? A crazy preacher? Some fucking dark angel? A risen angel?" He sneezed suddenly, as though he were allergic to the mere mention of preachers. "Should we go out into the congregations?"

"I don't know."

"What do you mean? You're the one who started this!"

"I haven't thought that much about him yet," Winter said. "I've been thinking about Paula."

"But she wasn't religious," Ringmar said. "At least not that we know of. Not deeply religious." He took out a handkerchief and wiped his nose. "She went to church a few times with her friend, but that was for the peace."

"There are other kinds," Winter said.

"Of religiousness?"

"Yes. It doesn't necessarily have to do with God," Winter said.

"Is there anything that has to do with God?"

"What do you mean by that?"

"Does God exist?" Ringmar said.

"I think we need a coffee break," Winter said.

That afternoon, Winter had a meeting with Birgersson. The boss stood at the half-open window, as usual. The light through the window made his office just bright enough to see. Before, Birgersson had always stood there to watch the smoke float out and off toward Ullevi.

When he'd stopped smoking he remained by the window anyway. It was like some sort of phantom position; in his hand was a cigarette that no longer existed. He was a boss who would soon no longer exist. One year, then Winter would take over, but Winter had already taken over. Nothing would change, other than formally. Winter would presumably move into this office. In any case, it would have to be cleaned thoroughly after Birgersson's cigarette smoke, but the poison would remain in the walls. It wouldn't be healthy to sit here. Cigarettes were not healthy, unlike cigars.

"You're welcome to smoke, Erik," Birgersson said from over by the window. "You know that."

"It wouldn't feel right, not in here," Winter said. "You know that's how I feel, Sture."

Birgersson rasped out a laugh. It was like tossing a shovelful of gravel into the room, right across the floor.

Winter could see Birgersson's silhouette in the pale light. Generally speaking, he had seen it for all of his adult life. He had been in here as a police officer, too. He didn't remember why that had been. But he had actually been afraid. That was part of his youth. Often being afraid. Sometimes he missed that. He was sometimes afraid because he wasn't afraid as often these days. It wasn't healthy.

"How's it going with our girl?" Birgersson said, turning back toward Ernst Fontells Plats outside. He could see all the traffic down there, to and from the police station, uniforms, marked cars, civilian cars, civilian clothes, women, men, old men with hats. It was as though he were personally responsible for all traffic in and out, had taken it upon himself to monitor it. "Have you checked all the crazies yet?"

"We're working on it."

"There are getting to be more and more of them," Birgersson said. He had turned back in toward Winter again. His face was indistinct in the gray light, as though he had already begun to disappear. "When I started here you could call them up before lunch. All of them."

"I know, Sture."

"There were no more than that. I had the whole gang in my Filofax there." Birgersson nodded toward his desk. "That was before cell phones. Before the Internet. It was a wonderful time."

"I think the crazies feel the same," said Winter.

"Yeah, yeah, we might have better electronic capabilities now, but that's balanced out by the fact that there are ten times more crazies on the streets now. Right?"

"Mm-hmm."

"So who is our particular crazy in this case?"

"I don't know. Not yet."

"Is he an old acquaintance?"

"I don't . . . think so."

"You're hesitating a little."

"Do you remember Ellen Börge?"

"Remind me."

"She disappeared. There was something fishy about it. We didn't figure it out. She never came back."

"Börge?"

"Yes."

"I recognize the name."

"Good."

"I'm old, but I'm not senile yet."

"It's the same hotel, the same room."

"Well, shit."

"Ellen, if it was really her, checked in there just before she disappeared."

"And?"

"Well . . . that's it. And the fact that Ellen was never found. Never came back . . . home."

"You hesitated about that, too."

"I don't think she wanted to come home."

"Home to her own home? Her apartment?"

"Yes. And to her husband."

"You remember this case well, Erik. Or have you refreshed your memory recently?"

"I looked through it a bit. It was one of my first cases, you know."

Birgersson nodded.

"Unsolved," Winter said.

"And you want to solve it now," Birgersson said.

"No, no."

"Don't try, Erik. I've seen it before throughout my years in the unit, with other people. With you, too. You all walk around with something unfinished that gnaws at you, something you think you missed. The case is cold as snow, but you try to blow on the damn coals anyway." Birgersson grew quiet, as though to ponder his metaphor. "And then comes a new case, and you start looking for similarities with the old one."

"I haven't been looking," Winter said. "I just said that there *are* some similarities."

"It was twenty years ago," said Birgersson.

"Eighteen," said Winter.

"See? You know exactly. Just don't take it out on Paula Ney."

"Don't insult me, Sture."

"No, no, I'm sorry, Erik. But you understand what I mean."

"Mm-hmm."

"A crazy from eighteen years ago. He did something to Ellen Börge and now, again, to Paula Ney? He waited for almost a generation? Well, that would be something new. We've never seen that before."

"There's a first time for everything," said Winter.

"Are you joking with me, Erik?"

"Never," said Winter.

"Find that damn lunatic," Birgersson said.

"Maybe he's in there," Winter said, nodding at the ancient Filofax on Birgersson's desk. "You do have all the crazies from eighteen years ago in there."

"Obviously you're not letting it go," said Birgersson.

"Can I borrow it?" Winter said.

Just as Winter left Birgersson's office, he remembered that he had forgotten to bring up his leave of absence again. He turned around in the middle of the corridor and went back. The door to Birgersson's office was still half-open, as he had left it. He could see Birgersson over by the window, with his back toward the room. Winter knocked on the door and stepped in. Birgersson turned around abruptly, as though Winter had knocked hard on his back. His face belonged to someone else. There was something there that Winter had never seen. There were tears on the older man's face. Winter felt as though he had stepped uninvited into Birgersson's most private space.

"What the hell do you want this time?"

"Excuse me, Sture," said Winter, "I'll come back later."

"Come in, for God's sake, and close the door behind you," Birgersson said, taking a handkerchief out of his pants pocket and blowing his nose and gesturing with his other hand toward the guest chair by the desk. "Shit, I guess I have September allergies," he said, sitting down heavily across from Winter. "My eyes are just running."

Maybe he's fooling himself, Winter thought.

"Has something happened?"

"Happened? What do you mean, happened?"

"Sture. You've smoked away every hint of an allergy. Or maybe it's the other way around. Anyway, something's going on. You don't have to talk about it. But I'm not going to sit here and pretend not to notice anything. I'm too old for that. And you're too old for it."

"You're not old, Erik. Not yet."

Winter didn't answer.

"I'm old," Birgersson said. "This is my last autumn. Then God knows. I was thinking about it as I was standing by that damn window. When you came in. Suddenly I just teared up. I didn't plan on it." Birgersson tried to smile. "It has to do with age. When you're old you can't control your bodily fluids. I can't ever be too far away from a urinal anymore. Or a handkerchief, apparently."

"Have you tried a catheter?" Winter said.

"Let me retire first," Birgersson said.

"Have we ever talked about anything other than work?" Winter said.

"Why do you ask?"

"Because it's important."

"For whom?"

"For you and me both, I think."

"I don't believe in that stuff," Birgersson said, and his gaze disappeared off somewhere. Someone who knew to look could still see traces of tears in his eyes, and Winter knew. He also knew that Birgersson was a lonely man. He refused to believe that the boss's whole life was *here,* here in this confined workroom, but sometimes it seemed that way. Birgersson never talked about his other life. No one knew how he lived it. He never invited anyone into it. Maybe he was paying the price for that now, here, by the window, during his last autumn.

"I know a nice place with good lighting," Winter said. "Let's go there."

"What will we do there? Cry together? We can't do that, not in good lighting."

"We'll talk a little."

"I told you, I don't believe in that stuff."

Their time is over, Winter thought. Those who didn't believe in "that stuff." Dead-silent men.

"Do what I'm doing," he said.

"What?"

"Take a leave of absence. Delegate once in a while."

"What are you saying? I should take a leave of absence six months before I retire?" Birgersson actually laughed. "And something like that coming from you? Inspector Winter preaches the virtues of taking time off. And for the second time in a short period." Birgersson stood up from his chair, abruptly, as though he was more vulnerable when he was sitting, vulnerable to words. "Besides you, no one here has applied for a leave of absence, as far as I know."

"You have three months leave left," said Winter.

"What will the others say? It goes against every unwritten rule."

"I'll settle for the written ones, Sture."

Winter thought of the others: Ringmar, Halders, Bergenhem, Djanali, Möllerström, other colleagues above and below. There would be mixed feelings.

"Besides, you have a case to take care of. If we don't solve this, there might be leaves of absence for everyone."

"We'll solve it," Winter said.

"In less than three months?"

Winter didn't answer.

Birgersson pointed at the Filofax.

"You just brought this up yourself. Sometimes even eighteen years isn't enough."

"We don't know whether it was a crime," Winter answered. "Ellen's disappearance. You just said so yourself."

"This isn't like you, Erik. Is this Spain thing Angela's idea?"

"No. It's mine."

"But why?"

"I thought we could talk about it at that nice place."

Halders and Djanali were watching the video. They saw the blond woman come and go, come and go.

"Black sunglasses are a great disguise," Halders said.

"And a wig," said Djanali.

"Is it a wig?"

"Yes."

"I can't tell. Do you have to be a woman to tell?"

"Yes."

"Would you figure it out if I were wearing a wig? If you didn't know me?"

"Yes."

"Would you still love me if I started wearing a wig?"

"No."

"Why not?"

"No woman can love a man who wears a wig."

"But women wear wigs."

"That's different."

"Why is she wearing a wig?" Halders said, pointing at the screen. The woman was leaving. "Is it a disguise?"

"For whom?"

"For us, of course. She doesn't want to be recognized. The wig and the sunglasses."

Djanali ran the tape forward and back again.

"I don't understand why she left the suitcase if she . . . knew what was going to happen to Paula. Or at least knew that Paula herself wouldn't come to pick it up."

"Keep going," said Halders.

"Why drop it off at all? If she's an accomplice? Why drop off a suitcase that your accomplice later picks up? And do it more or less publicly. It doesn't make sense to me."

"The alternative is that she did it for Paula. A favor."

"Then why hasn't she contacted us?" said Djanali.

"The usual old reason," Halders said. "She's afraid."

"Afraid of whom?"

"Of everything."

"Is someone threatening her?"

"Maybe."

"The murderer?"

"Maybe."

"But then there's some contact between her and the murderer."

Halders didn't answer. He studied the woman again. There was something about the way she walked. She wasn't limping, but it was like she was making an effort not to limp. There was something strange about her manner of walking. It didn't seem to be because of the digital jerkiness of her movements. It was also apparently the case that limps and things like that were intensified by the computerized resolution.

"Is she the murderer?"

Halders turned toward Djanali.

"What did you say?"

"Is she the murderer herself?"

Halders turned his eyes back to the person in the blond wig and dark glasses. She moved as though she were walking on footsteps that had been painted on the floor, a path. He counted her steps.

"No," he answered, "she hasn't murdered anyone."

Djanali followed his gaze.

"What are you looking at, Fredrik?"

"Do you see how she's walking? Isn't there something strange about how she walks?"

Djanali asked him to run the sequence again. The woman walked back and forth.

"Yes," Djanali said at last, "she doesn't really walk normally."

"What is it?"

"It's something about her feet."

"Are you sure?"

Halders looked at the woman's feet. She had dark boots, probably leather. They didn't look entirely comfortable.

"Boots too tight?"

"Maybe," said Djanali.

"What else could it be?"

"Some problem with her feet. Or toes."

"Her toes?"

"I think she walks like someone who has problems with toes." She turned to Halders. "Toe problems always cause problems with walking."

Halders nodded.

"I've heard that a person without big toes can't walk at all," he said.

"She can walk," said Djanali, nodding toward the monitor, "but it could be something about her toes."

"How old do you think she is?" Halders asked.

"What do you think?"

Halders tried to read the woman's face, what he could see of it. It wasn't much. They didn't have any close-ups yet. But there was something about her movements that pointed toward maturity. It wasn't just the way she walked.

"Much older than thirty," he said.

"Maybe over forty," said Djanali.

10

They found a nice place with worse lighting. Birgersson wanted it that way.

"So no one will see if my eyes water again."

Birgersson looked around inside and pointed at one of the leather booths behind the bar. Above the booth hung a picture that depicted nothing; at least, not that could be seen from where they were standing. As Winter sat down, he saw that a sea was rolling inside the frame, or maybe it was a field, or a forest, or a large city seen from a great distance.

"What time is it?" Birgersson asked, looking at the bar, where the bartender was polishing a wineglass. Aside from one man on one of the bar stools, they were the only guests.

"Quarter past four," Winter answered.

"Then I'll have a beer and a glass of akvavit."

"Is four the magic time?" Winter asked.

"I don't know if it's magic, but it's a respectable hour for a drink."

"I usually stick to seven."

"For whiskey, yes. I don't want that headache at four."

"The headache comes later," Winter said. "But it depends on the quality."

"When doesn't it depend on the quality?"

"Shall we order?"

Birgersson looked like he already had a headache. He rubbed a spot above one eye and studied the akvavit in his long-stemmed glass.

Winter took a sip of his beer.

Birgersson lowered his hand and looked around.

"I've never been here," he said. "One of your regular haunts?"

"No, no."

"And we've never sat down like this," Birgersson continued. "You and I, just the two of us, at a bar out on the town."

"They say there's a first time for everything."

"Who says that?"

Winter smiled in answer.

"But you should try everything at least once," Birgersson said, "except for incest and folk dancing."

"Who says that?" Winter asked.

"It's a wise old saying from where I'm from."

"Where are you from, Sture? You've never said."

"It doesn't exist anymore. So there's nothing to tell." Birgersson raised his glass. "This booze looks good."

Winter raised his beer glass. He had considered a whiskey, but it was a long way to seven o'clock. And one whiskey was often followed by another whiskey.

Birgersson took a sip and said "aahhh," set down his glass, and looked around the place again.

"A person could keep sitting here."

"So let's do that," Winter said.

"You have a family to go home to, if I remember correctly?"

Winter laughed.

"Didn't you have another child recently?" Birgersson continued.

"Just a year ago," Winter answered.

"Wasn't it a girl?"

"Yes. Her name is Lilly."

"Lilly? That sounds like an old aunt, even though she's only a year old."

"She could become an old aunt," Winter said.

"But it's a beautiful name."

"I think she's happy with it already."

"Reminds me of Sture somehow," Birgersson said.

Winter smiled.

"They're all still down on the sunny coast for almost another week," he said.

"Aha."

"Have you been there?" Winter asked.

"The sunny coast? Costa del Sol?"

Winter nodded. Birgersson was a legend in many ways at the police station, and the mystery surrounding his absences was great. No one had any idea where he spent his lonely vacations. If they were lonely. Birgersson had never had a family, not that anyone knew of, anyway, but there were many kinds of loneliness.

"Maybe," said Birgersson.

That was the correct, mysterious answer.

"You're welcome to come down this winter. Or this spring."

"Take it easy now, Erik. It's a long way to spring."

"Isn't it always?"

"That sounded depressed. Are you depressed?"

"Don't think so."

"It's enough that you think I am."

"Spring will always come," said Winter. "Does that sound better?"

Birgersson smiled.

"You're a strange devil, Erik Winter."

"Aren't we all?"

"The job leaves its mark," said Birgersson.

"Maybe. But we were strange from the start."

"Or nuts. Look at Halders."

"He's calmed down," Winter said.

"Since you landed one on him, you mean?"

"You remember that?"

"Like it was yesterday."

"It was in the fall," Winter said, "late summer, actually."

"That was the time of youth," said Birgersson. "Cheers!"

He knocked back the akvavit and put down his glass.

"I've recommended your leave of absence," he said.

"Thanks, Sture."

"But our friend the director of the county CID makes the decision. You know that."

"I don't have any problems with Leinert," Winter said. "And he owes me this."

"Why does he owe you a leave of absence?"

"All the overtime I never collected. Come on, Sture. You know how it is."

Birgersson didn't answer.

"Halders can take over," Winter said. "If he still needs to."

"Halders, lead the investigation? Is that such a good idea?"

"The prosecutor leads the investigation," Winter answered. "Don't you know that, Sture?"

Birgersson smiled a thin smile.

"When there's a reasonable suspect, yes," he said. "Is there a reasonable suspect in this case?"

"No."

"So Halders will lead everything, right?"

"I'm talking about after the first of December."

"Then Molina will take it up, you mean?"

"Maybe we'll all be taking it easy," Winter said.

"You'll have solved the whole thing?"

"*We'll* have solved it."

"Yeah, yeah."

Birgersson studied his empty glass with a concerned expression, as though it would never again be full.

"It's Fredrik's time now," Winter said. "He's more than ready for it."

"Imagine, hearing you say that," Birgersson said.

"People change."

"You? Or him?"

Winter saw two younger men come in through the door, walk through the small space, and sit down at a table nearby. They might be the same age he and Halders had been when they met each other.

"If he's going to replace me . . . possibly replace me, he has to be told now," Winter said.

"He might demand to be made a chief inspector, then," Birgersson said.

"So let him be one," Winter said.

"Oh, now I need an akvavit," Birgersson said, looking over toward the bar.

"I've spoken with Bertil," Winter said. "He hasn't got anything against it. Rather the opposite."

"Yeah, yeah," Birgersson said.

Winter followed his gaze and signaled to the bartender, who nodded. Birgersson held up two fingers and the bartender nodded again.

"Smart guy, that one."

"They all are," Winter said.

"Are you a barfly?"

"It's been a long time since I heard that word."

"Or king of the bar, I guess they say now."

"Just on payday."

"I'm sure your pay is plenty to cover the tab," Birgersson said.

"According to Halders's UN memories of Cyprus, the British officers' pay was enough to cover the mess hall tab," Winter said.

"Of course," Birgersson said. "Private interests paid for everything else. Just like in your case."

"It's not that much," Winter said.

"Depends on what you compare it to."

"Feel free to compare it to the British officers."

"Don't you still buy handmade shoes from London?"

"Only when I'm ordering suits."

Birgersson laughed. The man at the bar didn't move. Two women at a table closer to the exit turned their heads. The place had begun to fill up in the last fifteen minutes.

Two more beers and more akvavit arrived at the table.

"What's the time now?" Birgersson asked.

"Quarter to five. Why?"

"Another fifteen minutes left to the blue hour," Birgersson said.

"Mm-hmm."

"One almost always misses the blue hour." Birgersson raised his beer glass and seemed to be contemplating the color of the contents. "Instead, one is always sitting bent over an investigation report full of syntax that no God can help."

"Look forward to your blue hours, then, Sture."

Birgersson didn't answer. His eyes seemed to slide off somewhere, through the blue smoke that was beginning to rise in the bar.

Then he fastened his gaze on Winter.

"Be honest now, Erik: Are you tired of this shit?"

"Only when it comes up above my neck."

"It's well on its way," Birgersson said. "Haven't you noticed how hard it's become to move your arms?"

He lifted his arm at an angle. A ray of light from the ceiling landed on the glass, and color came into the liquor.

"Once when I was new, you said that this is a battle we can't win, but that we have to fight to the end," Winter said.

Birgersson drank, set down the glass, and made a little face.

"Did I say that? Have I said that?"

Winter nodded.

"That must have been when the heaviest drugs started. When heroin came in."

"No, it was earlier."

"Oh . . . well . . . what did you think about that?"

"Well, it wasn't exactly encouraging," Winter said.

Birgersson didn't say anything; there was nothing encouraging about the expression on his face, and it was an expression Winter recognized.

"And at the same time it was. Encouraging."

"Maybe I was having a bad day when I said it," Birgersson said. "Maybe there was some little twelve-year-old girl who had just been beaten to death."

"I don't remember anything about that day other than what you said."

"Apparently I was serious, anyway."

"I'm not accustomed to you joking about things like that, Sture."

"Have to fight to the end, huh? Yes, I suppose that's how it is."

"That implies that you'll get tired of all the shit," Winter said. "Because it is shit. Lots of it."

"A big pile," Birgersson said, raising his beer glass. "All the way up to the sky. Cheers to all the shithouses that make room for all the shit. That take care of it. All the shitheads."

Winter raised his glass in a toast, without really understanding what Birgersson meant.

"The reason I'm still tolerating a little shithead like you is that you're trying to avoid becoming a cynic," Birgersson said.

Winter didn't know what he should say in response to Birgersson's words. He had sometimes been worried that he wouldn't be able to become anything other than a cynic. That anyone who lived and worked in this segment of the world and humanity became a cynic. A cynic or an idiot. Or both.

"A cynic stops thinking," Birgersson said, as though he had read Winter's thoughts. "Your brain becomes automatic."

"A person might wish it would, sometimes," Winter said.

"Oh, no, kid. That's not for you."

"Not for you either, Sture."

Birgersson laughed his laugh again, a hiss that caused the two younger men at the table next to theirs to interrupt their low-voiced conversation and quickly cast a glance at the furrowed man in the white shirt with an open collar and rolled-up sleeves.

"No," Birgersson said after thirty seconds, "who would even think of calling me a cynic?"

Who would even think of calling Fredrik Halders a cynic? Quite a few people, to be frank. Everyone he had ever come in contact with, to be honest.

He considered himself to have reasons for his outlook on life, and not just the reasons he had come to through his work. But people undergo spiritual changes in their lives; some do, at least, and Halders had the good fortune of being one of them. He saw it as good fortune. He knew what was going on, and he didn't want to turn to stone before his children even grew up.

He was standing in Paula Ney's apartment again. What am I looking for here? Is it still the photograph? No. He was listening for something. It wasn't the wind outside the window, or the patter of rain against the pane, and it wasn't the cars in the roundabout down there, outside of Doktor Fries Torg. Not all the sounds of the city and nature. He didn't need to listen for them; they were logged into his brain after all these years on the streets, in cars, in houses, in parks, everywhere it was possible to set foot. He looked down at his feet; one was standing in front of the other, as though he were about to throw himself out through the window. The skies were gray out there; you had to fly high to reach the blue sky. Had she flown up there? And down again? Halders looked around for an answer. The shrouds were still there in the apartment. The silence was still there. He listened again but didn't hear anything. He knew that there were answers in there, maybe several. Necessary answers, tragic answers. In the answers he collected there was nothing that made the world a better place, more loving. It was just a battle.

The morning was brighter, as though the naked sky had one last need to expose everything. Winter pushed his bike into the rack, locked it, and walked toward the entrance. A bird of prey was circling high above the police station. The bird was sharply outlined against the blue. Suddenly it dove and disappeared behind the building.

Winter took the elevator past his own floor.

Torsten Öberg was waiting in his office. Winter had heard cameras flashing as he passed some of the rooms in the forensics unit. He had smelled a sharp scent. A woman had passed him with a plastic bag. It looked heavy.

"It will take another couple of days to get an answer from SKL," Öberg said before Winter had had time to sit down.

Winter nodded. He saw the rope in his mind. The knot. The fleck of blood that could have come from anywhere. If it was blood.

"You said you didn't want the VIP treatment."

"We wouldn't have gotten it anyway," Winter said.

He could see the city through the window behind Öberg. It was higher up; it was possible to see very far. He could glimpse the sea far off in the haze of heat, behind the Älvsborg bridge, which looked like the skeleton of a prehistoric animal from here. I should switch offices, he thought, upgrade a floor. The bird was back; might be a hawk. The perspective made it look like it was circling right above the bridge, a giant creature on prehistoric wings.

"We have a clue," Öberg said. "A shoe."

Winter leaned forward. He felt something across his scalp, like a sudden wind from outside.

"Someone had spilled soda pop in front of that storage locker," Öberg continued. "They had cleaned there, but not well enough. Which was good for us. Soda pop is good for a forensic investigator. There's a lot that gets caught in Pommac."

"Was it Pommac?" Winter asked.

Öberg smiled.

"We haven't finished analyzing it yet."

"A shoe print," Winter said.

"For what it's worth," Öberg said.

"There's a lot to suggest that our man made it," Winter said. "Depending on how old it is."

"It's fresh."

"How fresh?"

"One day. Two."

"It's our man." Winter thought about what he said. "If it's a man. Is it a man? A man's shoe?"

"Yes . . . this is the only print we have." Öberg opened the folder that lay on the table between them. "From what I understand, it's mostly men who wear shoes like this. Or wore them, maybe." He took out a few photographs and held one of them up in front of Winter. "Do you recognize this pattern?"

Winter took the photograph in his hand. At first the image looked like an uneven surface, maybe a deserted landscape. After a few seconds, he saw some kind of pattern. He saw stripes. At the edge there was something that might be part of a letter.

He looked up.

"Do you recognize it?" Öberg repeated.

"It looks familiar. I don't really know what it is."

"Not your brand?"

"No."

"But it was once on the foot of every man," said Öberg. "Well, besides yours."

"What is it?"

"Ecco."

"Ecco?"

"Ecco. Sound familiar?"

"Of course."

"Ecco Free. A very common brand of shoe. At least it was twenty years ago or so. But now apparently it's had some kind of revival."

Winter shook his head.

"Not what we were hoping for, is it?" Öberg said.

Winter looked down at the photo again without answering. The landscape looked less deserted now. The picture was more like a map that might be possible to make out.

"But the sole isn't new," Öberg said. "If we find the shoe, we can compare them."

"A twenty-year-old sole?"

"No. Not even Eccos last that long." Öberg nodded at the photograph in Winter's hand. "I used to wear them myself."

"Do people really still wear this kind of shoe?" Winter said, but it was mostly to himself. "I haven't seen ones like these for a long time."

"Maybe that's to your advantage, then," Öberg said. "Maybe there are only a few people who still buy Eccos in this city's shoe stores after all."

"Mm-hmm."

"But I think there were some knockoffs of that brand, from what I remember. Don't know if they're still around." He looked up. "I guess you'll have to find out."

"You didn't find anything else in front of the locker?" Winter asked, putting down the picture.

"Maybe this will do for a while."

"You never know," Winter said, getting up.

"I can't figure out that plaster hand," Öberg said.

"You're not alone," Winter said.

"The work was actually pretty clumsily done."

Winter nodded.

"Some kind of mold was used," Öberg said. "I don't know where you get hold of something like that."

"It can hardly be common."

"But plaster . . . normally I think there's some sort of plastic substance that you cast in forms like that. Like for mannequins and things."

"Mannequins," Winter repeated.

He closed his eyes and saw an empty face in front of him, and naked limbs in a color that wasn't found in people. There was nothing human about mannequins.

"There was no trace of plaster on her hand," Öberg said. "Only paint."

Winter opened his eyes.

"And nothing new about that, I understand."

"No, the most common semigloss enamel paint in the world." Öberg leaned back in his chair. "Can be bought even in the most poorly stocked paint stores." The haze of heat beyond the bridge had lifted. Winter could see the opening to the sea. "Tack-free after five hours." Öberg looked at Winter. "But it went faster than that on her body."

"Call me as soon as you hear from SKL," Winter said, getting up. "Give them a call and ask nicely if they can give us a slightly faster answer."

"I'm always nice," Öberg said.

11

Winter heard words, but that was all. He didn't understand what was being said. It was like one sound among others.

"Erik? Are you listening?"

It was Ringmar's voice.

Winter tore himself away from his daydream. He had been somewhere for a few seconds, but now he couldn't remember where.

"I'm listening."

"What did I just say?"

"Repeat," Winter answered.

"That's the kind of thing you can only get away with in the army," Halders said.

"Isn't this the army?" Djanali said.

"There you wear a uniform," Bergenhem said.

"Aren't there soldiers who wear plainclothes?" Djanali said.

"Yes, then you're in the CIA," Halders said.

"Or the KGB," said Bergenhem.

"The KGB no longer exists," said Halders.

"What's it called now, then?"

"The national murder squad."

"Just like we have in Sweden?"

"Yes. Same name, different meaning. There, the squad commits murder on the national level; here, ours tries to solve them."

"Perhaps we should try to solve our own murder," Ringmar said.

"Have we committed a murder of our own?" Halders said.

No one answered. It sounded as though Bergenhem sighed, or maybe it was just an exhalation.

"There's something in her apartment that we haven't noticed," Halders said.

"What do you mean?" Ringmar asked.

"I don't know if I mean anything," Halders answered, "It's mostly a thought, or a hunch, or whatever it's called."

"In your case it's probably a hunch," Bergenhem said.

"What?"

"Are you thinking of a postcard, Fredrik?"

That was Winter. He thought he understood what Halders meant. It was the same thought, or hunch, he'd had himself when it came to Ellen Börge. Something he hadn't seen.

"Not exactly a postcard," Halders answered. "It's just something I feel when I'm standing in that lonely fucking apartment." He looked around. "You should all stand there, too."

"Not all at once, though," Bergenhem said.

"I'm going to get sick of you soon, Lars," said Halders.

"I have stood there," Winter said. "I understand what Fredrik's saying."

"Finally," Halders said.

"Should we turn the place upside down one more time?" Djanali said.

"That's not what it's about," Halders said.

"Is there something that's there and not there at the same time?" Djanali said.

No one answered.

"I think we'll see it," Halders said after a little while. "And then we'll understand."

Ringmar followed Winter into his office. Winter was having a harder and harder time being in his office. It was starting to become difficult to think there, to give his imagination a chance. He had been there for many hours; the walls were like the ones up in the jail. They didn't let anything out; they gave no peace. He thought of Öberg's office. There was space up there. You could see the sea.

Ringmar stood by the window. He was starting to become like Birgersson.

"I called Paula's parents," Ringmar said. "The mom answered. Elisabeth."

Winter nodded.

"The question is whether she's getting over the shock."

Winter didn't comment on that. The injured and the shocked belonged together; they often came from the same family. Violence often ran in the family. In any case, it affected them forever. There were no exceptions. A simple break-in affected a person for a long time. Everything had an effect.

"Why did you call?" Winter asked.

"I want to see them again," Ringmar said. "Soon."

Winter nodded again.

"It's like what Fredrik was saying," Ringmar said. "There's something about them that we're not seeing. When we see it, we'll understand. Something they're keeping to themselves."

"It isn't necessarily something that will be useful to us," Winter said.

"What is useful to us, then?" Ringmar said.

"Everything," Winter said, smiling.

Ringmar looked out the window. Winter saw the drops of rain on the glass. It was a light rain; he couldn't hear it. It would be heavier in October, thud-thud-thud-thud against his windowpane.

"There was something breathless about her when she answered," Ringmar said, still looking out, his profile toward Winter. It was lit up by the gray light. Winter could see Ringmar's soft chin, or maybe it was the beginning of a double chin. He hadn't noticed it before. It wasn't visible from the front. Ringmar's face was starting to collapse, but only like a shadow, and only in a certain light.

It's worse with Birgersson. And then it's my turn.

"And it wasn't like she'd been running up the cellar stairs or anything," Ringmar said.

"She didn't expect it to be you," Winter said.

"Exactly. She didn't think she'd hear from us again so soon." Ring-mar turned to Winter and his chin became taut, almost narrow. "She was expecting someone else entirely."

"Was her husband home?" Winter asked.

"I asked to have a word with him; I made something up. And yes, he was there."

"They have relatives, friends. Could be anyone who was supposed to call."

"I don't know," Ringmar said. "I don't know."

Winter got up from the chair. He didn't want to sit there, never wanted to sit there again. He closed his eyes suddenly so he wouldn't have to see the door, the walls, the desk. He felt his pulse. He wasn't feeling very well. Is it a life crisis? he thought. I didn't have a forty-year crisis that I noticed. I'm forty-five now; that's right in the middle; I'm having my forty- and fifty-year crises at the same time.

"Let's go to their house," he said.

"Now?"

"Yes."

The sun was shining through the clouds as they drove down Allén; a yellow glow through the leaves, which were starting to change color. Winter still felt ill at ease, like a premonition of being sick. Ringmar was driving. Winter rolled down the window, let the air come in. It felt good on his face. It smelled like autumn, a wet smell. He felt a ray of sun in his eye, but it wasn't uncomfortable. He closed his eyes again.

When had he and Ringmar been out on their first job together? Winter couldn't remember.

He remembered the second job they were out on together.

She had called in herself. Winter had taken the call in the car. It had been transferred from the county communications center; they had been in the vicinity of her home. She had had a breathless voice. Very frightened. They had heard her screams inside as they stood outside. The sound of the family. The screams of a woman.

It wasn't the girl. It was the mother; they realized this later. The girl didn't want to do as her dad said. She had been out late a few nights. Now she wanted to go out again. Her dad reprimanded her with a kitchen utensil. Winter saw her face as he blinked his way through Allén. Why the hell did I start thinking about her? Mariana? What was her name? Maria? Bertil knows; he's good at names, better than I am. But I won't ask him. We thought we had her. She was alive in the ambulance. They came so quickly; I was surprised. The dad was gone, in another world now. The knife ended up in the courtyard. The window was open; it was the second floor. It had all happened in the kitchen. I noticed the color of the tablecloth; I would still be able to draw the pattern. Their dinner was still on the table; they had hardly started. He was the one who had asked. Where are you going? Where are you going now? If only he hadn't asked, the mom said afterward. If only he'd let it go and hadn't asked again. Shock, she was in shock, and why should she come out of it? She would never come out of it, of course. Elisabeth Ney wouldn't either.

"There's a draft," Ringmar said.

"It's mostly drafting on me," Winter said.

"Are you clearing your thoughts?"

"My memories. I'm clearing my memories."

"Good," Ringmar said. "That's good for you."

"Do you have an idea of what we should ask the Ney couple about when we get there?"

"Do you see them as a couple?"

"That's the question," Winter answered.

"And what's the answer?"

Winter looked at the shore on the other side of the river. It had been developed with condos, would be developed more until the balconies tipped into the muddy water. Just the balcony was worth more than the lifelong earnings of the shipyard workers who had built vessels in that same place a few decades ago. Winter had been a boy then, and he'd heard the racket that came from there when he took the ferry across the river. He had seen the ships, not built, half-built, finished.

He had stood on the pier at Nya Varvet and watched the ships glide away, out toward Vinga, off across the sea, toward the equator, even farther away, the South Pacific, Australia. They glided away as though they owned the whole world.

A person who passed the equator on a ship underwent a ritual christening. He had thought about that as a boy, thought a lot about it, but he had never done it; he had lived on the earth for nearly half a century, but he hadn't yet passed the midline of the globe on a ship.

"You should never look at a couple as a couple," he answered at last. "If you do, you're guilty of generalization."

"Some grow together," Ringmar said.

"Sorry?"

Winter turned his eyes to Ringmar.

"Some couples become like one," Ringmar continued. "It's like they grow together."

"That sounds horrible. You mean that as years go by they become like Siamese twins?"

"Yes."

"One can't even go to the john without the other?"

"That's what happens," Ringmar said. "It sneaks up. And one day it's a fact. Not one step without the other."

"I hope you're not speaking from experience, Bertil."

"I'm sitting here by myself, aren't I?"

"Nice."

"But it's worth thinking about."

They drove through Kungssten to avoid the rush-hour traffic out on the main roads. They were nearly crushed by a bus; they saw it coming, but there wasn't space for both of them. Ringmar heaved the car up onto a bit of sidewalk that was suddenly there. There were no pedestrians on it. In the rearview mirror, Winter saw the bus reeling forth toward the roundabout. Ringmar rolled back onto the street again.

"If we'd had a marked car, that hypocritical bastard would have driven like a normal person," he said.

"I got the number."

"Forget it. We don't have time."

Ringmar swung off onto Långedragsvägen. They passed Hagen School. Ringmar turned left at the intersection after the soccer field and crossed Torgny Segerstedtsgatan. Mario and Elisabeth Ney's apartment was in one of the apartment buildings in Tynnered. The redbrick buildings stood like walls facing the sea, far down in Fiskebäck. The wind was strong over the flat land; it was always windy here. Winter saw the buildings when they were up on the main road.

Ringmar swung into the OK station to fill up.

Winter went into the store and came back with an evening paper, the *GT*. He flipped ahead a few pages and held the spread up in front of Ringmar's nose as Ringmar pulled the receipt from the gas pump.

"Isn't that your bad side?" Ringmar said.

"I was thinking more of the headline," said Winter.

"POLICE WITHOUT CLUES IN HOTEL MURDER," Ringmar read from above the picture of Winter turning around, presumably after a short interview. "Is that proper Swedish?"

"Is that a proper conclusion?" Winter said.

"Essentially, yes," Ringmar said, "if we don't count the videotapes."

"And the hand," Winter said. "And the rope. And the shoe print."

"They actually should have had all of that already," Ringmar said. "What's his name, your friend at *GT*? Bry . . . Bru . . ."

"Bülow," Winter answered, "but he's not my friend."

"Anyway, he usually sniffs most things out. But not this."

"Our commissioner must have sealed up the cracks," Winter said.

"You mean by quitting?" Ringmar said. "You're talking about the Sieve, right?"

Winter nodded. Einar "the Sieve" Berkander, ex-police commissioner, had hooked up with a divorced reporter from *Göteborgs-Posten* during his ruling years. It got out, as did most of what the Sieve said in the woman's arms. The Sieve was also divorced nowadays.

"We can't forget that we often get help from the press," Ringmar said.

"Exploit it, you mean?"

"We need it," Ringmar said, studying the spread again.

"Is there anything there that's of use to us?"

"I don't know," Winter said, folding up the paper and throwing it into the backseat.

They drove out from the gas station and in among the houses. Ringmar parked. Winter checked the address.

It smelled like food in the stairwell, some indeterminate dish, almost no spices. It was the old stairwell smell. The new one was noticeably spicier, spices from all over the world, people from all over the world.

Ringmar rang at the door. No one opened it. He rang again. They thought they heard footsteps. They realized they were being observed through the peephole.

The door was opened a tiny crack. They saw Elisabeth Ney's face.

"Yes?"

"May we come in for a little while, Mrs. Ney?"

This was Ringmar. They didn't need any ID at this point.

"Well . . . what is it?"

They didn't answer. They had already asked to come in. A little while, Winter thought. What an expression. A little while could mean days.

"My husband isn't home," she said.

So they're separated right now, Winter thought. We're in luck.

"That's okay," Ringmar said.

How do you act when you're about to try to ask a mother what her relationship with her murdered daughter was really like? How do you act in a conversation like that when it's actually an interrogation?

Winter could see the courtyard through the kitchen window. A young mother was pushing her little daughter on a swing. The girl laughed as the speed increased. He wasn't unfamiliar with that. He had been pushing Elsa for years, and now it was Lilly's turn.

Elisabeth Ney couldn't be unfamiliar with that.

It couldn't be good that she was standing here and looking out this window.

The window in the living room was better, with its view of the gas station, the highway, the industrial area on the other side of the highway.

Ringmar had asked about Paula's long trip almost ten years ago.

"I don't understand why it's of so much interest," Elisabeth Ney said. "It was so long ago."

"Maybe that trip meant more than we understand," Ringmar said.

Ney didn't answer. She sat at the kitchen table in a stiff pose, as though she didn't know what she was doing there. As though she could have been anywhere. It didn't matter.

Winter gave a discreet cough.

"Your husband doesn't want to talk about his past," he said.

She looked at him.

"Surely that doesn't have any . . . anything to do with this?"

"We don't know," Winter said. "Think about it. We don't know. That's why we're asking."

We've tumbled right into this family's life. A week ago, I didn't even know that there was anyone named Ney in this city. Now I want to know everything.

"But I don't have any answers," Ney said.

"Was Paula upset about something?" Ringmar asked.

"You've already asked about that."

"Something that happened recently?"

"I've tried to answer that. No. I don't know. Good God, I don't *know*."

Winter saw the tears in her eyes.

Winter sat down on the chair in front of her. Until now, he had been standing at the window.

"Why didn't Paula want you or your husband to meet her boy-friend?"

"Pardon me?"

"According to a friend, she had a boyfriend. But Paula never introduced him to you."

"We didn't know that," said Ney. "I don't know anything about that."

"No," Ringmar said gently. "But why didn't you know?"

"Who is it?" she asked, looking at him. "Who is he?"

Ringmar looked at Winter.

"We don't know," Winter said.

Ney shifted her gaze.

"Don't know? What do you mean?"

"We don't know who it is."

"Then how can you be so sure that Paula actually had a boyfriend?"

"Her friend thought she did."

"And you believe her?"

"She seems pretty certain of it. But we can't know for sure."

"Where is he, then? Why hasn't he gotten in touch?" Her eyes moved between Winter and Ringmar. "What kind of boyfriend doesn't get in touch?"

They didn't answer.

Suddenly she understood.

Her hand went to her mouth, as though she was going to bite it. Winter could see all the awful feelings reflected in her eyes. He heard a laugh from down in the courtyard. It was the girl. They shouldn't be able to hear her laughter in here. The window ought to be thick enough.

"I thought that you . . . maybe . . . that she'd said something about him," he said, "or that you suspected something."

"But Paula didn't live here. Other than now, the last few days. If she . . ."

She broke off there. She put her hand to her mouth again.

"Oh God, I said last few days. I meant past. You say things wrong sometimes. I usually point it out when people say 'last' when they mean 'past.'"

Winter nodded. Ney looked at him with eyes that suddenly looked blind.

"I'm a teacher. I've taught Swedish and history in the upper levels.

I've always told my students that it's important to use proper language. Without language, you get nowhere."

"Elisabeth . . ."

"And then I sit here myself and say 'last.'" She looked from Winter to Ringmar and back again. Her eyes had still been blind, but now it broke. "Last! And I was right! It was her last few days!"

"Mrs. Ney . . . Elisabeth . . ."

"It's almost funny!" Her eyes had a sheen again. They flashed in a peculiar way. "I ha—"

"Elisabeth!"

She gave a jump on her chair, really jumped, as though a breeze, rather than Winter's words, had lifted her up, had defied the law of gravity.

"Elisabeth? Would you like us to help you get somewhere? Would you like to see someone? Elisabeth?"

She didn't answer. Her eyes were unfocused as she suddenly stood up and walked through the kitchen like a blind woman, her arms out in front of her.

She stood in front of the window. Winter and Ringmar stood up. Winter could see every furrow in Ringmar's face. It looked like a black-and-white photograph. It had to be the dusk.

"I can't hear the little girl any longer," said Ney. "Wasn't she the one who was laughing before?"

12

The door opened out into the hall. Winter heard a cough. The
door closed. Winter could hear the echo from the stairwell. Elisabeth Ney didn't seem to hear anything. They were sitting in the living
room now; Winter and Ringmar were sitting. Ney was standing at the
window, with her back to them.

There was no voice from the hall, no "I'm home" or "Hi" or anything like that. Just steps.

"What the hell?!"

Ney didn't say anything. She didn't turn her head. Maybe she was
still listening for the little girl.

"Good evening, Mario."

That was Ringmar. He had stood up. From where Winter was sitting, Ringmar mostly looked like a shadow. Dusk had begun to fall
while they were sitting there, and none of them had turned on a light.
There was an old phrase for that: sitting twilight. Winter had heard it
from his grandmother. It was an expression associated with comfort
and calmness. Awaiting the darkness in a state of peace.

"What are you doing here?!"

Winter couldn't really see Mario Ney's face.

"Elisabeth? What are they doing here?"

She didn't answer. Her eyes were still somewhere else, maybe out
in the courtyard, maybe nowhere.

"Elisabeth!"

She turned around slowly. Winter considered getting up and turning on a light, but he remained sitting. He could see Elisabeth Ney's
face clearly when she turned around; it was illuminated by the last of

the daylight before the sun sank behind the building on the other side of the courtyard.

It's like a mask, he thought. Like something that's been hung on her to patch up what would otherwise be a hole. No. A different face?

Then it was as though her eyes could see again.

She saw her husband. She gave a start, as he had done when he came into the room just now.

Winter saw a sudden fear in her face.

He looked at Mario Ney. The man was still standing there, a meter from the doorway. His heavy face was more clear now. It had the same strength as the first time Winter had seen it. When he came with the news of their daughter's death. That strength had remained in his face, under his grief.

"What are they doing here, Elisabeth?" Ney waved toward Winter. "I didn't know that they were going to come back."

"Your wife didn't know either," Winter said, standing up. "We're only here for a short visit."

"Why?"

"Couldn't you sit down for a bit?"

"Why hasn't anyone turned on the lights in here?" Ney asked.

"We forgot to," Ringmar said.

"The twilight comes quickly," Winter said.

"Twi—what kind of crap is this?" He took a few quick steps into the room. "Elisabeth? What have you all been talking about here?"

Winter noticed that she gave a start again. During the second when it happened, he tried to figure out whether it was because of her shock, her despair, her fear of everything. Or whether it was because of her husband.

It was hard to tell. But she is afraid. Bertil sees it, too, but barely, he thought. We should probably turn on the lights in here before we run into each other.

"You have no right to force your way in here!"

"Your wife agreed to let us in," Winter said.

"What does that mean?"

"That she agreed."

"I'm going to fucking check on that."

"We are also able to summon for interrogation," Winter said. "To bring a person in for questioning. Judicial Procedure Code twenty-three, paragraph seven."

"We know what we're doing," Ringmar said. "We don't break in."

Mario Ney didn't say anything now.

"Could you turn on a light, Mario?" Winter asked, as gently as he could.

Ney turned his gaze in Winter's direction. His eyes looked hard.

"Are you planning to stay for long? Should I start dinner?" He gave a laugh. "Should we start making the beds? Did you bring your sheets?"

"They're here for Paula," Elisabeth said.

It was like a foreign voice in there. Suddenly she sounded strong, clear.

She had left the window, had taken a few steps forward. The dusk had become red. At the moment, no one needed to turn on a light in the room. The light was everywhere.

Mario remained standing. He suddenly seemed to be at a loss.

"They're trying to figure out what happened to Paula, Mario. They're doing their job." She looked at Winter and back at her husband again. "If this helps . . . coming here . . . then they can do it whenever they like."

"Yeah, yeah." He seemed to shrink, become a few centimeters shorter. "Whenever they like. In the middle of the night."

"They wanted to know about Paula's boyfriend," Elisabeth said.

"What? What?"

He had given a start again. Winter couldn't tell if it was from surprise. The red light was gone again, as quickly as it had come. Now it was truly dark inside.

"Apparently she had a boyfriend," Elisabeth said.

Winter quickly walked around the sofa and turned on a floor

lamp with a large shade. The room lit up like a stage. He had thought of that a few times, that he was on a stage, when he was standing in a room asking questions of strangers and at the same time trying to study their faces, as though he would be able to learn everything about them in a few seconds. As though someone were observing them all, an audience. As though he would soon recite a line.

"We don't know," he said. "That's why we're asking."

"But didn't you have to get the idea from somewhere?" Mario asked.

His face was sharp and dark from the electric light.

"Should we sit down?" Winter said.

Mario looked at the furniture as though he were seeing it for the first time, and as though he were going to learn to sit for the first time.

He took a step and sank deep down into an easy chair and immediately sat up again.

"What is this . . . about Paula dating? When was this?"

"Had she been dating during those last few weeks?" Ringmar asked.

Oh God. Winter looked at Elisabeth, but she didn't seem to react to what Ringmar had just said. The strength had left her again. She was sitting on the very edge of the sofa, as though she was going to stand up at any time.

"No," Mario said.

"When was the last time Paula had a boyfriend?" Winter asked.

Mario didn't answer. His wife didn't hear. Winter heard sirens outside, an ambulance on its way here or there. A little while ago, he had considered calling one himself, when Elisabeth seemed to disappear far into herself, away from herself. He looked at her. She looked like she was on her way off again. Her husband looked at her. He didn't answer Winter's question.

Winter repeated it.

"I don't know."

"Try to think."

"There's no point."

"Why not?"

"She didn't date anyone."

"Sorry?"

Mario looked at his wife. She didn't hear, didn't see.

"I never met any boyfriend," Mario said. He seemed to have trouble pronouncing the word. "Never."

"Never?"

"Aren't you listening to me?" He looked straight at Winter. "Do I have to repeat it a thousand times?"

"Paula hasn't ever introduced a boyfriend to you?" Winter asked.

Mario shook his head.

"Mario?"

"How many times do I have to say it?"

Winter looked at Ringmar, who raised an eyebrow. Elisabeth didn't move on the edge of the sofa. The siren came back out there in the growing darkness, howling from the other direction this time. Winter again felt as though he were sitting on a stage. But he had no script. No one had written down what he should say. And what he said was important, perhaps crucial. What he asked. In that way, he wrote his own script, based on experience and emotion. Maybe it was sympathy.

"Did you talk about it?" Winter asked.

"I really don't understand," said Mario. "What do you mean by that?"

Winter looked at Elisabeth. He meant whether the parents had talked about it between themselves. He didn't want to say it. He wanted them to say it.

"Did Paula want to talk about it?"

"No," said Mario.

"Did you want to talk about it? You and your wife?"

"With whom? With her?"

"Yes."

"No . . . we didn't."

"Why not?"

Mario looked at his wife. She didn't seem to be listening. She couldn't help him.

"She didn't want to."

"Why not?"

"Why, why, why . . . that was a lot of damn whys."

"Paula was twenty-nine years old," Winter said. "According to you she'd never dated anyone. She never wanted to talk about it. You never asked her about it. You never talked about it. Is that right?"

Mario nodded.

"But you and Elisabeth must have talked about it?"

"Yes . . . I guess we did."

"Did you believe Paula? Did you believe her?"

"Why would she lie about it?"

Winter didn't say anything.

"That's not really something you lie about, is it? Isn't it more the opposite?"

"What do you mean?" Winter asked.

"Don't you get it? Why would she keep quiet if she had a boyfriend?" Mario looked at his wife. "We wouldn't protest, would we? What do you say, Elisabeth? We wouldn't have anything against it, would we?"

Elisabeth burst into tears. Winter couldn't tell whether it was because of what her husband was saying or whether it was something that had been coming anyway. On the other hand, he could tell that she needed help now, professional help. He took a cell phone from the inner pocket of his jacket and called.

A siren howled from down on Vasaplatsen, a police car. Winter had come in, hung up his jacket, sat down in the dark and had time to sit twilight for one minute before he heard the siren, and then the phone ringing.

He couldn't see the display in the dark. It could be anyone.

"Yes?"

"Hi, you."

"Hi, Angela."

The sound of the siren became louder, climbed up the buildings, came into the room.

"What is that noise in the background? Is there a fire?"

"An ambulance," he answered.

"What are you doing?"

"Right now? I just got home. I hung up my jacket and was about to grab the bottle of whiskey."

"You have to eat first," Angela said.

"I bought a little rack of lamb at Saluhallen."

"What did you do today?"

"Sent a woman off to the hospital," he answered, and told the story.

The siren disappeared up Aschebergsgatan, on its way to Sahlgrenska University Hospital.

"This girl, Paula, must have been very lonely," Angela said.

"If it's true," Winter said. "It doesn't have to be. Her friend didn't think it was."

"And you believe that there's a secret boyfriend?"

"If there is, we would really like to meet him."

"How will you find him?"

"We will, soon," Winter said. "If he exists."

"It could take time."

"Yes. It could take a lot of time. That, and the other thing. Lots of work."

"I have three days left down here before we travel home," Angela said. "I have time to let the clinic know."

"What? About what?"

"That I can't take the job, of course. That you don't have time to take paternity leave. Although I don't have to tell them that last part."

"Angela . . ."

"I have time to cancel the apartment, too. It will be easy, because I haven't signed the contract yet. That wasn't going to happen until tomorrow."

"I didn't know about the apartment. You didn't tell me that."

"I was going to now. And now I have."

"Where is it?"

"Marbella."

"Balcony? Terrace?"

"Does it matter?"

"We have a plan," Winter said. "Let's stick to it."

"Others might not," she said. "I don't need to say who."

No, he knew. The others were victims and perpetrators and parents and boyfriends and people who had disappeared. Maybe a winter on the sunny coast was a dream. Or maybe it was a good future working method to turn over a case in the middle of the preliminary investigation. Maybe the solution was near, the resolution, the dissolution. He knew even though he didn't know; it was like he had thought, and Halders—there was something they hadn't seen, hadn't understood. When they'd seen and understood, he could fly through the friendly skies straight to the sun.

He heard the siren again at night, after a dream. In the dream, he had met someone who had said that he'd chosen the wrong road at the crossing behind him. He couldn't see any face. Help me, he had said. You have to help yourself, the voice had said. Only you can help yourself. It was like it came from a silhouette. I have to turn on a light, he had thought. Then I'll see what he looks like. That voice seems familiar. It's someone I know. If I see the face, I can solve the case. I'll have time to solve the case before I have to go back to the crossing and take the other road.

When he woke up, the memory of the dream was still there. The siren was howling down there.

He lay awake with his eyes closed. What case had he been working on when he encountered the silhouette? There was no room for that information in the dream. Or who the stranger was. Except it wasn't a stranger.

Winter sat up in the bed. He wasn't really awake yet. This wasn't an unusual situation for him. His brain worked while he slept, while he dreamed. But could dreams show him the way at a crossroads? He didn't know; he still didn't know.

He had never seen the face he was looking for in his dreams.

The sound of the sirens moved off in the night. Winter leaned to the side and lifted his watch, which he had placed on the nightstand. Quarter past three; the night was on its way into the hour of the wolf.

He knew that he wouldn't be able to fall asleep again if he didn't get up and drink a glass of water and maybe stand on the balcony and smoke. It wouldn't be the first time. And he wouldn't really be alone out there. He had seen the glow of a cigarette on a balcony on the other side of Vasaplatsen a few times. It was always in the hour of the wolf.

The wood floor was soft and warm against the soles of his feet. He had refinished all the floors in the whole apartment during a week of vacation many years ago and given them three layers of varnish the week after, and after that he had immediately left for the sun, still drunk on sawdust and lethal fumes. In the sun, he had switched that out for a different drunkenness, mild but constant intoxication.

He had gone for a swim in the hour of the wolf, but it looked different on a beach on the Mediterranean. The moon was bigger.

Angela hadn't looked different on the beach. She was beautiful in any light, at any hour of the day.

They hadn't moved in together yet, then. But it was time. The floor was part of it. There was so much else. He didn't want to be alone anymore.

The loneliness was no longer an eternal and faithful friend. That's what he had thought as he drove the sander over his lonely floor.

Now he walked across it. There were a few toys here and there.

In the kitchen, he poured a glass of water from a pitcher with slices of lemon in it. He heard a siren again. The last twenty-four hours must involve some sort of record. He hadn't heard of any big accident. A sudden epidemic. He sat at the kitchen table. He tried to think of nothing for a second, but he failed. He thought of Mario Ney. What would happen to him when the shock subsided? What had happened to his wife had become clear yesterday evening.

Who would Mario become then? Who was he now? There was something about him that didn't have anything to do with shock. He refused any form of conversation with any form of therapist. The only conversations he was forced to have were with Winter, and even there the spaces between the words were too large. Like trapdoors. There was something about the Ney family that was a big, dark secret. Maybe many people had such things. But they seldom led to murder. Had the Ney family's secret led to murder? Directly or indirectly? He thought of Paula. He could see her face. A lonely face, if there was such an expression. Everyone was alone, faces, bodies, lives. You had to drag your own life around as well as you could. Winter had met too many people who couldn't handle it to be convinced about life. Life was a burden. Only an idiot would believe anything different. It was unbearable. It showed up in many ways. No, I haven't become a cynic. I still believe. Sometimes I even still believe in God, even go to church once in a while. What kind of self-professed cynic does that?

Winter didn't believe in Satan. He believed in people. It might have been the same thing. That was the awful thing about his job. The faces, bodies, lives, like him, like Angela, like the children, like his friends, the police. And still. Satan. The incidents were there. A face without life in a fucking hotel room in a small big city at the edge of the world. Good God, the white hand. There was a message there that he couldn't read. None of the fingers had pointed in any particular direction.

Yet he knew that he would find out. There would be an answer in the end, or part of an answer, part of a solution to the riddle. That's how it went. He trembled at the thought of that moment. He was already afraid of what he would find out then. It was something he didn't want to know in his lifetime, never, ever. Why am I thinking like this? How can I think like this? What is it I suspect? I don't want to know, he thought, looking up at the wall clock in the kitchen. It was the hour of the wolf again.

A group was playing morning soccer as he biked across Heden. The September sun was mild, and the light made the contours of the city rounder, almost like the ball; it flew into the air in his direction and aimed and bounced right against his front tire.

"Give the ball here, Winter!"

He looked up from the ball and the tire.

The goalie was waving. Winter recognized him again, and a few of the other players in their blue tracksuits. The SWAT team was taking a break from their kamikaze operations. But "break" was relative for this gang. It was always serious for them. Several of them would be injured on the field in the next half hour; knees to the tender ribs, elbows to the spleen, cleats to the wrist.

"Better for your health that I keep this," Winter shouted, picking up the ball.

"Watch out so your tie doesn't get stuck in your spokes, man!" one of the outfield players shouted.

A few of the others grinned.

Winter wasn't wearing a tie today, or even a jacket or a coat. But he had a reputation.

He threw the ball back onto the field without saying anything.

"Tell Halders we're ready when he is," his colleague shouted.

A few of the others grinned again.

Winter knew what he was referring to. The homicide unit had had a team in the intercompany league, but it had all ended after ten minutes. Halders had protested a call by kicking the referee in the ass. The team had been eliminated, and Halders had been banned for two years.

"He can play in two years," Winter called.

"He knows where we are!"

"He's longing for you guys," Winter called.

"You can play with us if you want, Winter!"

"I'll think about it."

He heard a couple of laughs again. The SWAT team was a cheerful group.

As he was placing his bike outside the police station, he met Ringmar, on his way in from the parking lot.

"That's not such a bad idea," Ringmar said.

"Then do it."

"Is it that simple?"

They moved past a marked car. Their colleague at the wheel lifted a hand in greeting. We're like one big family, Winter thought. And we have no secrets from each other.

He smiled.

"What are you grinning at?"

"Nothing, Bertil."

"It's not good when a person smiles at nothing."

"I was just thinking that we're like a big happy family at this station."

"Yes, it's wonderful."

"How's it going with our family in Tynnered? Did you go by Sahlgrenska?"

"She was sleeping. The pills were still working."

"How had the night been?"

"It was quiet. She hasn't said a word."

"Is she going to?"

"Say a word? I don't know, Erik."

Ringmar moved past another police car. The driver waved, the passenger waved, Winter and Ringmar waved.

"Maybe she has something to tell us," Ringmar said, following the car with his gaze as it swung out onto Skånegatan.

"This is her way of doing it," Winter said.

"Mm-hmm. And not doing it."

There was a message waiting for Winter on his desk.

He heard a cough inside the door before he knocked.

Birgersson was sitting behind his desk. That was unusual.

"Sit down, Erik."

"I think I'll stand by the window for a change."

Birgersson didn't smile.

"I got a phone call from Mario Ney half an hour ago."

"Oh?"

"He says that you and Bertil evoked a nervous breakdown in his wife."

"Was that his expression? Evoked?"

"What happened?" Birgersson asked.

"We made a mistake. But not yesterday. We should have made sure that she, Elisabeth, got help immediately."

"He says he's going to report us. You."

"Well, what am I supposed to say about that?"

"You could say something about how we should comment on this when the press starts writing about it."

"We? It'll be me, as usual."

"Why did you two go there again, Erik? Without making an appointment first?"

"You're asking me?"

Winter took a step away from the window and leaned over the desk.

"I have the impression that this is one of your methods. Don't give them a ring beforehand. Just ring at the door."

"Depends," Birgersson said.

"It really did depend this time," Winter said. "There's something about the Ney family that we have to get at. Soon, maybe immediately. Bertil and I didn't go there to give him a thrashing. His wife let us in. We asked a few questions. She agreed we could. He came home from God knows where and looked at us like we were burglars."

"Where had he been?"

"We didn't ask."

"How is his wife doing now?"

"She's sleeping. We're going to try to talk with her again. We have to, Sture."

"Hmm."

"I don't think he'll make any report. You don't think he will either."

"He has made one. To me."

"Let it stop with you."

Birgersson nodded.

Winter straightened his back. He got ready to leave.

"Erik?"

"Yes?"

"Uh . . . that thing we talked about the other day. Let's just forget it, huh?"

"What thing?"

"Exactly."

"Oh, that," Winter said in the doorway. "It was just a little jabbering about life."

13

The morning meeting was about Paula's loneliness. The list of her acquaintances was short. That didn't necessarily mean that she was a lonely person, but no one they'd met seemed to have been really close to her.

"It would be Nina Lorrinder if anyone," Halders said.

"Doesn't seem to be," Ringmar said.

"I was planning on talking to her this afternoon," Halders said.

"About what?"

That was Bergenhem.

"Her best pasta recipe," Halders answered.

"I'm serious," said Bergenhem.

"Don't always believe the worst of everyone, Fredrik."

That was Djanali.

"I think she knows more than she's saying," Halders said. "Both about Paula and her boyfriend. Or boyfriends."

"Or girlfriend," Djanali said. "Maybe that's what it was. Maybe that's why she was so secretive."

"In the twenty-first century?" Halders looked around the group. "Would anyone be ashamed of that this late in the game? Shit, the fags and the dykes are lining up to come out! There's a fucking crowd at the closet door!"

"Maybe Paula was different," Djanali said. "Maybe she didn't want to crowd in."

"But we've talked to her coworkers," Halders said. "No indication there."

Djanali shrugged.

"We've established that she seemed to keep to herself," she said.

"That's what I'm going to squeeze Nina Lorrinder on," Halders said.

"Don't squeeze too hard," Bergenhem said.

"Are you being serious now, too, Lars?"

Bergenhem nodded.

"When are you going to come out, by the way?"

Bergenhem winced. He opened his mouth.

"Lay off now, Fredrik!" Winter said.

"I was just joking," Halders said.

Winter and Ringmar sneaked out of the police station right after the meeting. Winter suggested a place where they could talk, maybe think.

Ringmar drove to Gullbergsvass and parked below the big gas tank. The scent of snuff from the tobacco factory was strong.

They walked across the street and continued along the quay. The rusty boats bumped back and forth in the water. Some were inhabited by society's dropouts. Ringmar nodded toward a houseboat that must have been able to sail at one time. Now it was red with rust, and it wasn't a home any longer. Its windows were empty and black. A gull lifted from its deck and flew with a hoarse cry toward the other side of the river. A barge passed in the background. A light rain began to fall. Winter turned up the collar of his coat. He looked up and saw the sky open up to the north as the rain cloud moved south. The rain stopped. Winter lit a Corps. The smoke floated out across the road, after the rain.

"That's where the stripper lived that Bergenhem fell for," Ringmar said as they passed the half-sunk houseboat.

Winter nodded. Bergenhem had fallen, hard, and several times— in the boat, on the floor in a bar, in a field. He had nearly died. That was a case that returned to Winter's thoughts more and more often recently. It was a gruesome case. He had moved on; they had all moved on. Sometimes he didn't understand why. It was like being in the middle of a war and surviving and then going out again and surviving and then going out again.

"Maybe you should be a little firmer during the meetings," Ringmar said, turning to Winter. "I mean, about meeting discipline."

Winter took the cigar from his mouth.

"Are you thinking of Halders?"

"Yes . . . and Bergenhem."

"Halders thinks better when he lets his mouth run." Winter smiled. "Look at you and me."

"It gets too personal," Ringmar said. "Bergenhem took offense."

"Mm-hmm."

"Halders went too far."

"Is Bergenhem gay?"

"I don't know."

"Well, it's his business," Winter said.

"Exactly. It's not, for example, Halders's business."

"Lars is a young man who's searching, but I don't think he's gay," Winter said, smiling again. "And if he is, I don't give a shit."

"Maybe he does, himself," Ringmar said. "Give a shit, that is."

"Does he need to talk about it, you think?" Winter asked.

Ringmar shrugged.

"Hanne will be back after Christmas."

"Will she?"

Hanne Östergaard had been the pastor and spiritual caregiver for the police. Winter had worked closely with her at certain times. Those had been complicated cases. She had been a help, to him and to others. For the past two years, she had been a seamen's chaplain in Sydney. When she got the job, she had told Winter about it. He had asked her if it was possible to get farther away from the underworld of Gothenburg, and she had said no. They hadn't gotten a substitute for her. That was how it worked in the police administration. His colleagues had to wait with their inner suffering. Maybe it would go away on its own.

A net of gray birds unfurled over the barracks on the other side. They looked like more rain. Winter heard the toot of a tugboat. The river had its own sirens.

"I don't want to be firm," he said, pulling in smoke and blowing it out. The smoke was floating over the water now; the wind had changed. "It almost always leads us the wrong way."

Ringmar kicked at a small stone. It flew into the water and skipped three times.

"Have you been practicing that long?" Winter asked.

"You should see what I can do with my left hand."

Winter saw the swarm of birds turn to the south and fly straight toward him. He still couldn't tell whether they were crows, magpies, jackdaws. He could hear the sound of their wings, like a second wind.

"She wrote that she would become like a bird," he said, following the birds as they passed overhead and continued to the south, becoming smaller, starting to disappear in the gray of the sky. "She would be like the bird who flew by outside."

Ringmar didn't answer. Winter took his gaze from the sky and looked at Ringmar, who looked like he'd gone pale. It could be the light. It made everything pale.

"We've analyzed the contents and surface of that letter but we haven't gotten much farther," Winter said.

"We've never run into anything like it," Ringmar said.

"Maybe that can help us."

"How would it help us, Erik?"

"We have no starting point. Sometimes that's good."

Ringmar kicked at another stone. It didn't reach the quay. They met a man on a flatbed moped. He didn't say hello. Winter turned around and saw him stop at one of the boats, a small trawler that had recently been repainted. It looked seaworthy. The man was wearing a red knitted cap. He disappeared belowdecks. That boat could pass the equator, Winter thought. It's up for it.

"Are there other letters?" Ringmar said, and he took aim at another stone but stopped himself.

"What do you mean?"

"I don't know . . . either that Paula had written something like this before . . . that wasn't about murder, of course, or kidnapping . . . but that she'd communicated like this before."

"To whom?"

"Her parents."

"They would have at least said *that,* wouldn't they?" Winter said.

Ringmar didn't answer. Winter heard the moped start. He turned around and saw the man in the cap swing around and pass them. There was a full garbage bag on the flatbed. It bounced with a nasty sound as the moped passed them.

"They can't keep quiet about everything, surely?" Winter continued.

"Where did the money for Paula's apartment come from?" Ringmar said.

Mario Ney had signed the contract of sale for the condo in Guldheden. He had nine-tenths ownership.

"Does that matter?" Winter said.

"It was a lot of money," Ringmar said.

"An inheritance from Sicily?" Winter said.

Ringmar smiled.

"Have you ever been there, Erik?"

"Yes. About ten years ago. Taormina. But I guess that's not really Sicily."

"What is it, then?"

"The dream of Sicily. That's not what it looks like in reality."

"I wonder what Mario's reality looked like."

"He doesn't want to talk about it."

"No, exactly."

"Has he done it before?" Ringmar said, and he stopped. The quay was wet and shiny and looked like a highway built of stone.

"The murderer? Has he murdered before? Is that what you mean?"

"Yes. And forced the victim, or victims, to write farewell letters?"

"Where are those letters, then?"

"Maybe never sent," Ringmar said.

Winter thought. Rain was falling again, but so gently that it wasn't visible as it hit the ground.

"Do you mean that there are families out there who are sitting with farewell letters from their loved ones that they haven't told anyone about?"

"I don't know if I thought that far."

"Say someone has disappeared from the family, left, has maybe run away, and then a letter about love and forgiveness arrives."

"But that person never comes back?"

"The family believes that he or she has disappeared of their own volition," Winter said. "He or she is alive, but wants to live in peace."

"Well, that's not unusual," Ringmar said. "And a last message is perhaps not unusual either."

"Are there ones like that?" Winter said. "That are like Paula's message."

"I hardly dare to think about it," Ringmar said.

"The question is how we find out," Winter said.

"Not the press," Ringmar said.

"No, that would be too much. People would be a little too panicked. Are there degrees? More or less panicked?"

Ringmar didn't answer. They had almost reached the base of the bridge. What had looked small at a distance was very large now. The traffic clattered up there with an awful noise.

"It's like with the hand," Ringmar said. "That's the kind of thing we can't just tell the public."

The white hand. Winter had looked at it again yesterday. It was one of the strangest things he'd seen in an investigation.

The hand was white like new-fallen snow. It was clean; it looked untouched. The word "innocent" had popped into his head. That wasn't a good word.

"I dreamed about it last night," Ringmar said. "It was waving at me."

They were standing under the bridge now. The din above them was like chains on iron. The gentle rain swept over the river like a fog. Winter could see the silhouettes of gulls through the mist of rain, gliding between the riverbanks. A boat siren tooted again. It sounded like the cry of a whale.

Paula had had her photograph taken two days before she was murdered. She had sat in a photo booth at Central Station. That was quickest, simplest, cheapest.

Winter was sitting with the four quick pictures in front of him. Paula's last face. He thought of her mother, and then about her again.

What was she going to do with these pictures? A trip? Photos are always good to have along on a trip. If you get lost.

He studied her face. It was the same, in four versions. She was possibly lowering her eyelids in one of the pictures. She wasn't smiling. She was just looking, straight at him. She didn't look like she was on her way anywhere.

Djanali wound the video forward and backward. Her eyes hurt from the green light in the images, the worthless light of Central Station.

She followed the woman's every movement from the second she became visible until she disappeared.

She followed the man's movements.

It wasn't cold in the room, but she was freezing. When she pressed the buttons on the remote control, her fingers felt like ice.

The woman's face was like a mask behind her sunglasses, under the wig. No way in hell that was her own hair. Now I'm starting to think in Fredrik's words. No way in hell. No way is enough. It's not necessary to swear so damn much.

The fake blond dropped off the suitcase between the times of 6:29 and 6:31 p.m. She was not alone in the area, but it wasn't crowded either.

Djanali began to look at the other people in there. They were faces of strangers, straight on, in profile. Strangers' backs.

She caught a glimpse of a coat.

A pair of shoes.

At the edge of the image.

The coat. A detail, but visible.

The shoes.

On the other side of the row of lockers. Someone was standing there, not moving. The room curved in sharply there. It turned into another room.

Djanali took out the video of the woman and put in the video of the man. Hardly six hours later he had come and taken out the suitcase. Put in the hand. Djanali looked at the coat, at the shoes. It could be the same coat. The shoes were black, wide. Large. Size ten or eleven. She switched to the other film. The shoes. Black, wide. Öberg had guessed size ten. They remained still. The camera's view didn't reach above the man's legs. The lower part of the coat flapped suddenly, as though from a gust of wind, but the shoes didn't move. What brand were they? She was no expert on men's shoes. But she was good at making observations.

She lifted the telephone receiver.

"Is he trying to hide by standing there?" Halders said.

"Or he's observing," Ringmar said.

"It's not really normal to just stand still in that place, is it?" Djanali said.

"Maybe he's warming up in there," said Bergenhem.

"There was a heat wave at the time," Djanali said.

"Run it once more," Winter said.

They ran it once more. The coat fluttered, the shoes didn't move. Winter saw that it could be the same coat, the same shoes.

"What is he doing there the first time?" Bergenhem said.

"Making sure, of course," Halders said.

"That the suitcase really ends up in the locker?"

"Yes, sir."

"Why doesn't he pick it up right away?"

"Don't know, sir."

"Why take the long way around the lockers at all?" Djanali said.

"Exactly," Ringmar said.

"The woman drops off what we think is Paula's suitcase. This man sees her doing it. Makes sure, maybe. Then he waits six hours to pick it up. Why?"

"And why double the risk of being discovered?" Ringmar said.

"That was the point," Winter said.

Everyone in the room turned to him.

"This is a movie that was filmed for an audience," Winter continued. "We're the audience."

"They directed it?"

That was Bergenhem.

Winter nodded.

"That's the only explanation I have. We are meant to see it. They knew that we would sit here and watch this and wonder what it's about."

"So what is it about, then?" Djanali asked.

"Some diabolical game," said Halders. "They're playing with us."

"But why?" said Bergenhem.

"That's always a very good question," Halders said.

"We have to get a closer look at those shoes," said Ringmar.

"Looks like Ecco Free," said Halders.

"Do those really still exist?" Bergenhem asked.

"Every well-stocked shoe store in the city sells about twenty pairs of Ecco Free per year," said Ringmar.

"That doesn't sound like much," said Bergenhem. "So they must have regular customers?"

"Maybe twenty years back," said Djanali.

"Why twenty years in particular?" Winter asked.

"What?"

"Why did you just think of twenty years back in time?"

"I . . . don't know, Erik. I could have said thirty."

Halders didn't say anything. He considered the shoes on the screen. They were waiting to be enlarged. The shoes looked clean, almost unused. The soles were thick.

"I've seen shoes like that," said Halders, "and quite recently, at that." He lifted his eyes from the screen. "Where did I see them?"

• • •

It was eighteen years earlier. Winter stood up from his chair. There was a strong scent of coffee in the small room, because he had just knocked over the plastic mug on the table in front of him. Halders had jumped to the side at the last moment to avoid getting the hot coffee on his thigh.

"Watch it, for God's sake!"

Winter went for paper towels.

"Please forgive me," he said when he was back.

"How clumsy can one person be?!" Halders said.

"It was an accident," Ringmar said.

"The guy is a walking accident," said Halders.

"I said I was sorry," said Winter, and he started to wipe off the table.

"What if there had been crucial evidence on this table?" Halders said. "Fingerprints, traces of blood, notes, signatures. Shoe prints."

Winter didn't answer. After a few months with the unit, he was starting to get used to Halders. And the coffee had been an accident. He suspected that Halders suspected otherwise, but that was Halders's nature.

The door opened and Birgersson stepped into the room.

"What's going on here?" he said.

"Nothing," said Ringmar.

"Do you have a minute, Erik?" Birgersson said, gesturing with his thumb toward the door.

Winter followed him through the corridor to his office. The path felt long, as though a reprimand awaited him when the march was over.

"Sit down," said Birgersson, who went to stand by the window. It was late October out there. From where Winter was sitting, it looked like a wall had been erected outside the window overnight, all the way from the earth to the sky. It muffled the sounds outside. The only thing that could be heard was Birgersson's inhalations as he pulled the smoke down into his lungs. His office smelled like tobacco, old and new. There was a used coffee cup on the desk, next to an overfull ashtray.

"Have a smoke if you like," Birgersson said.

Breathing in here is enough, Winter thought.

"I try to wait until after noon," he answered.

"Like Hemingway," said Birgersson. "The author."

"I know who he is."

"Although in his case it was liquor," Birgersson continued. "He didn't drink anything before noon, but then he drank a lot." Birgersson smiled. "But at the end of his career he was sitting somewhere in the world and started boozing at ten and someone pointed out that it wasn't noon yet, and then he said: Hell, it's noon in Miami!"

"Okay," Winter said, taking out his pack of Corps.

"Why do you smoke that crap?"

"It's become a habit."

Birgersson laughed and took another drag and blew out the smoke. The window was open a few inches, and the smoke glided out and disappeared among all the other shades of gray.

"I heard you had another chat with the husband of the girl who disappeared," Birgersson said.

"I'm working on writing out the interrogation right now," Winter said.

"No, right now you're sitting here. But tell me."

"Well . . . I didn't exactly get any farther. If it's possible to get further with him. He says that they quarreled from time to time, but that it wasn't anything serious."

"Mm-hmm."

"That she wanted kids but he wanted to wait."

"Do you think he's hiding something?"

"I don't really know. Like what?"

"That he's guilty, of course."

Winter saw Christer Börge in front of him. Could he have murdered his wife and hid the body and pretended that nothing had happened? Played the role of the worried husband after his wife disappeared?

"It's not all that unusual, you know," said Birgersson.

"I know," said Winter.

"Have you pressed him a little?"

"As well as I could."

"Do you want help?"

"You believe he's done something?" Winter asked. "You really believe that?"

"I don't believe anything, as you know. This is no church. I'm just asking if we should squeeze this Börge a little to see if anything else comes out."

"All right with me," Winter said.

"Bring him in," said Birgersson.

It was now. The wind had come up when Winter stepped out of the police station. He had needed a scarf. In addition, his throat had become sore during the last hour. It didn't seem tempting to bike home.

He heard a car horn and turned his head. Halders waved from behind the wheel.

Winter walked over.

"Do you need a ride?"

"Okay."

Winter climbed into the car and Halders roared off.

He drove through Allén. The trees would be completely bare in just a few weeks. Red leaves floated through the air.

Winter coughed.

"Got a cold?"

"I don't know."

"There's something going around. Aneta felt out of sorts this morning."

"We don't have time to be sick, do we, Fredrik?"

"No, boss."

"It's been a long time since you called me boss."

"Have I ever?"

"Would have been that first year, if you did."

Halders laughed.

"Yes, that's right. That's when we became friends for life."

Winter smiled.

"For a while I thought you spilled coffee on purpose," Halders continued. "It always happened when I was sitting next to you."

"So that's why you moved to the other end?"

"Naturally."

"I was just clumsy," said Winter. "And insecure."

"So what's new?" Halders said.

"We're older," Winter said, nodding toward the street. "You can stop here."

Halders pulled over.

"I'm going to see the friend now," he said. "Nina Lorrinder."

"Good luck."

"She has more stories to tell."

14

Nina Lorrinder had a headband that gleamed in a shade of red Halders was unsure he'd ever seen before.

He asked.

"Crimson," she said, giving him a long look.

"Just curious," he said.

"Are you interested in colors?"

"My dad wanted me to be a master painter."

Lorrinder looked over at the three-story building at the other end of the square. The bottom floor was of stone; the two upper floors were wood. It was called a *landshövdingeshus*, a type of building found only in this city. Two painters were standing on scaffolding, coating the facade in a shade of yellow that Halders had seen before.

"Like them," said Halders.

She turned her gaze back to him again.

"But it's not good for you in the long run," Halders continued. "At least it didn't use to be. The paint settles in your lungs. And in your brain."

She threw a glance at the painters again.

"You can become a bit stupid," said Halders. "Not that I think those guys are, or will be, but it's better not to take any risks."

She still hadn't said anything. Halders wondered when she was going to interrupt him.

"So I became a policeman instead," he said.

"Are you being sarcastic?" she said.

"Just a little."

She looked around again, as though she would take Halders's word about anything and wasn't expecting anything other than to sit on the bench and listen to whatever was going to come. It wasn't cold. Halders could even feel the weak sun on the back of his neck. He could see some elderly people on a bench on the other side of the fountain. The sun looked strong on their waxy faces. Their faces were approximately the same pale yellow shade that the painters were painting up and down on the wall of the building. Halders could hear music coming from there, rock music from a boom box that was balanced on the second story of the scaffolding, but he couldn't tell what song it was. The distance was too great. The old people couldn't tell either. They belonged to the generation before rock 'n' roll, the generation before him.

When he was sitting like that himself, with stiff joints and a yellow face, he would be able to move his skull carefully to rock 'n' roll if there were some workmen nearby with their eternal boom box. But they wouldn't be playing rock 'n' roll then. God knows what they would be playing. Maybe there wouldn't be anything left to play.

"I thought you had some questions," said Lorrinder.

"How long have you known Paula?"

"You talk like she's still alive. Like I still know her."

Halders didn't say anything. Lorrinder looked over toward the painters. They were on their way down from the scaffolding now. The music had been turned off.

"But I guess I do," she continued, without looking at Halders. "You could look at it that way. It sometimes feels that way." She looked at Halders. "Do you understand what I mean?"

"Yes."

"How can you understand?"

"My wife was killed by a drunk driver. We have two children."

"I'm sorry."

"I was, too. Goddamn sorry, and goddamn angry. So I can understand."

"I've been angry, too," she said.

"Why?"

"Because it was so . . . awful. So awful. And so pointless."

Halders nodded.

"Who could do something like that?"

"That's what we're trying to figure out."

"And why?"

"We're trying to figure that out, too."

"But how can you?"

"By doing what I'm doing now, among other things."

"But it goes so slowly," she said. "Asking questions. And then you have to go through the answers. Doesn't it make you crazy that it goes so slowly?"

"Not like a painter," said Halders.

The painters had left for the day. Half the wall was a shade of yellow, but the sun was shining on the unpainted part of the house, and the wall there looked even more cheerful.

The old people on the bench across from them had also left for the day.

"But it goes so slowly," Lorrinder repeated.

"It's the only way," said Halders.

"I want to know now," Lorrinder said. "Who. And why."

"So how long have you known Paula?" Halders asked.

His cell phone rang as he crossed Kungstorget. He saw his mother's number on the display. Or the dis*playa* if you wanted to be witty. Siv had said that. Winter had been surprised. Elsa had added the new word to her vocabulary.

"Papa!"

"Hi, honey!"

"What are you doing, Papa?"

"I'm going to go buy some food at Saluhallen."

"What are you going to buy?"

"Some kind of fish, I think."

"We ate fish yesterday."

"That's nice."

"I fried it!"

"Good job, Elsa."

"Lilly had a little piece. She spit it out."

"What a shame."

"That's what I told her!"

"Then what did she say?"

"Blehhowehhh!"

"What does that mean?"

"That she wants milk from Mama instead."

"Ha-ha!"

"But Mama says that she can't have any."

"I know, honey."

"I think that's mean of Mama."

"Lilly has to start eating a little fish now. She's starting to get big now."

"She's not big at all!"

"No, not like you, Elsa."

"Will you be there when we get home, Papa?"

"Of course I will."

"We're coming tomorrow!"

"I think it's the day after tomorrow, actually."

"Oh."

"I bought a present for you. And one for Lilly."

"I bought a present for you, Papa!"

"That will be exciting."

"Here comes Mama. Hugs and kisses!"

"Hugs and kisses, honey."

He heard a clatter in the background, and the scream of a small child. He heard his mother's voice. Siv had her hands full.

"Well, there we go," Angela said. "Dinner's out of the way."

"Not mine."

"From what I understood, you were standing outside Saluhallen."

"That got through?"

"The art of reasoning. Does that sound familiar?"

"No."

Lilly bawled in the background again.

"Everything is set now down here," Angela said. "It's going to be expensive if we don't come back this fall."

"It's all set," he said.

"Has it been cleared with everyone involved?"

"Yes," he lied.

"You're lying."

"No."

"Yes, you are. What does Uncle Birgersson think of all this?"

"I don't know what he thinks, to be honest, but he's recommended my leave of absence. And he has his own retirement crisis to think of."

"But you're not retiring, are you, Erik?"

"Of course not."

"I don't want this to be the end of your career. That's not my intent . . ."

"Whiting," Winter interrupted. He was reading the board outside the fish shop at the west end of the hall. "It's going to be whiting fillets."

"You interrupted me."

"Lightly dipped in flour, flash-fried in olive oil with garlic and lemon and a bit of parsley. Creamed potatoes. The Riesling from Hunawihr."

"Sounds like you're doing fine without us."

"I'll be fine until the day after tomorrow and not a day longer."

"Good."

"I miss you all."

"Don't drink up all the bottles to feel better."

"Only the 2002 is gone. Or will be gone tonight."

"We should probably end it here. Lilly is getting a little sick on Grandma."

"What's wrong?"

"It's nothing."

"It's always nothing for doctors," Winter said. "One might start to wonder if we really need the medical profession."

"Are you going to do away with me just like you're doing away with yourself?"

"Take care of Lilly now," he said, and they said good-bye and hung up.

He went into the shop and bought the fish and then walked home through Kungsparken. The tops of the trees were turning red and yellow, like dyed hair that was starting to go back to its original color. And soon that hair would fall to the ground. And then it would grow out again. It was a strange world.

Vasaplatsen was deserted. It was almost always deserted around the obelisk. Sometimes someone was sitting on one of the benches at the south end, but not always. Vasaplatsen wasn't a place of rest; it wasn't even a park, even though it was green. But this neighborhood was a place of rest for Winter. This was where he always returned, to the center of the city. It was calm at the core. In the eye of the storm.

He unlocked the front door and took the old elevator up to the apartment. The elevator was a hundred years old and decorated as though it were going to an evening at the House of Nobles. As long as Winter had lived here it had climbed reluctantly up with him to the third floor. It had never broken, as far as he knew, but it always sounded as though it might happen at any time.

In the kitchen he placed the package with the small fillets on the counter and took olive oil, garlic, and a potato out of the pantry. He peeled the potato and cut it into small pieces. He opened the Alsace wine and drank a first glass. It was cool and calming, as though someone he trusted had placed a hand on his forehead. As though everything would work out in the end.

It smelled good in the kitchen as he grilled the fish with sliced garlic in the olive oil. He tossed in a small handful of chopped parsley and squeezed in half a lemon. He ate the fish with the creamed potato, which tasted of butter and coarse salt, and a few fresh string beans. He drank two glasses of wine with his meal and brought the bottle into the living room when he'd cleared the table.

There still wasn't anyone down on the lawn of Vasaplatsen. He smoked on the balcony, but didn't see anyone doing the same on the balcony across the park. Dusk was falling fast. Many people were waiting for streetcars down there under his window. The tracks ran together under him. The whole city had its intersecting point down there, its breaking point. Everyone in the city passed under his window at some point in their lives. If they looked up they would see him.

He went in and sat down in the easy chair. He poured a glass of wine and clicked his laptop on. He searched his way through the files. The light from the screen was the only light in there.

The phone rang.

"I think it was two years," Lorrinder said.

"You've known each other for two years?" Halders asked.

She nodded.

"But I told the other officer that."

"I know."

"And you're still asking?"

"Where did you usually hang out? Aside from at church?"

"Oh . . . at some café. The movies, sometimes. The bar, once in a while."

Halders nodded.

"Sometimes at the Friskis & Svettis gym."

"Which one?"

"The one on Västra Hamngatan."

"Is there really time to hang out there?" Halders asked.

"What do you mean by that?"

"Well, there's so much huffing and puffing."

Lorrinder almost laughed.

"There's a small café there, too," she said.

"And you met up there?"

She nodded.

"How did it happen?"

"I don't understand."

"Were you alone?"

"Yes."

"Every time?"

"Yes."

"Was she in shape?"

"Does that really matter?"

Halders didn't know. Did it? No one else knew, either.

"I'm just trying to learn as much as I can about Paula," he said.

"I don't know if I . . . did," she said. "Know her very well, I mean."

"Why not?"

"She . . . didn't seem to want to let anyone get very close, I guess."

"Why not, do you think?"

"She . . . was just that kind of person, I guess."

"What kind of person?"

"Oh . . . withdrawn, maybe. Or a bit reserved." Lorrinder looked straight across the table at Halders. "Not everyone is the same."

"No, certainly not."

"I guess she mostly wanted to be by herself."

"But she went to Friskis & Svettis," Halders said.

"You can be by yourself there, too, for the most part, like you said yourself just now."

"The huffing and puffing."

"Exactly."

"Everyone fighting for himself."

Lorrinder didn't seem to hear that last part. All of a sudden she looked like someone deep in thought.

"How often did the two of you work out?" Halders asked.

"Uh . . . what did you say?"

Halders repeated the question. Lorrinder seemed lost in her thoughts. Her gaze was far away.

"Are you okay?" Halders asked.

"I thought of something . . ."

Halders waited.

"When you asked if we sat in the café alone."

"Yes?"

"I think she met someone at the gym."

Halders didn't say anything. He just nodded.

"A . . . man."

Lorrinder seemed to be staring into the past so hard that it would help her remember. She closed her eyes, as though to make herself see more clearly. She opened her eyes. They were clearer now.

"I might be wrong."

"Just keep going."

"She talked to someone a few times."

"Where."

"When we . . . at the gym. In the fitness studio."

"Is that so unusual?"

"For Paula it was."

"In what way?"

"She just didn't talk to people. Not like that."

"Maybe she wasn't the one who started it. Maybe he stepped on her foot and apologized. Maybe it happened several times."

"I don't know . . ."

"Maybe that's one of the ways to pick someone up at Friskis & Svettis."

"Is it?"

"Isn't that one of the city's biggest pickup locations?"

"I don't actually know. I haven't thought about it."

"But you noticed that Paula was talking to someone."

"Yes."

"Enough for you to think about it," Halders said. "Remember it."

"Maybe it doesn't mean anything."

"What else do you remember? About Paula's encounter."

Lorrinder closed her eyes again. She was really trying. Halders could almost see the thoughts moving inside her forehead. A nerve began to twitch. She tucked her hair back over one ear. Her temple continued to twitch.

She opened her eyes again.

"It was like she knew him."

Winter lifted the receiver of the phone, simultaneously looking at the clock.

It was Torsten Öberg.

"It might be late," he said, "but I thought you'd want to know. A girl at SKL was working overtime and she thought I'd want to know, too."

"What have we learned, then?"

"It's blood, and it's hers," Öberg said.

"What?"

"Something of a disappointment, isn't it?"

"But wasn't the fleck old?"

"Yes. They can't say exactly how old, but more than a month."

"So she brought the rope herself," Winter said.

"That I don't know," Öberg said. "That's your job."

"And no other traces? On the rope?"

"No other traces."

"We don't know if she tied the noose herself," Winter said.

"No. The fleck could have ended up there at any time."

"Damn it. I'd had high hopes for this."

"You're not the only one."

Winter heard the streetcar outside. It was no later than that. It was a lumbering sound, homey, calming. When the streetcars stopped running for the night, the city became a more troubled place.

"Could we have missed anything in that room?"

"Is that an insult, Erik?"

"I was talking to myself."

"Not quietly enough."

"Come on, Torsten. Talk to yourself a little, yourself."

"Could we have missed anything in that room?" Öberg said.

"Could we?"

"Missed what, Erik? Clues? Marks? Flecks? Don't think so. I would like to say that in all probability, I don't think we did. But there's no way I can know."

"Mm-hmm."

"It was a neat room. A clean room. That makes it harder."

15

So that bastard might have leapfrogged next to her!"

"Leapfrogged?" Ringmar asked.

"Or whatever the hell kind of exercises they have at Friskis & Svettis," Halders continued.

He had called Winter right after he spoke to Lorrinder.

"It's probably time for you to see for yourself," Winter said.

"That'll be interesting."

"How specific is the description?" Bergenhem asked.

"Vague," Halders answered.

"She can't have been mistaken?" Ringmar said.

"Mistaken, mistaken, everyone can be mistaken." Halders stretched his arms backward, as though he were already at the gym. "But she saw Paula talking to someone, apparently several times. She got the idea that they'd met before, somewhere else. And Nina Lorrinder doesn't seem to be an airhead." Halders brought his arms down. "I had to pry all of this out of her with pliers."

"We like that kind of witness," Ringmar said.

"Once they start talking, sure," said Halders.

Ringmar changed position in his chair, and changed position again. Halders's arm motions were contagious. Soon they would all start doing aerobics in the conference room.

"Could be anyone at all," Ringmar said.

"That's what we're going to rule out, isn't it?" Halders stretched his arms out behind him again. His joints cracked like dry wood being snapped. "Or vice versa."

"You really need the gym," Bergenhem said.

"Phys ed with team sports and games," Halders said. "I was always best."

"At which one?"

"You're too young to understand, kid."

"I'm confused."

The door opened. Djanali came into the room and closed the door behind her.

"Back already?" Halders said.

She sat down beside him without answering and took out her notebook and looked up.

"I showed the pictures to the staff at Leonardsen and at Talassi, and everyone agrees that it's Ecco."

"You've only been to *two* stores?" Halders asked.

"No, but I wanted to give you an idea of what things look like."

"What do things look like, then?"

"How many have they sold?" Winter filled in.

"If we're talking about size ten or eleven . . ." Djanali read from her notebook, "seven pairs at Leonardsen and ten at Talassi. That's this year."

"Last year, then?" Bergenhem asked.

"The shoe wasn't for sale there last year."

"Why not?"

"No doubt they thought that no one wanted them anymore. That they could offer other brands."

"That the Ecco Free era was over," Halders said.

"How many used charge cards?" Winter asked.

"All but two."

"Those are the two we're after," Halders said.

"I'm not so sure of that," Ringmar said.

"Should we bet on it?" Halders said.

"The shoes we saw in the video might not have anything to do with the case," Ringmar said.

"Should we bet on that, too?" Halders said.

"Let's go with what we have right now," Winter said. "Get going."

• • •

Christer Börge didn't look scared as he sat in the interrogation room. He looks like he's been here before, Winter thought. But he hasn't.

The interrogation room had a small window that let in the September light. There was a microphone on the felt tabletop. It was like a microphone in a studio. And the room functioned as a studio.

"Why are we sitting here?" Börge asked. He hadn't asked that before. He hadn't said much when Winter called and asked him to come in.

"It's calm and quiet," Winter said.

At first he hadn't wanted to conduct the interrogation. He was no interrogator yet. It took experience. But Börge wasn't a suspect. And Winter had talked to him more than anyone else had. That could be an advantage. At least, that's what Birgersson had told him before he'd walked into the interrogation room.

Börge turned toward the light from the window. Suddenly it looked like he was starting to feel cold. He rolled down the sleeves of his shirt and then placed his hands on the table. His hands were very white against the green felt surface in the faint light inside the room. Winter thought they looked like they'd never been exposed to sunlight. They looked like white plastic, or plaster.

After the formalities, he prepared himself for the questions. Börge looked at the window. There was only sky outside. No trees reached up this high. Winter cleared his throat one time.

"Do you believe Ellen will come back?"

Börge turned his face toward him.

"What kind of question is that?"

"Try to answer it."

"Does it make any difference what I *believe*?"

Faith can move mountains, Winter thought. But a policeman can't think like that. A pastor can think like that.

"Sometimes it makes a difference in how you handle the shock."

"What do you know about it?"

"What was the last thing she said when she left home that afternoon?" Winter asked.

"I don't remember."

"Try."

"Would you remember what your wife said when she went to buy a magazine?"

"Think about it."

"About what?"

"About what I just asked. What Ellen said when she left."

"She probably didn't say anything."

"Was that how it usually was?"

"I don't understand what you're trying to get at."

Winter didn't answer.

"Are you trying to get at that she said some kind of good-bye or something?"

"I'm just trying to help you," Winter said.

"Help *me*?"

"To remember."

"But what if there's nothing to remember?"

There's always something, Winter thought. If you want to remember. You don't want to. And I want to know why.

"Earlier, you said that you had an argument before she left."

Börge didn't say anything.

"That that's why she went out."

"Surely that's not what I said."

"That it wasn't the first time."

"Wait a minute now," said Börge. "Take it easy now."

Winter took it easy. Börge had taken it easy, until now. His answers might have seemed aggressive when one read the transcribed interrogation, but his attitude wasn't aggressive. In that sense, a transcription of an interrogation was inadequate. The words were only one component. Sometimes, the words were the least significant part. Everything ought to be on film, Winter thought. In the nineties, we'll film everything.

"Did Ellen ever threaten to leave you?"

Börge gave a start. His eyes had sought the window again but had only gotten halfway.

Now they were back on Winter.

"No. Why would she do that?"

"She wanted to have children. You didn't want to have children. Isn't that a reason?"

"No."

"You don't think that's a reason for divorce?"

"You don't understand," Börge said. "Have you been divorced yourself?"

"No," Winter answered. He had made up his mind not to answer any questions, because he was the one who was supposed to ask them. When the person being interrogated started asking the questions, the interrogation had gone in the wrong direction. An interrogation was one-way communication disguised as a conversation. An interrogator must never give anything. Never let anything go. Never say anything that revealed himself. It was always take, never give. Listening. And at the same time, it was about forming trust. Listen to the story, Birgersson had said: Everyone has a story they want to tell; it wants out of them and in the end they can't stop it.

"Are you married?" Börge asked.

"How often did Ellen say that she wanted to have children?" Winter asked.

"So you're not married," Börge said. "Make sure to get married. Maybe you'll learn something."

"What will I learn?" Winter asked.

"Well . . . how women are, for example." Börge's gaze moved away and reached the window. "You learn stuff like that."

"How are they, then?"

"You'll have to figure that out for yourself." It seemed to Winter that Börge was smiling. "You have to figure *something* out for yourself."

"Do you mean that all women are the same?" Winter asked.

Börge didn't answer. He seemed to be studying what was outside the window, but there was nothing there.

Winter repeated the question.

"I don't know," Börge said.

He didn't seem to notice the contradiction in his words.

"What was Ellen like, compared to other women?" Winter asked.

"She loved me," Börge said, looking straight at Winter again. "That's the only thing that matters here, isn't it?"

Now the lobby was deserted, as though the hotel had already closed down. The young clerk who had found Paula Ney was standing behind the reception desk. Bergström, his name was Bergström. It sounded like a name from Norrland, and he had a Norrland accent. Everyone up there was named something with "ström"—stream—combined with something else from nature. It was wild up there; it was beautiful. Sometime Winter would head north. Past Stockholm. He wanted to show his children what snow was for real. Elsa had seen snow during a total of two weeks in her five-year-old life. Lilly had never seen snow. It wouldn't happen this winter, either. But there would be other winters.

"We're closing in two weeks," Bergström said.

"That was fast."

Bergström shrugged.

"The hotel already looks closed," Winter said.

Bergström shrugged again. Once more and it would be some kind of spasm.

"How's it going?"

"Not great," he answered, "I shouldn't actually be here."

"Why not?"

"I'm off sick. But don't tell the insurance office. Salko has the flu and there's no one else left."

"Are there any guests, then?"

"A couple of salesman types. But they're out doing sales."

Winter saw the man smile faintly. It disappeared as quickly as it had come.

"You can keep the cordon up until the place closes up," Bergström said.

"That's kind of you," Winter said.

"I didn't mean it that way."

"I'm going up," Winter said, and he left the lobby and walked up the stairs.

He climbed over the cordon and opened the door.

He stood in the middle of the floor and listened to the sounds from outside. They were faint but distinct through the double-glazed windows.

Had she brought the rope along herself?

Had the murderer brought the rope?

Did they know each other?

He looked around. Room number ten. Everything was familiar in there, like in a cell. A place a person knows well but doesn't want to spend a second of his life in. He looked up, toward the beam that the rope had been wrapped around. She hadn't done it herself.

Winter hadn't seen her hanging; Bergström had seen to it that he didn't have to see. But he had wanted to. What a fucking wish. I wish I had been standing here then, to see her swinging from the rope.

Would I have learned anything? Understood anything?

He felt the familiar tingling on his neck and across his scalp. He closed his eyes and saw the image he wanted to see and didn't want to see. At the same time, he felt a draft from the window, as though someone had opened it while he stood there. As though someone were observing him.

He opened his eyes. The window was closed. The room was closed. But he knew that he would come back here.

He remembered her words, all of them: *I love you both and I will always love you no matter what happens to me and you'll always be with me wherever I go and if I've made you angry at me I want to ask for your forgiveness and I know that you'll forgive me no matter what happens to me and no matter what happens to you and I know that we will meet again.*

• • •

Elisabeth Ney's face was pale and closed. She had opened her eyes a little while ago, but she still looked . . . closed in. Closed off. Closed up. Winter didn't know. He was sitting on the chair next to the bed. There was a vase of red roses on the nightstand. He couldn't see a card.

"Oh, it's you," she said.

"I pop up everywhere," he said. "I apologize for that."

She blinked once, as though to accept the apology.

"How do you feel?" he asked.

She blinked again. That must mean yes. Two times was no.

"I don't know what I'm doing here," she said after a little bit. "How I ended up here."

"You needed to rest," Winter said.

"Am I sick?"

"Haven't you spoken with a doctor?"

"They say that I need to rest."

Winter nodded.

"But they let you in."

She said this in the same slow way as everything else. There was no accusation in her voice.

"I wanted to see how you felt," he said. "And I admit that I wanted to ask a few questions, too."

"I understand. And I do want to help. But I don't know what I should say." She moved her head on the pillow. "Or what I should remember."

Her brown hair looked black against the pillow. The light fell in through the blinds and gave her circles both above and under her eyes. Her chin looked like it was in two parts. There was a particular characteristic in her eyes that Winter thought he'd seen before, on someone else. It was a pretty normal observation. There were people everywhere who weren't related at all but still resembled each other. That's the way it was with Ney. He had seen those eyes on someone else. He didn't know who, or where, or when. Someone he had met or had seen on the street, at the store, in a bar, in a park. Anywhere and anytime.

There was green in her eyes.

"It's possible that Paula met a man at the gym," Winter said.

"At the gym? What gym?"

"Friskis & Svettis. Didn't you know that?"

"Uh . . . yes. Of course."

She didn't look certain. But that didn't have to mean anything. This time, it might be the words themselves that were the truth.

"Didn't Paula ever say anything about it?"

"That she worked out?"

"Whether she met someone there."

"Well, she didn't even say that she'd met anyone at all. In general. I told you that before."

Winter nodded.

"She would have told me about it, if it were true."

"Is there any reason that she wouldn't want to say anything?" Winter asked.

"I don't understand."

"Maybe she wanted to tell you that she had met someone. But she couldn't do it."

"Why wouldn't she be able to?"

"Maybe she was afraid to."

"Why would she be afraid to tell me?"

"I don't know."

"Do you mean that she was with someone who forced her to keep it a secret?"

"I don't know that either. It's just a . . . manner of questioning."

Ney had raised her head from the pillow. Winter could see the depression her head had left on the pillow. It was like a shadow.

"She should have told me. Whatever it was."

Winter nodded.

"Do you think she went to that hotel voluntarily?" she asked.

"What's voluntarily?"

"Do you mean she was drugged?"

"Right now, I guess I don't mean anything," Winter said.

But Paula hadn't been drugged. The autopsy had shown that. Maybe she had been paralyzed. Scared into motionlessness. The autopsy couldn't show something like that.

"But if someone dragged her into the hotel . . . into that room . . . then surely someone else must have seen it?" Ney was sitting up now. She was almost on her way down from the bed, with her feet on the floor. Winter realized that some of the shock was finally beginning to subside. The questions were starting to come. "Surely someone would have seen?"

"That's what we're hoping, too," Winter said. "We're looking for witnesses. We're working on that all the time."

"Well, there are people who work at the hotel, aren't there? What did they say?"

"No one saw her," Winter said.

"What about the maids? Don't they see everything? Don't they go into the rooms?"

"Not into . . . that room," Winter said. It felt like a personal failure to say it. "They hadn't cleaned there in the past day."

"Oh, God."

Winter didn't say anything.

"If they had, Paula might be alive!"

Winter tried to disappear, become part of the air, let his face become inscrutable. Color had suddenly come to Ney's face. She looked younger. Winter again had the vague sense of recognition.

"And how can someone check into a hotel without being seen?" she said, moving to the edge of the bed. Winter extended a hand to steady her, but she waved it away.

"She didn't check in," he answered.

"Why wouldn't she do that? Why didn't she do that?" Ney's face was close to him. Her head began to fall forward. She tried to bend it back again with a jerky movement. Winter thought of the taped sequences from Central Station. "Why didn't anyone see her in the lobby? Why?"

"We're trying to figure that out, too. But as I said, we don't know how it happened."

"Do you know how anything happened?"

"Not much."

"Oh, God."

She lurched, and now Winter extended a hand and steadied her. She sat down on the edge of the bed again. Her nightgown was large, like a tent. She could have had any body type at all under the nightgown. Her hands were small and sinewy; they looked like they were made of some kind of brittle wood that had been subjected to wind and rain.

"Her hand!" Elisabeth Ney burst out. "Why her hand?"

Winter ran into Mario Ney in the hall.

Ney nodded as they passed each other but showed no sign of stopping.

Winter stopped.

"What is it?" Ney said, still walking.

"She's coming out of the shock," Winter said.

Ney mumbled something that Winter couldn't hear.

"Sorry?"

"So it got better here, I said."

"Now listen, she had to come here. For a bit."

"Are you a doctor?"

Winter looked at the café at the other end of the hall. It was only a few tables with a large plant in the middle. No one was sitting there now.

"Can we sit down for a little bit?"

"I'm on my way up to Elisabeth."

"Just for a few minutes."

"Do I have any choice?"

"Yes."

Ney looked surprised. He came along almost automatically as Winter began to walk toward the café.

"She's waiting for me," Ney said as he sat down.

"What can I get for you?" Winter said.

"A glass of red wine," said Ney.

"I don't know if they have that here," Winter said, looking over toward the counter.

"Of course they don't," Ney said. "What did you think?"

"We can go to a bar," Winter said.

"I'm going to see Elisabeth."

"I mean after that."

"Okay," Ney said, standing up.

"I'll wait here," Winter said.

Ney nodded and left.

Winter's cell phone rang.

"Yes?"

"The clerk from the hotel was looking for you. Hotel Revy."

It was Möllerström.

"Which one of them?"

"Richard Salko."

"What did he want?"

"He didn't want to say."

"Did you give him my cell number?"

"No. Not yet. I asked him to call again in three minutes. It's already been two."

"Give him the number."

Winter ended the call and waited.

The telephone vibrated in his hand. He had turned off the ringtone.

"Winter."

"Hi. It's Richard Salko."

"Yes?"

"There was some dude standing outside the hotel today. He stood there for a while."

"A dude?"

"A man. A weird guy. I saw him through the window. He looked up and side to side and up again."

"Young? Old?"

"Pretty young. Thirty. Maybe a young forty. I don't know. He had some hat on. I didn't see his hair."

"Have you seen him before? Did you recognize him at all?"

"Don't think so. But . . . he stood there for a while. Like he just wanted to stand there. Do you know what I mean? Like the place meant something to him, or whatever. Like he'd been here before."

"Did he come in?"

"No. Not that I noticed."

"He might have?"

"Well, only for a minute, if he did. I had to do something in another room, but I was only gone for a minute or two."

"Maybe it was one of your regular customers," Winter said.

"Maybe. But no one from my shift. Like I said, I didn't recognize him."

"A tourist?" Winter said.

"He didn't look like a tourist," Salko said.

"How do they look?"

"Stupid."

"How's it going with the list?" Winter asked.

"The list?"

"I'm still waiting for a list of all the employees you've ever had."

"I am, too," Salko said.

"What the hell kind of comment is that?"

"Sorry, sorry. But it takes time. We're talking about a long period of time here. And a lot of turnover."

"If we had enough people we'd have done the whole job ourselves," Winter said.

"I know how it is," Salko said.

"Oh?"

"I'll do my best. Keep doing my best. I called you just now, didn't I?"

16

Tourists. The city was full of tourists; they were still there even far into September: pointing, asking, spying around, eating, drinking, laughing, crying. Winter had nothing against tourists. He was happy to give directions. The city might go under without tourists; soon it would be the only industry left. Tourism and crime. Organized, unorganized. Heroin had finally reached Gothenburg. It had only been a question of time, and now, in the late eighties, the junk was here.

"Comes with our friends from faraway lands," Halders said.

They were sitting in a car on the way along the river. No matter where you were going, you ended up along the river. In the autumn sunlight, it looked oily and black. A ferry was gliding out toward Vinga, on its way to Jutland. The risk that it would come back with the junk in its belly was great. Or the chance, if you preferred. There were great profits to be had for the entrepreneurs. I packed my suitcase and in it I put . . .

They had talked about the drugs, and the more serious violence that the drugs brought along. Big money. Big violence.

Halders drove along Allén. The scene around them was still of the old-fashioned, safe sort. Scattered groups were smoking up on the grass, and the smoke spread over the canal along with the fumes of everything else that was gliding around in the air. But the sweet and spicy scent of hash floated above all the other smells, and Winter could smell it as he walked over the canal bridges on late afternoons.

"You lie down in Allén one day in the September sun, and light a little joint and have yourself a little fun," Halders sang, keeping rhythm on the wheel.

"That was very good," Winter said. "Did you write it yourself?"

Halders turned his head.

"Haven't you ever heard of Nationalteatern?"

"Oh, them."

"You have heard of them?"

"Of course."

Halders smiled a mean smile but said nothing. He stopped for a red light. Two guys in old-fashioned dashikis looked up from what they were doing out on the grass and looked over at the police car. Halders raised his hand and waved.

"Don't forget, sneaky sneaky ding-dong, like on pins and needles, one two three, the pigs are up and trawling," he sang.

He turned to Winter.

"Trawling is our thing here in Gothenburg."

"Trawl on, then," Winter said.

"I don't give a shit about that small-time crap," Halders said, nodding toward the dashikis, who had lit their pipe. They began to disappear into the haze.

"Mm-hmm."

"But the other stuff. That's a different story."

He stopped at the next red light.

A man walked by in the crosswalk. He had dark hair, sharp features, looks from the Balkans, maybe Greece, Italy, somewhere south of Jutland.

"Could be a mule," Halders said, nodding toward the man.

Winter didn't say anything.

"They're going to take over," Halders said. "In ten, fifteen, twenty years the city will be full of mules, and criminal gangs from faraway lands." He turned to Winter. "And do you know what? A lot of them will have been born here in the city!"

"You know your future, Fredrik."

"It's necessary, man. You have to be able to see into the future. It's called imagination. It's the only thing that separates us from the psychopaths."

"Will you and I be sitting here then, Fredrik?" Winter said. "In a government car on our way through Allén? In twenty years?"

"Twenty years? Well, why not? If we're not dead, of course. Slain in a shootout with drug dealers from the north suburbs."

"You said faraway lands before."

"It's the same thing."

In twenty years. Winter might be able to think twenty years ahead, but he didn't want to. The 2000s were more than a faraway land and a faraway time. They were like a planet that had not yet been discovered. If he made it all the way there, a lot would have happened on the way; a lot of water would have run under the Göta Älv bridge.

Halders stopped for the third red light.

A man walked by in the crosswalk. This one looked very Swedish. He moved stiffly and stared straight ahead, as though he were walking in a dream.

"That guy there," Halders said. "He needs to buy himself an alarm clock."

"Hey, that's Börge," Winter said.

"Börje? Börje who?"

"Börge, Christer Börge. His wife disappeared about a month ago. Ellen Börge. I interrogated him up at the station day before yesterday."

"Why?"

The light was still red. Börge had passed them and was now on his way down toward Rosenlundsplatsen. Winter watched him. Börge still wasn't turning his head to either side. He was walking quickly, but not in any particular direction. It was a feeling Winter had. At that moment, Börge had no direction.

"Why?" Halders repeated.

"There's something I can't put my finger on with that case," Winter said, turning toward Halders as Börge's coat disappeared behind the yellow branches.

"Case? There is no case, is there?"

"I think there is. I think there's a crime behind it."

"You think she's dead?"

Winter flung out his hands.

The light changed and Halders accelerated.

"You must have something to go on, right? What makes you think it's a crime?"

Winter tried to find Börge again, but he had vanished.

"Him," he said, nodding toward the empty branches.

"Do you think he did it? Killed his wife?"

"I don't know. There's something I *could* understand here, but that I don't understand."

Halders laughed.

"That might not be because of him," he said, "it might be because of you, man."

"I wish I were like you, Fredrik."

"I know just what you mean. Lots of people wish that."

"Happy and unconcerned and ignorant."

"Imagination is better than knowledge," Halders said.

"That's Einstein," Winter said. "You quoted Einstein."

"I didn't know that," Halders said, and smiled. "But there you go."

"I wish I were like you," Winter repeated.

"Flattery doesn't work on me."

"You're a lucky person, Fredrik."

Halders stopped for the fourth light.

"So you brought Börge in for questioning, Einstein? What did Birgersson say about that?"

"He's the one who suggested it."

"What the hell are you talking about?"

"But I had talked about it earlier myself."

"I guess you really sucked up to the boss."

"Haven't you ever gotten to conduct an interrogation, Fredrik?"

"So Birgersson is that interested," Halders mumbled, without answering Winter's question.

"I guess he suspects something, too," Winter said.

Halders didn't say anything. He was driving on Första Långgatan now. A streetcar whistled by on its way west. Halders rolled down his window. Winter felt a cool breeze. The level of sound increased. There was scratching from their police radio, mumbling, talking, but nothing was directed at them.

"Did you get anything out of him, then?" Halders asked as he turned right, down toward the river, and stopped at the fifth light. Semi trucks from the West Germany ferry roared by on Oscarsleden. "Did a light bulb come on while questioning Mr. Coat?"

"Just that he loved his wife."

The light turned green and Halders made a flying start and drove west. Winter watched the ferry pass under the Älvsborg bridge. His perspective distorted the image. It looked as though the smokestacks were going to crash right into the span of the bridge.

"Did he say that? During the interrogation?" Halders turned his head. "That he loved her?"

"Yes."

"Then he's the guilty one."

"It was the second time he said it," Winter said.

"Then he's doubly guilty."

It was quiet in the cafeteria, giving a sense of reverence. A man had shuffled down in his hospital pajamas, surrounded by his family. They conversed in quiet voices and Winter couldn't hear any words. Some teenagers came in from the street and sat down without ordering anything. They looked around with big eyes, as though they had chosen the wrong door somewhere.

Mario Ney was back in thirty minutes. Winter had worked on his notes during that time. By now they had questioned all the guests who had been at Hotel Revy at the time of Paula's death. There weren't very many, and all of them could be crossed off the investigation. Some of them would land in other investigations. The hotel was going to close down, and no one knew yet what would come in its place. For Winter's part, they could just as soon tear down the whole thing. But not yet.

Ney sat down in front of him, but it was clear this was tempo-rary—he was sitting on the edge of the chair. Winter could have decided on a different meeting at a different time with Ney, but there had been something about the man that made Winter decide on now. It was an expression on Ney's face. Winter recognized it, but in a dif-ferent way than with Elisabeth. It was the restlessness of someone who is suffering from knowing something. Who wants to get rid of it.

"Where are we going?" Ney asked.

"Do you still want a glass of wine?"

"Yes. But if you . . ." Ney said, but he didn't finish his sentence.

"I always want a glass of wine," Winter said. "I'm just going to get rid of the car."

The bar was near Winter's apartment. He had put the car in the park-ing garage after he let Ney out on the next block.

They each ordered a glass of wine of high quality. A girl of about twenty served them. She set down a glass of water for each of them without being asked. Winter didn't recognize her.

"I'll get this," Winter said when the woman had left the table.

"You mean the police will?"

"Won't be approved, unfortunately."

"Do you work like this often?" Ney asked. "You'd become an alco-holic."

"I'm working on it," Winter said.

"Watch out. It can go quicker than you'd think."

Winter nodded.

"I've seen it with people around me," Ney said.

"Around you where?"

"Nowhere in particular," Ney answered, letting his gaze float out around them.

It was peaceful in the bar. It was another blue hour. Winter didn't recognize the bartender. The man had a black circle around his eye, and he wasn't just wearing it because it was twilight. He had definitely been hit, but probably not in here. It wasn't that kind of place.

"I have to apologize for being brusque earlier," Ney said. "At our house, I mean." He looked at Winter. "And I'm not just saying that because you're buying me a drink."

"I can buy you two."

"Do you understand what I mean?" Ney said.

"I understand if you overreacted. It's normal."

"Is it?"

"When something like this has happened, everything is normal," Winter said. "And nothing. Nothing is normal anymore."

He looked around the bar again. Its corners had started to grow darker in the last few minutes. The contours began to dissolve, as though he had already had a few glasses. Everything became dimmer, and would continue to do so until someone got the bad idea of starting to turn on lights. They could sit in twilight until then. The wineglasses still stood on the table. It's as though neither of us wants to lift the glass, Winter thought. That's not why we came here.

"But why?" Ney said. "I just don't get it. Why?"

"That letter . . ." Winter said.

"Don't talk about that damn letter," said Ney.

"But we have to."

"I don't want to. Elisabeth doesn't want to. No one wants to."

Winter lifted his glass and drank without bothering to smell any of the wine's bouquet. This made the wine lose its taste. Ney drank. He didn't seem to be smelling the bouquet either. They could have been drinking swill from a box. Winter had never done that. Wine belonged in glass bottles. Someone who drank from a box might as well also drink wine from a paper cup for the sake of consistency.

Ney put down his glass.

"I don't understand this guilt she's feeling," he said, without meeting Winter's eyes. "Because it seems to be something like that. Like she wants to beg for forgiveness. She *is* begging for forgiveness. She had nothing to beg for forgiveness for. Nothing."

"Nothing that once happened to all of you? Your family?"

"Like what?" Ney asked.

"Something she was thinking about," Winter said. "That she couldn't let go. Something you might not remember yourself."

"I can't do this," Ney said, looking straight at Winter now. "I can't remember anything like that. There isn't anything. What could there be that . . . would make Paula write a letter like that? In such a . . . situation. Oh, my God."

"She went away on a trip," Winter said. "A long trip."

"That was a long time ago."

"Why did she go?"

"She was young. Younger. Oh, God. She was still so young."

Ney suddenly looked frightened of his own words. It was as though they had attacked him. He had recoiled as though he'd been hit. It was as though someone Winter couldn't see were standing there. There was a sudden cold draft from the door, maybe from the window. Ney's eyes turned inward. His face closed like a heavy door.

"For a long time, you didn't know where Paula was," said Winter.

"We knew where she was," said Ney.

"Oh?"

"We knew she was traveling in Europe."

"Italy? Did she go to the place where you grew up?"

Ney didn't answer. That was answer enough.

"Sicily?"

"There's nothing left there," said Ney. "Nothing for her to see."

"But did she go there?"

"It doesn't exist," said Ney. "There's nothing she could find there."

"Find? What was she searching for?"

"Searching . . ."

Ney seemed to be searching for words, himself. He looked as though his own background was so far away that he couldn't remember it or put it into words. I'll have to be careful here, thought Winter. If Paula traveled to Sicily, it might not have anything to do with her death. Why am I even thinking that it does? Is it because of her father's silence? And her mother's? She is silent, too, in her own way.

"Paula didn't even know Italian," Ney said, as though that were a crucial factor in deciding not to go to Italy.

"But didn't Elisabeth say that Paula spoke Italian?"

"Just a few words," Ney answered.

The trip, Winter thought again. What happened during that trip? What happened after it? Ten years after it?

What happened in this apartment? Winter walked from room to room. Paula had lived in her apartment for the past seven years, and that was a very long time. Who had come here? Not many people. Paula and her loneliness. She'd had her parents. Her family. Her job. A few friends. Was that a lonely life? If it was, then Winter was lonely, too. That was what he had. It was enough for him. It wasn't loneliness.

He walked over to the window. Guldheden was outside; the tall buildings, the slopes and the hills, the city squares, which were modern and yet belonged to a different time. Squares that were built in the fifties will always be modern, Ringmar had once said. The fifties and sixties. We'll never have a more modern time. Winter thought about when he had turned twenty. He was going to become a lawyer. He became a cop. When he'd become one, he had stood as he was standing now, right now, and looked over Guldheden from a different angle, a different point, but it had been the same buildings and hills.

His own apartment had been sparsely furnished, bare, unfinished, and that was somewhat natural. He wasn't finished with anything yet. But this . . . Paula's apartment was still covered, draped, and there wasn't much that told of a life under there. Her apartment was as sparsely furnished and bare as Winter's had been; when she died she was only two years older than Winter had been back when he became a cop, and he felt a sudden despair. Yes. The feeling came and went very quickly. No modern 2010s for Paula; no more twenty-first century. Nothing would be finished in this apartment, or anywhere else.

He saw a small van weaving its way along down there among the tall brick buildings. It stopped in front of a mailbox and a woman got out. It wasn't Paula's fault; she hadn't had any fault in the matter. A pen had been stuck in her hand. That bastard. Her hand didn't exist. It was hidden behind all the white.

The mailwoman emptied the mailbox, placed the sack in the yellow vehicle, got behind the wheel, drove into the roundabout, and disappeared northward. Winter had seen her white hands turning the wheel as she drove through the roundabout. He remained standing at the window. The leaves were beautiful. They were mostly yellow, but a different yellow.

Suddenly, the city out there felt bigger than ever. You could hide out there. Do some deed and then hide. But I will get you, you bastard.

He knew that it would be dangerous.

The plane glided down with the usual slow landing and the loud noise. Winter was standing in the east parking lot, and he saw the plane touch down like a giant bird on a course to the north. The wrong course. But later this evening it would turn back. In less than two months he would be sitting onboard. *They* would be sitting onboard.

He went in and waited outside Arrivals. People were standing in a half circle outside the doors. He thought he recognized a few faces, and that wasn't unusual. He was one of many with relatives in Costa del Sol. Málaga wasn't far away.

Lilly was sleeping in her stroller and Elsa was carefully pushing it ahead of her.

"Papa! Papa!"

Elsa let go of the stroller and Winter caught it with one arm and Elsa with the other. She could jump high, higher than she could just two weeks ago.

She gave him several kisses; he didn't have a chance.

He caught Angela's waist and gave her a kiss on the lips.

"Welcome home."

"Hi, Erik."

"Did the trip go well?"

"Lilly's ears hurt a little, but it stopped."

"She cried a whole lot," said Elsa.

"Enough to sleep until tomorrow," said Angela.

Winter bent down and gave his younger daughter a kiss. She didn't wake up. She smelled good; he had almost forgotten that scent.

Elsa and Lilly were sleeping when he uncorked another bottle and carried it into the living room. Angela was sitting in the easy chair next to the balcony. The door was cracked and they could hear the traffic down there, like a distant roar. The curtains moved in the breeze.

"The weather is warmer than I thought," Angela said. "And the city looks bigger. It's funny."

"It's easy to forget," said Winter.

"How warm Gothenburg is?"

"Yes. Warm and tender."

"Like your cases."

He drank the wine. It was cool; it tasted of the minerals in the Alsace soil.

"Paula."

"Yes. Do you know anything more?"

"I don't know if I know," he answered, and he told her about the past few days.

"My leave of absence went through," he said afterward. "The boss at county didn't have any objections."

17

They lay in the bed and listened to the sounds of the night. There weren't many. No sirens, hardly any noise from cars. Winter looked at the clock; soon the hour of the wolf. The wind had come up outside; the temperature had dropped. There was a draft from the half-open window. He got out of bed and walked across the room and closed the window. The wind was tearing at the branches of the trees around Vasaplatsen. He could see the leaves falling even in the dark. He tried to see whether anyone was standing and smoking on the balcony across the park, but there was no glow. He walked back to the bed and felt the warmth of the wood floor. That was one of the reasons to stay in the apartment. The children could play on that floor without the risk of catching cold. A new heated floor wasn't the same thing, and this quality of wooden floor didn't exist anymore.

"Soon it will start to get light," Angela said.

"It's hours until then."

"I don't think I can sleep."

"Why not?"

"My head is spinning."

"Do you want a glass of water?"

"Yes, please."

He got out of bed again, passed the hall, took a glass from the shelf in the kitchen. Familiar noises were coming from down in the courtyard. It was the paperboy. In three minutes the paper would plop down in the hall. Angela might take it and start reading right away, local news without an extra day's delay.

Winter guessed that Paula's murder was hardly newsworthy any longer. Too little was happening. At least for the journalists. At the same time, some of them understood that the less they got out of the CID, the more there was to get. Silence was telling, in its own way. But in this case, the silence spoke in a different way. The silence surrounding Paula. It was a silence he couldn't get at. There was something suppressed about it that he'd never really come across before. Like a silence that's only a false front. That you know something tremendous is hiding behind. You can see the silence, touch it, but it's not real. It appears to be connected to everything else, and all the details, for their part, seem to be real, but it doesn't fit together. It's like reading the instructions for a dream. They don't exist. They can't ever exist.

He went back with the glass of water.

"Thanks."

"Why is everyone so quiet?" he said, sitting down on the edge of the bed.

"What do you mean? Here?"

"Paula. Everyone around Paula. It's so quiet."

"Well, you talked to her father. Didn't he open up a little?"

"I don't actually know. I don't know what he wanted."

"Your work is hurting you, Erik. You think that everyone has a hidden agenda behind what they say."

"Well . . ."

"That everyone lies. Or tries to hide the truth."

"Isn't that the same thing?"

"You know what I mean. And then, when someone just tries to tell it like it is, or just wants to . . . well, get something off their chest, maybe, then you don't believe that either."

"The chief inspector as psychotherapist."

"Now you're starting to understand," she said, and he saw a smile flash in the dark of the bedroom.

"I've understood that for a long time. I even invite it."

"Yes, I know, Erik. But try to *see* it like that again sometime. Not everyone lies."

"People lie until there's proof to the contrary," he said.

"Isn't it the other way around?"

"It used to be."

"You promised me once that you wouldn't become cynical."

"I've kept that promise."

They heard a new sound in the hour of the wolf.

"Lilly," said Angela. "She's started to wake up early."

"I'll go."

He went out into the hall again and into the girls' room. They had asked Elsa whether she wanted her own room, but she wanted to share with Lilly. She thought that it would be "fun." Lilly moved in. She had already crawled up into a half stand when Winter lifted her up and whispered into her ear.

He walked by Ringmar's room before the morning meeting. Ringmar was reading from a thick pile of documents in front of him.

"You look full of energy," Ringmar said as Winter sat down.

"My family came back yesterday."

"Aha. No more bachelor life."

"That was long ago," Winter said.

"Everything was long ago," said Ringmar, and he looked down at his document again.

"What are you reading?"

The telephone on Ringmar's desk rang before he could answer.

"Yes?"

Winter heard only a voice, no words. Ringmar nodded twice. He looked at Winter and shook his head. Winter leaned forward.

"Where is he now?" Ringmar said into the receiver, and listened. "We'll have to hope he stays there."

Winter saw a wrinkle deepen between Ringmar's eyes.

"Elisabeth Ney has checked herself out of the hospital but she hasn't come home," Ringmar said as he hung up the phone.

"I'm listening," said Winter, and he felt his skin tighten at a spot above his right temple.

"That was Möllerström. Mario Ney called here and as Möllerström was about to transfer the call to you, he disappeared."

"To me? He wanted to talk to me?"

"Yes."

"Where was he?"

"Möllerström asked right away, like the good policeman he is. Ney is at home. He had called the hospital and found out that Elisabeth had checked out at her own request and that she hadn't asked for anyone to meet her."

"No one asked, probably," Winter said. "Or they thought she would be met by someone."

"In any case, she hasn't come home. It's been three hours since she left the hospital. She doesn't have a cell phone."

"When did Ney call the hospital?"

"Just now, according to Möllerström. And then he called here right away. Möllerström tried to get hold of him again when he disappeared into the ether, but no one answered at the house."

"She could be walking around the city," Winter said. "Sitting in a café. Shopping. Riding around on the streetcars."

Ringmar nodded.

"All so she wouldn't have to go home again," he said.

"Or she could be disoriented."

"She could have disappeared," said Ringmar.

"That word can mean many things, Bertil."

"We're going out to Tynnered," said Ringmar.

"Isn't there any supervision?" said Mario Ney even as they were in the stairwell. He had been waiting with the door open; he must have been standing at the kitchen window and saw them park down below. His words echoed through the stairwell. There was sweat on his forehead. "How could she just be discharged like that?"

"Can we come in, Mario?" said Winter.

"What? Yes . . ."

They walked into the hall. Ney closed the door with a bang. Winter could hear it echo through the stairwell. It sounded like it turned around down at the front door and came back up again, like a lost soul.

"Can we sit down in the living room, Mario?"

"Sit . . . sit down? But we don't have time to sit down!?"

"We have people out in the city looking for Elisabeth," said Ringmar.

"In the city? But what if she isn't in the city?"

"Where else would she be?" Winter said.

Ney didn't answer. They went into the living room. Ney sank down into an easy chair. He looked at Winter.

"She's been gone for more than three hours," he said after ten seconds.

"When did you last speak with Elisabeth, Mario?"

"You know that. It was before you and I went and drank wine."

Ringmar looked at Winter.

"Why did you call the hospital?" Winter asked.

"Call . . . I call every day. What's so strange about that?"

"Nothing. But you usually visit her. Every day."

"Call and then visit, yes."

"What did she say to the staff when she left?" Ringmar asked.

"Don't you even know that?"

"We have people who went over there," Winter said. "But Bertil and I wanted to come out here right away."

"She must still be disoriented," said Ney. "Otherwise she would never do this. Never."

Earlier, it was a mistake to admit her, Winter thought. Now it's wrong that she was released. Either he's learned his lesson or something else is going on.

"Did you speak with Elisabeth earlier today?" Winter asked.

"No."

Winter looked at Ringmar.

"Did someone else talk to her?" Ney asked.

Winter didn't answer.

Ney repeated his question.

"We don't know yet."

An hour later they would know. Someone, a man's voice, had

called for Elisabeth Ney, and a nursing assistant had arranged for her to take the call by going into the hospital room and bringing her to a telephone discreetly placed next to the common room.

Half an hour later she had left the floor. No one at the reception desk remembered her going out through the shining doors. It was like a hotel, Winter thought. Strangers came and went.

"Where did he call from?"

Halders had come into the room a few minutes after the others.

"Gothia," Winter answered. "The hotel."

"Oh, shit. We're sticking to the hotel theme."

"The call came from a telephone in the lobby," Ringmar said.

"But of course it wasn't any of the employees who called?" Halders said.

"Not that we know of," Ringmar said.

"Smart bastard," Halders said, "just go in and look like it's raining and borrow a telephone and call."

"If he isn't staying there," Bergenhem said.

"Hardly," Halders said.

"Can you do that? Just call from a hotel phone like that?" said Djanali. "Is it possible?"

"We've just seen the proof," said Halders.

"And no one has seen Elisabeth Ney at the hotel?" Bergenhem asked.

Winter shook his head. They had sent people there when they found out about the phone call. None of the staff recognized her.

Now they would go through the list of guests. And try to check out the employees. This list could expand to any size; he had seen that many times. The case expanded outward but simultaneously shrunk inward. It became more difficult to see what was important and what was just air, wind.

"What should we do?" Halders asked. "Should we ask Prosecutor Molina about a search warrant so we can open all the hotel rooms?"

Molina was hoping to start a prosecution against someone, but he wasn't optimistic. He was never optimistic. Winter seldom had occasion to cheer him up.

"It's going to be like with the lockers, for God's sake," Halders said. "How many rooms are there at Gothia?"

"We won't get it," Winter said. "Molina will never go along with it. And anyway, we don't have the resources."

"The only chance of getting a search warrant for a big hotel is if there's suspicion that a terrorist is hiding in some cleaning closet," Halders said.

"A particular room might be okay," said Winter, "but not all of them."

"I remember we had to wrestle the warrant out of Molina when it was just a question of those couple of rooms at Hotel Revy," Ringmar said.

"Would Elisabeth Ney really be in a room at Gothia Towers?" said Djanali. "Isn't that the last place we should look for the very reason that that's where he called from?"

"He's smart," said Halders. "He's going with the penalty-kick method."

"What's that?" Bergenhem asked.

"The penalty taker knows that the goalie knows that he usually aims for the right corner, so therefore he aims for the right corner because he counts on the goalie thinking that he'll aim for the left corner instead of the right."

"But what if the goalie thinks a step further?" said Bergenhem.

"Then maybe the penalty taker will already have thought yet another step ahead," Halders answered, smiling.

"So then where does the ball end up?" Bergenhem asked.

"No one knows," said Winter. "That's why we're going to keep looking for Elisabeth Ney. Even at Gothia Towers."

"Where the hell is she?"

Ringmar paced back and forth in the lower part of the lobby. Through the wide windows into the corridor inside, Winter could see groups of people milling back and forth. Many of them were carrying large plastic bags that probably contained books, because there was a book fair going on.

"She's not here, anyway," he said in answer to Ringmar's question.

They no longer believed she was at Gothia.

"Maybe she's just disoriented," Ringmar said. He stopped and looked at the masses of people on the other side of the glass. "Maybe she's in there."

Winter shook his head.

"Like looking for a needle," Ringmar said, turning to Winter. "A disoriented needle. She could wander all over the city."

"What's the alternative?" Winter said.

"We don't want to know."

"Is there an alternative?"

"If there is, all of this is more connected than we think."

"Will it help us, if it is?"

"Not necessarily," said Ringmar.

"It's high time to put out a missing-person report," Winter said.

"Well, good luck to us," said Ringmar.

"Was that a cynical comment?"

Ringmar studied the people on the other side of the glass without answering. The corridor was full; everyone was forced to move slowly. Hundreds of faces passed like a river. Some of them looked out, looked at Ringmar and Winter.

"Like a needle," Ringmar repeated while he observed the haystack on the other side. "Birgitta and I were thinking of going there on Saturday." He nodded toward the mass of people behind the glass. "But now I don't feel like it."

There was chaos outside. The fair was about to close, and everyone was trying to leave at the same time. It had also been very crowded in the lobby. Winter had realized how simple it would be to place an anonymous call from an anonymous telephone.

"We might as well go back," Ringmar said.

They had been driven there in a patrol car.

They followed Skånegatan straight north, past Scandinavium, Burgårdens secondary school, Katrinelund secondary school, temples of knowledge for those who would carry the city into the sweet future. The pillars of Ullevi looked slimmer from this perspective. Winter had stared at them from another direction for nearly twenty years.

"Mario could have been anywhere," Ringmar said.

"He could have kidnapped his own wife, you mean?"

"I don't know. You're the one who goes wine tasting with him."

"What makes you think that, Bertil? That Mario Ney is behind this?"

"Sometimes it feels like he could be behind an awful lot," Ringmar said.

"I don't think he's that good an actor," said Winter.

"Actor? He could be a raving psychopath. That doesn't take any acting talent."

"No."

"He could be from a degenerate mafia family in Sicily."

"He could be from Mars," said Winter. "We don't know much about his background."

"Exactly."

"But we're talking about his own wife here. And his own daughter." Winter shook his head. "No, Bertil."

"Never rule out the family," Ringmar said. "Have you given up on rule 1A?"

"It's someone else," Winter said. "It's not him."

18

It became late afternoon, evening. Where was Elisabeth Ney? No one could see the leaves falling after dark, but they did fall. The crowns of the trees became more and more sparse. Soon it would be possible to see through them, over to the next street, over to the next square, up to the next building. Was she there?

They did what they could, what they always did in these kinds of situations, and a little more. A woman had disappeared. Her daughter had recently been murdered. She was deeply in shock, disoriented, despairing; no one knew how she felt right now. Her disappearance was connected to the murder in that way. Were they connected in any other way?

"Are you saying that I have something to do with this?!"

Mario Ney had started to get up. He sat down again. Neither Winter nor Ringmar needed to do anything. And Ney didn't look as though he were going to strike out. More like he might leave.

"Did I say that you do?" Winter said.

They were sitting in Winter's office. It wasn't a formal interrogation, but naturally, it was an interrogation.

"More or less," Ney said.

"I'll be frank with you," Winter said. "When people disappear, we want to know what their family members were doing at the time of the disappearance. Where they were."

"Can't you think of anything better?"

"It's often the best thing."

"I don't believe that," Ney said. "I don't believe that at all."

Winter didn't say anything. Ringmar was silent. Something rattled against the window, as though some of the autumn leaves were trying to get in, or entire branches.

"In any case, you know where I was," Ney said. "I was home."

"Was there anyone who saw you?" Ringmar asked.

"I was alone. My God. You know I'm alone now. What is this? How can you keep doing this?"

"I mean whether you ran into a neighbor," Ringmar said.

"Or whether you made another phone call," Winter said.

"Where would I go? And who would I call? Anyway, can't you check that? Whether I made a call?"

"Yes."

"Yeah, yeah, I get it," Ney said.

He suddenly looked even more tired, as though it was all over after all. Hope had left this city when it became dark. Or as though he wanted to say something more. Winter thought he wanted to say something more. That was why they were sitting here. Winter's intuition was strong there. He often depended on it. Ney knew something but didn't want to say. Whatever had happened, and was happening, he didn't want to say it. His secret was deep as an abyss. What could it be? What the hell could it be? Could he wear Ney down and find out?

"What do you think of Elisabeth's disappearance?"

"What . . . what do you mean?"

"Why has she disappeared?"

"She's disoriented, of course. She never should have been allowed to leave the hospital, like I said before."

Winter nodded. Ney had also said that she never should have gone there.

"That's what this is about," Ney continued.

Winter nodded again.

"You're not saying anything, Winter. You don't seriously think that Elisabeth's disappearance has to do with . . . with . . . Paula's murder, do you? That someone . . . that someone . . ." He didn't continue the sentence. "Surely that's not what you mean?"

Winter didn't answer right away.

"That it's *me*?" Ney suddenly stood up. "Say it right out if you think it's me!"

"Sit down," Winter said.

"Say it!" Ney cried.

Ringmar had stood up. Winter made a motion with his arm, but Ringmar remained standing there. Ney didn't move. He looked undone, as though he was about to see something he didn't want to see. Are we going to solve the mystery now? Winter thought. Will we get answers now?

Ney sat, or rather fell, down on his chair.

Ringmar walked across the room and looked out through the window. There's nothing there, Winter thought. It's just dark there. Ringmar turned around.

"Is there anything more you want to tell us, Mario?" he asked.

Ney looked up. He looked like he was having trouble focusing on Ringmar's form over by the window, directly across the room, which was half dark. It was a room that was always half dark, Winter's office. It was the same with the Ney family's living room.

"Tell us now," Ringmar said.

Ney looked at Winter, as though for help. As though Winter were the nice cop and Ringmar the bad one. But Winter couldn't be nice now.

"Tell us, Mario," he said, nodding slightly. "Just tell us."

"You all are not right in the head," Ney said, but his voice was very slow, almost a drawl, as though he was repeating something he'd just thought of but hadn't believed. This was something Winter sometimes experienced as an interrogator. The thought was one thing, but the words that would convey it were somewhere completely different, at the other end of the brain, the room, the city, the world.

Winter waited. Ney could get up and go, he had every right to; they weren't planning to put him on a six-hour hold, or double that. But Ney was waiting, too, as though his thoughts would soon tell him what he should do.

And then he got up again.

"I want to go home now."

"Shit," Ringmar said. "We almost had him."

They were still sitting in the half-dark office, sitting twilight again. Everything became quieter when the lights were low. Maybe that's when you think best. Winter observed the slow movement of the trees. I need a smoke out in the fresh air. I'm not going to get up, not yet.

"We almost had it," Ringmar continued.

"What was it we had?"

"A secret."

"What kind of secret?"

They tested their method again, the routine: questions, answers, questions, answers, a quick tempo, straggling sometimes, sometimes on the way to a single point.

"About him."

"Just about him?"

"His family."

"His wife? His daughter? Both of them? One of them?"

"Both," Ringmar said. "It's connected. They're connected."

"In this case?"

"Yes."

"More than as mother and daughter?"

"Yes."

"In what way?"

"I don't know yet. So we have to dig further into the past."

"In this family's background?"

"Yes."

"Have we not been observant enough?"

"No."

"In what way?"

"We'll see. We'll find out."

"Does it have to do with Mario's background?" Winter said.

"Maybe. But that could be a dead end. Italy, Sicily. It could be the wrong direction."

"Does it have to do with Elisabeth's background?"

"Yes."

"Why?"

"She has a secret."

"Is she the only one who knows it?"

"No."

"Who else knows?"

"Mario."

"So that's his secret?"

"Yes."

"But it's about her?"

"Yes."

"Is it about Paula?"

"No."

"Are you sure?"

"No."

"What if it is about Paula, then?"

"Yes, what then?"

"Is it her adult life?"

"I don't know. We still know too little about her."

"How can we find out more?"

"You know how, Erik. We just have to keep working."

"What if this is about Paula's childhood?"

"Why do you say that?"

"I don't know."

"Something from her childhood? That's connected to her murder, you mean?"

"Yes."

"Is it connected with the family?"

"Yes. No. Yes. No. Yes."

"You said yes last."

"It is connected with her family."

"Only her family? Or someone else outside the family?"

"I don't see anyone. But there could be someone."

"Is it connected to Mario's childhood?"

"No."

"Elisabeth's childhood?" Ringmar repeated.

"Yes."

"Why?"

"I can see Elisabeth. This is about her. Mario showed us that, without saying anything."

"Elisabeth's childhood?"

"Yes. Maybe."

"We haven't gone back to her childhood."

"We haven't had time."

"Do we have time? Do we have the energy?"

"Is it a good idea?"

"What could there be in Elisabeth's childhood that would shed light on this?"

"A shadow. The past always casts shadows."

"Should we search their apartment again? Really search it?"

"We won't find anything there, I'm afraid."

"Where should we look, then?"

"Only one place left."

"Paula's apartment?"

"Yes."

"We've gone through the place twice."

"Then there will have to be a third time. Third time's the charm, as he said."

"Who said that?"

"It was me."

"Now it's time for a break."

The break room felt like a blinding operating room compared to the twilight in Winter's office. They drank vending machine coffee that was far too hot. Winter let the plastic mug stand. This was routine, too. Everything was routine, necessary routine. In the same way, imagination was also routine; intuition was routine. Thinking was routine. Some people had just never learned it. You had to learn how to think. Even thinking badly could be trying, and it was infinitely more difficult to think well.

Ringmar took a sip of the cooled poison and made a face.

"Let it stand," Winter said.

"It'll be the death of me," Ringmar said.

"My cappuccino machine is coming next week," Winter said. "I'm going to have it in my office."

"Really?"

"Maybe."

Ringmar smiled and lifted the mug again but set it down. A colleague from the city desk came in and pressed out his coffee and nodded and left again with the hot cup balancing between his fingertips.

They heard the wind outside. It had come up as they were sitting in Winter's office. He had seen it in the trees outside the window, and he could see it now. The wind tore at the trees outside the entrance to the police station. They swayed with half-naked branches. The branches were like hands, slowly waving farewell. Winter followed their movements. Ringmar did, too. He turned to Winter.

"Are you thinking what I'm thinking?"

"Presumably."

"Is it a symbol we ought to see?"

Symbol. The white hand. Where was the symbolism? In the hand itself? The fact that it was a hand? In the paint, the white paint? In the reproduction itself?

"The white hand," Winter said, but it was as though to himself.

"I went down and looked at it this afternoon," Ringmar said.

Winter nodded.

"As though I would learn something more this time."

"The white paint," Winter said.

"Yes?"

"It could be the paint." He took his eyes from the trees and turned to Ringmar. "The color. White. What does it stand for?"

"Well . . . innocence. Something innocent."

"Mm-hmm."

"Purity."

"Yes."

"What are you thinking now, Erik?"

"Is it the color, Bertil? Is that what we should concentrate on?"

"How far will we get with that?"

"Love," Winter said. "Doesn't white stand for love, too?"

"I suppose it depends on what you mean," Ringmar said. "In this case, it could stand for anything."

Winter nodded.

"It can stand for death," Ringmar said. "White is also the color of death. At a funeral, you wear a white tie."

Winter wiped a string of saliva from Lilly's mouth. The child turned in her sleep. He leaned forward and kissed her cheek. Her skin was soft, like a summer cloud.

Elsa was snoring faintly. He turned her carefully and the snoring stopped. But he knew it would come back. The polyps. It might mean an operation. There would probably be an operation.

Angela was lying on the sofa with her feet on the armrest.

"Do you want a whiskey?" he asked.

"Are you asking because you want one yourself?" she said.

"Me? Why would I want a whiskey?"

She put down her feet and sat up. "You can give me a glass of the red wine from last night. There's a little left."

He went out into the kitchen and poured the rest of the wine into a large glass and poured a Glenfarclas, two centimeters. There could be another two centimeters a little later, but no more.

He went back to the living room.

"Maybe tomorrow you'll be home before the girls fall asleep," Angela said, taking the wineglass.

"It was Bertil. We ended up sitting there with questions and answers."

"Sure, blame him."

"You know how it can be."

"Twenty questions and answers?"

"If only it stopped there."

"Siv called."

"Oh?"

"She was in the apartment today. They switched out the stove."

"Did it go well?"

"I guess we'll have to see when we use it." She lifted her glass. "But it seemed okay."

He nodded. The stove in Marbella, the kitchen in Marbella. Just over a month left. He lifted his glass and thought about how he would be there in the apartment when Angela began her job. He wanted to be there already. No. Yes. No.

"I talked to Siv," Angela said.

"Yes, you said that."

"About December. She's ready."

"Ready?"

"Ready to help me with the children. When I'm working. And if you're still working here."

"I'm going to be there," he said, "with you. My leave of absence has been approved, as you know."

"It might be delayed."

"No."

"I know you, Erik."

He didn't answer.

"Better than you know yourself," she continued.

"Would you be able to go down by yourself with the children?" he said after a little while. "If I am . . . a little delayed?"

"I've done it before, haven't I?"

• • •

Möllerström transferred the call.

"She seems a little jittery," he said.

Winter waited as Möllerström put it through.

"Hello? Hello?"

It sounded like a cry.

"Yes, this is Winter."

"Yes . . . hi, it's Nina Lorrinder."

"What can I help you with, Nina?"

"I . . . I thought I saw him."

"Who?"

"The guy who . . . who Paula was talking to at Friskis & Svettis. I thought I recognized him."

"Where?"

"At church."

"At church? Domkyrkan?"

"Yes. I went there last night during evening prayer. I just wanted . . . to sit there for a while. I wanted to think . . ."

She stopped talking. Winter could hear her breathing. It sounded as though she had run to the telephone.

"Yes?"

"I thought it was him. He was sitting diagonally across . . . on the other side of the aisle."

"Yesterday evening? Was it yesterday?"

"Yes."

"Why didn't you call right away?"

She didn't answer.

Winter repeated the question.

"I don't know. I guess I wasn't sure enough. I'm not now, either."

"What happened after that?" Winter asked. "When prayer was over."

"I . . . kept sitting there. He got up and left. He walked past me. Then . . . I left, too."

"Did you see him outside?"

"No."

"Have you seen him at church before?"

"No. Not that I remember."

"How often do you go there? To Domkyrkan?"

"It's been a while now. I haven't . . . I don't know. After Paula died . . . she and I were, you know . . . it was something we did together . . ."

"Do you want to go there with me?" Winter asked.

It was peaceful; it was beautiful. Winter was no stranger to churches. It was a good space. The light was good. The world outside disappeared. The windows of the church let in their own version of the city out there.

It was the third evening prayer. He listened, but not too attentively. The first time, four days ago, he had been surprised that there were so many people in the church. Maybe more people had begun to seek out churches recently, during the past year.

Maybe it was just here, in Domkyrkan, downtown. An alternative to the shopping district on Drottninggatan just outside.

The man in white over there said something that Winter didn't understand.

The congregation sang, stood up and sang. Winter observed the congregation. Lorrinder stood beside him with the hymnal in her hand. She wasn't singing.

She was doing what he was, watching the other people in there. There weren't enough people for someone to be able to hide.

The song ended. They sat down.

"He's not here tonight either," she said in a low voice.

Winter nodded. It was an experiment. They would keep coming here; maybe he wouldn't, and they couldn't force Lorrinder to come here day after day, prayer after prayer. But sometime. One fine day.

Then the time was up. People began to stand up in the pews.

Maybe that was it . . . that people had to bend forward to get out of the pews . . . Winter kept his eyes on the rows diagonally across the aisle, just ten meters away, maybe twelve, and a man who had been sitting by himself got up and Winter saw his profile before the man turned his back and left the pew from the other side and walked along the far wall toward the exit of the church. Winter could see the right half of his face now, but from farther away.

He had seen it before, had seen that man.

It must have been a long time ago. It was someone from a long time ago. Who is it? What was it . . . that had happened back then?

Winter turned in the pew, but the man had disappeared behind a pillar that obscured the exit.

"What is it?" Lorrinder asked.

"I thought I recognized someone."

"Who was it?"

"I don't really know."

Talked to him, Winter thought as they stood up. I've talked to him.

Interrogated him.

Yes.

It was him.

It was many years ago.

Outside, no one was left. The streetcars came one after another over on Västra Hamngatan.

"I'll drive you home, Nina," said Winter.

Halders visited Friskis & Svettis along with Lorrinder, at the same time that Nina and Paula used to work out two evenings a week for the past year.

"And before that?" Halders had asked as they walked up the stairs from Västra Hamngatan. "Didn't you work out then?"

"Sometimes. But it was mostly me."

"Why?"

"I don't know. Paula jogged a bit. I don't actually know."

There were lots of people everywhere inside the gym. Most of them were exercising, or were about to start. It smelled a little bit like sweat, but mostly it smelled like different kinds of lotion. This isn't the wrestling gym of my youth, Halders thought. It smelled like sweat there, decades of accumulated sweat. Here it was more like the bodies around him were emitting sweat for the first time but didn't really want to let it out, as though it might be dangerous to sweat. In the large studio inside the glass, many people were exercising in many different ways, carefully, exaggeratedly, shyly, narcissistically, ergonomically correctly, or completely incompetently. Halders could have stood at the very front in place of the beautiful boy and shown them what it should really look like. Not now, but ten years ago when he was in perfect shape.

He had spoken with the staff earlier. He had talked to them along with Lorrinder, too. They had left a description of the man that Paula had spoken with. It was vague, verging on invisible, despite the fact that Lorrinder thought she had recognized him in Domkyrkan. Halders hadn't hooked up Lorrinder with a portrait artist yet. Maybe he ought to, even if it was old-fashioned and seldom led anywhere.

None of the staff remembered Paula Ney. No one remembered Lorrinder, either.

"We have quite a lot to do," said a woman with a red sweatband. She was dressed in a tight leotard. Halders avoided lowering his gaze to her large breasts by fixing it on her sweatband. It wouldn't look good if she thought he was staring at her breasts. "It's not easy to remember a face."

No, Halders thought. It was mostly about bodies here. He felt uncomfortable here, and he would feel even more uncomfortable in a leotard. He had neglected his workouts.

"What does someone have to look like for you to remember them?" Halders asked.

She looked at him and smiled. That was answer enough.

As they walked toward the café he asked:

"Would you recognize him if you saw him now?"

"I think so," Lorrinder answered.

"Was he in good shape?"

"I didn't see him in workout clothes. Or maybe it was just during the workout."

"What do you mean?"

"Maybe she talked to him when there wasn't a class going on. I mean, before or after."

"Where did they stand?"

"Well, it was only a few times, a couple of times."

"Show me where."

"Once in the café. I've told you that."

"And where else?"

"Here. In the hall. There." She pointed over toward the other end, where there were a few chairs and a small table. The hall continued on toward several entrances or exits. Halders could see the aerobics continuing in the studio behind the glass wall. Feet, arms, legs in the air, back and forth, up, down. Hands. If he wanted to, he could look at it as hands flapping around in the air and . . . nothing else. Hands that turned white in the bright light. He was nearly blinded in there. When he had blinked and closed his eyes and looked again, it was still hard to see clearly. He wondered whether Nina Lorrinder had really seen someone in there, or whether she just thought so. She had had a great deal of uncertainty, in some ways unnecessarily great. Her memory ought to be sharper. Maybe it was just a wish he had: Paula knew someone and that would help them find her murderer. Not because it would help Paula. She had left all sounds and groans and jumps and arm motions and blinding lights behind.

It could also be that Lorrinder wanted to help because she wanted to help. Halders had seen that hundreds of times. Someone wanted to help, but there wasn't anything to help with. All they got was disinformation; it delayed the investigation, the search. Maybe he shouldn't be here. He should be back in Paula's apartment, continuing to search for what they still hadn't found.

"How many times were you at Paula's house?" he asked.

They were standing next to the puny table and the spindly chairs. Everything here was for slight bodies. Perhaps it was an encouragement. You can be like us. You come in here as fat-asses and leave as models. We have been like you, you shall be like us. The saying suddenly popped into Halders's head. He had seen it in a cemetery somewhere in southern Spain. It was on one of his first vacations with Margareta, before the children were born. It had been very hot; the rental car hadn't had air-conditioning. He had stood for a while and looked at the writing above the gateway that led into the cemetery. We have been like you, you shall be like us. Inside, the black sarcophaguses towered toward the incredibly blue sky. An old man had walked by and explained the words, though Halders hadn't asked. The old man had spoken English like an American. That was no surprise. He looked like he was straight out of a Western. Halders had thought of the words over the gateway on the way back to Granada. They were scornful words.

"I was almost never there," said Lorrinder.

"What?"

"At Paula's place. You just asked me about it. I was almost never at her place."

"But when you were there. What was it like?"

"What do you mean?"

"Was it cozy? Homelike? Did she look like she felt at home there?"

"Well . . . I don't know. There wasn't much furniture."

"Do you need that to feel at home?"

"I don't know. I guess it's also a matter of money."

"But she had a comfortable income, right?"

"I think so."

"Did she talk about her job often?"

"Never."

"Never."

"No. Just as little as I talked about mine."

"And just as little as I talk about mine," said Halders.

"I thought police officers often talked about their jobs at home," said Lorrinder.

"We prefer not to. But we think about it. Unfortunately."

"Why unfortunately?"

"Because you would rather drop it just like you drop your coat right on the floor when you come home."

"You drop your coat right on the floor?"

"That guy," Halders said without answering. He nodded toward a man who had just come out of one of the exercise studios and was now starting to walk toward them. He looked like he'd finished a session. There was something familiar about him, despite the fact that Halders had never seen him. "Could be him."

"It *is* him," said Lorrinder.

"The night has a thousand eyes that follow you every step you take." Halders was singing quietly as he drove through the nighttime city. "The night has a thousand eyes, so it's best if you stay right here."

"Stay right here where?" Winter asked.

He had begun to get used to the strange company of Fredrik. Absurdity was only the beginning. Sometimes it was like being in a play by Beckett. *Waiting for Godot.* Eternally driving on their way from different nowheres. Crime scenes to the west, crime scenes to the east. Sometimes evidence sites, worse than crime scenes. What the hell was the point of it? Maybe better to keep it at bay with the harsh type of humor that Halders had. A little melody in the middle of the chaos, on the way to and from the abysses. Yes. The night had a thousand faceted eyes; they were shining and flashing and blinking out there. Neon dusks became neon dawns, and sometimes it felt like he'd been awake for a month when the daylight came.

"Stay right here in the car," Halders answered.

"What will we do when we get there, then?" Winter asked.

"Call for backup," said Halders.

"Are you joking?"

"Naturally."

Winter had known Halders for a few months now. They didn't fight anymore. They traveled through the nights together. They went up strange and frightening stairwells together, with weapons drawn. Bled together, but it was always someone else's blood; it was impossible to avoid *that*. Blood was their workday. He saw blood every week: some weeks every day, some days every hour. What the hell was the point of that? The point was that he went up stairwells. That he drew his weapon. That he was standing there, *being* there. But it was almost always over. If only he had gotten there before. They seldom arrived in time.

"Is it here?"

Halders turned his head. Winter read from his notes and looked up. He hadn't been born on Hisingen. This was far beyond Vågmästareplatsen, which was closer to downtown. A person who hadn't been born on the island never really learned his way around. It was as though it moved every time he came there. The points of the compass were no longer valid.

Halders had stopped beside a five-story building. There were six or seven identical buildings around it in a spiny half circle. There was a number above each entrance, and each building had three entrances. Winter read the number in his notebook aloud. Halders started the car and drove alongside the buildings. It felt as though they were leaning over the car. It was the shadows. The shadows at night were different compared to the daytime ones; they were artificial shadows, and they could be dangerous. You lost perspective. One night, Winter had run in the wrong direction because of the false shadow, and that could have ended in a way he didn't want to think about.

Halders parked beyond the entrance, possibly out of sight of the windows. Winter wasn't thinking about that right now. He looked up at the windows. They were dark.

"I would have preferred the lights to be on up there," Halders said.

"I would have preferred this to be over," Winter said, and he drew his Walther and checked the bolt.

"I like you, Winter," Halders said, smiling. "You're already looking ahead."

"What did he say when he called?"

"A fucking racket. Heavy fucking traffic."

"It can't get any calmer than this."

"Makes a guy nervous, huh?"

"Maybe we should think about that backup you were just talking about," said Winter.

"It doesn't exist. Are you ready?"

"Are we both going?"

"One after the other. You first."

"Why me?"

"I'm the only one of us with eyes in the back of my head," Halders said.

They got out of the car, continued together along the facade of the building, and went in through the front door, which was apparently not equipped with a lock, or maybe the lock was not working. They didn't turn on the light in the stairwell. They couldn't hear any sounds from any of the apartments as they passed the doors on the way up. Winter hadn't seen any lights in the windows next to this entrance. It was as though the entire stairwell had been evacuated. The guy who had called hadn't said anything about that. He had only told them about the fucking racket, the fucking traffic. Traffic was down right now. There was an awful silence in the stairwell, the worst kind; it was like it was waiting for them. Winter had learned to recognize it. It would start to roar sooner or later.

"Next one," Halders whispered.

Winter nodded toward the rough wall. The meager light in the stairwell came from the streetlights outside. This was a long way for the light to come. They stood beside the door, one on each side. There was a peephole in the middle of the door. Halders pressed the doorbell. The ring sounded very loud; the sound was enhanced by the darkness. It was a shrill ring, like in an old-fashioned clock. There was no melody to the ringing; even Halders's singing earlier had been melodic compared to this ringing. Halders pressed again. Again, there was shrieking and rasping in the hall beyond the door. That was what they heard. No voices, no steps. Winter bent down and carefully lifted the metal flap over the mail slot. He saw only darkness. After about ten seconds he saw the contours of the rug that lay inside the door. A faint light was coming from somewhere inside the apartment, presumably from a window. It was the same worthless light.

19

Winter lifted his head and nodded at Halders.

Halders pounded his fist against the door.

"Police! Open the door!"

Winter listened for sounds from inside. It was almost always possible to hear something. No silence was completely quiet.

"Open the door," Halders repeated. He tapped his fist lightly on the veneer of the door. It sounded thin, hollow. Another blow and Halders would be through. They were still standing in the gloom of the stairwell. No one stepped out of any of the doors to turn on the lights and ask what in God's name was going on.

They didn't hear anything from inside. There was a rushing sound outside; it could be the wind or the building's ventilation system.

Winter thought of the agitated voice on the telephone:

"They're screaming in there! There's a woman screaming!"

Halders placed his ear against the door.

Winter felt the door handle, pulled it down.

The door opened when he tugged at it.

"Shit, it's not locked," said Halders.

"Take it easy."

Halders nodded. He slowly opened the door. Winter felt his pulse, as he felt the weapon in his hand. It felt like now. This was now. This was nothing you could practice for, not in any real way. There could be anything at all in the darkness, inside the apartment. To go in there could be to say farewell to this world. That was what he was feeling right now. He hadn't had that feeling very many times yet.

"I'm going to turn on the light," Halders said. "Be prepared."

The hall suddenly lit up, as though there had been an explosion. Winter shielded his eyes with his left hand. They waited for ten seconds and then stepped in. There were clothes lying on the floor, outerwear, innerwear. Shoes.

They walked carefully from room to room. There was no one in the apartment.

There were red stains on the floor in the kitchen. There were newspapers lying on the floor. The red stuff had run down onto the newspapers like paint. The papers lay there like a protective layer, as though the red stuff were paint. Winter could see a headline, but it didn't tell him anything. He could see pictures.

"What the hell is this?" Halders said.

Winter didn't say anything. He bent down. He looked at the stains. It could have been paint. He could have been a painter.

"There's a lot," Halders said, and he turned around and looked at Winter. "Do you feel sick?"

"No."

"You're pale, kid."

"What happened in here?" said Winter.

Halders turned around again.

"Whatever it was, it's over now."

"There was no blood in the stairwell," Winter said.

"We don't know that yet, do we? Forensics hasn't been here yet, have they?"

What would they look for? Winter thought. What kind of crime had taken place here? If it is a crime.

"Someone could have cut himself on the arm when he was cutting a ham," Halders said. "Or butchered a few chickens. What do you think?"

"Where's the knife?"

"He forgot to toss it," Halders said.

"Where is he, then?" said Winter.

"He doesn't remember," Halders said.

Winter didn't say anything about Halders's absurd comments.

"We'll have to have a chat with the witness," Halders said.

"He doesn't live here, does he?" said Winter.

"On the other side of the courtyard."

"What was he doing in this stairwell?"

"Was going to visit a friend on the floor below, dispatch says. Guess the friend wasn't home. But our witness heard a fucking commotion from in here."

Winter nodded. Now there was only fucking silence there. Sometimes it could seem as though screams remained in a room he came to, but that's not how it was this time. Whoever had been here had taken their screams with them.

Halders looked around again.

"Fucking weird," he said.

"I guess we'll have to go talk to that guy," Winter said.

"I'll call for another car," Halders said. "We can't leave until someone else is here."

"I'll look around a little more," said Winter.

He went out into the stairwell and read the nameplate on the door. Martinsson. No first name. He knew absolutely nothing about Martinsson, him or her or them. There hadn't been time for that. He knew nothing about what had happened here. It was fucking weird, as Halders had said. Without a victim, they knew nothing.

He went into the hall and continued into the closest room. The double bed was unmade. It looked like two people had lain in it; there was a depression in each of the two pillows. It could have been this morning, yesterday, the day before yesterday.

There was blood in the bedroom. He saw it the second time he looked. At first it looked like part of the pattern on the pillow. It looked as though it had ended up there on purpose. You had to look at least twice to tell.

What had happened here?

He went back to the kitchen.

They waited for forensics, and then they walked across the courtyard to the building on the other side. Winter heard a dog barking from a grove of trees at the north end of the row of houses. It looked like a forest for children. The trees stood close together, but there didn't seem to be many of them.

The barking continued as they walked in through the entrance. Winter could still hear it as he walked up the stairs.

They rang at another door. Winter read the nameplate: Metzer. It sounded German, or maybe French, or maybe Italian. Quite a few people from other countries lived in this part of town, southern Europeans, Finns. The Finnish colony was large. They had big parties with lots of akvavit, but his colleagues in patrol seldom had to come out here. The Finns took care of their own drunks; they were probably the best in the world at that, they and the Russians. The Swedes were worse at it, even though the country was in the middle of the vodka belt.

Winter remained standing a few stairs down. The man who might be named Metzer opened the door. Winter didn't know the name of the guy who made the call. Halders had taken it. Halders and Winter had been in the vicinity. They were investigating a gang that was suspected of smuggling narcotics. Yes, they could go an extra kilometer. The gang wasn't there anyway.

"Metzer?" Halders said.

Winter couldn't see the man. He was still standing inside the door. There was a draft through the stairwell, a breeze from below, as though someone had opened the front door and was holding it open. Winter could hear the dog barking again; it came up with the wind. The door must be open down there.

"May we come in?" Halders said.

Winter heard only a mumble from the door. He still hadn't seen the man's face, just Halders's back.

"I just have to check something," he said, and he started to go down the stairs.

"Did you forget something?" Halders asked, and he turned around.

"You go in," Winter answered. "I'll be right back."

The door was open downstairs. He could see that someone had propped it open; the chain was tight.

A boy with a dog on a taut leash was standing in front of the building. The boy looked at him without saying anything. The dog was quiet now, but it wasn't calm. It was straining to get to the small collection of trees, as though there were a magnet there.

"Did you see anyone open the door?" Winter asked.

The boy shook his head. He might have been eleven, maybe twelve.

"Do you live here?" Winter asked.

The boy pointed at the building they had been in earlier. The forensics team was still in the apartment on the fourth floor. Winter could see the light through the windows, and a sudden shadow as one of the technicians moved around inside. We won't be long, they had said. What kind of crap is this?

"Do you live over there?" Winter asked. "In that building?"

The boy nodded.

"Can't you talk?"

The boy shook his head. His hair was dark, yet still light in the glow from the streetlight. Winter suddenly felt it. The boy knows something. He's standing here because he knows. He's seen something.

Winter could see his eyes even from this distance. It was as though they were illuminated from within.

Winter felt a faint shiver. It passed over his hair like metal. The boy is watching me. Those eyes. The dog is tugging at its leash. The boy is pointing again. What is he pointing at now? He's nodding and pointing. Toward the grove of trees. His hand is trembling like the leaves in the wind. It's just as thin as they are. Now the dog is barking. It's like it's crazy. What did they see, the boy and the dog? The grove of trees. He wants me to go there. He can't say it. It looks like he's trying.

"Is there something you want to show me?" Winter asked, and he pointed. "Over there? In the grove of trees?"

The boy nodded.

"What is it?"

The boy didn't answer.

Winter looked around. There were no other people outside. The wind tore at whatever it could grab. The branches made shadows on the facades of the buildings. It looked like a film being shown at double speed. It was fifty, maybe sixty meters over to the trees. It was only a small grove, like an oasis in a brick desert. The birches swayed like sparse palm trees.

The boy's eyes were large and frightened. Winter didn't want to expose his pistol to him. He held his hand over its butt in his pocket. He looked over at the car. It was closer than the grove.

"I'm just going to grab something," he said, and he walked to the car, opened the passenger-side door, and took out a flashlight. Halders had the other one. The flashlight was heavier than his weapon. Winter held it up so the boy could see. It was like a calming object. An unlit flashlight conveyed calmness. A lit one did, too, but mostly for the person holding the flashlight. A pistol could be calming in the same way. But not right now.

As they walked across the playground, the dog began to bark and tug on its leash again. It looked like a mix of God knows what breeds. It was on the hunt; it was a natural instinct. It could smell scents in the wind that no person could smell.

He shone the light in among the trees and looked at the boy. The dog had stopped barking, but the leash was taut. The boy was having trouble keeping the dog at the edge of the grove.

Winter walked closer with the beam of light pointed down. Everything on the ground turned white: leaves, dirt, grass, sand, stone. That was what he saw. The boy was still standing outside. Winter walked back.

"I don't see anything," he said.

The boy pointed again.

"Where?" Winter asked. "Where is it?"

The boy stood a few steps in among the bushes and it looked as though the dog flew ahead through the air as it got a few meters of freedom. When the leash tightened, the dog was jerked backward, like it had been hit by a gust of wind.

The boy nodded down toward the ground. Winter shone the beam around down there: leaves, dirt, grass, sand, stone. Several stones lay in an undefined half circle. It was probably the remains of an open fire. Winter bent down. There were darker stains on the stones, but it could be the humidity, or moss. He looked at the boy again.

"Did you see something here?" Winter asked.

The boy didn't answer; he kept staring downward.

"There's nothing here," Winter said.

"A . . . a . . . hand," said the boy.

"What?" Winter was still crouching down. "What did you say?"

"There was a hand there."

They sat at a kitchen table with a vase of cut flowers that Winter didn't know the names of. Flowers, birds, plants, he wasn't good at that stuff. Leaves, dirt, grass, sand, stone; that was more his area.

The boy was eleven years old. His name was Jonas. He looked just as frozen in here as he had outside. There was a mug of hot chocolate in front of him. His mother was sitting beside him. She looked young, but she must have been older than Winter, at least over thirty. Winter could see her features in the boy's face; not all of them, but there was no dad at the table he could compare with.

"We weren't home," said the mom. Her name was Anne. Anne Sandler. Both Jonas's and her names were on the nameplate on the door. No dad there, either.

Winter had asked about times. When the witness named Metzer had reported the possible fight in the Martinssons' apartment, Anne and Jonas hadn't been home.

"We were at the pool."

Winter nodded.

Jonas drank a sip of hot chocolate. Winter had said no thanks to hot chocolate, but yes to a cup of coffee. It was strong and hot.

"He doesn't usually make things up," Anne Sandler said, nodding to Jonas.

The boy hadn't said much since they came in. The dog was quiet, too. It had done its duty.

"It was a hand," he said.

"Oh my God," Anne Sandler said, looking at her son.

Winter nodded down at the boy. He didn't look as frozen anymore.

"There were fingers and everything."

"I believe you," said Winter.

"It stopped here," Jonas said, aiming at his wrist.

"Oh my God," Anne Sandler repeated.

"Was it big?" Winter asked. "Like a grown-up's hand?"

"I don't know . . . pretty small." The boy looked at his own hand, as though he was comparing. "But it was pretty dark out."

"Can't we stop now?" Anne Sandler said, and she looked at Winter. Her eyes were pleading.

"Soon," he said, looking at the boy.

"Did it look like a child's hand?"

The boy shook his head.

"Like a . . . lady's hand? A woman's hand?"

"Maybe," Jonas said.

His mother looked at her hands, removed them from the tabletop, placed them in her lap.

"It was dark out," Jonas continued.

"But you could see anyway?"

"Yes. There's a streetlamp there. And Zack was barking more than he usually does."

"That dog," Anne Sandler said. "He doesn't do anything but bark."

"I'm working on training him," Jonas said, looking at his mother.

"It's too late," she said. "He's too old." She looked at Winter. He realized that talking about the dog was calming her down. "It's like they say: You can't teach an old dog new tricks."

"Zack knows good tricks," said Jonas.

"You saw the hand clearly?" Winter asked.

The boy nodded and looked at the dog, who was performing the trick of sitting in the middle of the kitchen floor, and drank hot chocolate again. He looked up.

"But it didn't look real."

"What do you mean, Jonas?"

"It was so white. Like plastic. Or a cast."

"That's enough," his mother said, and she got up and took Winter's half-drunk coffee cup with her into the kitchen. Winter heard the coffee land in the sink.

They drove back over the Älvsborg bridge. The downtown glittered to the east like there was a festival. To the west, the river widened to the sea. The blackness became wider, and larger. The temperature had sunk in the last few hours. Maybe it will snow, Winter thought. Snow in October. White on the ground.

"Is the boy credible?" Halders said.

Winter shrugged.

"I think so." He held on to the ceiling handle as Halders spun through the roundabout down toward Karl Johansgatan. "But it could have been anything. The light wasn't the best."

"But you did see stains?"

"Yes. but it could have been anything."

"I guess our friends from forensics will have to tell us what it is."

Winter didn't answer. Soon he wouldn't have any friends in forensics, if he ever had. They were out on the thoroughfare along the river. The dead shipyard cranes on the other side stretched far into the sky. They should be reminiscent of something, but soon no one would remember what it was. It had been part of this city. Now all of that was gone, everything that should form the face of a city. Gothenburg had a lot of faces now. Many of them were turned away. It was impossible to see them.

"They sure were happy, our friends," said Halders. "Another discovery site, and only fifty meters away."

"Yes, they were really glowing."

The neon lights became brighter the closer they got to downtown. Eastern Nordstan wasn't lacking for anything. Halders stopped at a red light. A group of people dressed for a party passed on their way to Lilla Bommen. No one even glanced at the two young detectives in the anonymous car.

"Now we just need to find the Martinsson couple to see if either of them is missing a hand," said Halders.

"The woman, in that case," said Winter.

"The mom and the boy didn't know them, you said?"

"No, no. That's no cozy little row-house neighborhood, Fredrik. People don't even know each other if they live in the same stair-wells."

"But they must at least see each other, right?"

Winter shrugged. That was the second time this evening. He didn't like to shrug. He would have to quit.

"How is it for you?" he said. "And me? Quite honestly, I don't give a shit about people in my building up in Guldheden. I wouldn't be able to point out a third of them."

"And yet you're an expert," said Halders.

He swung into the half circle around Central Station. The line for the taxis outside the main entrance was long. Winter could see people's breath. That's how cold it had gotten. Shit. Then it would be November, and December, January, February, March, half of April. That was the white winter. Then the green winter would start. His father had talked about leaving this part of the world once and for all, and then he had. That had been quite recently. He had taken his money with him and he'd forgotten to pay the taxes. Winter understood that his father wanted a life in the sun, but he didn't understand the other part. They no longer spoke to each other. Maybe they would in the future, but Winter wasn't sure. First he wanted an explanation. But that wouldn't be enough.

"Metzer wasn't much help," Halders said. "He got nervous because it sounded so bad, he said. And that was all."

"Did he know the Martinssons, then?"

"No."

"No one knows anyone here, apparently."

"That's how it is," said Halders.

"So what do we do now?" said Winter.

"Wait for the Martinssons to call," Halders said. "Or be found. Maybe just one of them."

Winter didn't answer. They waited at a red light outside the *GP* building. Maybe he would be able to read about what had happened out on Hisingen in the paper the next day.

"After that we'll just have to see what the guys in forensics come up with," Halders continued.

"One of the guys was a girl," said Winter.

"Well, it's just like they say," Halders said. "If a chick is good enough, she becomes one of the guys."

He parked outside the police station. They were going to go in and write, and then this day would be over.

"Are you coming along for a brew after?" Halders said.

"Not tonight."

"A lady waiting for you?"

"Yes, actually."

"Be careful."

"Of what?"

"Of getting stuck. It can go fucking fast."

"No chance," Winter said.

"Is she cute?"

"None of your damn business, Fredrik."

"I'm just curious. What's her name?"

"Hasse."

"Hasse? Come on now, for fuck's sake."

"She's one of the guys."

"Ha-ha. Come on, Erik. What's her name?"

"That's none of your damn business either."

• • •

Angela took a step back from the crosswalk. It might have been at the last second.

"Did you see that?!"

Winter didn't answer. He tried to read the license plate, but it was too dirty. It was an S40, a later model. He hadn't had time to see the driver as the car passed at sixty-five or seventy kilometers per hour.

"He ran a red light!" said Angela.

The S40 turned right and drove the wrong way on Chalmersgatan, maybe on its way toward the local police station at Lorensberg. Winter took out his cell phone, called right away, explained quickly.

"Yes. Yes. He might be on his way to you right now."

He waited, with the cell phone against his ear. They were still standing at the crosswalk. Angela had taken two steps back.

"Yes? Okay. Oh? Well, there we go. Thanks." He put away the cell phone. "They got him."

"Serves him right."

"A thief."

"Did they say that?"

"A real celebrity," Winter said.

"Could they tell so quickly?"

"We live in speedy times." The light turned green again. The traffic stopped, nice and proper. "Should we be brave and cross?"

They walked through the park and down toward Salutorget.

"Hasn't it always gone quickly?" Angela said after a little bit.

"What do you mean?"

"Haven't you always felt like things go too quickly? Too quickly through life?"

"What kind of question is that?"

"Can't you answer?"

"Well . . . yes, I guess I can." He slowed down. "Maybe I have . . . felt like that before."

"With us, for example?"

"No, no, no."

"You know, we were actually seeing each other for only five years before we moved in together," she said without looking at him. "It went very fast."

They were walking on the bridge across the small river. It was black in the night light. It was hard to see where you were walking. He felt for Angela's arm.

"Did we live apart for such a short time?" he said.

"The time really did fly by."

"I like it when you're being sarcastic," he said.

"Although you did stay with me up in Kungshöjd an awful lot," she continued.

"There you go."

"You said that you felt more at home there than in Guldheden."

"Yes. And then I got the apartment at Vasaplatsen and then it was like there wasn't really much to discuss, was there?"

Angela's cell phone rang.

"Yes? Yes? Yes. Yes. No. Yes. No. Yes. Yes. Yes. Exactly. Exactly. Of course. Yes. Yes. Yes."

She hung up and put the phone in her purse.

"The babysitter," she said.

"I could tell. Problems?"

"No."

They continued across the square to the restaurant on the east end. Angela had made a reservation yesterday. The table was by the window. From the inside, it looked very cold outside. Winter smelled good smells in the room. He ordered a dry martini; Angela ordered a Kir Royale. The martini was very dry; there had only been a few drops of Noilly Prat on the ice before it ended up in the glass.

They clinked glasses.

Winter looked out through the window. It looked like winter out there. He could see his mirror image in the glass. It was blurry. He saw the glass in his hand. He saw Angela.

"Do you know what we're celebrating tonight?" Angela said, looking up from the menu.

"Of course."

"But you didn't say anything when I booked the table. Or the babysitter, for that matter."

"Did you want to test me, Angela?"

"Of course."

"Do you believe me, then?"

"No."

He took the box from the inner pocket of his jacket and handed it over. It wasn't large. He could have hidden it in his hand.

"So do you believe me now?"

"How could you hide your true intent for so long, Erik?"

"'Intent'? Don't you mean 'present'?"

"How could you keep it up like that?"

"That's my job."

20

Winter's cell phone rang at the same time the appetizer was placed on the table. He smelled the fresh, oven-browned herbs that lay like a little brush on the plate. He would use them to paint the scampi.

He answered reluctantly.

"Where are you, Erik?"

It was Halders.

Winter told him where he was.

"I'm not far from there," Halders said. "Västra Hamngatan."

"The fitness center?"

"You could put it that way."

"What do you want?"

"I met Paula's boyfriend here. Or whatever we should call him. He didn't like that term."

"Are you sure?! Is it him?"

"Nina Lorrinder's the one to ask. She's sure."

"What does he say?"

"He's not saying much. He doesn't like this."

"Where is he now?" Winter asked.

He saw Angela's questioning look over the table. He could still smell the scents of everything that was on his deep, oblong plate. But not for much longer. Another thirty seconds and it would all be ruined.

"He's standing two meters away," Halders answered.

"Do you want to bring him in?" Winter asked.

"I think I'll question him a little more first," Halders said. "Then I'll see. I don't think he'll leave the city."

"Call me in an hour."

"What will Angela say?"

"Just call me."

"I might call before then," said Halders.

The boyfriend looked like a man of thirty. He still had his hair. Halders was suspicious of men who still had their hair; that went for everyone, from drunks to financiers. For that matter, most financiers were drunks.

The boyfriend didn't look like a drunk. He had an open face. There was something unfinished about it, some features that hadn't been outlined yet. It would take a few years. Some people drank their way to a face, especially actors; there was a particular purpose for it. But that took time, too.

Halders wasn't sure that he would have remembered this face if he'd seen it only a few times. And anyway, it looked like so many other faces in this place. Maybe it was the exercise that did it, the aerobics. Their appearances became streamlined.

"I only spoke with her a few times," the boyfriend said. "That was all."

"Listen here, Johan . . ."

"Jonas."

"Listen here, Jonas. We're just trying to find out as much as we can about Paula."

They were sitting in the café. Halders wanted it that way. It was far enough from the next table after he'd rearranged things a little in there.

"I'm happy to help," said Jonas.

"What do you do, Jonas?"

"What?"

"Where do you work?"

"Uh . . . I'm unemployed right now."

"How well did you know Paula?"

Jonas looked confused. That was the point. Not all questions needed an immediate follow-up. Jonas looked somewhere, as though the witness who'd pointed him out would step forward and explain that it had all been a mistake. But he hadn't met the witness. Lorrinder had left without showing herself after she'd recognized him.

"But I already told you that I didn't know her."

"You were just talking to Paula a little?"

"Yes."

"Isn't that what knowing someone means?"

"Well, it—"

"How did you two happen to start talking?"

"Can't you take it a little slower?"

"Is this moving too fast for you, Jonas? Don't you have time to think?"

"What, I ca—"

"What did you talk about, you and Paula?"

"Nothing, really."

"Is that common?"

"What part?"

"Talking about nothing? Is that what you usually do?"

Jonas looked around in the café, as though the other patrons might hear him, or rather Halders. Halders was leaning over the table.

"Don't you like this, Jonas? Should we go to my place instead?"

"To your place?"

"You know what I mean."

"I don't understand your . . . tone. I haven't done anything."

"You didn't contact us after Paula's death."

Jonas didn't answer.

"Did you hear what I said?" Halders asked.

"Yes. But . . . what could I have done? Or said? Said to you?"

"She was murdered. Did you know that?"

Jonas nodded and mumbled something.

"I didn't catch that," Halders said.

"Yes. Yeah. I . . . read it."

"Read it where?"

"Where? It was . . . at home."

"In which paper?"

"It was . . . *GP*." He looked around and then at Halders again. "I think."

"A woman you know is murdered. It wasn't a car accident or something. She was murdered, for God's sake! It happened a quick ten- or fifteen-minute walk from here. It might have happened the same week you met her." Halders leaned closer. "Maybe it happened the same day?"

Jonas recoiled. Halders could see drops of sweat on his forehead. It might have been left over from working out, but the kid hadn't done his workout yet. He probably wouldn't get his workout tonight.

"What do you mean?"

"I don't mean anything. I'm asking."

"I didn't meet her that week."

"So you checked out what week it was?"

"I read—"

"You read, but you didn't react?"

"Yes, I did re—"

"No, Jonas, you didn't react. You didn't contact us."

Jonas didn't answer.

"So what did you and Paula talk about?"

The appetizer was gone; the main course was on the table. Turbot, melted butter, horseradish, simple as hell and just as expensive. A grand cru from Bergheim.

"Are you waiting for Halders to call?" Angela asked.

"Yes."

"Try to eat a little now, my friend."

"I'm glad you understand," Winter said.

"I have a few questions, but I'll wait for the coffee."

"If there is any coffee."

"Have a bit of fish now, Erik. Doesn't it look nice?"

He looked down at the fish. A whole turbot, the skin partially rolled down, the wonderful flesh underneath, like a silk sheet under a velvet coverlet. He lifted a large piece onto his warm plate, sprinkled horseradish over it, ladled on the frothy butter. The boiled potatoes were good here. Good potatoes were rare in Swedish restaurants. Potatoes were this country's national food, but they were worthless at restaurants. It's strange, he thought. In Alsace the sauerkraut is almost always perfect. He took a little sip of the wine. Not to mention the wine. He put down his glass. Best to take it easy. The telephone might ring at any time with any damn manner of bad news. Or good. They run together. The worst news is often the best news.

"Have you talked to Siv yet?" Angela asked.

"Yes . . . I guess I have. Are you thinking of something in particular?"

"Is she feeling better?"

"I didn't know she was feeling worse."

Angela didn't say anything.

"Isn't she feeling well?" Winter asked.

"She's been feeling dizzy again."

"Well, what is it?"

"I don't know, Erik. We've talked about that. She needs to take it easy. And she needs a real, thorough examination."

"Examination of what?"

Her body, he thought in answer to his own question. The shell of thoughts. Yes. Reinforced with nearly fifty years of alcohol and nicotine. If I keep at it, I'll become my mother's son.

"We're going down together," he said. "You know that."

Angela lifted some fish over to her plate. She gave him only a quick glance.

"Think of that little place by the old soccer field," Winter said, pouring more wine for her. "Those two tables on the sidewalk."

"Are you in Marbella now?"

"I sure am. That grilled pepper salad. The garlic shrimp. Those were no average garlic shrimp."

"Was that where we went one time after midnight? Was it that place?"

"It sure was."

"Mmm."

"Exactly. That about sums it up." He smiled. "The cook blew fresh life into the coals again. There were still a few sea bass on ice."

"Wasn't it the waiter?"

"They helped each other."

"The waiter looked like he had a chimney sweep's face when he brought the fish," Angela said.

Winter's cell phone rang.

"Yes?"

"We're up in the department," Halders said. "Perhaps you could come over here pretty soon."

21

They finished their dinner. They didn't want dessert after all. Winter drank his espresso while he paid.

"Halders doesn't call if he doesn't need to," he said, out on the square.

Angela nodded.

"Will you be there all night?" she asked.

"If I am, then maybe it will all be over tomorrow."

"Do you think that guy will admit to anything?"

"Halders wouldn't have brought him into the station if he didn't suspect something."

"Maybe he was just nervous." She looked at him. "Anyone could get nervous when Halders is asking questions, couldn't they?"

"Now I'll be the one asking questions," Winter said.

Halders had sent a car and they went via Vasaplatsen.

"Good night, then," Angela said as she climbed out.

"I'll call in a few hours," he said.

"Call my cell," she said. "Elsa has trouble falling asleep again if she wakes up."

She would set her phone on silent. It would light up the room when he called. She would read something, maybe tropical medicine. No. Marbella isn't tropical yet, she'd said just now, as they were sitting at the restaurant. But soon, he had said. It's getting warmer everywhere on earth, he'd said, and looked out into the Nordic night. Except here, he had added, up here by us. Incidentally, do you know what malaria means? Bad air, he'd answered, before she had time to open her mouth. Everyone knew that.

The car turned down from Vasaplatsen and continued east on Allén. This is the street I've driven on more than any other in this city. The pigs are trawling.

The city lights flashed by, light and dark, sun and shadow, dawn and dusk. That was what he liked most of all down south: the dawns and dusks over the Mediterranean. Over Africa.

"Okay," said the police inspector at the wheel, braking outside of the main entrance.

"Thanks," said Winter, and he climbed out and the car drove off, turning back out into the October night. A fog had suddenly swept in from the sea. The car disappeared off into the gray before Winter had made it through the doors. He inhaled the moist air. It didn't feel good. He would exchange it for cigar smoke later.

The air was lighter in the interrogation room, as though someone had opened a window that looked out onto a different evening.

The guy was sitting on the chair. His hair hung down over his eyes, as though he had combed it forward to hide his identity. But it was known. His name was Jonas. The name didn't tell Winter anything; first names seldom did. He didn't recognize the guy, or the man: Winter knew that he was thirty years old.

The question was what he was doing here.

"My name is Erik Winter," he introduced himself. "I'm a detective chief inspector."

The man nodded without saying his name.

Winter picked up the form that lay on the table and read the topmost lines. The man's name was indeed Jonas. He had a relatively unusual last name, which didn't tell Winter anything either. Yet he read it again, along with the first name. There was something vaguely familiar about the name. He lifted his gaze and observed the man. There was nothing in his face that Winter recognized.

"Why am I sitting here?" said Jonas Sandler.

"We just want to ask a few questions."

"That's what your colleague said, too. Now you're saying the same thing. But I still don't understand why I'm sitting here."

"It's quieter here," said Winter.

"Surely you don't think that I had anything . . . anything to do with Paula being murdered?"

Winter didn't answer. He observed the man's face again. It wasn't just the name. There was something else, too.

"Do you really think that?" Sandler repeated. "Then you're crazy."

"Have I seen you before?" Winter asked.

"What?"

"Have we met before?"

"What do you mean?"

"Exactly what I'm saying." Winter sought the man's eyes. "I think I recognize you."

"You think I'm some old thief, you mean?"

"No."

"Is this a new method of interrogation?"

"Have you ever had anything to do with the police?" Winter asked. "Before. When you were younger, maybe." He put down the form. "Where you were . . . a witness to something, for example?"

Then he saw it. Then he remembered. The boy's face, and his name, and the place they had stood. A few quick pictures came into his head, click, click: The dusk. The grove of trees. The dog. The hand.

It's him. This is that boy.

"Now that you mention it . . ." Sandler said, looking up. "When I was ten or so I talked to a policeman about something . . . that I'd seen."

"It was me," Winter said.

"That was almost twenty years ago," said Sandler.

Winter nodded.

"I don't remember what you looked like," said the boy who had now become a man. Winter remembered the boy. He would be able to describe his face now.

"I don't remember the faces of any adults from when I was a child." The boy swept out with his hand. "I have to look at a picture."

"It's like that for me, too," said Winter.

"But how could you remember me?" Sandler asked. "Isn't it the same if you turn it around?"

Watch out now, Erik. This is an interrogation. You can't let it meander off into different sorts of memories.

"I was working," he said. "There was something to connect it with." He stood up from his chair. "We had gone out to investigate something."

"I remember," said Sandler. "But what happened? What was it that happened in that apartment in our stairwell?"

"We never found out," Winter answered.

"Hadn't there been some kind of fight?"

"We never found that out, either."

"They said that there was blood in there. In the apartment."

"Who said that?" Winter asked.

"The neighbors."

Winter nodded without saying anything more. At the moment, this was a conversation, not an interrogation. Maybe that was good.

"So nothing happened, you mean?" Sandler asked.

"Not that we know of."

"What about the blood?" The boy leaned forward. Winter saw him as "the boy." "You're not allowed to answer that, are you?"

"According to the man who lived in the apartment, there had been an accident," Winter said.

"So you found him? The guy who had an accident?"

"Yes. The same night."

"What about his wife? I remember that he had a wife."

The boy made that gesture again, as though he were wiping away something in the air. "I don't remember what she looked like, but there was someone."

"We found her, too."

"What kind of accident was it?"

"Kitchen accident," said Winter. "I won't say any more."

"Kitchen accident," Sandler repeated. "Did someone die?"

"No."

"That's good."

It was as though the boy was saying it to himself. But he should know. He lived there.

"We didn't find the hand, either," said Winter.

The boy gave a start.

"We didn't find any hand," said Winter.

"No," said the boy curtly, as though it went without saying that it couldn't be found.

"Did you really see it?" Winter asked.

"Yes."

"It could have been your imagination. Or something else that you saw. A tree branch."

"No."

"We didn't find it."

"I saw it. Zack saw it. It was like he went crazy. I don't know if you remember that. If you remember Zack. My dog."

"Of course I remember."

Sandler didn't say anything more. He had once said everything he knew about the hand he'd seen.

"How is Zack?" Winter asked.

The boy didn't answer.

Winter repeated his question.

"He disappeared," the boy answered.

"What happened?"

"I don't know. He was just gone one day."

"That's too bad."

"Don't try to be polite."

"I'm not trying to be polite."

"Zack was old even then."

Winter nodded.

"I looked for him for a long time. I was still little then. But I never found him. And no one else did either." Sandler looked Winter straight in the eye. "Maybe he just forgot where he lived."

"Maybe."

"Weren't there stains on those stones in that grove of trees?" the boy asked. "Or whatever it was. I know I remember some stains."

"I can't say anything about that," said Winter.

"So there were stains."

"Where do you live now, Jonas?"

"Not far from there." He named an address. "We people from Hisingen don't leave the island."

"I've heard that."

"That's how it is with island folk."

"I've heard that, too."

The boy was moving in a slightly spasmodic way now. He was speaking spasmodically, nervously. More than usual, Winter guessed.

"But not everyone knows that it's actually an island. Sweden's third largest, I think."

"And yet there are bridges and ferries to and from it," Winter said.

"There are bridges on the mainland, too."

"How is your mother?" Winter asked.

"Good."

"Does she still live on Hisingen, too?"

"In the same apartment."

Winter nodded.

"It looks the same out there. Even the grove of trees is still there."

"Did you ever show it to Paula?" Winter asked.

"Oh, that's what this was all about," Sandler said.

"What do you mean?"

"You asked about Zack and Mom and all of that before just so you could ask about this."

Winter tried to watch the boy's face. He didn't look paranoid. It seemed more like just a statement.

"I didn't know that it was you sitting here when I came into the room," Winter said.

"I don't believe that," said Sandler.

"Did you show her the grove?" Winter asked again.

"Why would I?" The boy looked even more like a boy now. It was as though he had changed in the last few minutes. His facial features had become more vague and simultaneously more clear.

Winter thought about the boy's story, the one from before. He thought about Paula. He hadn't seen any connection between Paula's hand and the hand Jonas had told him about eighteen years ago. He hadn't even thought of it before. Why would he have? He had thought about Ellen Börge. That was a more concrete connection back in time. No, not concrete. He couldn't find the right word. Maybe there wasn't one.

"Why would I?" the boy repeated.

Winter was smoking outside the front doors. The fog had lifted. The silhouette of Ullevi was visible on the other side of Skånegatan. The pillars of the floodlights rose toward the sky like the abandoned cranes on the other side of the river. The Hisingen side.

I'll have to go over there, he thought, and he blew the smoke out into the air, which had become clearer, as the boy's face had inside. He thought of him only as the boy. He couldn't picture him with a woman, not that way. Maybe because there was nothing to see. I'll have to go over there. Hisingen. I don't know why. Maybe I'll know when I get there.

He heard someone come out through the door and turned around.

"What did he say?" Halders asked.

"Do you remember the Martinssons?" Winter asked back.

"No. What's that? Who?"

"The Martinsson couple. Their kitchen in Hisingen. We went out there eighteen years ago. Some guy had reported a fi—"

"Yeah, yeah, now I remember," Halders interrupted him. "He had cut his wrist."

"So he said."

"It was his blood."

"Not all of it," said Winter.

"That sure was old," Halders said.

"What do you mean, Fredrik?"

"Another old kitchen injury," Halders said.

"With who involved?"

"Hell, Erik, we're talking about a generation back."

"The new generation is sitting in there. The guy. Jonas."

"I'm not following."

Winter explained.

"I never met him as a boy," Halders said.

"He's sitting in there."

"What do you mean, Erik?"

"It's like the boy he was is sitting in there now."

"Oh."

"Do you know what I mean?"

"No, but you don't need to explain."

Winter smiled.

"I remember the hand, of course," Halders said. "Or rather, the boy imagining it."

"You think it was his imagination?"

"Erik, we didn't find anything."

"Like this time," Winter said under his breath.

"What? What did you say?"

"Like now," Winter said, "we can't figure out what the hand means. Paula's hand."

Halders didn't say anything. He seemed to be studying the concrete arms that held the floodlights in place up in Ullevi's sky. Within the next few nights they would shine like the sun.

Halders turned toward Winter.

"There are coincidences in the world, Erik."

"Like this boy, you mean? He's a walking coincidence?"

"I don't know what he is. I guess that's what he's going to tell us, right?"

Winter could see a film of sweat at the boy's hairline. This time it couldn't be left over from his workout. It wasn't particularly warm in the room. The air in there was not so good now. It had a particular smell, like nowhere else. Many people had sweated in this room. Maybe there was the scent of everything that had been said here, all the words that had been spoken. All the lies, excuses, evasions. A library of lies? Why not? Without books, with just the stench of sleazy words.

Once in a while the truth had been spoken. Had sprung forth like a sudden light in the darkness. A floodlight. After that, everyone had been able to go home, to their cells, to their apartments, to houses in the suburbs. To their graves, he thought suddenly. The real protagonists were always there at the interrogations. The dead. The victims. When the rare truth was illuminated, they were at peace.

"How did you meet Paula, Jonas?"

"I've told you, haven't I?"

"No."

"Haven't you asked?"

"How did you meet?" Winter kept his voice neutral. "Just answer the question."

"Meet . . . we talked to each other a few times. A couple of times. I did say that to your . . . colleague." Jonas looked up after having studied the surface of the table for a long time. "I told him everything I knew."

"How did it happen, when you met?" Winter asked.

"I don't actually remember. It was probably in the café. Maybe we were sitting at the same table." He looked around the room, as though it had transformed into the café and he was trying to find the table where they'd sat. "Yes, that's how it was. I was sitting there and she came up and sat down. It was probably the only free chair."

"Was she alone?"

"Yes . . . I think there was just one chair free."

"What happened then?"

"Happened . . . nothing happened. I guess we said something, I don't remember what. Just being polite. I don't know. And then I guess I left. Or maybe she did."

"When did you meet the next time?"

"We didn't *meet*, as I've told you a hundred times. We ran into each other a few times over there. At Friskis & Svettis. That's all. How many times do I need to say it?"

A hundred times, Winter thought. You might need to say it one hundred times, and then a hundred more.

"But you became acquainted with each other, didn't you?"

"Not more than that we talked a little. About like the first time."

"Being polite?"

"What?"

"What did you talk about?"

"Nothing that I actually remember."

"Did you talk about seeing each other another time? Outside of Friskis & Svettis?"

"No."

"Never?"

"No."

"Why not?"

"I don't know how to answer that."

"Weren't you interested?"

"I don't know what you mean."

Winter met his eyes. The boy didn't look like he was challenging him. He didn't look stupid, either.

He wants to buy time. He's trying to think. Think about what?

"Interested in seeing her without workout clothes," Winter said. "Or without any clothes at all." He leaned forward. "You know what I'm talking about, for God's sake."

"We . . . didn't get that far."

"Did you see her talking with anyone else?"

Winter switched tactics, tried another one, a looser one. He could see the boy relax; his body became looser, hardly noticeably, and yet it was body language. Sometimes it was a hundred times more obvious than the other language. It was like a voice. It reveals a hundred times more than the words themselves. But Jonas Sandler's voice didn't reveal much. Maybe it was just revealing the truth, or parts of it.

"Others? No . . . not that I saw."

"What about her friend?"

"Didn't see."

"You never saw her together with her friend?"

"I said no. I never saw her with anyone."

He looked at Winter again. "Although there were always a lot of people, of course, so you couldn't say that someone was alone, exactly."

"Do you have a girlfriend, Jonas?"

"What . . . no."

"Boyfriend?"

"What kind of question is that?"

"Please answer it."

"No, I don't have a boyfriend. I'm not gay."

"Do you live alone?"

"If I don't have a girlfriend, then I guess I live alone, don't I?"

"You can share an apartment. Rent out half the floor. Rent a room. Live in a co-op."

"I live alone," Sandler said. "And you know the address." He moved his shoulders, as though to show that he'd become stiff from sitting there. "I want to go home now. When can I go home?"

"What were you doing the night Paula disappeared?" Winter asked.

"I don't actually know."

"Why don't you know?"

"I don't know what night it was."

"What are you saying?"

Halders was sitting on the other side of Winter's desk. The desk lamp illuminated the lower portion of his face. He didn't look nice. Soon it would be Halloween, a new tradition of fear in Scandinavia. Halders wouldn't need a mask.

"We're letting him go home."

"Mm-hmm."

"But we're not letting him go."

"So he doesn't have an alibi," Halders said.

"There's something I can't put my finger on," said Winter.

"When isn't there?"

"It's about . . . then. The past."

"When isn't it?"

"Have you thought any more about that trip to Hisingen? Eighteen years ago?"

"No. Why would I?"

"I never met the witness," Winter said. "The one who called it in."

"Not much to meet," Halders said. "He had walked by the door and heard the racket and called. He didn't know the Martinssons."

"Who was it he was supposed to visit in that stairwell?"

"Don't remember," said Halders. "I'll have to look in the archive. Don't even know if I wrote it down."

"Would you be able to check?"

"When? Now?"

"Yes."

"Okay," Halders said, getting up. "But what's the hurry?"

"I don't know."

The traffic was starting to thin out on the Älvsborg bridge. There were a hundred times a hundred lights down there. The evening sky was cloudless, deep blue over the North Sea.

Metzer. His name was Anton Metzer. He had been on his way to visit a man in Martinsson's stairwell, but he didn't make it all the way there that night. Winter had written down the name. It told him nothing. He hadn't interrogated everyone who lived in the stairwell. After half a day there hadn't been anything to interrogate about. No one had asked questions about a hand that had been seen by an eleven-year-old boy and his dog.

No one had talked to Metzer after Halders's visit the same evening. There hadn't been anything else to talk about, and there wasn't now, either. Still, Winter felt a slight agitation, no, not that . . . a foreboding. A foreboding about the past. Could you say that? Why am I driving out there right now?

The interrogation of the boy had told him something that he didn't yet understand but still had the sense to follow up on. His primary reason for going out wasn't to talk with the boy's mother, but he would also try to do that.

He would walk into that strange little grove of trees. Strange? Yes. It had been strange to stand there. The boy's evident silence. Fear. Yes. The dog's teeth. The dog had also become strangely silent.

Winter parked in the parking lot alongside the buildings. He could be anywhere in the city at all. There were a hundred times a hundred residential areas like this one. He recognized the place because he knew he'd been here, but that was the only reason. He walked across the yard. The playground was in the electric half light, a glow that was more white than black. The grove of trees lay at the far end, and now he knew where he was for real, as though the last time he had been here was yesterday.

He walked in among the few trees and turned on his flashlight. He suddenly heard a dog barking somewhere. The ground turned white when he shone the light on it. They had stood here. Somewhere down there had been something the boy said he'd seen.

They hadn't found anything.

Winter shone the light on the ground for a long time, but he didn't see anything that didn't belong there. Just stone, dirt, gravel, dead leaves. A new autumn, one of many since the last time.

He walked back toward the playground. It was like coming out of the forest.

He felt the breeze in the stairwell, like the last time he had been here. He remembered it. It remained even when the door down there swung closed, whirling up and down like a lost soul.

He rang the doorbell. It said "Metzer" on the nameplate, no first name. He rang again. It pealed inside, a ring that was left over from the past. Winter hadn't given notice of his arrival. Metzer could be out.

The door opened a few inches.

"Mr. Metzer? Anton Metzer?"

Winter could see a pair of eyes, part of a forehead. Dark hair.

"Yes?"

Winter introduced himself.

"May I come in for a bit?"

"Why?"

"I have a few questions I'd like to ask."

"What is this about?"

"May I come in?"

The door opened. The man took a few steps back. He was dressed in a white shirt and brown pants that looked like they were made of gabardine. The slippers he had on his feet looked comfortable. His face was aged. It smelled like food in the hall, a late dinner. Winter heard voices from somewhere within, a television. There was an old rotary phone on a small table in the hall.

"Well . . . I guess you should come in, then," Metzer said, gesturing into the apartment.

They went into the living room. There was a debate program on the television; people were sitting on two facing benches and Winter heard an agitated voice say, "That's the stupidest thing I've ever heard" and saw that it was a woman with large hair. Stupid things were always being said on TV, but few people dared to say so on the tube itself. Before Winter had time to hear any defense of the stupidity, Metzer turned the debate off with a button on the TV.

Winter explained the reason for his visit.

"That was a long time ago," Metzer said.

Winter nodded.

"I don't remember you," Metzer said.

"It was my colleague whom you spoke to."

"Mm-hmm."

"Did you know the Martinssons?"

"No, no. I never exchanged a word with them."

"But you became concerned when you walked past their door?"

"Yes."

"What did it sound like?"

"Like someone was about to kill someone else."

"Have you heard anything like that before?"

"Here? No."

"Did you talk to them afterward? Either of them?"

"No. Why would I do that?" Metzer changed position on the sofa. "And they moved just a few weeks later, you know, or maybe it was even sooner."

Winter nodded.

"I just became concerned. That was why I called the police."

"Who was it that you were supposed to visit that evening?" Winter asked.

"It was a neighbor over there. I told them that then, didn't I?"

"Yes."

"Well, there you go."

Winter read the name from his notebook. He remembered it, but he still used the notebook. It looked as though he had done his homework, prepared himself. He didn't want it to look as though he'd fluttered across the bridge by chance.

"He wasn't home, I believe?"

"No."

"So you had time to ring the doorbell that evening? At his place?"

"Yes . . . I think I did, didn't I?"

"You don't remember?"

"No . . . It probably says in the witness statement, or whatever it's called."

"It says that you didn't visit him."

"Then that must be how it was."

Metzer looked at Winter. There was a line on his face that ran from one temple down across his cheek. It looked like a scar left by a sword. Metzer. He could be of German nobility.

"It wasn't . . . actually him I was going to visit," Metzer said after a little while.

"Sorry?"

"His name was on the door, but he didn't live there."

Winter nodded. He felt something across the top of his head, a faint excitement. That was how his body reacted. It came without warning.

Please tell me, Anton.

"There was a woman living there, subletting. And her daughter. It was just for a little while."

Winter nodded again.

"They only lived there for a month or two."

He fell silent.

"Yes?" said Winter.

"I talked to the woman a little bit out in the yard. And the girl. And I . . . helped them a little. They needed help. Nothing was going on between her, the mom, and me, nothing like that. I was too old for that, even then. But I guess I felt sorry for them."

"Why?"

"I don't know. They were a little . . . lost. Alone." He seemed to give a small smile. "Like me, maybe."

"You were on your way to visit them that evening?"

"Yes."

"Why didn't you say anything about that then? Eighteen years ago?"

"No one asked." Metzer rubbed his chin. It looked newly shaven. "And it wasn't important. After all, surely it wasn't something that would be of interest to the police, was it?"

22

Winter was standing in the yard again. He heard a dog barking again, from behind the grove of trees. The barking was carried by the wind. It circled around the playground as though it had wings. As Winter passed the playground, he thought of the boy. He must have sat there many times. The wind moved the swings in a faint back-and-forth motion. It was as though someone were sitting there, an invisible child.

As he walked up the stairs, he had a strong sense that he would learn something important in the next hour. Something *important,* something he had suspected when he'd stood out in the yard and sat in Metzer's apartment where the scent of loneliness and quiet desperation had sat over everything like dust.

He rang the doorbell. It must be the same one as back then. Nothing seemed to have changed here; there was nothing new about what he saw around him. Nothing had been renovated, improved, spruced up. The money had run out before it had reached out here. There was none of that money for those who lived here. There was no money at all.

Winter rang the doorbell and heard a single chime.

The woman who opened the door had a towel wound around her hair. He recognized her immediately.

She recognized him.

"How may I help you?" she said. And then: "Has something happened?"

"May I come in?" Winter said.

"Has something happened to Jonas?"

It was as though he were back in this place eighteen years ago, in this stairwell. He had only gone out for a little while, and come back, and the boy had disappeared.

"You recognize me?" he said.

"Winter," she said. "I remember that name."

"I recognize you, too," he said.

"It's been many years." She looked behind his shoulder, as though to see whether he had come alone. "Many years have gone by."

"May I come in?"

She took a few steps to the side, as though to let him pass. He stepped into the hall. All these halls I've stepped into during all these years. I could have sold vacuum cleaners, or encyclopedias. May I come in for a moment and sell you something? Steal something. Steal time.

Winter saw the playground through the window, or maybe it could be called a French balcony. The glass went all the way down to the floor.

"What is it that's happened?" she asked again. She had removed the towel from her head in the bathroom, and she'd come back and sat across from Winter. Her hair was still damp. The lighting in the room made it shine.

"Is it about Jonas?" she continued.

"Why do you ask that?"

"Is it that strange?" She looked straight at him. "Why else would you come here?"

"Nothing has happened to him," Winter said. "But I ran into him. Recently."

"Why?"

There was alarm in her eyes, but Winter couldn't determine why. There could be several reasons for it, most of them natural.

"Have you heard about the murder of a woman by the name of Paula Ney?" he asked. He could have chosen to ask her whether she recognized the name, just the name, but he wanted to see her reaction.

"Paula? Paula . . . who? A murder? Why would I have heard of that?"

"Paula Ney. N-e-y."

"How awful. No . . . I don't know. Might I have read about it? Might it have been in the paper?"

Göteborgs-Posten was on the table. Winter could see that it was open to the TV-guide portion. He could see the TV in the corner, to the right of the French balcony. It was an older model, but Winter couldn't tell how old it was. He didn't know much about televisions.

"There's been quite a bit about it in the paper," he said, nodding toward the television, "and they've talked about it on TV."

"I might have seen something . . ." She looked down at the paper and then toward the TV. "But why did you come here to say that?"

There were several answers to that question. It would be a long story.

Her face had transformed during the last minute. He had said that a woman had been murdered. And that he had recently run into her son. The alarm had spread out from her eyes.

"Surely Jonas doesn't have anything to do with this?" She leaned forward. "He doesn't, does he?"

"He met this woman a few times," Winter said.

"Oh, God."

"Have you met her?"

For a second it looked as though she would say yes, just because it might help her son, without her knowing why or how. But maybe it would be just as well to say no. Maybe the truth was better now.

"No," she answered.

"Paula Ney," said Winter. "Jonas never talked about her?"

"No."

"Are you completely sure of that?"

"Yes. What is this? What has he done? Surely he hasn't . . ."

Winter didn't say anything.

"Is he"—she searched for the word—"a suspect?"

Winter told her about Friskis & Svettis. He told her portions of Jonas's story.

She appeared to relax.

"Well, then that's what happened."

Winter heard a dog barking again and turned his head.

"You believe him, don't you?" she said. "Why wouldn't you believe him?"

Winter turned back toward her. Anne. Her name was Anne. It said so on the door, Anne Sandler.

"All I did was talk to Jonas," Winter said. "That's all. We talk to many people when we're working on an investigation. We have to. Jonas is one of the witnesses, an important witness. He was one of the last people to see Paula."

He saw her relax. Her alarm left parts of her face. He had seen a twitch at her temple, and a nervous movement across her mouth. Now the alarm was creeping back into her eyes again. It seemed to remain there.

"When did you last see Jonas?" he asked in an easy tone.

"Would you like coffee?" she said, and began to stand up. "Why, I forgot to ask you if you want a cup of coffee?"

"Yes, please," Winter answered. "Can you just tell me when you last saw each other?"

It had been some time since they'd seen each other. She hadn't been able to tell him exactly how long. A month or so. That was a long time. She couldn't give Jonas an alibi for the time that Winter was working with. He didn't mention anything about an alibi. That might come later, another day, week, month.

Winter didn't ask why she so seldom saw her son, or why he didn't see her. If it was, in fact, seldom. Who was he to judge? How many years had it been between the next-to-last and the last time he saw his father? And then it had been too late. How many times had he seen his mother in recent years? More and more often, at least. And maybe too often, this coming winter.

They were in the kitchen now. Winter had suggested it. They had sat here eighteen years ago. The chair where Jonas had sat was empty.

Winter remembered which chair it was. Memory sometimes worked that way.

He had a few more questions.

"I understand that a woman and her daughter lived on the fourth floor in this building?"

She turned around with a few buns on a plate that she'd taken out of the microwave oven.

"That time," Winter continued, "when I was here the first time. Eighteen years ago."

"I see . . ."

"Is that true?"

"Yes . . . I think it was . . ."

"How well did you know them?"

"It wasn't long. They didn't live here for more than a month or so, I think, maybe two. It was a very short time."

"But you still remember that woman, and her daughter?"

Sandler nodded.

"Why is that?"

"What do you mean?" she said.

She was standing at the kitchen counter.

"If it was such a short time," Winter said.

"Well . . . I suppose we saw each other a few times out at the playground. Or in the yard. And I suppose Jonas played with that girl a little bit. They were about the same age." Sandler took a step toward the table. "There weren't very many children here then. It was mostly older people here." She walked up to the table and sat down. "And now they're even older. Or we are, I should say."

"What were their names?" Winter asked. "What was their last name?"

"I . . . don't remember."

"Was it a difficult name to remember?"

"I don't actually know. Isn't it easier to remember a difficult name?"

"What was the woman's first name?"

"I don't remember that either." She pushed the coffee cup forward a bit on the table. "That's strange. I really ought to."

"What was the girl's name, then?"

Sandler appeared to consider this.

"I think her name was Eva," she said after a bit. "I think I remember because Jonas said that name."

"Did you ever visit them? Did you go to their home?"

"No."

"Why not?"

"It . . . just never happened. I suppose we didn't have time to get to know each other well enough." She looked around in the kitchen. "And they were never in here." She looked suddenly at the empty chair beside Winter, as though it reminded her of something, too. "No, wait, I think the girl was here once."

"Was there any man in the family?"

"Not that I know of. I didn't see anyone. She never talked about any man."

Winter could see in her face that it had suddenly become painful to talk, that he had reminded her of something else that she didn't want to think about, or talk about.

"Why are you asking about her? About them?" she said, looking at him. "What do they have to do with . . . the murder?"

"It's about that night," Winter said. "When we came here. When there was a fight in the Martinssons' apartment."

"I remember that you asked about that. Back then. I think I told you what I knew about them, the Martinssons. It wasn't much, I remember that."

Winter nodded.

"But what do they have to do with it? With that fight? Or with anything else? The mom and the girl, I mean."

"I don't know," Winter said. "Probably nothing."

"And what do we have to do with all of this?" she asked. "Other than that Jonas apparently spoke a few words to the woman who . . . died?"

"What happened to them?" Winter asked, without answering Sandler's question. "The mom and the daughter. Do you know? Where did they move?"

"I don't know. One day they were just gone."

"Did she say anything beforehand? The mom?"

"No."

"Or the girl? She didn't say anything to Jonas?"

"No. I asked him but he said that she was just gone." Sandler looked out through the French balcony. She saw what Winter saw: a playground faintly lit by the electric light, like a yellow shadow. They could see the swings from here, and some kind of jungle gym. Behind the jungle gym was a slide.

"He was sad because she just disappeared, without saying good-bye," said Sandler.

Mario Ney called Winter's cell phone as he was on his way back over the bridge. The traffic was light. It was past ten o'clock. Winter could see a ferry on its way in, abreast of Älvsborg Fortress. It was a clear night.

"Have you learned anything else?" Ney said. "Has anyone seen Elisabeth?"

"Not yet," said Winter.

"Someone must have seen her."

"Where are you now, Mario?"

"I'm at home. I'm sitting here by the telephone. She might call. Or someone else. You, for example. You might call. You said you would call me."

"I was going to do it tonight. In a while."

"You're just saying that."

Winter could still see the ferry in the corner of his eye. A floating ten-story building bathed in its own light. As the ferry glided into the harbor it looked like it was on its way to a party. From up here, the whole city looked like it was on its way to a party.

"How long have you lived out there, Mario? In the apartment in Tynnered?"

"What? Why do you ask?"

"How long have you had the apartment?" Winter repeated.

"The ap— Oh, we've had it for a long time. Since Paula was little. Why?"

"How little?"

"What is this? What are you getting at?"

"How old was she when you moved in there?"

Winter heard Ney mumbling something, as though he was talking to himself.

Winter repeated the question.

"Five," said Ney. "I think she was five."

The sheets were on the third shelf on the right. But in order to get to them, the maid had to pass another shelf and then follow the wall to the right as it curved like a bow. For that reason, one could say that the supply closet was almost made up of two rooms. A person standing in the doorway couldn't see the inner room.

The maid had had her hands full of what was now on the floor, spread out where she'd dropped it. She had screamed. It had been heard out in the stairwell and down on the floor below and up on the floor above.

She hadn't been able to move for the first minute, just stood there and screamed, just a loud and long scream.

Elisabeth Ney's body lay on a bed of blindingly white sheets. Almost everything in the supply closet was blindingly white.

Winter tried to see everything at once.

He was the first one inside.

One of the hotel managers had called the police, and three colleagues had been waiting outside the door when Winter arrived. Ringmar was on his way, along with Aneta Djanali.

The maid was resting in one of the hotel's staff rooms. It was uncertain whether she would be able to say more than a few words to Winter tonight.

She had never seen anything like this.

He walked carefully around the body. The bed of sheets was fifteen or twenty inches high.

This wasn't a coincidence. The murderer had prepared it. When? While Elisabeth Ney . . . waited? Or earlier? In preparation for something the murderer knew would happen? Yes. No. Yes. Yes. Someone with access to this room. This hotel. Someone with access to hotels. An old hotel. Right in between Revy and Gothia Towers, which was a long way. Not luxurious and not shabby. A hotel for the average citizen. Like Elisabeth Ney. How did she get in here? In this damn closet? She hadn't checked in to the hotel, he knew that already, and above all she hadn't checked in here. Winter waited for the doctor. The doctor. Start healing. Tell me whether she died here. Winter studied the body. He thought it had happened here. How else would it have happened? He got up and walked back through the strangely shaped closet. Two police officers were standing guard out in the stairwell. Winter asked them to move so he could push open the door to see its front side. There was nothing there, it was blank; no signs, no numbers. Why here? he thought.

"Why here?" said Ringmar. Djanali was standing next to him. She was observing Ney's dead body and her surroundings. It was a scene.

"He wanted us to see it this way," she said. "This is how we were supposed to . . . encounter her."

Winter nodded.

"He must have planned it carefully."

"The supply room door wasn't locked," Winter said.

"Why not?" Ringmar asked.

"Inconvenient," Winter said, "the cleaning staff ran in and out of here all the time."

"Well, he must have been here," Djanali said, looking around again, "he must have come here earlier. Maybe several times."

Winter nodded again.

"Someone must have recognized him."

"We'll see," Winter said.

"Or is he so well-known here that no one recognizes him?" said Djanali. "He could come and go as he pleased."

"Good point," said Winter.

"Maybe he still is," said Djanali.

"Could this be where the murderer works?" Ringmar said.

No one commented on what he said.

No one believed it. They would question everyone who worked here; but that was part of the routine. They might get other answers; maybe some would help them.

"Why here?" Ringmar repeated, mostly to himself.

"Because it's a hotel," said Winter.

"This isn't a real room," said Ringmar, "and above all, it's not room number ten."

"That doesn't matter anymore," said Winter, "to him."

"What do you mean?"

"This isn't . . . the same type of murder as Paula's murder." Winter looked down at the body. "It resembles it, but that's not important here. Not that way." He looked up. "It was planned, but not the way he planned Paula's murder. This came afterward. He might not even have planned it this way."

"We don't even know if it's the same murderer," said Ringmar.

"Do you mean that the murderer was . . . forced to murder Elisabeth Ney even though he hadn't planned to?" asked Djanali.

"We'll see," said Winter, and he looked at the body again. It was an unusual situation: leaning over a dead person he had met earlier, had spoken to, asked questions of, listened to. A murder investigation was unusual in and of itself. Most murderers were known minutes after the crime. Sometimes before they even committed it. But even when a murder was investigated, it was very unusual for the investigator to have met the victim previously. It had happened to him before, but only once. He had felt . . . shocked then, and he felt shocked now. The feeling didn't hamper his thinking. Maybe it helped him to think clearly. It got his blood flowing.

Winter left Ringmar and Djanali and walked out into the stairwell. The air felt healthier out there, even if it wasn't. He couldn't think of anything healthy here. All the shades of white reminded him of illness and death. Everything was white in a hospital, a morgue. In a church. White was the color of death in every shade.

His cell phone rang.

"I'm outside now," said Halders.

"Come up," said Winter.

He waited in the stairwell.

Halders went straight into the storeroom when he arrived. The doctor had arrived just before him. It was a man Winter had never met before. He was young, maybe ten years younger than Winter. He appeared to take a deep breath before he stepped in. Winter had had a few words with him.

Halders came out.

"Well, shall we go?"

Mario Ney was waiting at the apartment. Winter had sent a car there from the Frölunda station.

Halders drove through the Tingstad tunnel. The voices on the radio took on another tone, as though they were suddenly speaking another language. Winter had never liked going through tunnels. Once he had gotten stuck in a traffic jam in one of the kilometers-long tunnels in Switzerland, and it hadn't been a pleasant experience. A claustrophobic woman a few cars ahead had gone crazy and started to jump from car roof to car roof toward light and freedom.

Once they got out, Winter had driven into the first rest area and got out, stood still on the firm ground and inhaled as much air as there was, fresh or not. It had been like coming down from a great height.

"It didn't look like it had happened very long ago," Halders said.

"We'll have to see what the doctor says."

"I didn't recognize him," said Halders.

"Neither did I."

"What did Mario Ney say?"

"I haven't told him yet."

"Did he wonder why you wanted to see him?"

"I didn't give him time to," Winter answered.

"I don't think it's the same murderer," Halders said. "That's what I don't think."

Halders turned off of the highway. Winter could see the gray highrises of Västra Frölunda a kilometer away. They rose to the sky like building blocks. A social structure that had gone to hell. Everything was gray today. Gray was yet another shade of white, some kind of white.

"Or the same motive," Halders continued. "That could be it."

"What are the motives?" Winter asked.

"Maybe they don't exist," said Halders. "Except in the murderers' heads."

"The murderer's," said Winter. "They're one and the same."

Halders parked in one of the many empty spaces in the parking lot below the apartment buildings. Winter got out of the car. It wasn't so long ago that I was here. Never thought I'd be coming back with this news.

"Is it possible he'll become violent?" Halders asked.

"I really don't know, Fredrik."

"If he accused us before, he has even greater reason now."

Winter nodded. He had made the decision that Elisabeth Ney needed care. He hadn't put her under guard. He hadn't protected her. Perhaps he hadn't considered it fully, or far enough into the future. How far ahead can you think? To the next murder? He walked across the courtyard. Is that where the boundary lies? Or should you think farther? They passed the playground. It was larger than the one up in Hisingen. There were more swings. He thought of the boy again, and the girl. They had done a search for renters who had subleased an apartment that had been rented by a man whose name Winter didn't know. That renter had moved away a long time ago. Most people had moved away; it was a passing-through area. Could one call it that? Most people moved through, and on, but Metzer had remained, and the boy's mother, Anne.

One of the swings moved in the breeze as they passed, just one, as though an invisible child had started swinging there, too.

Paula sat in that swing, Winter thought.

"The boys are in their places," Halders said.

Winter saw the marked car outside the front door.

"They haven't called, so it's probably okay," Halders continued.

Winter looked up. He saw the windows that belonged to the Ney family's apartment. There were three windows; he remembered that there were three windows that looked out onto the courtyard. There had been three people in that family. He suddenly saw a face in the dark middle window. The face was like a white shadow.

23

"What the hell is this all about?" Mario Ney was already out in the stairwell as Winter and Halders were on their way up. Winter could see the two police officers from Frölunda flanking Ney like bodyguards in uniform. "What's going on?"

"Can we go in?" Winter said.

Ney turned around abruptly, as though to verify the location of the door, that he was standing outside his own home.

"It's Elisabeth? Something's happened to her? Where is she?"

"Mario . . ."

Winter extended his hand, but Ney was already on his way back over the threshold, as though he understood that it was in there that he would get his answers.

"Can we go now?" one of the police officers asked.

"Thanks," Winter said.

"What did he say when you got here?" Halders asked.

"He didn't say anything."

"Nothing?"

"We just came up here. He opened the door and stared at us and then he went back into the apartment again."

"And then you got here," said the other officer. "But he was calm."

"He was acting quite differently just now," Halders said.

"He saw us through the window," Winter said. "He recognized me."

"So you triggered the reaction?"

"He probably feels that he has quite a bit to blame me for."

"He doesn't know the half of it yet," said Halders.

Winter didn't answer. They were on their way into the hall. He could hear his colleagues' footsteps as they clomped down the stairs like elephants in uniform. If none of the neighbors had noticed their visit yet, they would now.

Winter saw Ney's back. The man was standing at the window, as if he was waiting until he could see the uniforms down in the courtyard. He turned around. He looked calmer now. It was as though he knew.

"Can we sit down?" Winter said.

"Just say what you have to say."

"We found Elisabeth. She's dead."

First the good news, Winter thought. We found her. Then the bad. Ney didn't seem to react at first. He looked like he was still waiting to hear Winter's news. He looked from Halders to Winter, back and forth, as if one of them was going to say something.

"Mario . . ."

"How?"

Just that. How. Ney was still standing at the window. It was impossible to see the expression on his face; the light from the window was shining on his back. Winter could see the police car start up beyond the playground, make a U-turn in the parking lot, drive slowly out onto the thoroughfare toward Frölunda. He wished he were sitting in it. Then he could have avoided describing how. He couldn't do that now, wasn't allowed to do that.

"Where?"

Two questions now. The second question suddenly made it easier to answer the first one.

"Odin," Winter said. "Hotel Odin. She ha—"

"What was she doing there?" Ney interrupted. "Where is it?"

"Kungsgatan. But—"

"Another hotel! What the hell is going on?"

Winter heard the increase of sharpness in Ney's voice. He still couldn't see the man's face clearly. It was completely necessary to see it.

"Sit down, Mario."

"I ca—"

"Sit down!"

It was as though Ney understood. He took a few quick steps forward and sat down in the nearest easy chair. Winter sat on the sofa across from him, next to Halders, who had sat down right away.

"We still don't know how," Winter said.

Ney placed his hands over his face. He bent forward. Winter and Halders could see the bald patch on the top of his head.

He dropped his hands and looked up.

"But . . . dead?"

Winter nodded.

"What had she . . . done? What has she done? What happened? How did she die?"

"She was murdered," Winter said.

"When?"

"Sorry?" said Halders.

"When did it happen? Did it happen just now? Today? Did it happen yesterday?" Ney leaned forward. Winter could see the taut skin of his face, the red eyes, the moving hands. "When did it happen?"

"We don't really know yet," said Winter.

"Don't know? Don't know?" Ney was on his way up again. "What *do* you know? You don't know a damn thing!"

"Is there anything we should know?" Winter asked. "Something that you know?"

"What?" Ney sat down again, or fell down, into the easy chair. "What? What?"

His eyes were moving back and forth now, from Winter to Halders. First his daughter and then his wife, Winter thought. He has the right to ask how, and where, and what. Maybe he's right. But we have to ask questions, too.

"I think you understand that we have to ask you what you've been doing for the last twenty-four hours," Winter said.

"What? Me? What does it matter what I've been doing?"

He stood up.

"Other people should be answering that question. Shouldn't they?"

"Like who?" Winter asked.

Ney didn't answer. He looked like he was still waiting for an answer from Winter.

Halders drove back through the tunnel. The traffic had increased; headlights illuminated walls that looked better in darkness.

Mario Ney had refused help. "We'll send over someone for you to talk to," Winter had said. "If you want to stay here."

"I want to be alone," Ney had said.

It was a difficult situation. They could take him in for six hours, maybe six more if he were under suspicion for anything. Under suspicion, the lowest degree. Is he? Winter thought of the fleck of blood inside the knot of the rope that had been tightened around Paula's neck. His daughter's neck. The drop of blood was hers. And there was nothing else to compare it with. No one else. Winter hoped that something would come of the new analyses at SKL. A drop of saliva on the rope that had been wrapped around Elisabeth's neck. Soon they would know. And he would ask Mario politely about a DNA test. A simple test, a swab along the inside of the cheek, across the gums. Something to compare to.

But perhaps Mario needed someone to talk to, to protect him from himself.

"I really want to be alone," he had repeated.

"Don't you have someone you can talk to?" Halders asked. "A friend or a relative."

Ney had shaken his head.

Halders drove out of the tunnel. The October afternoon was slowly sinking into evening. The streetlights had already come on.

"He shouldn't be left alone," Halders said.

"I know."

"Are you going to send someone?"

"Let me think for a minute."

Halders spun through the roundabout and turned onto the highway. The river became visible. A merchant vessel was gliding into the harbor. Winter thought he could see people on the deck, despite the long distance.

"Your minute is up," said Halders.

"There was something about his reaction that made me react," said Winter.

"Didn't he express enough sadness?" Halders turned toward Winter. "Or too much?"

"What did you think?"

"I've seen too many reactions like that," Halders said. "I can't decide until I see him again."

"No."

"Sadness shows up in a thousand different ways. Reactions, delayed reactions. Shock. You know that."

Winter nodded.

"Soon he'll call with all the questions he wants to ask," Halders said.

"We have enough already," Winter said, changing position in his seat. His knee had been rubbing against the dashboard. "A mother and a daughter murdered."

"At least there's a connection there," said Halders.

"Is that some kind of gallows humor?" Winter said.

"No."

They passed the Stena terminal. The lines of cars to the ferry were long. The exhaust fumes rose like smoke from the semi trucks.

"We've tried looking back in Paula's life," Winter said after a little while. "And we haven't gotten very far. But Paula's past probably isn't enough."

"What do you mean?"

"Her mother, Elisabeth. We have to trace her life backward, too."

Halders mumbled something Winter couldn't hear.

"What did you say?"

"Soon we'll be moving more backward than forward in this case. These cases."

"Is it the first time?" Winter said.

Halders didn't answer.

"The whole family's past," Winter said. "There's something we're not getting at there. A big secret."

Halders nodded.

"A big secret," Winter repeated.

"Maybe not just one," said Halders.

Winter didn't need to take out the white hand to look at it. He could see it already. It wasn't like it was for Ringmar; it wasn't waving at him. It was closed, clenched. Something he couldn't reach. Like the remains of a statue.

He was sitting at home with the whiskey in his glass. Statue. The remains of a statue. What do we have here? We have a hand from a body. It's the opposite. What do you see when you look at an ancient statue? A body, a torso. No head. No hands. The opposite now. Hand. No torso. Something is wrong.

The middle finger on Elisabeth Ney's right hand had been painted white. The right middle finger. There hadn't been any cans of paint in the white storage room.

Just one white finger. Not a whole hand.

Winter looked at the clock. There was someone at Ney's house now. Maybe he wouldn't make it through the night. Up to the emergency room. Maybe the same bay.

Winter drank his Glenfarclas. There was a scent of whiskey around him. It was a good scent. It stood for the goodness in the world. In life, too. The word "whiskey" came from the Gaelic usquebaugh. The water of life. There had still been moisture on the floor in the storeroom where they found Elisabeth Ney. The cleaning rooms had to be cleaned, too. The maid had been there shortly before the murder. Oh God, he must have waited. With her? How could the timing work out like that? Winter looked at the clock again, almost midnight. The girls were sleeping. Elsa had woken herself up with her own snoring an hour ago. The polyps. She would have an operation soon, but he pushed that thought away. It was easier for Angela. She was a doctor, and she knew everything that could go wrong but didn't say a word about it; maybe she didn't even think about it. There must be something compulsive about doctors: Nothing happens to anyone, especially not those in one's own family. Elsa would be okay by the time they were on the plane to Málaga. Would he be okay? Would he be there?

"Aren't you coming to bed, Erik?"

He lifted his gaze from the whiskey glass. The liquor was a beautiful color when the flame of the candle shone right through the glass.

"Come and sit down," he answered, making room on the couch.

She yawned over by the door.

"I'm just going to get a glass of water."

He heard the tap out in the kitchen. He heard a car go by down on Vasaplatsen, and the hoarse protests from a gang of jackdaws that were breeding in the maples. Soon the last streetcar would clatter by and people would go to rest.

Angela came back with the glass in hand.

"Come here," he said, opening his arms.

"It smells like a distillery in here," she said.

"Yes, isn't it lovely?"

"Don't you have to work tomorrow?"

"I'm working now."

She cuddled up against him. Winter put down his glass and pulled her even closer.

"Are you cold?"

"Not anymore."

"You smell like sleep," he said.

"What does that smell like?"

"Innocent," he answered.

"Yes, I'm innocent."

"I know you are, Angela."

"Innocent until proven guilty."

"You don't need any proof here."

"Mm-hmm."

"And you don't need this, either," he said, and he unbuttoned the top button of her nightgown, and then the other buttons.

He dreamed about two children swinging, each on their own swing, in perfect symmetry. He was standing alongside. There was no stand for the swings; they were flying free in the air, there didn't seem to be any law of gravity. This is a lawless land, he thought. The children laughed. He couldn't see their faces. They laughed again. He woke up. He fought it; it was an involuntary awakening. One of the children had said something to him just before he left them. He wanted to go back to hear clearly what he hadn't understood. Now he didn't remember.

Winter placed his feet on the floor. The wood was soft and warm. Angela moved in the bed behind him and mumbled something. Maybe she was dreaming. He walked across the floor and into the living room and sat down on the sofa. It was dark and quiet out there, the hour of the wolf. November first tomorrow. Scandinavia was entering the hour of the wolf that would last until next year. The merciful snow usually blew past this city to fall farther inland. The gray winter was left behind. Nothing ought to be able to be hidden in it. There was nothing to use as cover. And yet, so much was hidden. Everything, more or less. There won't be much more sleep tonight. There won't be much more sleep until this is over. When will it be over? Angela had asked, just before she fell asleep. But it wasn't a question. They were planning for the immediate future, and she didn't say anything because he didn't say anything. He didn't say that he might come later. That he would leave the winter, green, white, gray, but that he would leave it later because he had something he had to do first. Someone he had to meet.

Suddenly Lilly began to scream. Another dream in the night, a nasty one. It had happened a few times. He wondered what she was dreaming. What was there that was nasty in her life, or her dream life? What was it that threatened such a small person? What was it that was allowed to threaten someone so little?

He got up and quickly went to her and lifted her up and felt her tears against his cheek.

"There there, sweetheart."

She quieted and snuffled and he carried her into the living room. She weighed nothing, a weightless daughter. She started to nod off right away as he rocked her back and forth in front of the big window that looked out onto the city that would soon awaken. He felt her hand move against his neck. It was weightless, too, like a feather.

The dreams didn't want to come back. Winter got up out of the bed again and tried to sneak out into the kitchen without waking anyone. Elsa moved in her bed but didn't wake up.

He sat down at the table with a glass of water. He wasn't thirsty. Maybe the water would help him nod off. It had become more difficult to sleep.

The shadow on the facade of the building across the courtyard formed a pattern that could depict anything. A figure, two figures. He suddenly thought of Christer Börge. A figure on his way out of the church. Börge hadn't looked in his direction, but Winter had sensed that Börge knew that he'd been sitting there. The way he didn't move his head. As though he could only stare straight ahead.

Börge hadn't changed so much that he became someone else.

Winter hadn't sat next to Nina Lorrinder during their visit to the church. But he had exchanged a few words with her in there last time. He wondered now whether Börge had seen it.

·   ·   ·

The sun hung low above the hills. In the distance he could see the facade of the hospital. It cast a large shadow, but it didn't reach this far. The room he was standing in was very bright in the sunlight. There was a worn-out expression that said that something was bathed in light, but he had never seen the image before him. Exactly how did things bathe in light? Today, in Paula's apartment, everything was light; there were no differences. As he stood in the middle of the floor, it struck him that the sun out there had always been hidden during the three or four times he'd been here before. It had been that kind of autumn.

Had Paula felt threatened? Was she hiding from someone? When did the threat begin? Did it exist? He had thought about it as he had held his daughter's little bird-body close. Maybe he had begun to think about it even as he had held her mother's body in the same way. A long threat. No. An earlier one. No. Recent? No. A current one? No. Yes. No. Yes. Her loneliness. Paula's loneliness. She didn't choose it herself. Winter looked around in the shrouded apartment. Soon the shrouds would be removed and someone else would receive permission to live her life here. To live her life. It was a right.

He walked up to the window. He could see the house he'd lived in as a young man. The chief inspector as a young man. There had been winter and summer and winter again here, but he had hardly noticed wind and weather in those days. There wasn't time for things like that in his life. His life flung him along toward the new challenges in his chosen career. That was his life. Crime. He had had a long way to go toward a method and an attitude. His whole world was discipline; he thought like a threshing machine; he was promoted. Yes, he was promoted. What had he thought when he became chief inspector? Didn't they say that he was the youngest in the country? Thirty-seven years old. Had he cared? Yes. No.

He turned away from the window and walked across the plastic mat on the floor. It was, in turn, covered by a layer of plastic.

His cell phone rang.

"Yes?"

"Do you see anything I didn't see?" Halders asked.

"There's better light this time," Winter answered.

"Blinding," said Halders.

"No, the opposite. But I don't know what I should be looking for, Fredrik. We've looked everywhere."

"Letters," said Halders, "photos."

Words, pictures, things that could describe a life, a past. That's what they always came back to. The before, as Elsa had said last week. Children created the concrete language that meant what it really meant. There was the now and the before and in Winter's world, they existed simultaneously, and all the time.

He walked out into the kitchen as he spoke to Halders on his cell phone. The kitchen wasn't shrouded in the same way as the other two rooms in the apartment.

"Maybe she kept a diary," said Halders.

"It could be in the suitcase," said Winter, "if there is one."

"Everything we need is in that suitcase," said Halders.

"And yet here I stand," said Winter, "and you've stood here, too."

"Look around again," said Halders.

He looked around. The white paint in there was whiter than ever, applied in another layer, or several. Along with the sunshine coming through the window, the color made the kitchen blinding. Had the murderer been here? Had he sat at this table? It was the same table. Everything in this kitchen was the same as before the renovation.

"Who talked to the painters?" Winter asked.

"Sorry?"

"The painters. The ones who were doing the renovations when Paula was murdered? Who talked to them?"

"Damned if I know, Erik. Wasn't it Bergenhem?"

"Can you find out?"

"Of course. But if he got anything out of them, we would have known. Bergenhem doesn't miss things like that."

Winter didn't answer. One ray of sunlight reached farther than the others and shone against one of the cupboard doors above the stove. The door looked like a piece of a sun.

"Do you mean that they saw something we ought to know?" Halders continued.

"They were here," said Winter. "I don't know how much they had to clear away before they really got to work. But they were here before us."

24

The conference room was just as illuminated as Paula's apartment. The November sun hung above Ullevi as though it had gotten the wrong season and the wrong point of the compass. No one had lowered the blinds. Halders had put on his sunglasses.

Djanali took her hand from her eyes, got up, walked over to the window, lowered the blinds, and shrugged her shoulders at Winter, who was still standing there. He saw an airplane on its way south through the friendly skies. People still had the sense to leave; their brains hadn't frozen to their craniums yet.

This wouldn't last. The sun would come to its senses again and head south, too.

Ringmar discreetly cleared his throat and Winter turned around.

"Feel free to speak," he said.

"Well, thanks," said Halders.

Even Ringmar smiled. And Halders was right. It was a crappy expression. In this context, everyone should always feel free to speak. Free speech was like a tradition in this part of the world, he thought. It was different down south.

"So take advantage of that freedom," Djanali said, nudging Halders in the side with her elbow.

"We have someone who seems to be obsessed with hotels," said Halders.

"Or rather, killing people in hotels," said Bergenhem.

"That kind of goes without saying," said Halders.

Bergenhem didn't answer.

"Room number ten," said Djanali.

"What?"

"Paula was in room number ten," Djanali repeated, and turned toward Halders. "And . . . Börge . . . Ellen Börge had checked into room number ten."

She looked at Winter, who was still standing by the window. He seldom left that position during these talks. It was good to stand a bit apart; the words sometimes worked better if they could fly a bit farther, and it might be the same with thoughts. The point was that the thoughts should fly. Sometimes it worked.

"Yeah, yeah, her," said Halders. "I guess she's still missing, from what I understand."

"Is she still part of the background of this investigation?" Bergenhem asked.

"Has she ever been part of it?" Halders said. "Erik? Are you still thinking about her?"

"I haven't for a while," said Winter.

"That's a coincidence," said Halders.

Winter didn't answer.

"She's gone," said Halders.

"Elisabeth Ney is, too," said Djanali.

"What does that mean?" said Halders.

"I don't really know. But she's the one we're talking about here, first and foremost."

"You're the one who mentioned room number ten," said Halders.

"You're the one who mentioned hotels," said Djanali.

"How did he get in?" said Winter, and every head turned toward him. "Elisabeth's murderer. He must have moved around the Hotel Odin. Presumably several times. How did he get in without anyone noticing him?"

"Maybe someone did," said Bergenhem. "We haven't questioned everyone yet."

"A disguise," said Halders.

"How?" Bergenhem asked.

Halders shrugged his shoulders.

"It doesn't matter. And it doesn't matter what anyone saw. It wasn't him, anyway."

"It was someone," said Djanali. "That might be enough."

"The long coat?"

"It works better in October, anyway," said Ringmar, "compared to August."

"It's November now," said Djanali.

"Of course, the question is also how she got in," said Bergenhem.

"And what shape she was in then," said Halders.

"She was murdered in there," said Ringmar. "We know that much."

"How could he arrange a meeting with her in there?" said Bergenhem. "Why did she go along with meeting there?"

"Maybe that's not where she thought she was going," said Ringmar. "He could have carried her, shoved her."

"So their rendezvous was out in the stairwell?" said Halders, looking around. "Well, if that's the case, it clears this right up."

"Your sarcasm is really a big help to all of us, Fredrik," said Djanali.

"Rendezvous," said Winter. "Do you know what that word actually means, Fredrik?"

"Yeah, what about it? . . . It means meeting. A planned meeting."

"An arranged meeting, yes," said Winter. "Most often in the sense of an arranged meeting between lovers."

It was quiet around the table for a few seconds.

"She went there to meet her lover?" Djanali asked.

"Well, it's a thought," said Ringmar.

"She was gone for just over twenty-four hours," said Halders. "Where was she during that time? If she had a lover, shouldn't she already have been with him? Maybe that's where she was. We couldn't find her. Presumably she wasn't wandering the streets. She was somewhere."

"Maybe in that storeroom," said Bergenhem.

"Without being discovered?" said Halders.

Bergenhem shrugged.

"No," said Ringmar. "We've checked the maids' routines. They come and go pretty often. At least a few times a day."

"As long as someone didn't ask someone else to keep away," said Halders, lifting his hand and rubbing his thumb between his index and middle fingers. "Maybe hinting at a little lovers' tryst."

Winter nodded.

"Anyway, we need to talk some more with those two who used the storeroom. The stairwell was their territory. Maybe they remember more now."

"Speaking of territory," said Djanali. "We started by talking about hotels. So: Why hotels?"

"Exactly," said Halders.

Everyone suddenly looked at Winter, as though he were standing there with the answer at the ready. Don't you think I've thought about that? he thought. There's a reason for it.

"There's a reason for it," he said.

"You just need to tell us which one," said Halders.

"Give me a few days," said Winter.

"You have a month," said Ringmar.

Winter's leave of absence wasn't a secret. Halders had slowly taken part in leading the investigation. He would continue to do so until the prosecutor took over for him. But for that they needed a reasonable suspect. Winter would be happy to leave a suspect behind when he got on the plane. He didn't want to keep leading this investigation via cell phone from Nueva Andalucía.

"Has anyone we've questioned worked at a hotel?" Djanali asked. "I don't mean just those from these hotels. Hotels in general."

"Not that we know of."

"Maybe we don't know enough," said Djanali.

"The johns and the Social Democrats at Revy," said Halders, as though those two types of people were cut from the same fabric. "Are we really finished with them?"

"Of course not," said Ringmar.

"But you know how long it takes."

Halders looked like he was planning to say more, probably something bitter, probably about politicians, but he refrained.

"The connection," said Bergenhem, "we have to try to see the connection."

"Well, there's an obvious connection here," said Halders.

"Yes?" said Bergenhem.

"The family connection. We're working on two murders in the same family, in case no one had noticed."

"And?" said Bergenhem.

"The head of the family," said Halders. "Where do you usually start looking for the perpetrator?" He turned to Bergenhem. "Do you remember that lesson at the police academy? Or did you have the shakies and sickies that day?"

Mario Ney looked like he had the shakies and sickies in the room where Winter had met him several times. It looked like Ney was starting to fall apart.

They had tried to piece together a potential alibi for Ney, but one didn't exist. That didn't have to mean anything; it might even be to his advantage. He hadn't sought out company during the recent chaotic times. He had sought his own solitude, at first along with Elisabeth, then alone here in the apartment. Winter had looked for answers in the man's face, in his words, in his manner of moving. He expressed sorrow, sorrow and despair. Other feelings would come later. He might become suicidal; maybe he already was. The Ney family might disappear from the earth. Someone wanted that to happen.

"I have some questions to ask," said Winter.

Ney looked out through the window. He had been doing so since Winter had walked into this room, a room that smelled closed up, a sweetish smell that might also be sweat, fear, despair.

"She looked like she was sleeping," said Ney.

His eyes were still fastened on nothing outside.

He turned his head.

"My little Elisabeth. Like she was sleeping."

Winter nodded. He had let Ney see his wife's body. It wasn't an obvious decision. They hadn't let Ney see her neck, only her face.

Winter didn't want Ney to see something he might have seen before.

Ney's face looked almost peaceful for an instant. As though he had encountered death and accepted it. Another's death, accepted another's violent death.

"She was missing for over twenty-four hours before we . . . found her," said Winter. "I have to ask you again, Mario." Winter leaned forward. "Do you have any idea where she might have been during that time?"

"Ab-so-lute-ly-no-i-de-a," Ney said, with emphasis on every syllable in every word. It was like a new language. Then something seemed to happen to his eyes and he searched for Winter's gaze. "Why would I?"

"I don't know, Mario. But she was somewhere. Indoors, somewhere. No one saw her out anywhere."

"Just because no one saw her doesn't mean that she was indoors the whole time," said Ney.

"Could she have traveled somewhere?" Winter asked.

"Traveled? Where would she have traveled?" He threw out his arm and hand, a gesture that could contain everything they could see. "She lived here. This was her home."

"Where did she come from?" Winter asked. "Where did her parents live?"

"I think it was . . . Halmstad."

Halmstad. Another city to the south, along the coast, halfway to Malmö, Copenhagen. Winter had a vague idea of how people from there talked; he had a few colleagues from Halland, but he hadn't heard that kind of dialect in Elisabeth Ney.

"But she moved here when she was young," Mario continued.

"Did you meet her parents?"

"Yes. But they're gone now."

"Does she have any siblings?" Winter asked.

"No."

Like Paula, Winter thought. No siblings.

"Is her family still in Halmstad?"

"There's never been anyone there," said Ney. "They moved to the city when Elisabeth was pretty young, or half-grown, or whatever it's called. I don't think they knew anyone there then."

"But didn't they make any friends?"

"Yes, I think they did. But no one I know."

"But Elisabeth did."

"Do you mean she might have gone there? To Halmstad? And then straight back again? Why would she?"

"I'm just trying to figure out where she was," said Winter.

"I know where she is," said Ney.

"Sorry?"

But Ney didn't answer. He looked out at the courtyard again.

"What do you mean, Mario?"

"She's at home," Ney said, his eyes on the sky.

Dusk was falling like rain outside. Winter could almost hear it, or maybe it was the rush-hour traffic out on the highway. Everyone wanted to go home.

On his way home, Halders bought crispbread, *filmjölk,* whole milk, apples, and smoked sausage at the ICA store on the corner. He knew he'd forgotten something but couldn't come up with it during the whole trip to his house five blocks away, and then it was too late anyway.

"Where are the eggs?" Djanali asked when he'd taken everything out of the bag and placed it on the counter in the kitchen.

"I knew there was something."

"I promised Hannes and Magda pancakes for dinner," said Djanali. "You can't make pancakes without eggs."

"Have you tried?"

"Don't try to get out of this, Fredrik."

"I'll go now," he answered.

So it was never too late. And he went. Dusk would turn to evening in a few minutes. Evening came before the day was over. In a month it would take over completely, evening and night. Everyone would light Advent candles, and Christmas lights at the same time, a month early. Magda had already asked him about his wish list. She had always gotten a head start. But Hannes would put in his requests the week before Christmas Eve. He, on the other hand, would give his wish list to the children before the end of November. He knew what he wanted.

It was nice to walk. Halders exercised at work because it was part of the job, but he wasn't an enthusiast. It had been a long time. He carried what some people called "a healthy weight." It didn't feel healthy to him. When this winter finally decided to go the hell away, he would pull on his workout clothes and go out and pound the asphalt. Maybe run the Göteborgsvarvet, a half marathon. Astound the whole world.

He carried the carton of eggs home as if it were the last drop of water.

Djanali was making pancakes as though it had been her job for years. She hadn't done it before, not at Halders's house. He wondered whether that meant anything. Whether she had decided to stay, and not just for tonight. She still hadn't moved in. The house was big enough. There was room for everyone. It was home.

"Is there more blueberry jam?" Hannes asked.

"Both blueberry and strawberry."

"Where did you learn to make pancakes like this?" Halders asked.

"At home, of course."

"You had pancakes at home?"

"Why wouldn't we? We loved pancakes."

"Your parents escaped from Ouagadougou in Burkina Faso. I didn't think pancakes were their thing," said Halders.

"Their thing?" Djanali said, pancake turner in hand. "Their thing?"

"Isn't it everyone's thing?" Magda said. "Pancakes are everywhere. Didn't you know that, Dad?"

"I was mostly thinking of blueberry jam."

"You were not," said Magda.

"Strawberry jam, then."

The curtain moved, but it was barely visible. Must be the ventilation, he thought. The air intake was up there, to the left of the window, or the air blower, depending on how you looked at it.

Room number ten looked like last time he had stood here. And the first time, eighteen years ago. At least it felt that way. Time moved in both directions, as though it met itself halfway. As though he himself were standing there, and here at the same time. Standing halfway. As far backward as forward. Equally difficult to see in both directions. Or equally easy.

He walked up to the window and looked down at the street. It wasn't very easy to see it; faint light from a streetlight that was reminiscent more of the fifties than a new century. If it was the fifties. He hadn't been born yet in the fifties. He was born in 1960, and that was the best decade yet in the world, if you could believe what most people said. Ellen Börge was born in the sixties, the year after him. How had the sixties been for her? Winter turned around. The room lay mostly in darkness; the only illumination was the fifties-era lights outside.

Paula Ney had sat in this darkness; she must have. Waited. Listened. Suffered. That letter. Winter took a few steps into the darkness, as though to test it out, maybe challenge it. It was the same darkness now as it had been then. It was a witness to what had happened. There must be more letters. From other times. Why haven't I read any other letters from Paula? The first things I learned about her were in a letter. She wrote it. Where are her letters? At home? No. Not at home and not . . . at home. If it's possible to say that she had two homes. Her parents haven't saved anything. Isn't that strange? Is that connected to the silence? With a secret? What is the secret, this family's secret? If I knew that, I'd know everything.

He heard voices out in the hallway, maybe whores, johns, Social Democrats. A woman's laughter, a man's laughter. No children's laughter. This was the place for people who had left all of that behind.

It's gone, lost and gone forever. And now Revy is in its final days. The child. The child that was Paula. Why am I thinking of Paula as a child? Is it the swings? The playgrounds? The woman and the girl in the miserable apartment building in Hisingen? Why am I thinking about them right now? I've got so much else to think about. Others who were children once. Some who are now. My own, for example.

A door slammed hard farther down the hall. Life went on as usual all over, such as it was. A car went by down on the street; the red taillights cast their light all the way up to room number ten. Everything suddenly looked older in there, like something from a film from the past, the fifties, the sixties, the seventies, the eighties. The eighties. What a little greenhorn I was then. I stood here and didn't know anything more than that I was standing here. Ellen, I thought. Where are you, Ellen? Though I knew even then that she was gone, probably dead. Just as dead now. Wonder how it's going for her husband now? Christer. It's about time I talked to him. It's been a long time. He goes to evening prayers at the church. He was my age, too. Everyone was my age; I guess there's just one age. Paula was my age, when I was green, and Ellen before that, and Christer. And Jonas. And his mother that time when the boy was a boy.

A laugh rolled past outside, like gravel on the floor, no pearls. They had looked for secrets in room number ten but hadn't found more than what they already knew. There were no more letters in this room. The one that existed was enough. He had read it before he came here. There was a macabre power in the words that was impossible to avoid. There was a message in those words that he couldn't see. A secret. Like this room; he knew that it was a room and he knew what was there, but he couldn't see anything really clearly.

Winter opened the door and stepped out into the hall. It was lighter there, but not by much. The red wallpaper dampened what light there was. Of course it was red. There was gold here and there. All was as it should be at Hotel Revy.

He walked down the curved staircase. Even that looked like something from another epoch, a belle epoque.

The desk clerk looked like something from another epoch and yet didn't.

It was the same desk clerk as throughout the years.

"So the room is free again, then?" he said.

Winter nodded.

"It feels nice somehow," said the man. "It's like it will be a bit normal again here."

"Normal?"

"You know what I mean."

"I'm not sure I do." Winter turned around to leave. "And anyway, this place is closing down soon."

A man came in through the revolving door with a suitcase and a laptop bag. He looked like he'd come straight from the train; maybe he'd walked from Central Station. It wasn't far. His cheeks bloomed red. The temperature must have fallen outside when the sun went down. It was winter now. The man had a winter coat on. Winter was wearing his winter coat. The man announced he had arrived, filled in a form, went up the stairs with his bags. No bellhop here.

"A normal guest," said the desk clerk.

"In what way?"

"He's here to sleep and work."

"What room did you give him?"

"Not ten, if that's what you're thinking."

"Do you have the list?"

The desk clerk reached for a paper next to the cash register.

"I don't know how complete it is."

Winter took the paper without answering.

He quickly read through it.

"There are more than I thought," he said.

His cell phone rang out on the stairs. He nearly lost his balance as he took it out. It had certainly become slippery outside, but he was inside. It was colder in the wind.

"It's the same type of paint," said Torsten Öberg.

"But we don't have a can," said Winter.

"He does."

"Did you find anything more in the room?"

"Traces of paint?"

"Yes. Or anything."

"It's the same type of rope, as you know. We'll see what they come up with in Linköping."

"I don't exactly feel optimistic," said Winter.

"Well, at least you know about the paint."

"I guess he must have brought a can in with him," Winter said.

"We can't be entirely certain of that."

"I understand what you mean, Torsten."

"But how it happened, I can't explain. I'll leave that to you."

"Thanks."

"But it seems unbelievable."

Unbelievable. Yes. No. Maybe Elisabeth Ney had walked through the city to her rendezvous with a white-painted finger. Maybe there was an explanation. There always were explanations, but many of them were not at all relevant. There was a lot that could never be explained. The most inexplicable things were almost always a result of human actions.

25

Winter took shelter under an awning that had extended far out over the sidewalk since the summer. The rain fell harder. Ringmar stuck out a hand and it looked like it was being hit by a water cannon.

"Well, I guess we'll be standing here for a while," he said, shaking off his hand.

"I can think of better places," said Winter.

"Don't be so impatient," said Ringmar.

Winter laughed. Bertil had been trying to get him to be more patient ever since they first met. Was that two years ago? No, three. Crazy how time flies.

It was hard to keep up, hard to hold himself back for the sake of patience. He looked up at the sky. It wasn't holding back right now. The rain increased, the wind increased. November was sweeping in with its customary arrogance. Here I am. I'm taking over now. If you don't like it, leave.

"Gothenburg is not for weaklings," said Ringmar.

"Have you ever considered moving away?" Winter asked.

"Only a few times a day."

"The South Pacific, perhaps?"

"Do you mean Skåne?"

"Yes. Or Tahiti."

"What would I do there?"

"Walk around in shorts," said Winter.

"I don't look good in shorts. And it rains in the South Pacific, too. Rains like hell, sometimes."

"Have you been there?"

"No. Have you?"

"Only in my dreams."

"Dream on, man. Come on, let's get out of here."

As though nature were answering Ringmar's words, the skies opened up completely and all the rain in the universe poured down on the city, or maybe just on the street where Winter and Ringmar were standing.

They were on their way to a meeting. Maybe it was important, maybe not. No one would know until afterward. This was something Winter was in the process of learning as a half-green detective. You knew afterward. Maybe it was too late by then, and maybe it wasn't. But their routines were necessary. First the routines, then the thoughts. He was also slowly beginning to discover that it was possible to think during the routines. That it was possible to think at all. At first he had been skeptical. Now he was starting to realize that perhaps he hadn't taken a wrong turn in his life.

The rain wasn't falling as hard anymore. It was more the sound than anything they could see; the roar against the awning above them diminished.

They had been standing there for five minutes.

Winter suddenly realized where they were standing.

A compartment of memory that had been filed away, not too far from the center of his thoughts.

Now it was coming back.

He turned around, toward the stairs up to the door. The words were still there on the glass, the gold etching. The hotel hadn't changed names since the last time. He could see the sign that said "Hotel" on a wrought-iron stand a meter out from the wall of the building. It looked like a beetle on its way up the wall. He looked up at the facade. The windows were like black holes, story after story.

Three years ago, autumn then, too. He had been inside that room. He hadn't come with a warrant, he hadn't gotten one of those: Ellen who? Missing, you say? Stayed in a hotel room for one night? You want to inspect the room? No, nothing like that. I just want to look at it.

That wouldn't work.

Instead he had asked the clerk whether he could see the room, whether it was empty. It was two days after she'd disappeared. He had stood in the room and listened to the traffic outside. No one had stayed here since Ellen Börge. That was the closest he ever got to her.

"We're standing under Revy's awning," he now said, and he turned back toward Ringmar.

"Oh?"

"Ellen Börge, the woman who disappeared. She checked in here the night before she disappeared for good. Do you remember?"

"Now that you mention it. I remember her, not the hotel. But I guess you haven't forgotten."

Winter didn't answer. He had a sudden urge to go up the stairs and ask whether he could see the room again, whether it was empty. But that would be pointless. He would never see that room again. Would never need to.

The coat moved back and forth. The picture was as bad as ever. The shoes hadn't changed since last time.

They hadn't been able to connect anyone to the shoes. Aneta Djanali thought about the shoes. There weren't that many people with shoes in Africa. She had been back there, back to where she came from; she hadn't been born there, but still she came from Burkina Faso, as it was called now. Not many shoes in the villages, more in the capital. She came from a village just outside the capital. There had been dust everywhere. Feet became covered with a layer that could get thicker and thicker and maybe provide protection.

Halders was sitting next to her.

They were studying the woman now, her particular way of walking. A limp that wasn't a limp.

"She's hiding her face, but I'm not sure why," said Halders.

"What do you mean?"

"Maybe she always hides it," said Halders.

"Keep going," said Djanali as she watched the woman.

"She's not hiding it from the camera, if she even knows there's a camera. She just looks like that. That's how she looks," he said, nodding toward the monitor.

"Why?"

"I don't know."

"So she wouldn't be involved in a . . . conspiracy?"

"Conspiracy?"

"You know what I mean, Fredrik."

"She's involved in something," Halders said. "She's involved in dropping off that fucking suitcase, which I would really like to open."

Djanali followed the woman's movements for the thirtieth time.

"She's doing it for Paula," she said after a little while. "She's dropping it off because Paula told her to." Djanali turned to Halders. "Paula was on her way somewhere, and she helped her with her suitcase."

Halders nodded.

"Paula was on her way somewhere," Djanali repeated.

"Two questions," said Halders: "Where? And why?"

"One more question," said Djanali, nodding at the screen: "Why hasn't this woman contacted us?"

"And one more," said Halders: "Who is she?"

"And," said Djanali: "Where is she?"

"Here in town," said Halders.

"But why in God's name hasn't she made herself known?"

Halders studied her movements again.

"Might be dead. Might be afraid."

Winter and Ringmar were on the way back from their meeting. But there hadn't ended up being any meeting. The person they were to meet hadn't come.

"Impolite bastard," said Ringmar.

Winter laughed.

"Maybe there weren't any cars to steal up in Bergsjön," he said. "In which case, he can't be expected to come on time."

"There are always cars to steal," said Ringmar. "They swiped mine once. Have I told you about that?"

"No."

"In the police station parking lot. In broad daylight."

"It's almost impressive," said Winter.

"I found it under the Göta Älv bridge the next week."

"Isn't that how it always goes? The gas always seems to run out for the fuckers right under the bridge."

"They'd swiped the radio."

"That's too bad."

"Didn't matter. There wasn't anything good on it anyway."

Winter smiled. He liked Bertil. It wasn't a father-son relationship, but it wasn't too far from one either. They could talk to each other, which fathers and sons maybe couldn't always do, and they had found a way to have discussions that worked. It was always a question of conversation. There was almost always an opening in a conversation that started with some distant point and slowly moved toward something. Silence was never enough, just thoughts weren't sufficient. Conversations. Loud and quiet. Jargon. Discussion. Arguments. Crying. Yells. Whispers. Cries. Everything.

The rain had stopped and a pale sun glimmered behind the haze like a flashlight with a dying battery. They walked across Gustav Adolfs Torg. The fat king on his pedestal pointed his finger down at them as they passed. He wasn't much of a warrior. A soldier pointed with his whole hand.

The wind swept the remaining leaves along with it across the square, pages of newspapers, a red and gold piece of wrapping paper. The Christmas tree would be put up here soon. There would be lots of wrapping paper all over. All the good children would get what they deserved, and the bad ones would, too. Candles would burn in homes. Winter had gotten the annual invitation to his parents' house in Nueva Andalucía, and he would give them his annual rejection. Lotta would go down with the girls. His sister needed it; she could dip her recently divorced toes into the Mediterranean and try to forget a little bit. For his part, he would work. It was better than staring out at a gold-decorated Guldheden on Christmas Eve and listening to Christmas songs on the radio and toasting himself. There was nothing good on the radio anyway. He had friends, but most of them had their own families now and he didn't want to be a bother. It's no bother, for God's sake, Erik. Anyway, I'm working.

"Should we get some coffee?"

Ringmar pointed toward Östra Hamngatan with his whole hand.

"Why not?"

This was another thing he had learned, and learned to appreciate. Sometimes they left the police station and had their conversations at the city's cafés. Once in a while at a bar, after the workday was officially over. Being among people, regular people, gave them a sense of reality that could get lost in this line of work. In the end, everyone was abnormal, subnormal, a criminal, a madman. A perpetrator. A victim. And nothing in between. Spending a day as a detective, or as any kind of police officer, was almost always strange. In reality, it was frightening. It was not something for regular people.

A cup of coffee and a Danish were comforting.

They walked across the street and into the café.

The line at the counter was long.

"Let's go someplace else," said Ringmar.

At that moment, a table opened up near the large windows that looked out onto the street. Through the glass, Winter could see that the rain had begun to pour down again. It was April weather in November.

"Let's take that table," said Winter. "I'll get in line. What do you want?"

"Regular coffee, no milk, two sugars, a napoleon, and a glass of water."

"Nothing else?"

"Get going before the line gets even longer, kid."

But it was shorter when he got there. It was as though some of the people in line had disappeared into thin air. The line moved slowly. When it was his turn, he gave his order. The girl behind the counter placed Ringmar's napoleon on a small plate and turned to him again:

"The princess cakes just ran out."

"Oh, no."

"I'm sorry," she said, and Winter followed her glance to the small plate with the last princess cake. It was on the tray ahead of him. Winter looked up and met a pair of green eyes.

"If it's as bad as it sounds, you can have it," said the woman in front of him in line. "I guess I got the last one."

"No, no."

He thought he saw a smile playing somewhere on the edge of her lips. He felt dumb as hell. She was pretty as hell. A few years younger than him, maybe five, or four. Her hair was golden brown.

"This cake doesn't mean that much to me," she continued. "I could just as well have ordered something else."

The girl behind the counter followed the conversation with interest. People were waiting behind Winter in the line, but that didn't seem very important right now. But he had to decide and go on his way so that life could continue as usual at this counter.

"Come on, take it," said the woman with the green eyes. "I haven't touched it."

"But . . . but I have to pay." He felt half-unconscious. Apparently he would say anything, go along with anything. "I ha—"

"I'll have one of those instead," she interrupted him, nodding at the napoleon on Ringmar's plate.

Okay, okay, Winter thought. I guess that's the quickest way to get out of this.

He threw a glance over to the window. Ringmar raised his eyebrows.

"It's more expensive," said the girl behind the register. "Napoleons are more expensive."

She, too, appeared to find something amusing in all of this. Winter himself felt like his throat was dry. He considered grabbing Bertil's glass of water from down on the tray and emptying it in one gulp.

"That will be another two-fifty."

"I'll pay the difference," said Winter, taking out his wallet.

The woman turned to him again, studied him for a second or two, and smiled again. He felt even more idiotic. He wasn't used to this feeling. The last time he'd felt even more idiotic was when he'd met Halders for the first time and Birgersson grabbed him by the ear.

"Okay," she said with a gentle tone, as though she were doing him a small favor that he'd been nagging her about for quite some time.

She received her napoleon and took her tray and walked toward a table that had opened up a bit farther inside the café.

Winter paid and balanced his tray back over to Ringmar.

"What was that all about?" Ringmar said.

"Forget it."

"How can I forget something I don't know anything about?"

Winter didn't answer. He cast a glance past the line, back into the café, to the small round table where she was sitting. She smiled again. It seemed to be a bigger smile now.

If it had happened at a bar counter, he would have asked her name.

"Cute girl," said Ringmar, taking a small gulp and grimacing. "This coffee is a little cool."

"I'm sorry, Bertil, it's my fault." He got up and took Ringmar's cup. "I'll get more."

"Don't you have to pay for a refill here?"

"Don't worry about it."

He walked straight past the line and took the six steps to her table. She saw him coming and waited with a forkful of pastry raised halfway to her mouth.

"You haven't changed your mind, have you?" she said.

That little smile again.

"Yes," he said, "I just decided to ask you your name."

"Why?"

"Because you . . . were so nice. That's not so common these days."

She laughed, quickly and loudly. Maybe he smiled, he didn't know. But he knew that the people at the two tables on either side of them were following the drama attentively.

"What's your name?" he asked.

"Angela," she answered. "Angela Hoffman."

"Where's my coffee?" Ringmar asked when Winter came back to the table.

Winter walked down the stairs with the thin piece of paper in his inner pocket. The wind found its way down his neck and he turned up the collar of his coat.

His cell phone rang. The display said "private number" and he guessed who it was.

"Hi, Angela."

"Can you be home by seven tonight, Erik?"

"I really hope so."

"Lilly has something she wants to show you. Preferably before she falls asleep."

"What is it?"

"She'll show you herself."

He was home at five thirty. Lilly showed him right away, in the hall.

She could take four steps.

After the formalities, Jonas Sandler leaned back in his chair. It wasn't an arrogant motion. It was more like he didn't know what to do.

"There are some dates I'd like to discuss with you, Jonas."

"Discuss?"

"Yes, discuss."

"Okay."

Winter told him the days. He meant the evenings, too, and the nights.

"I was out at a few places," Sandler said. "That evening. It must have been that one."

He named the place.

Winter made a note.

"They must recognize me there."

"When were you there? Between what times?"

"I think it was probably late. From midnight on, maybe one."

"From one on?"

"Something like that."

"Are you out often? At clubs, bars?"

"It happens."

"Isn't it expensive?"

"It depends."

"Depends on what?"

"Where you are. What you take."

"Take?"

"Drink. Or something else. You know what I'm talking about, right?"

"Are you talking about drugs?"

"The clubs are full of drugs, that can't be a secret even from the police."

His voice suddenly had a sharper tone. It was as though he'd become older.

"You're unemployed. How do you get money?"

"I don't get anything," said the boy. "It's cheaper that way."

"Is it as fun that way?"

"Is what as fun?" Sandler asked in turn, and he changed position on the chair.

I'm not falling into that trap, Winter thought, looking at the tape recorder in front of him on the blond wood table.

"Not having money," he said.

Sandler shrugged.

"I talked to your mom the other day," Winter said.

He could tell that Sandler gave a start, a barely visible shudder across his shoulders, but he was trained to see such things.

"Oh?"

"She hasn't mentioned anything to you?"

"No. Why would she?"

"When did you last talk to her, Jonas?"

He shrugged.

"Try to think back."

He appeared to be thinking back. Maybe he knew.

"Quite a while ago."

"Aren't you wondering why I visited her?"

He shrugged again. He transformed before Winter's eyes, regressed, one could say. He became defiant.

As though Mom's shadow had fallen over the room.

"When you lived out there as a boy," Winter said, "you played with a girl who lived in the same stairwell. Can you tell me a little about her?"

26

I don't remember that," said Sandler. He looked down at the table. "A girl? There were a lot of children there." He raised his eyes.

"Were there?" Winter asked.

"Yeah, so what?"

"According to your mom, you were the only children in that stairwell."

"Yeah, so what? There were probably a ton of other kids in those yards. That's what I remember, anyway."

"But you don't remember this girl? Or her mom?"

Sandler didn't answer. He appeared to be thinking back. Winter waited for him to say something. Maybe the boy has something to say. Or something to hide.

"Did they live in the same stairwell?" Sandler asked.

"Yes."

"What about them? Why are you asking about them?"

"Just try to remember."

"What am I supposed to remember?"

"Come on, Jonas, shape up."

"Huh?"

"Shape up!"

Sandler jumped. His eyes slid back and forth, and out to the corners of the interrogation room, as though they were looking for something to hold on to, as far away from Winter as possible.

"You don't have to yell," he said at last.

Winter waited. The ventilation system buzzed like a swarm of flies up under the ceiling. The room's blinds let in a light that hardly deserved the name. The daylight couldn't really handle the time of year any longer. Last night a smiling weather woman had half promised snow for the weekend. In the morning, Halders had said he'd thrown a slipper at the TV when that chick had grinned out her prediction.

"How old was she?" Sandler asked.

"About your age. Eleven."

"She couldn't have lived there for long. I . . . ought to remember."

Winter had thought through the interrogation before setting foot in the room. What did he himself remember from when he was eleven? Quite a lot. He had hung around the streets of Kortedala, and later, western Gothenburg, with a gang that split up when adult life began, earlier for some and later for others. Some grew up when they stopped teasing the girls, and after that they never returned to childhood. It was gone forever. Winter had tried to stay there as long as possible. When he thought of that time yesterday, and this morning, he remembered images and individual episodes. But he hardly remembered any names. There were one or two left in his memory, but his other childhood friends had lost their names. Maybe there weren't very many of them. They had also lost their faces.

"How long did she live there?" Sandler asked.

"We don't really know."

"What was her name?"

"We don't know that either," Winter said.

"Are you really sure that she really lived there?"

"Your mom is sure, Jonas."

He didn't answer.

"Shouldn't we believe her?"

Sandler didn't answer that either.

"Could she be wrong?" Winter asked.

"I don't know what she remembers and doesn't remember." Now Sandler looked Winter in the eye. "What was this girl's name?"

"I don't know, either."

"No? Well."

"I thought you could help me with that."

"I never remember names."

"Try to remember her. When you leave here, try to remember if you played with her."

"But why?"

"Try to remember, Jonas."

Winter and Ringmar snuck out on the town just before lunchtime.

The café on Östra Hamngatan had become their regular place. The table at the window had become their regular table. Sometimes Winter and Angela came here, at first alone, then with the children. The table inside the place had been moved a time or two during the last twenty years. It was a table and a place to remember.

"She must have kept hidden somewhere," Ringmar said when Winter came back with coffee and two napoleons.

"Mm-hmm."

"It's more difficult than many people think."

"Or easier."

"She must have had an apartment," said Ringmar.

"Or a hotel room."

"Not here in the city."

"No, it doesn't seem like it," said Winter.

"She must have been at someone's house. Someone she knew."

"We've gone through all her acquaintances. The few there are."

"We'll have to go through them again."

Winter looked out through the window. The first snowflakes of the season suddenly came falling down to the ground.

"It's snowing," he said.

"Don't worry about that. You're heading for sunshine soon."

Ringmar looked at his watch.

"You have three weeks." He looked up. "Then we'll take over for real."

The falling snow picked up outside; the air became thicker. A woman hunched over a stroller. The child was holding its hands out to the snowflakes. For children, snow was real precipitation. Winter remembered the snow of his childhood, especially because it had been so uncommon in western Gothenburg. The sea was too warm and too big.

"How did it go with the boy?" Ringmar asked.

"I don't actually know."

"What do you think?"

"He doesn't want to remember."

"Why?"

"He knew her."

Ringmar didn't say anything. He understood what Winter meant.

"He knew Paula then," said Winter. "He doesn't want us to know that."

"And we don't know it."

"Why the hell can't I figure out who they were? Where they went?"

"Mm-hmm. And where they came from."

Winter stared down at his pastry. He hadn't touched it. The red raspberry jam suddenly looked unappetizing. He pushed the plate aside.

"They wanted it like this," said Ringmar. "I'm certain the woman wanted it like this. No one would know anything about them."

"But people did know! Sandler knew, Jonas's mom. Metzer. Others must have seen them."

"Well . . . of course they couldn't sit in their apartment night and day," said Ringmar. "That would have been even more suspicious."

Winter nodded.

"I think it's even more shady that we can't find the person who held the lease."

"Well, we know his name, at least."

"But where is he?"

"And is it his real name?"

Ringmar stabbed his dessert fork into the top layer of the pastry. It turned into a mess.

"Why do they make pastries that you can't cut up nicely and neatly?"

"You should pick something other than a napoleon if that's what you want."

"I like the taste."

"Jonas played with her as a child," said Winter. "I believe that. And he remembers her."

"And he doesn't want to tell us that," said Ringmar.

"Because he met her again as an adult."

"Which he doesn't want to tell us either."

"Because he saw her more times than he wants to tell us."

"Which he's lying about."

"Because he . . . murdered her," said Winter.

"Okay."

"He's too cold not to have done it."

"Okay."

"Give me a counterargument," said Winter. "It can't be that hard."

"He's just a scared boy," said Ringmar.

"Keep going."

"He happened to talk with a poor girl who happened to get into trouble. That's all. He never knew any little girl who could be our Paula because she never existed."

"Who?"

"The mysterious little girl, of course. At least, she never existed for him. Maybe she lived there, but he's forgotten. It was such a short time. It didn't mean anything."

Because she never existed. Winter thought of what Ringmar had said, of the illusion, the interpretation. She had never existed. Not as they knew her. She was someone else. Always had been.

Ringmar had been contemplating his napoleon, and now he looked up with his fork suspended above the rest of the pastry's simultaneously delicate and hard shell. He looked around, as though someone had caught what they'd said and was now continuing to listen. But they were sitting far from all the other patrons, and relatively near the clattering counter and the hissing coffee machines behind it.

"Why did he murder her?" Ringmar asked. "I'm not saying I agree with you. I'm just asking."

"Because he's sick," Winter said. "Is there a reason when that's the case?"

Winter and Ringmar left the café. The sun stung their eyes. Winter reached for sunglasses he didn't have. They belonged in the other season, the green winter.

"Did you exchange phone numbers?" Ringmar asked.

"I don't know what you're talking about, Bertil."

"Hitting on girls at a café. In the middle of the day. During working hours. You're going to be a legend in the department, kid."

"She was the one who . . ." Winter said, without finishing his sentence.

"Talk about shifting the blame."

"Okay, fine, I have her number."

"What's her name?"

"Angela."

"That's unusual." They were walking through Brunnsparken. A drunk on a bench saluted the plainclothes officers, his bottle in the air. "Sounds English."

"Or German. She had a German last name."

"Was she German?"

"I don't know any better than you do, Bertil. She spoke Swedish, anyway. Sounded like she came from here in town. Downtown dialect."

"What does that sound like?"

"Not like your Hisingen talk, anyway."

"I'm proud of my background, kid."

"Wish I could say the same."

"Forget that dad took off with the money. He hasn't murdered anyone, any—"

"Hey, that's him there," Winter interrupted, nodding at the mass of people who were passing in front of them, on their way into Nordstan. Ringmar followed Winter's gaze.

"Who?"

"Börge. Christer Börge." Winter nodded again at the mass of people as they stopped at the crosswalk. A streetcar passed, creaking wretchedly. "Ellen Börge's husband. We talked about her a little while ago, Bertil."

"Oh, right," said Ringmar. "She hasn't turned up, as far as I know."

"No, she hasn't turned up." Winter nodded at the mass of people again. "That's him, farthest out to the left. In the blue stocking cap."

The man turned his head, as though he heard them talking about him. But that was impossible; the distance was too great. Winter could see his eyes fell on them, moved away, went back to what he had been looking at before. It was definitely Christer Börge.

"Are you sure?" Ringmar said. "Do you remember faces that well? Even when they're wearing stocking caps?"

"I remember this one. I'm worse with names."

"But you know that that one's name is Börge."

"I remember this one," Winter repeated.

"Poor bastard," said Ringmar, looking over toward Börge's hat. It looked as though it had been put on to attract attention.

Winter didn't answer. People began to move as the light changed, and they walked quickly across the street. Börge didn't turn around. The mass of people disappeared in through the doors of the gigantic shopping center as though it were a tunnel.

"I think I'll pay him a visit," said Winter.

"Why?"

"It's a shame about him. You said it yourself."

"You can't let this case go, Erik."

"No."

"What can you accomplish by visiting this poor guy and picking at an old wound?"

"I don't know. But I feel like I ought to do it."

"Is it intuition?"

"Call it whatever you want."

"Do you still believe he had something to do with her disappearing?"

"I don't believe anything. That's our motto in the department, isn't it? Like Birgersson says: Believing is for church."

"I think we have to make our way back now," said Ringmar.

"Go ahead," said Winter. "I'll be back in an hour or so."

He left Ringmar and crossed the street on green.

There was a chance he could find Börge again, as long as blue stocking caps hadn't suddenly come into fashion. But it wasn't necessary to find him. Winter had his address, if he hadn't moved. Apparently he was still in town.

Why am I doing this? Winter thought.

He saw the stocking cap outside Åhléns, in front of one of the display windows. Börge was standing in front of the toy department. He was turning his head in different directions, as though he were looking at everything except what was in the display window. The Christmas display would appear in a few weeks, and then Christmas, and then the New Year, and simultaneously the new decade, the nineties.

Börge walked quickly toward the north exit.

Winter followed him at a distance of thirty meters.

Börge went into Systembolaget, the liquor store. Winter waited outside. Börge came out with a bag. Winter could see the contours of the necks of a few bottles. Börge continued toward the exit and took a right after the automatic doors and he was gone.

Winter went out. He could see Börge crossing the thoroughfare at a crosswalk fifty meters away. He must have walked quickly. Winter could see him stop at a bus stop next to a handful of other people. No one else had a blue stocking cap. The bus was already approaching. Börge got on last and the bus drove off. Winter couldn't find him as it passed. The sun cast reflections straight across the black windows. It looked like fire.

27

Perhaps it was Börge's face he saw in the back window of the bus, a white fleck in the dirty glass.

Winter kept walking east, past Central Station, the *GP* building, Gamla Ullevi.

He checked a car out from the police garage and drove to Börge's address. There was an empty parking space a block away.

The name was still at the front door.

Winter looked around. Things mostly looked the same. No one dared to touch the patrician villas in the central parts of Gothenburg. The streets here were left unmolested by idiotic Social Democrats. The suburbs and the central hubs of the small cities had to take the brunt of the changes.

He walked in through the doors and up the stairs. Börge lived on the third floor. The stairs were well kept and the stairwell let in light through painted windows. It was like a church.

Three years ago. Three years ago, he had walked up these stairs a few times. After that: four or five phone calls to see how things were, maybe fewer. Börge had called him once or twice. He had sounded subdued, as though he had placed a handkerchief over the receiver.

As Winter extended his finger toward the doorbell, it hit him that Börge might not live alone any longer. That maybe he should have called before showing up, after all.

But he didn't want to.

He rang the bell, and Börge opened the door after the first ring, as though he had been standing and waiting just inside the door. Maybe he had seen Winter enter the front door, maybe he'd seen him even from the bus, or inside Nordstan.

Börge didn't look surprised.

"Oh, so it's you."

It was mostly a statement. A tiredness in his voice, like after an illness. Börge had aged in three years, maybe in a normal way. A few crow's-feet around his eyes. But I probably have some, too, Winter thought. I see my own face every morning and don't notice the changes.

"May I come in?"

Börge gestured in toward his apartment, turned around, and walked back through the hall.

"You'll have to take off your shoes," he said over his shoulders. "It's just been cleaned."

Winter didn't know whether this was some sort of joke, but he pulled off his handmade English shoes and placed them beside a few pairs that stood on a shoe rack under the coat rack in the hall. Winter hadn't thought of them before; maybe they hadn't been there. The pairs appeared to be identical. It was a good idea, maybe not to always wear identical shoes, but to switch shoes regularly. Winter had had this carefully impressed upon him by his shoe dealer in Mayfair. He went over once a year and always got the same advice. He didn't need to buy shoes every time. The shoes he wore were made to last. Börge's shoes were simpler, of course, but not junk.

Börge was already sitting down when Winter stepped into the living room.

There was a bottle of red wine on the table, and a half-full glass. Winter had smelled the wine on the man's breath out in the hall.

Börge nodded toward the bottle of wine.

"Would you like a glass? It's not crap."

"I can see that."

"Do you want a glass, then?"

"No thanks. I'm driving."

Börge smiled, possibly a sour smile:

"Good excuse."

He was dragging out his syllables a bit, a sign of mild intoxication. Maybe a few glasses on an empty stomach. Winter could see from the level in the bottle that Börge was onto his second glass. Maybe this was a regular afternoon treat.

"Sit down," said Börge.

Winter sat in the easy chair across from Börge. A few blackbirds drifted around outside the window, as if searching for a home. Winter could hear their cries through the glass.

Börge lifted his glass.

"Well, it looks like we're sitting here and celebrating something."

"Are you, then?"

"What do I have to celebrate?" He put down the glass. "This is more like a nice way to get through the day."

Winter nodded.

"You don't have any opinions on it?"

"No, why would I?"

"Well, you know . . . you're a policeman."

"It hasn't yet gone so far that we step into people's homes and take their bottles."

"But you did step in here," said Börge.

"Do you want me to leave?" said Winter.

"No, no. It's nice to have company."

This was the second time he'd said the word "nice." But it felt anything but nice in there. It suddenly felt cold, as though all the warmth had left the radiator and drifted out through the window, to the birds who were still flying back and forth. Must be trees on each side of the window, Winter thought. I didn't think of that when I came in here.

"How's it going, Christer?"

Börge had reached for his glass of wine again, but he stopped in the middle of his movement.

"Are you really interested, Winter?"

"I wouldn't be here otherwise."

"What are you interested in?"

"I don't understand."

"The hell you don't. I remember that you suspected I had something to do with Ellen disappearing. I wouldn't be surprised if that's why you're here now, too."

"That's not why," said Winter.

"She's still not lying in any of the closets here," said Börge. "You can check once more if you want to."

"I saw you today," said Winter.

Börge didn't answer. He took a quick gulp of wine and put down his glass. The foot of the glass had left behind a red ring on the blond wood of the coffee table. Börge didn't seem to notice it. His movements had become a bit broader. The bottle was barely half-full.

"I saw you in town. At Nordstan. I happened to see you." Winter leaned forward. He could smell the faint barn aroma of the wine from the bottle. It was a relatively expensive Pessac. Apparently, if Börge was going to drink, he was going to do it in style. "It was a coincidence."

"You don't think I saw you?"

"I wasn't sure. I wasn't hiding."

"I wasn't, either." Börge contemplated the wine bottle and then looked up. "Don't you think I expected you would show up?"

"It did actually seem that way," said Winter. "When you opened the door."

"Nothing for three years, and then the detective pops up."

"It was a sudden inclination," said Winter, "that I showed up."

"What does that word mean? Inclination?"

"Well . . . I don't know exactly," said Winter. "It's when you—"

"We have to find out right away," said Börge, and he hastily stood up and swayed and had to grab the back of the sofa behind him with one hand so he wouldn't lose his balance. Winter looked at the bottle again. It struck him that it wasn't necessarily the first bottle of the day. Börge seemed relatively sober, but maybe he had the tolerance of an alcoholic.

Börge walked across the room to a wide bookcase on the wall next to the window. He studied the spines of the books and reached for one.

"Swedish Academy's list of words," he said, holding the thick volume out to Winter. "Indispensable."

He began to page through the book.

"In . . . incli . . . in-cli-na-tion." He looked up. "There's no explanation." He looked at the book, held it up to the window as though to a source of light. "Not so indispensable." He tossed it straight across the room in a high arc. It landed behind Winter.

Winter got up and walked to the bookcase. Börge was still standing there, steadying himself against the spines of the books with his other hand. He stared after the book, as though to see where it had landed.

One of the shelves was half-empty. There were three framed photographs, very close to one another. They hadn't been there three years ago, not that Winter could remember. Or maybe they had been. He recognized two of the photos; he had seen them when he had been here. On one, Ellen was smiling at him from a chair that could be standing anywhere. She had an expressionless smile on her face; it revealed nothing. In the other photograph, one could see Christer and Ellen standing together under a tree. It could be the trees outside. It was in a city. The buildings looked familiar. Maybe one of them was the building he found himself in now.

In the third photograph, Ellen was smiling along with another girl. The girls might be about fifteen, maybe a bit older.

"Who is that?" Winter asked, nodding at the photograph.

"Huh?" Börge said, turning his face toward the bookcase. Winter realized that the man was drunker than he thought. The bottle standing on the table wasn't the first one. He must have been drinking before he went to the liquor store, unless he had downed a whole bottle in twenty minutes, before Winter arrived. It was possible.

"Who's the girl standing next to Ellen in that photo?"

The girls appeared to be standing in an arbor. The bushes were close around them. They had their arms around each other, four arms, four hands. It was summer; their clothes were thin. At the edge of the picture, Winter could see something shimmery. It might be a piece of sky or water, a lake, the sea.

Börge fixed his eyes on the photo. He swayed again but wasn't about to lose his balance.

"That's Ellen's sister."

"Oh?"

Börge fixed his eyes on Winter now. He squinted slightly. His speech was even more drawn out, thicker but not slurring.

"Didn't you talk to her when Ellen . . . disappeared?"

"It wasn't me."

"I see."

"It was another of my colleagues. But I knew about her, of course." Winter looked at the girl again.

"Ellen never showed up at her house. We had someone down there who talked with her, too. Malmö, I think. She lived in Malmö at that point."

"I haven't seen her since . . . then," Börge said, nodding toward the photograph again.

"Why not?"

"I don't think she likes me." He looked at Winter again. "I know she doesn't like me." He nodded, as though to himself. "She thinks everything is my fault."

"And yet you took out a photograph of her. And placed it on the shelf."

"It's not for her," Börge said, waving a sweeping finger in the direction of the photo. "It's for Ellen, of course!" He took a cautious step closer. "She looks happy there, don't you think?"

Winter looked at the photo again.

"I found it just a month or so ago," Börge said. "I was going through a few things and there it was."

"Did you find anything more?"

"Like what?"

"Any more photos of Ellen? Or something else. Some kind of memento."

"No, no, nothing."

Winter kept his eyes on the girls' faces. Perhaps there was a resemblance, but he had trouble finding it. Maybe something about their eyes or their hair. Maybe in the very way they held their bodies. Both were tall, thin, with an angularity about their bodies that would change with time.

"They were only half sisters, as you might know," Börge said.

Winter nodded.

"Never see her anymore," Börge mumbled. "But I guess I said that before."

"Where does she live?" Winter asked.

"No idea."

"I seem to have forgotten her name at the moment," Winter said.

"Eva," said Börge. "At least, that's what she was calling herself then."

"What do you mean?"

"She used different names," Börge said.

"Why?"

"How the hell am I supposed to know that?" He detached himself from the shelf and took a few steps to the left, toward the sofa. Maybe it wouldn't work this time. "I guess you'll have to ask her if you see her."

The morning meeting began with a moment of silence. It didn't have anything to do with showing respect to anything in particular, it was more like a moment of concentration. Then Halders's cell phone rang. Winter had just started his run-through.

"Hmm?" This was Halders's way of answering the phone. "Yes? Yes, it's me."

He got up and walked out into the corridor and closed the door behind him.

"It could be someone who used to work at one of the hotels," said Winter.

"Have we had time to go through the whole list you received?" Djanali asked.

"Not yet," Winter answered.

"How about the list from the Odin? Is there anyone we know?"

"Some small-time punks," Ringmar said.

"Aren't there always?"

"It's not many, just a couple," Ringmar said. "But a position at a hotel seems to function as some sort of through station sometimes."

"Why?" Djanali asked.

"Well . . . people don't seem to ask very many questions at a hotel. Among the staff, I mean. They don't seem to be very curious."

"No, we've definitely fucking noticed that," said Bergenhem.

The door was wrenched open.

Halders stepped in with his cell phone still in hand.

"That was one of the painters," he said.

"From Paula's apartment?" Bergenhem asked.

"No, van Gogh."

"What did he say?" Winter asked.

"When they got there, Papa Mario was there." Halders sat down. "It happened a few times."

"So?"

That was Djanali.

"Well . . . he may have had access to his daughter's apartment. I don't even know if we've asked him about it. But anyway."

"But anyway, what?"

"He had a bag. He was carrying a bag when he left there."

"A suitcase?"

That was Ringmar.

"No, we aren't that lucky. It was some kind of duffel."

"Why?"

That was Bergenhem.

"The painter didn't ask if he could look in the bag, Lars. So the contents will remain a mystery."

"He was probably getting something for his daughter," said Djanali.

"When did this happen?" Winter asked.

"After she disappeared, the first night," Halders answered. "We hadn't stopped the renovation yet."

"What was he doing there?" said Bergenhem.

"I suggest that we ask him," said Halders.

"I just wanted to see if she was home," said Mario Ney.

"You could have called," said Winter.

"Maybe she couldn't have answered. She could have been sick. That's what I wanted to check."

"But the painters were there."

"I didn't know that. I didn't know whether they were still there."

"You had been there a few times."

"Yes, so what? Paula wanted me to get a few things."

"What kind of things?"

"Clothes. A skirt, I think. A blouse."

"Why didn't she do it herself?"

"I . . . she asked me. I don't know. I did it."

"What did you get the second time?"

"The second time?"

"Didn't you understand the question, Mario?"

"Uh . . . yes. The second time . . . I don't really remember . . . it was some more clothes, I think . . ."

"But Paula was gone then. What did she need those clothes for?"

"I must have been . . . I don't know . . . I must have been confused."

He looked Winter in the eye. His gaze didn't waver. He looked as though he really was trying to think back.

"No," he said, after a little while. "That's not what it was. I just wanted to go back there to see if I . . . could find anything that could help me. Us. Help us find her."

"What would that have been?"

"I don't know. Anything. Something that could help us."

"Did you find anything?"

"No."

"Nothing?"

"No."

"Were you looking for anything in particular?"

"No."

"What was in your bag?"

"You mean the duffel?"

"Yes."

"There was nothing in it."

"Whose was it?"

"It was mine."

"It wasn't Paula's?"

"It was mine, I said."

"What did you have it for?"

"In case I found anything. If I was going to take anything with me."

"What did you take with you, Mario?"

"I just said I didn't take anything with me! I just said it!"

"We asked one of the painters. It looked like there was something in that bag."

"What does he know? Who? He couldn't tell. He was standing on a ladder up by the ceiling."

"Was the bag closed?"

"I don't even remember. Probably not."

"Why not?"

"It doesn't close, not all the way. The zipper is broken."

"You took a bag with a broken zipper with you?"

"I just took it. I hardly knew what I was doing. What does it matter if the zipper is broken or not? What the hell does it have to do with this?"

"Why didn't you tell us that you were in Paula's apartment those times?"

"Why would I? It's not important, is it?"

"Is it important?" Birgersson asked.

For once he was sitting behind his desk. A toothpick was sticking out of his mouth. That was a bad sign. It would likely be exchanged for a cigarette soon.

"He was keeping it to himself."

"It might actually be like he says," said Birgersson.

"I'm inclined to agree," said Winter.

"Inclined? That's a funny word. You don't hear it so often. Do you know what it means, exactly?"

"No, not exactly," Winter said.

"Then I guess we'll have to find out," said Birgersson, getting up.

"Is that necessary?" Winter asked.

"I think better when I'm focused on looking for answers to questions," Birgersson answered, walking over to the narrow bookcase, on which stood about thirty volumes. He took down one of them.

"Let's see," he said, flipping through the pages.

"This is the second time this has happened to me," Winter said.

Birgersson looked up with a questioning glance.

"Fifteen years ago or so. At Christer Börge's house."

"Christer Börge? The missing wife?"

"He looked up a word in the Swedish Academy's list, too."

"Well, there you go."

"Strange," Winter said.

"Maybe it's more common than you think," Birgersson said, and he kept flipping pages.

"Wonder if he's still alive," said Winter.

28

N o explanation," Birgersson said. He closed the book, placed it on the bookcase, walked back, sat down in his chair again, and nodded at Winter. "That's how it goes sometimes."

"That's how it went then," Winter said.

"Sorry?"

"There was no explanation."

"For what?"

"I don't remember what word it was," Winter asked. "Give me a minute."

"I'm not thinking of the word," said Birgersson.

"I can't stop thinking about that case, Sture. Or whatever I should call it. Ellen's disappearance."

"You'll probably have to live with it for the rest of your career," said Birgersson.

Winter didn't answer.

"Career," Birgersson repeated, and he picked up a new toothpick, looked at it, stuck it in his mouth, looked over the table at Winter. "Next fall I'll be rid of mine."

"Congratulations are in order," said Winter.

"Yes, aren't they?"

Birgersson leaned over the photographs they had placed out on the desk. There were more of them on a bench along the long side of the room.

They depicted mother and daughter.

Birgersson had placed the two faces alongside each other. It was approximately the same angle, lighting, distance. The same silence. In their own way, the same faces.

Birgersson looked at them in silence.

"Who does she look most like, Erik?" he said at last, looking up. "Of her parents?"

"I don't actually know, Sture."

"Her mom? Her dad? I don't really see any resemblance here."

"Why are you asking?"

"Just hit me that I've hardly seen any photos of this family."

"There are hardly any," said Winter.

"What does he want with . . . the white trophies?" Birgersson said, looking down at the pictures again, other pictures. "It's as though he's collecting something. But he . . . leaves it there."

"It's got something to do with ownership," Winter said.

"He had the right to them? The hand? The finger?"

Winter nodded.

"Is that how you see it?"

"He felt that he had the right to everything that was them," said Winter. "He could take what he wanted. And leave what he wanted." Winter nodded toward the photographs. "Do what he wanted."

"The plaster hand, then?"

"A confirmation," said Winter.

"Confirmation of what?"

"Of what I just said."

Nina Lorrinder had called Halders during the early afternoon. Halders looked at the clock as he picked up the receiver: two thirty, and outside the darkness was coming. In two hours he would drive Hannes to bandy practice. The kid had chosen the calmer bandy rather than the more aggressive ice hockey. Halders had played hockey. Hannes took after Margareta, Halders had thought when Hannes told him what he wanted to do this fall. That's good.

"Homicide unit. Halders."

"Yes . . . hi. It's Nina Lorrinder."

"Hi, Nina."

"Yes . . . there's something . . ."

Halders sat up straighter in his chair and reached for a pen.

"Tell me, Nina."

"I don't know how to say this . . . but when I walked by the building where Paula lived. Well, you know that I live a little farther away. I was on my way to the streetcar stop. And then I saw someone standing in among . . . the bushes below the building. It's right across the square. There's a playground there."

"I know what it looks like, Nina. Who did you see?"

"I don't know if it means anything. Maybe it was dumb to call. But it was . . . him. It was starting to get dark but there's a streetlight right above there and he turned his head as I walked by and I saw that it was him."

"Him? Who was it?"

"The guy Paula met at Friskis."

"Are you completely sure that it was him?"

"Yes."

"What was he doing?"

"He was just standing there. It looked like he was looking up at the building. At the window, up a ways."

"Then he turned his head, you said?"

"Yes. It was probably because he heard me. As I was walking on the path behind there."

"Did he see you?"

"Yes . . . he might have. But I don't think he recognized me. It was pretty dark . . . and it was raining a little. I had a hood." Halders heard her swallow. It was audible. "And then he turned his head again."

"When did this happen?" Halders asked.

"The day before yesterday. About four thirty."

"Why didn't you call right away?"

"I . . . I don't know. At first I was sure it was him. And then . . . I don't know."

"Were you afraid?"

"Yes."

"Afraid of what?"

"That he saw me." Halders heard her breathing. "That he would . . . I don't know . . ."

"Even more reason to call me right away. If you thought he would try to find you."

"Yes . . . I know."

"Have you seen him other times?"

"No . . ."

"You're hesitating, Nina."

"I've . . . felt like I've been . . . I don't know . . . being stalked recently."

"Stalked?"

"Yes . . ."

"Have you seen anyone?"

"No . . ."

"What do you mean, then?"

"I . . . how should I put it . . . it's like someone is following me. Or spying on me. Watching me. Is that just silly of me? Maybe it's nothing at all."

"And you haven't seen anyone?"

"No . . . not exactly. I've thought that I caught a glimpse of someone outside the window. Someone . . . who was standing out there. But I'm not sure. And one time the phone rang but no one said anything. But the line was open. And there was a siren from an ambulance outside, or maybe a police car; I heard it in . . . the room, and I also heard it on the phone. It seemed to be the same sound . . . at the same time. And it was really close by."

"Why didn't you say something about this earlier, Nina?"

She didn't answer.

"Nina?"

"Is it . . . could it be dangerous? For me?"

"Is there anyone you could get hold of?" Halders asked. "A friend, or family? Whose house you could go to?"

"I guess I can . . . call someone."

"Do it."

"Do you mean now?"

"Yes."

Halders heard the fear in her voice. He didn't want to scare her. But he took her fear seriously.

"Nina . . . are you completely sure that you haven't seen him any other times? The guy Paula met, I mean."

"I . . . think so."

"Not in town? Anywhere?"

"No."

"At Friskis & Svettis?"

"I don't go there anymore. Not since it happened."

"What happened after you passed him that time? When you saw him?"

"Nothing . . ."

"Did you turn around? Was he still standing there?"

"I turned around a bit farther on. But I didn't see anything then. The bushes were in the way."

"And then you took the streetcar?"

"Yes."

"And you've never seen him before in that neighborhood? Near where Paula lived?"

"No."

"Okay, Nina. Thanks for calling."

"What . . . happens now?" she asked.

"We'll have to have a little talk with him," Halders answered.

No one opened up when they rang at Jonas Sandler's door. No one had answered the telephone that was somewhere inside. No one answered Jonas's cell phone. Halders tried again.

There was a small, handwritten sign on the door: No ads, please.

"No Jonas, thank you very much," said Halders.

"He's probably out taking a walk," said Winter.

"Sure that's what he's doing," said Halders, putting his cell phone into the inner pocket of his leather jacket. "Walking and stalking."

"It's too bad when people are unemployed," said Winter, ringing the doorbell again. "You can't get hold of them at work when they're not home."

Halders laughed.

"A case for the Social Democrats," he said.

"We'll have to take it to the national police commissioner," Winter said, and he turned around and looked down at the stairwell.

"Isn't he a Social Democrat, too?" said Halders.

"Don't you like Social Democrats, Fredrik?"

"If I got to know one for real, maybe I would like him, or her. No doubt there are female Social Democrats, too. No doubt there are also nice ones."

"I'm a Social Democrat," Winter said, starting to walk down the stairs.

"Are you joking?"

"Yes."

"What are you, then?"

"A feminist."

"Are you joking?"

"No."

"I'm a feminist, too," said Halders.

"I know, Fredrik."

"It's true. I'm not joking."

"You've tried to hide it, but you can't fool me," said Winter.

"No one can fool you, can they?" said Halders.

They were standing outside the front door. It closed behind them with a creaking sound. The sound made Halders think of a Social Democratic politician who had to make decisions that didn't necessarily help his own career.

"Jonas," Winter answered. "He may have fooled me."

"We'll wait until tonight," said Ringmar.

Winter nodded.

"He might be out roaming the streets," Ringmar continued. "Sounding the alarm now . . . well . . ."

"He might have roamed a good bit of the way to hell at this point," said Halders.

"If that's the case, we have our man," said Ringmar.

"Not necessarily," said Winter.

Anne Sandler didn't answer the phone. Winter had called the first time as they stood in the yard outside Jonas's apartment. He had kept calling. She didn't have an answering machine.

Winter passed the swings in the empty playground. He hadn't yet seen any children there. It was as though that time was forever gone. The only children he knew who had sat on those swings were Jonas and the girl. But even that was uncertain. Anne Sandler could have been mistaken. Maybe that family never lived here, or at least not in her same stairwell. How was Jonas supposed to remember a girl from one month in a distant childhood? For many people, childhood was very far away. For many, it had never even existed. In his work, Winter had met many people who missed a childhood they'd never had, who were looking for it, desperately searching for it.

That could have horrible consequences.

Had Jonas had a childhood? Winter didn't know. He had met the boy that was Jonas, but he didn't know the other one. Had Paula had a childhood? He didn't know that, either. Yesterday he had thought: This is about childhood, or what could have been childhood. Paula's. Someone's. Several people's. Ellen Börge's. Or Elisabeth's, Mario's. Ellen's, he had thought again. I can't get away from it. I-can't-get-away-from-it. Why won't she leave me alone?

The swings were swinging in the wind again. The invisible children. It was as though the wind were swinging through time, and time was the same. Nothing was old or new. Everything was there.

No one opened up when he rang at the door. He hadn't expected anyone to. And yet he came out here. It's like a magnet. Is it the swings? The grove of trees? Yes, it's the grove of trees.

Winter walked out of the building and over to the small group of trees and bushes. It wasn't possible to see anything in there. It was like a room with walls, without doors. Dusk was falling again; it was always falling at this time of year, falling and remaining like a black light.

He took a few steps toward the trees. He heard a sound, a noise. Was there a dog in there, digging in the earth? It sounded like something was digging, or moving around in the dirt. It was a sound you recognized. Winter pushed aside some bushes and took two steps farther in. He saw a movement behind the large tree. He saw another movement, a hand. He heard the sound of something digging in the ground. Then he heard a sniffle.

Jonas turned around as Winter stepped forward behind the tree.

He was on his knees, digging in the ground with his hands. It must be hard work. The earth had begun to freeze for the winter. The autumn leaves lay like a tough skin on the ground.

He didn't stop digging.

"Jonas?" Winter said, taking another step.

He didn't answer. There was nothing in his face that didn't remind Winter of the first time he'd seen him. That had been a powerful experience for Winter. Sandler was sniffling, breathing hard, digging, digging. Winter could see blood on his knuckles. It was still light enough that he could see the red color. All the other colors around them had begun to creep down into the ground for the night.

"Jonas!"

He looked up but kept on digging, scratching at the crust of dirt. Winter took the last few steps and placed his hands on the young man's shoulders. It was like touching stone. Sandler kept moving his arms, his muscles. He was like a machine.

"Jonas, calm down."

Winter could feel the movement slowly cease; this was a mechanical movement, too. The sniffling didn't stop.

"Jonas."

He turned his face up to Winter. There was great terror in his eyes. Winter knew that this wasn't about him. Jonas hadn't been afraid of being discovered. He seemed to be beyond that now. He had been

searching for something, looking for it in here. Digging for his childhood, something in his childhood that had never left him in peace. It
wasn't necessarily the crust of dirt. That was only the top layer.

"Paula," the boy said, turning his face toward the ground again.
"She's here."

29

Sandler held up his hands as if they were proof of something. Winter didn't see any proof, not yet. He saw the young man's intense agitation, as though he were about to be blasted to pieces.

"Jonas," Winter said, extending his hand.

"Paula!" said Sandler. "I saw her!"

"Where did you see her, Jonas?"

"Here!" he said, waving at the ground with his arms. "She was here!"

"When did you see her?"

"She was here!" he repeated.

"When did you see her, Jonas?"

"You saw her, too!" he said. "You were here, too!"

"That was a long time ago, Jonas."

"No!"

Sandler's agitation increased even more, as though he would lose consciousness, or his senses, at any second. Maybe he already had. Something had happened in the last few days. Or hours. The boy had been yanked from his lethargy. That was the word that came into Winter's head. He suddenly had an image of Christer Börge in his mind, with the book in his hand, under the bookcase in the creepy living room where time stood still. Lethargy. It meant a trancelike state, Winter had looked it up once himself. There was nothing trancelike about the way Jonas Sandler was acting now. Perhaps he found himself in a nightmare, but it wasn't a trance.

And time had frozen in the grove of his youth.

Now Sandler was back there.

"Paula!"

Winter got down on his knees. He tried to place his hand on the young man's shoulder, but Jonas twisted himself away from it. He had stopped digging now. He had made only a shallow pit, like a bowl among the leaves. His hands were covered with wounds, rasped, as if a pattern had been pulled over them. The light was gone now. The scratches on his hands were black. Winter thought of the black stones he'd seen here eighteen years ago. They were no longer here, or else Jonas had tossed them aside. He thought of the hand that only Jonas had seen. That wasn't here either. The white hand that the boy had described with large, frightened eyes. Maybe he would always see it, whether or not it was gone. And Paula wasn't here, either. But Sandler was just as convinced now as he had been then. What did he know? What had he done? What had someone done to him? What was there, in this black earth?

Sandler had begun to cry, a quiet sound. Winter suddenly heard the distant hum of the traffic on the island. Now it felt very small, as though the island consisted of nothing more than this grove of trees. Above them, a bird screeched. The boy gave a start. He looked at Winter as though he recognized him now. It was as if he was waking from the nightmare. The boy turned his face toward the ground, as though it had been part of the dream, too, but was now foreign to him. It wasn't an act, a role. He didn't repeat her name. Winter did.

"The girl you played with here was Paula, wasn't it?"

Sandler was calm as he sat in Winter's office. It was a better place right now than the cold interrogation room, which was reminiscent of a nightmare. Winter was afraid that Sandler would return there. Then it wouldn't be possible to reach him.

The light over Winter's desk was warm. Sandler appeared to be warming himself in it. Winter felt himself beginning to thaw from the iciness he'd experienced among the trees. He had driven straight here, with Sandler as a silent passenger. He glimpsed Sandler's hands under the desk. He was holding them in his lap. His knuckles were covered in gauze. It looked like he was wearing white gloves.

"Tell me about Paula," said Winter.

Jonas tried to say something, but no words came out. It was like a weak breeze. He tried again.

"There's . . . nothing to tell."

"You played together."

Sandler nodded slightly.

"Did you play with Paula when the two of you were little?"

"Y-yes."

"Are you sure of that?"

"Yes."

"How can you be so sure?"

"I don't understand," Sandler said, looking up at Winter. The boy was leaning forward in his chair, with his head near the surface of the desk.

"How can you be so sure now? You said earlier that you didn't know her."

"I . . . knew her."

"Why didn't you say so before, Jonas?"

He didn't answer.

Winter repeated the question.

"I don't know."

"You know, Jonas."

He looked up again.

"You're afraid of something," Winter continued. "What are you afraid of?"

"Nothing."

"Who are you afraid of?"

Sandler didn't answer.

"Has someone threatened you?"

"No."

"Who has threatened you, Jonas?"

"No one."

"Did Paula threaten you?"

"Wh-what?"

Sandler raised his head.

"Did you feel threatened by her?"

"N-no. Why would I?"

"Did you feel threatened when you met her again, Jonas? When you were adults? Did she know something about you?"

"N-no. Like what?"

"Why did you go out there? To that grove of trees?"

"I . . . don't know that either. It's like . . . I don't know why I did it." He searched for Winter's eyes. "It's like the other thing. That we had played . . . out there."

"Did you talk about it when you saw each other?"

"Yes . . . once or twice."

"So what did you say?"

"Nothing in particular. We . . . just remembered it."

"How did you meet, Jonas?"

"You know that. At the gym."

"How did it happen?"

"What? Happen?"

"Did you recognize her?"

"Yes."

"Just like that?"

"Yes. She . . . was the same."

"What do you mean? The same?"

"She looked like she did then."

"After eighteen years?"

"Is that so long?" Sandler said.

"Did she recognize you?" Winter asked.

"No . . . not at first."

"When did she recognize you?"

"I don't understand."

"Did she ever recognize you?"

"Yes."

"Was she as sure as you were?"

"Yes."

"Where did you meet the next time?"

"What?"

"Where did you meet the next time?" Winter repeated.

"There. At the gym. Friskis."

"I mean outside of Friskis."

"We never met . . . outside."

"I don't believe that, Jonas."

"It's true." The boy sat up straight. It had been like a slow awakening of his bodily function. "We didn't. It's true."

"No coffee on the town? A pub?"

"No."

"Why not?"

"She didn't want to."

"Did you ask?"

"Yes."

"Did you invite her home?"

"Yes."

"What did she say?"

"She said no."

"Why?"

"I . . . I don't know."

"Did you ask?"

"What?"

"Why she said no?"

"No . . . yes . . . she didn't want to. I couldn't nag her."

"But you knew where she lived?"

"Yes . . ."

"Have you been there?"

"I . . . don't understand. I just said I wasn't . . . invited."

"You were seen outside," said Winter.

Sandler didn't answer.

"Have you been there?" Winter asked.

"Yes."

"When?"

"The other day . . . several times."

"What were you doing?"

"No-nothing. I just stood there."

"Why?"

"I . . . don't know." Sandler looked at Winter again. "I don't know that either." He looked somewhere else, maybe toward the window. "I missed her. I had met her again and then she was gone." He looked at Winter. "She was gone."

"Why was she gone, Jonas?"

"I don't understand."

"Have you thought about why she was gone?"

"Oh . . . thought . . . I don't know . . ."

"She was murdered, Jonas. She wasn't just gone. Who could have murdered her?"

"I don't know." Winter noticed that Sandler's lower lip began to tremble, a spasm. He had also seen this out in the grove, among all the boy's other movements. "Oh God, I don't know."

"Do you know Paula's parents, Jonas?"

"Parents? No."

"But you knew her mom."

"No . . ."

"You didn't know her mom? They lived in the same building, didn't they?"

"Paula said that it . . . wasn't her mom." He looked across the table again, straight at Winter. "Not her real mom."

"So he says that Paula lived there as a child," Ringmar said. "And what if she did? It doesn't have to mean anything."

"Oh no?" Winter walked back and forth in the room, which was unusual. "It might mean everything."

Ringmar was sitting outside the circle of light on Winter's desk. Fifteen minutes ago, Jonas Sandler had been sitting there. Now he was sitting in an examination room one floor down. He had become a boy again and begun to shake; his lips had suddenly turned blue in the warm light, his eyes had started to flutter like a flame. Winter had called for a doctor. After him, there would be a psychologist. Then they would see. Maybe a prosecutor. Maybe a clergyman.

"This means everything to him now," Winter said. "It's become his entire life."

"He might be crazy."

"No."

"Why not?"

"There's a lot of pressure," Winter said. "He's under a lot of pressure. It's something else."

"That kind of thing can lead to craziness."

Winter didn't answer.

"If he murdered her, we'll find out," Ringmar said. "Maybe even today."

Winter stopped in the middle of the room and looked out the window. It wasn't daytime anymore; it hadn't been for a long time.

"What about Elisabeth Ney? The mom? Did he murder her, too?"

"Well, according to Jonas, she's not her mom," said Winter.

"Are we supposed to believe that?"

"Why else would he say it? Why would Paula have told him that?"

"If she said it."

"Mm-hmm."

"Maybe it was something she made up," Ringmar continued. "Children can say things like that."

"So can adults."

"Like Jonas," said Ringmar.

"Mm-hmm."

"Maybe it's all in his imagination," Ringmar said. "There was never any Paula when he was growing up. He invented her later, when he met her. No, when she died. A fantasy about her."

Winter didn't say anything. He thought of the boy's face when he met him for the first time. The boy and his dog. What had its name been? Zack. That was a name he remembered. Zack. It was a good name.

"He really doesn't seem to be very clear about what he sees and doesn't see," said Ringmar.

"I don't know," said Winter. "It's not that simple."

"Who said it was simple?"

"He saw something out in that grove of trees," Winter said.

"You mean twenty years ago?"

"Eighteen."

"That hand? Is that what you're talking about?"

"Not now. I'm talking about what he saw now. Today."

"He said that Paula was there?"

"Yes. But was that why he was there? To look for Paula?"

"Maybe he was looking for himself," Ringmar said. "And I don't mean that as a joke."

"Is it the hand he saw as a boy?"

"Not Paula's hand, anyway. We've managed to keep that out of the media."

"Which means what?"

"That very few people know about it," said Ringmar. "And only one of them is outside this unit."

Winter's cell phone rang.

He answered, listened, nodded, hung up, and put back his phone.

"It's time," he said, reaching for his coat.

A patrol car had been directed to the grove of trees after Winter had called. He had called while he was still in there, in the dark, and he'd waited for the car to come before he drove to the police station with Sandler in the seat next to him.

Winter and Ringmar arrived one minute after their colleagues in forensics.

One of them was a veteran.

"I can't believe it's true," he said as Winter got out of the car and walked toward them. "The same yard and the same grove."

"You have a good memory, Lars."

"Sometimes it's a burden."

"History always repeats itself," said Winter.

"If that's the case, then we won't find anything this time either."

"If that's the case, I apologize," Winter said.

"You didn't last time."

"Shall we begin?" Winter said, starting to walk toward the familiar trees and bushes. Soon I'll recognize them as though I grew up here myself. Those swings are mine. The only thing that's gone is the merry-go-round. There had been a merry-go-round in the middle of the playground when he was here the first time. It was gone now, for safety reasons. Children might injure themselves, be dragged along by scarves that got stuck; they could trip and fall under the merry-go-round.

The swings swung in the never-ending wind. It must always blow from the same direction here, coming in from the northwest between the two buildings that leaned above the playground and shaded the grove of trees.

They were standing in the middle of it now.

The two forensics technicians began to set up spotlights. They wouldn't do much more this evening. Get an idea of the place. Put up a tent over everything. Come back early tomorrow morning. That was the routine. In the dark, they might destroy more than they found. Digging in the dirt was a sensitive archaeological task. At times, Torsten Öberg and his technicians had even worked with archaeologists from the university, right at the site of evidence. Forensic technicians and archaeologists had the same job: digging for the past. Digging for death. And Winter could stand beside the pit and be part of the whole thing. He was an archaeologist of crime, too. He dug in his own way.

Lars Östensson tested one of the spotlights and the small area exploded in a white light that made it more naked than ever. So this is what it looks like, Winter thought.

"Where is it?" the veteran asked.

Winter pointed toward the hollow in the leaves. In the powerful light, Winter could see that it was deeper than he thought. Sandler must have been here longer than he knew. Or be stronger than he thought.

"What are we looking for?"

"I don't know," Winter answered.

"Last time we were here it was a hand some kid had seen."

"You remember that?"

"How could I forget? After that girl was murdered. I'd probably forgotten, but it reminded me."

Östensson had been the one to take in the plaster hand. He would never forget it.

"Are we looking for something big or something small?" he asked.

Winter threw out his arms. It was also a motion toward the place on the ground. Search. Find. It might be everything or nothing.

"I can't wait until tomorrow," he said.

"We'll do more harm than good now, Erik. You know that."

"I want to bring the dog here."

The Gothenburg police had a crime-scene search dog. They called it the corpse dog, not a very nice name. Its actual name was Roy. It was trained to sense the odor of a cadaver.

Now it was standing on the playground, its tongue visible through its sharp teeth. The dog's eyes shone in the spotlight. Or the moonlight. It was bright tonight.

The spotlights shone above the grove of trees and the black earth it stood on. The earth became even blacker in the light, as though it had already become a deep hole. Winter thought of when he had stood here with his flashlight so many years ago. The boy's white face next to him. The dog's heavy breathing, and the bark that had suddenly exploded, stronger than any spotlight.

The dog's keeper's name was Bergurson; he was Icelandic. He spoke with Roy in a language that sounded ancient.

They were on their way to the grove now. The dog looked like a wolf. Winter could see the breath of the men who were standing around.

The place seemed less illuminated now, as though a cloud had sailed in front of the spotlights. Winter saw the dog. It was the first time for Winter. He heard the dog.

A long time seemed to pass.

Winter closed his eyes. He wasn't tired. It was as though he would never be tired again.

"There's something in the earth here," said Bergurson.

They made their way down through the topmost layer of leaves, which had stiffened into a brittle hood. Dawn came with a mild light. Four technicians were working inside the grove, under Östensson's leadership. Winter was there, too. The technicians had divided the surface of the ground into a pattern of squares. They would work their way through the layers section by section with trowels that looked like regular gardening trowels. They would sift all the dirt, look at it. They would try to get closer to what Roy sensed in the air. It might take a long time, or a short time.

"It's almost like I recognize this dirt," Östensson said, scooping away a layer. His closest colleague was named Arnberg, a younger man. He got up and adjusted one of the spotlights. The light of dawn was still like half night. "How deep do we have to go?" Östensson mumbled to himself.

Winter walked out of the grove, passed the playground, went in through the front door, and rang at Anne Sandler's door. He knew it would be in vain. The windows had been black. She was probably still down at the police station, with her son. He rang at the door anyway. No one else opened it, and no other door was opened.

He walked back down the stairs. His cell phone rang as he was standing in the yard.

"Yes?"

"Mario Ney had a position at Hotel Odin a hundred years ago," came Halders's voice. It sounded thin and metallic, as though the reception were coming only halfway through because it was only half-way morning.

"Has he confirmed that?" Winter asked.

"Hell no. He doesn't know anything."

"Where is he?"

"Don't know. Should I call Molina and ask what he says now?"

Until now, the public prosecutor hadn't found reason to detain Mario Ney. Winter hadn't seen a reason to either, nor had Halders. The conversation with Molina had been routine.

"Who substantiated it?" Winter asked.

"An old housekeeper. I think that's what it's called. She recognized him."

"His name?"

"No. His picture. Bergenhem was the one who talked to her. I've praised Bergenhem."

"She recognized an old picture?"

"Ney's face has held up well through the years," said Halders.

"What did he do there? At the hotel?"

"He was an all-around man of action, as she put it."

Winter continued to walk toward the grove as he spoke with Halders.

"Let's figure this out when I come back," he said.

"How's it going out there?" Halders asked.

"Nothing so far."

"Sandler doesn't seem to be doing very well," Halders said. "His mom is with him now."

"Yes, I know. She's not here."

"Are you digging deep?"

Winter didn't answer. Ringmar had stepped out of the grove. He signaled toward Winter. There was something in Ringmar's eyes.

30

A bird screeched. It was the same screech as always. Winter looked up and saw the bird high in the sky, a black scribble against the gray. It must have been circling this grove of trees for eighteen years.

Ringmar waited at the edge. The odd look in his face remained. Winter knew what it was. Ringmar knew that he knew.

Winter followed his older colleague without a word. A small twig had become stuck in Ringmar's hair. It almost looked like a piece of jewelry.

Östensson, the veteran, looked up from the pit as they stepped into the glade. Winter couldn't see anything in there that he hadn't seen before.

"We were waiting for you," said Östensson, turning his head toward the pit.

Winter nodded.

Pia Eriksson Fröberg, the medical examiner, raised her hand in greeting. She was standing at the ready next to the pit.

"There's someone lying in the ground here," said Östensson.

He reached forward and made a circle with one hand above part of the excavation. That was the word that came into Winter's head. Excavation. And ground. There's someone lying in the ground. It isn't consecrated ground.

"I can feel a hand here," said Östensson, holding his own hand a little above the ground.

"Let's see what it is," said Winter. He felt calm, almost cold, but not as though he were freezing. It was a different sort of chill. It was a confirmation. Something he had known all along. Like the boy had known. But it was something more than this pit, this grove of trees.

Nothing had lain here eighteen years ago. The vision the boy had had was because of something else. Maybe he didn't know what. Maybe they would never find out.

The forensics technicians carefully began to scrape their way down into the square pattern, the layers of dirt.

Östensson didn't need to dig deep.

The hand became visible.

"This here is going to take some time," said Östensson.

Winter nodded. Suddenly he felt restless, as though he either had to start digging himself or leave the place.

He walked out of the grove and lit a Corps. The fog had begun to lift and the dampness seemed to rise along with the fog toward the treetops. It was like low clouds out there. Winter inhaled smoke and blew it out and watched the smoke rise with the clouds. Suddenly he heard voices, bright and high voices, and a few seconds later he saw two children come running to the other side of the playground, and each hopped up onto a swing and started swinging, pumping their legs vigorously.

It was a good sight. They were the first children he'd seen there. Somehow, in that moment, it made him very happy. He felt as though he would suddenly start laughing like a madman. He felt tears in his eyes. It could be the smoke from his cigar. He moved it away from his face and wiped his eyes with his arm. The children might be looking over at him; he couldn't really see. For a few seconds, it was foggy around him.

It felt like he was going to start crying.

Now he could see better.

The children were still there. The bird was still there, up in the sky.

He stubbed out his cigar and went back into the grove.

There was more to see now. More of the hand. The technicians seemed to be working faster now.

Winter saw an arm.

A shoulder.

"A woman," said Östensson in a low and steady voice. "Here comes her head."

She wasn't deep. The body had been carefully covered with leaves.

The autumn, too, had done its job. But Winter couldn't tell how long she'd been lying here. No one could determine that just yet.

Her head became visible. Winter saw her hair, her cheek, part of her chin. A profile. It was a ghastly sight.

"She can't have been lying here long," he heard Östensson say in a calm, low voice. It seemed to calm everyone who was standing or kneeling at the grave. But this was no grave. It was everything but a grave. They called it a grave, but that was their police jargon. Routine.

Winter got down on his knees in order to see the face better. Her hair covered her forehead and part of her left cheek. Her hair was white in the spotlight; perhaps it had been blond while she lived. Winter wasn't an expert, not like Östensson and his colleagues from forensics, but he could tell approximately how long someone had been dead. He had experience with that. The woman had not yet returned to dust; from the earth you were taken, and to dust you will return. Winter leaned closer. He was almost face-to-face with her. Her eyes were neither closed nor open. The lower part of her face lay in shadow from a tree, a bush, anything. Yet Winter could see her mouth, her chin, her throat. Suddenly he was freezing, as though a wind from the sea had stormed in among the trees. Several thoughts crowded into his head simultaneously. One of them said: This is also a confirmation.

"It's Ellen Börge," he said.

So he had found her. How could he recognize her? Her face. Ellen's face. Almost a generation had gone by since she had disappeared and Winter had studied her face in a picture for the first time. It had stayed in his mind. He had returned to the photographs a few times through the years. It was as if Ellen's face had been frozen by time and by dirt. Her features had been smoothed by death, and her face had taken on a younger appearance. That wasn't unusual. Death could lead to an effective face-lift. Winter had heard forensics techs joke about it. But he didn't feel like joking now. He was standing before Ellen. She was no longer lying in the ground. The light was different here in the morgue, still electric but bluer, even colder. She still looked young; her face looked even more naked in this light. She was missing the middle toe on her right foot. He didn't know when she'd lost it. An accident, Christer Börge had said. Winter had recently read that he'd said it. He hadn't talked to Börge but he would do that soon. He heard someone come in through the door, and he turned his head. It was Halders. He walked up to the table, stood beside Winter, looked at the woman.

"I went through the video again," he finally said, without taking his eyes from the woman's face. He looked only at her face.

"Yes?"

"The woman at Central Station looks a little older," Halders continued, "but sunglasses can't hide everything." He nodded slightly at the face below them. "Not when we can make a comparison."

Winter nodded.

"You don't seem surprised."

Winter didn't answer. He closed his eyes and saw a photograph before him.

"You've never let go of the Ellen Börge case," Halders said. "And you were right not to."

"I had let it go," said Winter.

"In that case, it never let you go," said Halders. "Or us."

"I let it go too early," said Winter.

"Erik . . ."

"I didn't see clearly enough." He turned to Halders. "I didn't listen to what people said."

"Come on, Eri—"

"You said it yourself, Fredrik," Winter interrupted him. "Here is something we can't see, but it's there." He lifted his eyes from Ellen's face. "Or was there."

"What are you thinking about?"

Winter looked at the clock. It wasn't yet midnight.

"I'm going to Börge's house," he said.

"Now?"

Winter didn't answer.

"Aren't you going to call first?"

"It doesn't matter to him, does it? Won't he want to know what happened to Ellen?"

Halders turned his eyes to Ellen's face again.

"He might know."

Winter nodded.

"Is that why you're going?"

"I don't know yet."

Winter started to walk away from the damned steel table. He had stood at it before. It was the most god-awful part of the job. It was worse than photographs.

"What'll we do with Mario?" Halders asked.

"Where is he now?"

"At home." Halders took a step away from the table. "We haven't knocked at his door, but Frölunda is keeping a discreet eye on him." Halders walked across the room. "There are lights on in his apartment. They can see him walking around in there. I talked to them ten minutes ago."

"Let's wait and see," said Winter. "I'll go to Börge's house first."

"Do you want company?"

"Aren't you going home to your family?" Winter asked.

"What about you?"

"It's walking distance from Börge's flat to my place," said Winter.

"Well, that changes everything."

Winter couldn't help smiling.

"You're welcome to come along, Fredrik."

"I wouldn't go alone," Halders said.

They stood out in the corridor. The cold light was the same out here as it was in there, as though you weren't allowed to let go of the sight of death too soon.

"It's all coming together," Halders added. "We have to be careful."

Winter got a call before they left.

"Hi, Pia here."

"Yes?"

"There's considerable damage to her ankles and wrists," said Fröberg.

"What does that mean?"

"She was bound for a long time. Tied up, somehow."

"Oh God."

"A relatively thin rope."

Winter didn't say anything.

"And she was horribly emaciated," said Fröberg.

They drove through the darkness. The night outside was empty and swept in fog. The streetlights were powerless. It was as though the sea had taken over the city. The few cars that were out on the street drove in and out of the fog like ships. Winter stopped at a red light and let three men of early middle age cross the street. They were nicely dressed; their coats were open, but one of the men seemed a bit disheveled. They stopped suddenly in the middle of the crosswalk and made obscene gestures at Winter and Halders. The men laughed as the light changed. They didn't move.

"Might be different if we had a marked car," said Halders.

Winter crawled slowly toward the men. His Mercedes was the only car on all of Allén.

"Hell, run them over," said Halders. "I promise to shut my eyes. I haven't seen a thing."

"Another time," Winter said, heaving the car onto the sidewalk and passing the men and the crosswalk on two wheels.

Halders turned around.

"That scared the shit out of them," he said, laughing. "Hopefully they'll be robbed by a gang of kids before the night is over."

Winter took a left.

They passed Vasaplatsen.

"I see there's light in your windows," Halders said, peering at an angle up at the building facade.

"Lilly's learned how to walk," Winter said.

"Just now?" said Halders.

"She can't stop," said Winter, turning onto Vasagatan. "I suppose it's the most fun thing that's happened to her so far."

Winter parked next to the sidewalk outside of Börge's building. His cell phone rang.

"Yes?"

"Hi, Winter. Östensson here."

"What is it, Lars?"

"We kept digging in that pit."

"Yes?"

"There was the skeleton of a dog half a meter down."

Winter didn't answer.

"Are you still there, Winter?"

"Yes."

"A small dog. It's been there for decades, I'd guess."

"I think I know its name," said Winter.

"How could you know that?"

"We'll worry about it later, Lars," said Winter, hanging up.

"What was that?" Halders asked.

Winter just shook his head in answer.

Halders looked up at the facade of the building.

"Which floor does Börge live on?"

"The third," Winter said, switching off the engine and opening the door.

"There's light in a couple of windows on the third floor. Right above the door."

"That's Börge's place," Winter said, climbing out of the car.

Halders climbed out on the other side.

"Maybe he's expecting us," Winter said.

Halders looked up at the facade again. It was rough with stucco and decorations.

"There's someone in the window," said Halders.

31

The shadows moved back and forth in the stairwell. The weak light in there came from a source that was impossible to see, like a distant sun. They walked up the worn stone stairs. They were like the ones in Winter's building. A hundred years of feet in the stairwell.

"I'll go in alone," said Winter.

Halders nodded.

"I'll wait one floor down."

Winter rang at the door. Maybe he recognized it. It was built of solid wood, with stylized door panels. The sound of the doorbell echoed inside, muffled by the door. It was an old bell, a hundred years old. Winter waited. He rang the doorbell again. As the sound subsided in there, he heard steps. He looked at his watch. It was past midnight now.

"Who is it?"

The voice sounded weak, as though it had lost its strength by coming through the door. Winter didn't recognize the voice.

"Erik Winter," he answered. "Chief Inspector Erik Winter. We've met before."

"What do you want?"

The voice sounded more clear now, as though it had come closer. Winter heard Halders in the stairwell behind him. He looked down, saw Halders's raised eyebrow, turned back to the door:

"Can you please open up, Christer?"

He heard the bolt move slowly and then click. There was a rustling at eye level as the door opened slightly. Winter could see the chain lock. He didn't remember it being there when he was here last. That was fifteen years ago. The face inside was mostly a shadow. It was impossible to recognize anything in that face.

"Winter . . . is that you?"

"Sorry it's so late. May I come in?"

"What's going on? What do you want?"

"May I come in?" Winter repeated.

The door swung open with such force that Winter had to take a quick step back. The weak light in the stairwell shone on the figure in the doorway, and now Winter could recognize Börge. It was the same face, fifteen years later. He had only seen his profile in Domkyrkan, but it was the same face. He wasn't sure that he would have recognized him on the street, in another context. But now he knew. Would he have recognized Ellen? In life? He didn't have to think about it. It was one of the few things he didn't need to think about.

"Well, come in," said Börge.

Winter stepped into the hall. He heard music, a classical piece at a very low volume. He didn't remember Börge playing music any other time.

Winter began to take off his shoes.

"Don't bother with that," said Börge, who was waiting farther away in the hall. It was long, like a room whose walls had ended up too close to each other.

There were no shoes on Börge's shoe rack.

Winter suddenly remembered the three pairs he'd seen there when he was here the last time. They had been identical, hadn't they? At least two of them. Oh, God. He turned his head and saw Börge's back. The man was on his way into the living room. The shoes. He had seen the shoes standing here fifteen years ago. The shoes. That brand. Take it easy now, Erik. But now there was nothing here. Did Börge walk around barefoot on the November streets? Were his shoes in a closet? Could I be wrong? Yes. No. Yes. Ecco Free was a common brand. But where are Börge's shoes now?

Börge suddenly turned around, as though Winter had spoken to him. Winter noticed that he was in stocking feet. That was an old phrase, stocking feet. In only his socks.

"You've found her, haven't you?"

Winter sat on Börge's sofa. It was the same sofa. The air felt very thick, as though it, too, were left over from before. The thoughts in Winter's head moved quickly. Börge hadn't sat down. He stood behind an easy chair, as if poised to go. No. That was just one of Winter's thoughts.

"I don't believe it," said Börge.

Winter didn't say anything. He had said what he'd come to say. But he hadn't told the whole story. It wasn't possible to, after all; there was no end, not yet.

"After all these years," said Börge. "It's impossible."

"I drove straight here," said Winter.

"It's impossible," Börge repeated.

He stretched, pulled up his shoulders, and then sank down again. Winter could see the damp night air through the window behind Börge. It was as though a wall had come up out there, right through the street. A stone wall.

"Why is it impossible?" Winter asked.

"What? What?"

Börge looked straight through him, as though it were the first time he realized that Winter was there. That he had brought his message tonight.

"You said that it's impossible, Christer."

"It's impossible," Börge said, for the third time.

"What is impossible?"

"How could you have . . . seen someone who has disappeared?" Börge answered. "It doesn't . . . fit."

Winter stood up.

"Do you think I was lying?" Börge said.

Winter didn't answer.

"Do you think I . . ." Börge said, taking a step away from the easy chair, and another step, toward Winter.

"What do you think I think?" Winter said.

Börge didn't answer. His eyes roved back and forth between Winter and the bookcase, still standing where Winter remembered it had stood last time, too. There was a photograph there, one of three,

Winter recalled. I remember that Ellen was smiling in the photo, along with her sister. They were about fifteen, I remember that, too. I asked Börge who the other girl was and he answered that it was Ellen's sister. What was her name? I don't remember. It was something with *E.* They hadn't looked very much alike, the girls. They were half sisters. Börge said that he'd never seen her again after Ellen disappeared. Why can't I remember her name? Börge said that she liked to use different names, I remember that. Eva. Her name was Eva. Is Eva. Börge had found that photo a month or so earlier, he said. He had gone through a few things and there it was, he said. I remember that, word for word. But I don't remember the shoes.

Winter looked over at the bookcase. The three photographs were still there, presumably on the same shelf. They would presumably be the same photographs if he went over there and checked.

He took the few steps across the room to the bookcase. Börge followed his steps but said nothing.

The photograph he was looking for was still there. It was the same picture. The girls appeared to be standing in an arbor; the bushes were close around them. They had their arms around each other, four arms, four hands. It was summer; their clothes were thin. At the edge of the picture, Winter could see something shimmery. It might be a piece of sky or water, a lake, the sea.

Winter kept his eyes on the girls' faces.

There was a resemblance. A resemblance between then and now.

Jesus!

He hadn't seen it then. How could he have seen it? He hadn't known back then. But now. He saw something that he knew meant something.

Meant everything.

The girl beside Ellen was Elisabeth Ney.

They were sisters.

"My God," said Ringmar. "Sisters."

"That's Börge's word," said Winter.

"But you said you recognized her."

"I recognize Elisabeth," said Winter. "That's her. She didn't change that much. Or however the fuck I should put it."

The phone on the desk rang. Winter lifted the receiver, answered, listened, hung up.

"That was Möllerström. He got hold of an aunt down in Halland. Ellen's sister's name was Elisabeth. Among other things."

"Among other things?"

"She called herself Eva, too. That was the name Börge mentioned."

"Was there anyone who ever talked to her?" Ringmar asked. "Back then, when Ellen disappeared."

"I'm not sure," said Winter.

"We concentrated on Christer Börge," said Ringmar. "Although maybe not as much as we should have."

"Maybe we expected that someone would get in touch if her missing sister turned up again," said Winter. "That's what would happen in a normal world."

"Mm-hmm."

"I still didn't know that nothing is normal in this world."

"Which world is that?"

"The one you and I live in, Bertil."

"Then I didn't know, either," said Ringmar.

Winter thought back. What had he done in the days, the weeks, after Ellen disappeared? He had call—

"Oh shit, we talked to her!" Winter sprung up from the desk. "We knew that there was a sister. One of our colleagues talked to her. That has to be somewhere in the records."

"She probably just confirmed that Ellen hadn't been seen," said Ringmar.

Winter didn't answer.

"Surely it couldn't have been anything sensational."

"But that sister was Elisabeth Ney," said Winter. "Elisabeth Ney!"

Ringmar nodded.

"Help me out here," said Winter.

"How should I help you, Erik?"

"What's the connection? Is there a connection?"

"Of all of us, you're probably the one who's thought the most about it," said Ringmar.

"Just give me the connection," Winter repeated.

"Ellen and Elisabeth are sisters. Were sisters. Paula is Elisabeth's daughter. Was Elisabeth's daughter."

"Keep going," said Winter.

"Ellen disappeared eighteen years ago. No one has seen her since, as far as we know. A few months ago, she carries a bag into Central Station and puts it in a storage locker. We're not sure that it was her, but we think it was." Ringmar looked up. "And then she isn't missing anymore. We find her body."

Winter nodded.

"Before that, we found Elisabeth's body." Ringmar paused. "And before that we found Paula's body."

"Three bodies," said Winter.

"Three murders."

"And three men," said Winter.

Ringmar didn't answer. He knew the names of the men Winter was talking about: Mario Ney. Christer Börge. Jonas Sandler.

"Let's have a little talk with Jonas," said Winter. "And his mom." He stood up. "We're going to show them something."

Anne Sandler stood up from the bed when Winter and Ringmar stepped into the room. Jonas was lying with his head toward the wall. He hadn't moved when they came in. Anne Sandler took a step toward them.

"How is he doing?" Winter asked.

"I think he's sleeping," she said. "He seems completely exhausted."

Winter looked at the back of Jonas's head. It was half-hidden behind the blanket. The young man didn't move.

"Was it really necessary to bring him here?" she said.

Her words could have been accusatory, but Winter didn't hear any accusation in her tone.

"We have him under observation," he said.

"What kind of observation is that?"

"Medical, of course."

"Then couldn't you have taken him to a hospital instead of here?" she said.

"I'd like to ask you to come with me to a different room," said Winter. "Bertil will stay here with Jonas."

She followed him out into the corridor without a word. Once outside, she turned to him.

"You don't really think that Jonas had anything to do with that . . . that awful thing, do you?" she said.

Winter didn't answer. He gestured toward the far end of the corridor. His office was down there.

Once there, she asked her question again. She looked like someone who had suddenly stepped into a world where everything is unfamiliar and who was starting to realize that it wasn't a dream.

"Please have a seat," said Winter, gesturing at the chair in front of his desk.

"Jonas can't have done anything . . . bad," she said, and she sat down abruptly.

"What was he actually doing out there?" Winter asked. "He hasn't been able to explain. Been able to talk about it."

He had sat down, too.

"He's in shock," she said. "He's shaken up! Who wouldn't be?" Her eyes became larger. "A . . . body . . . a dead body in the grove. In our grove?"

"I found Jonas in there," said Winter. "It was before we found the body."

She didn't answer.

"That's what I'm wondering about," said Winter.

"I don't know," she said after a few seconds. "He doesn't know either. He isn't feeling well."

Winter opened the envelope that was on the desk. He took out a photograph and held it up for her.

"Do you recognize this woman?"

"Who is it?"

"Just tell me whether you recognize her." He held the photograph out farther. "Here. Take it."

Sandler took it and held it up in front of her. Winter adjusted the light from the lamp on the desk.

Sandler looked up.

"Is it her?"

"Sorry?"

"Is it the woman in . . . the grove?"

"Do you recognize her?"

Winter saw her eyes become even larger. It looked as though the skin was stretched tight over her face.

"There's no rush," said Winter.

"No," she said after a little while, and she put down the photograph. "I don't recognize her. Who is she?"

Winter didn't answer. He took out another photograph and handed it over without holding it up first.

"Have you seen this woman before?"

It could be a worthless question.

"Yes," she said almost immediately. She looked up. "It's her. She's younger here. But it's her."

"Who?"

"The woman who lived in our stairwell. The mother of the girl."

"How can you be so sure?"

She looked at the picture again.

"I don't know. I just recognize her." She looked up. "It . . . I don't know. I recognize her."

"That's Ellen," said Winter. "Ellen Börge."

He had chosen to reveal the name to Sandler. It could be a mistake, but he had made his choice. It was the same thing with the photograph.

"Is that her name? Ellen?"

"Yes."

"That wasn't her name . . . she had a different name . . ."

"Eva?"

"Yes!"

"Her name was Eva when you met?"

"Yes. Her name was Eva."

"Have you seen her picture anywhere else?"

"No. Where would I have seen it?"

Winter didn't answer.

"No . . . I've never seen a picture of her before."

Winter nodded.

"So that's the girl's mom." Sandler looked up from the photograph. Her skin looked very thin in the light from the desk lamp, as though the blood was about to leave her face.

Her eyes reflected her sudden thought: "Is that her? Is she the one who . . . who . . ."

Winter didn't answer.

"Where is she, then? If it isn't . . . her? And where is her daughter?"

"If it is her daughter," said Winter.

"I don't understand."

"The daughter said that she wasn't her real mother."

"I don't understand. Who told you that?"

"Your son," said Winter.

32

Mario Ney stood up immediately when Winter stepped into the interrogation room. His face was whiter than chalk. The circles under his eyes looked as though they were made of soot. He tried to say something, but Winter couldn't hear a sound. The words that caught in Ney's throat caused him to cough suddenly and then gasp for breath. Maybe they were big words, important words.

Ney's coughing fit stopped as quickly as it had started. He steadied himself against the surface of the table and looked at Winter with watery eyes.

"Why . . . why am I here?" he finally asked. "What has happened?"

"How do you feel?" Winter asked.

"What . . . what's happened?"

Ney wiped his mouth. Winter could see sweat gleaming on his forehead.

"I can tell by looking at you that something has happened."

"Would you like a glass of water?" Winter asked.

Ney shook his head. He took a step away from the chair and appeared to lose his balance. Before Winter made it over to him, he caught the top of the table and regained his balance, as he had just regained his voice.

"Have you found him?" Ney asked, looking at Winter. There were still tears in his eyes from his fit of coughing. "Is that why you're here?" He looked around suddenly, as though he had finally become conscious of where he was. "Is that why I'm here?"

"Sit down, Mario."

"I'm good standing here," he said, suddenly swaying again. "Just tell me what's going on."

"Sit down," said Winter.

Ney turned his head, looked at the chair, looked at Winter again, took the few steps up to the chair, and sat down. The legs of the chair scraped against the floor. Winter's thoughts suddenly flew to cleaning, grit on a floor, a broom, a vacuum. A cleaner, a maid, a room, a hotel.

Winter sat down in front of Ney. His chair scraped in the same way. The director of the county CID had drawn back on the cleaning of the interrogation room. He was better at taking leave than at cleaning.

"Tell me about your job at Hotel Odin," said Winter.

"What?"

Ney had given a start, as though he was about to have another coughing fit. But his voice worked this time:

"What about it?"

"Tell me about the job," said Winter.

"How do you know that?"

"How do we know what?" Winter asked.

"That I worked there. It was many years ago."

"Tell me about it," Winter repeated again.

"Well . . . what . . . it was a long time ago . . ."

"What did you do?"

"Oh . . . everything. I don't know what that has to do with anything."

"Don't you understand?"

Ney didn't answer.

"Don't you understand why I'm asking, Mario?"

Ney looked down at the table. He seemed to have frozen where he sat.

"Mario?"

He looked up.

"You're . . . thinking of Elisabeth," he said. "But I . . . I swear that it didn't occur to me that I . . . that I once worked there. And anyway, I wasn't there for very long. I swear that I didn't put . . . didn't put that together."

Swear, Winter thought. That's a big word. But swearing is for church. No, that's believing. Or you do both. Swear to your belief. The church offers that opportunity.

"Do you remember what you did at the hotel, Mario?"

"What do you mean, did? When?"

Winter didn't answer. Ney appeared to become more conscious of what he was saying. His eyes became more alert, as though his thoughts were moving around more quickly inside of them.

"I mean when as in during the time I worked there," he said. "That is, many years ago." He waved his hand. "That's what I meant."

"And when was that?"

"I don't remember." He seemed to relax; perhaps his eyes became calmer. "I was young then; it was twenty years ago, twenty-five . . ."

"When you lived with Elisabeth," said Winter.

"Yes . . . but my God, surely you don't think that I . . ."

Winter didn't say anything.

"Is that why I'm here? Because you all think . . . think that I killed my own wife?" His eyes came to life again, his thoughts. His words became faster, too, with no pauses aside from the audible dot-dot-dot at the ends of his sentences and after words in the middles of his sentences. "How could you think something like that? My own wife? How could someone do something like that?"

"Did you do it, Mario? Did you kill her?"

Ney didn't answer. He was staring straight at Winter, as though to emphasize his words with his eyes.

"Did you kill her, Mario?"

"*No!*"

Winter had stood up and walked over to the door and asked for some water. Then he had walked back and adjusted the recording equipment on the table. This time he had chosen to do without the video camera. He thought that it might be too distracting for this interrogation. Had he expected anything from the interrogation? Yes. No. Yes. No. Not a confession. Maybe something else. Some sort of truth.

Part of one. It wasn't too late yet. The water had arrived. Ney drank it thirstily and set down the empty glass.

"Do you want more?" Winter asked.

Ney shook his head.

"Who is Ellen Börge?" Winter asked.

Ney slowly raised his head. Winter could see the answer in his eyes. But there was also something he couldn't decipher.

"Why didn't you tell us earlier?" Winter asked.

"What would I have told you?" Ney answered.

"That Elisabeth had a sister. That Ellen was her sister."

"I . . . don't understand. Why would I have told you that? What does it matter? What does it matter to Elisabeth? It doesn't have anything to do with this, does it?"

He isn't mentioning Paula, Winter thought. He isn't saying her name. Why isn't he?

"If it doesn't matter, then I don't understand why you didn't tell us about it," said Winter. "Neither you nor Elisabeth did."

Ney threw out one hand as though to say "I don't know, it never occurred to us, I didn't understand."

"And you didn't tell us about the time when Ellen and Paula lived together in an apartment on Hisingen," said Winter.

Ney gave a start. Winter's words appeared to have hit him like an electrical shock. Maybe he had thought the worst was over. That Winter didn't know what he knew. Or that he would guess like he was doing now. But these weren't just guesses. This was something else. Experience. Intuition. Imagination. Maybe something more. Maybe luck. Or bad luck. We'll see.

"Why did Ellen and Paula live together?" Winter asked.

Ney didn't answer. He appeared to accept Winter's words, to receive them without fighting them.

"Why did they live in an apartment you rented, Mario?"

Ney started again.

Winter had gotten lucky again.

"Why did you rent that apartment, Mario?"

"It was only for a short time," said Ney.

His words were short, direct, with a dark tone. But they answered the question.

"You never lived there yourself, did you?"

"No."

"Why did they live there?"

"It was only for a short time," Ney repeated, as though he had forgotten that he had just said this.

"Why?"

Ney didn't answer. Winter couldn't see his eyes. The sweat on his forehead was back. Ney's graying hair looked like steel wool in the cold light. His eyes were somewhere else. When they come back, maybe he'll tell me everything, Winter thought.

"Why, Mario?"

"Ellen wanted to spend a little time with Paula." Ney looked up. Winter could see that there was something very painful inside him. That didn't necessarily mean that he was worthy of sympathy. Or empathy. "Just a little time."

"But why?"

"Because . . . because Paula was Ellen's child."

Winter felt himself give a start.

Maybe Ney hadn't seen it. He didn't seem to see anything anymore. His eyes were open, but he wasn't seeing. They seemed fixed on the wall behind Winter, or on a place or a time that was far beyond the walls and the doors in this ugly brick palace. All the silence Winter had encountered. Here was the source of it. Maybe more hidden silence, more lies, were streaming out of it. An even greater darkness.

"Paula was Ellen's daughter?" Winter asked slowly.

Ney nodded just as slowly, as though in reply to each and every one of Winter's words.

"Why didn't she live with her parents?"

Ney stopped nodding. Winter saw that he gave another start. Parents.

"Christer," said Winter. "Christer Börge."

Ney looked at Winter. Winter saw the answer in his black eyes.

"Paula was your daughter."

Ney nodded slowly, in the same manner as before.

"Yes. Paula was mine."

"You . . . and Elisabeth adopted her?"

Ney nodded again.

"Why?"

"Ellen . . . was weak. She was sick. She couldn't manage."

"Ellen disappeared," said Winter. "Ellen has been gone. She's been missing."

Ney didn't answer.

"When did you meet Ellen for the first time, Mario?"

"It was a long time ago. At the hotel. When I worked at the hotel."

"Odin?"

"Yes."

"Did she work there, too?"

"Yes."

"Did you live with Elisabeth then?"

"No."

"Did you know Elisabeth then?"

Ney didn't answer.

Winter repeated the question.

"Yes, a little bit."

"Were you together? Were you a couple?"

"Yes."

"Why didn't you and Ellen become a couple?"

"She . . . didn't want to," said Mario. "She couldn't manage it."

"She lived with someone, too, right?"

"Yes."

"Christer Börge."

"Yes."

"Why didn't she leave him?"

"But . . . she did."

"Much later. Long after Paula was born."

Ney nodded.

"How well did you know Christer Börge?"

"Not . . . not at all."

"Didn't you ever meet him?"

"Yes."

"Where?"

"At the hotel."

"Odin?"

"Yes, there, too."

"What do you mean, Mario?"

"You're asking about the hotel. Which hotel do you mean this time?"

"Did you meet him at more than one hotel?"

"Yes."

"Did he work at Revy?"

"Well, he was there when I picked things up a few times, anyway. They shared things. Odin and Revy."

"Why was Börge there?"

"Why? He worked there, I think."

"Doing what?"

"It was probably some sort of janitor thing. I don't really know."

"Why didn't you tell us that earlier?"

"No one asked. And why would I say anything about it?" He looked at Winter. "I didn't even remember it until you started asking."

"And you also saw him at the other hotel?"

"Odin? Just for a short time. A few weeks."

"Did Christer Börge work there, too?"

"Yes."

"As what?"

"I . . . don't really remember that, either. Janitor. I don't know."

That can wait, Winter thought. But something else can't wait.

"Why didn't the two of you tell us that Paula was adopted?" Winter asked. "Why didn't you ever tell us?"

"It didn't seem . . . necessary," Ney said. His voice had lost its strength again. "It . . . didn't matter then. The only thing that mattered was that she was . . . gone. That she was dead. Nothing could change that." He looked up. "We didn't have the strength."

"But we haven't found anything about adoption," said Winter. "There's no information about it. No documents. No papers."

"There . . . aren't any papers," said Ney.

"What?"

"There are no documents," said Ney.

"Why aren't there any documents?" Winter asked.

"We . . . they . . . switched . . . identities." Ney looked up. His eyes were clearer now, as though revealing this lifelong lie drew the veil away from his eyes. He was on his way to confessing a lifelong lie. Maybe it was the end of the whole story.

"Elisabeth became . . . Ellen. Officially. At least when it came to . . . the authorities. As though she had given birth to Paula. And I became Paula's father. Which of course . . . I was."

"Christer Börge, then? What did he become?"

"He didn't know."

"He didn't know?"

Winter had raised his voice more than he thought.

"Ellen left him," said Ney, "it was during those . . . months. But it was a longer time than that. It was more than a year. And she had the baby . . ."

"And moved back?"

Ney nodded.

"She never said anything to Börge?"

"No."

"And she continued to live with him?"

"Yes . . ."

"Up until she left him for good?"

"Yes . . ."

"This isn't possible," said Winter. "This can't be possible."

"That's how it was," said Ney.

"Why did Ellen disappear?"

"She wanted to get . . . away from him," said Ney. "She was afraid."

"Why didn't she just move? Leave her husband? More . . . officially?"

"She was . . . afraid," Ney repeated.

"Where did she go?"

"A few different places."

"Where?"

"Italy."

"Italy?"

"My old . . . neighborhood. Sicily. Outside Caltanissetta. It's in the mountains. South of Palermo."

That sounded logical. That's why they'd been so secretive about Mario's background. Sicily. Anyone could hide for as long as she wanted in a Sicilian mountain village.

"Did Paula know?"

"Know what?" Ney asked.

"About Ellen. That Ellen was her mother?"

"No . . ."

Winter waited for him to continue. He saw in Ney's eyes that there was more.

"Not at first. That came . . . later." Ney suddenly leaned over the table, as though a severe pain in his chest had increased. "We . . . told her later."

"How did she react?"

Ney didn't answer.

"When she took her long trip, did she go to Ellen? To her mother? Did she know that she was visiting her mother?"

Ney nodded.

"And then they continued to keep in touch?"

"When it was possible."

"Why wouldn't it be possible?"

"They were both . . . afraid."

"Afraid? Of whom?"

"I don't know."

"I think you do know, Mario."

"No." He looked up. "I didn't understand."

"Do you understand now?"

"Yes."

"Who were they afraid of?"

"Christer Börge," said Ney.

"Did he know about their existence? Did he know about Paula? Did he know where Ellen was?"

"I don't actually know," said Ney.

"Didn't they say anything to you?"

"No."

"Maybe you were the one they were afraid of?"

"No."

"They were trying to escape you, Mario."

"No," he said, lifting his head again and looking Winter in the eye. Winter couldn't decipher what was in there. It was impossible. It was the most difficult thing he'd encountered.

"When did you last see Ellen?" Winter asked.

"It was . . . probably a couple of years ago."

"Where did you see her?"

"At home."

"Where is home?"

"In Sicily."

"Why did Ellen and Paula live together when the girl was ten years old?"

Ney seemed to give a start at the sudden change in the interrogation.

"It was Ellen. She just wanted to live . . . with the girl for a little bit."

"Did she tell her then that she was her mother?"

"No. Not that I know of. For Paula, at that time, Ellen was a friend of the family."

Winter thought. According to Jonas, the eleven-year-old Paula had said that Ellen wasn't her real mother. It could be like she said. Ellen wasn't her real mother, because Elisabeth was her real mother. That was her world and her life. There weren't yet any lifelong lies in her life back then.

But Winter still couldn't understand the silence, and he couldn't accept it. These were some of the deepest secrets he had ever encountered in people he'd met in his job. A large part of his work was people's secrets. From him. From each other. They ran deep.

There was something more behind all of this, something Ney didn't want to talk about.

Ellen had left everything. Just left. That's what it looked like, anyway. She had gone underground many years ago. Good God. As Winter thought that thought, he realized what he was thinking.

"Why did Ellen leave everything?" Winter asked.

"I've never completely understood that," said Ney. "You'll have to ask her yourself."

33

The November sky was crying as though all hope for the world were gone. The wind tore at the windows as though it wanted to break into the police station. The October storms had come a month too late. Winter felt the wind through the pane, as though it were flowing through the glass.

"The Älvsborg bridge is closed to traffic," Ringmar said behind him.

"No one in his right mind would drive on it anyway," said Halders.

Winter turned around.

"Watch out over there," said Halders. "The glass could give out."

"Then we'd be in the middle of a disaster movie," said Bergenhem.

"Maybe we're the stars," said Halders. "Maybe we have the lead roles."

"There can only be one lead," said Bergenhem.

"Then I'm the one we're talking about here," said Halders.

Winter walked over to the oblong table and sat at the narrower end. He could feel the wind even there. It had taken over the ventilation system. Ringmar's tie was moving. The knot of Ringmar's tie was loose, almost undone. Winter wasn't wearing a tie. It had recently begun to chafe at his neck. He couldn't breathe. Maybe he would never wear a tie again.

Ringmar cleared his throat. It wasn't only because he wanted to have the floor and get back to their discussion. The violent change of weather had brought with it the first cold of the autumn. He hoped that it would be the only one.

"What are we going to do with this?" he said.

"The man doesn't seem to be a marvel of reliability," said Halders.

They had been discussing Mario Ney for half an hour. Everything he had revealed to Winter. If "revealed" was the correct word.

"If he has a motive, he's hiding it well," said Bergenhem.

"Isn't that always how it goes?" said Djanali.

"Isn't that the whole point for a murderer, after a crime?" said Halders. "To keep the motive secret?"

"The motive and the crime itself," said Bergenhem.

"If there is a motive," said Winter.

"So he's mentally ill?" said Halders.

"He isn't well," said Winter, with a dry smile, "and he hasn't been for a very long time."

"He's a hell of a lot better than his daughter and his wives," said Halders.

"Is that what you're calling them? His wives?" said Djanali.

"I don't know what I should call them," said Halders.

"There's one thing we can be sure of," said Ringmar. "It's still possible to cheat the system."

"There are starting to be too many people in this country," said Halders.

"You don't mean that," said Djanali.

"I was only speaking from a purely surveillance-based standpoint," said Halders.

"You mean Big Brother is starting to lose his grip?" Bergenhem asked.

"It's been almost a generation since Paula was born," said Winter. "A lot has happened since then in the authorities' version of Sweden."

"There's always a way to cheat the system for someone who wants to," said Ringmar, "the social system, the financial system."

"Yes, if the guy's story is true," said Halders, "but there's starting to be a shortage of people who can verify it."

"So what should we do?" said Djanali.

"Question him again, naturally," said Halders. "Detain him for another six hours. He could be under suspicion for a crime, couldn't he?

He has no alibi whatsoever. He's part of the family. That's all. And the fairy tale he told Erik makes him even more of a suspect, in my book."

The room became quiet. Winter could hear the winds tearing at the window. In two weeks, the plane to Málaga would take off. He would be sitting on it, whatever happened. Halders was in the process of taking over. They did have cell phones and all that. But he wouldn't be all the way on that plane, and, accordingly, it would be wrong to go. He wouldn't be there. It would be a halfhearted trip in the sunshine. No. Yes. No. The children would be there, and Angela. His family. The world would keep on turning, and so on. There would be hope. He would have his children around him. There would be a sea, a horizon, a sunset, a dawn, and a dusk. Everything in between.

That was enough for him.

His cell phone rang. Everyone had been so engrossed in thought that they all appeared to jump when the ringtone sounded in the room. It drowned out the roar of nature outside.

Winter listened, asked a few questions, hung up.

"She was hanged," he said. "Ellen."

"When?"

It was Ringmar who asked.

"No later than two weeks ago," Winter asked.

"She was well preserved," said Halders. "It was good dirt."

"We still don't know where it happened," said Ringmar.

"And how he transported her there," said Halders.

"While no one was watching," said Ringmar.

"What's the latest from the door-to-doors?" Ringmar asked, turning to Bergenhem.

"No one has seen anything. Of the people we've talked to so far. Or heard anything."

"How many were unavailable?"

"Six addresses, last I heard from the guys."

"And when was that?" Winter asked.

"Two hours ago."

"Get us a list of the unavailable," he said.

Bergenhem nodded.

The unavailable. It sounded like the name of a movie, Bergenhem thought. A thriller. A disaster movie.

"I'm going to have another conversation with Jonas," said Winter, standing up.

"Is he still here?" Halders asked.

"Yes," Ringmar answered. "He wanted to stay."

"Why?"

"He said he was afraid."

Jonas Sandler was sitting on the bed. It looked as though he had tried to make it up. One of the two pillows was on the floor. Winter could hear the wind outside the windows in this part of the building, too. Through the streaked glass he could see Gamla Ullevi. No one was playing soccer there this afternoon. The grass was oddly green, as though it had been painted, and with a very wide brush. He could see across the river to the other side, to the big island. Hisingen was swept in dark clouds. Beyond them was only darkness. Behind the darkness, the sun was about to go down, but no one could see it. It was only something you hoped, that the sun was still there.

"How's it going, Jonas?"

The boy didn't answer. His face was no longer that of a man, and it probably never would be. Too much had happened in the past.

"Tell me," said Winter.

The boy looked up.

"What am I supposed to tell you?"

"The grove of trees. Why did you go out there?"

"I told you, I don't know."

"What were you thinking when you went there?"

"Nothing."

"What made you get on the streetcar?"

"I . . . don't know."

"Who are you afraid of, Jonas?"

He didn't answer. It was like he suddenly couldn't hear.

"Tell me, Jonas."

"I . . . that's what I'm doing."

"Did you talk to anyone before you went out to the grove?"

"I don't understand what you mean."

"Did you talk to anyone before you left?"

"No."

"Your mom? Weren't you going out there? To see her?"

"No. Not to see her. I didn't go there."

"Were you planning on going to her place after?"

"After? After what?"

"When you'd been to the grove?"

"No, no. I wasn't thinking of anything."

"You were thinking of Paula," Winter said.

"Yes. Paula. Yes."

"Why did you think she was buried there?"

The boy didn't answer. Winter could tell that he was thinking about what he was going to say. But he had said all along that he knew. Something drew him there. Or someone. It hadn't let him go.

"It was like that . . . hand I saw once," Sandler said, looking up again. He didn't search for Winter's eyes. He looked at the window behind Winter, the storm, the wind, the rain. Freedom, maybe. No. He seemed to be looking for that in here. Or for protection.

"I really thought she was there this time," the boy continued. "That Paula was there." He rubbed his eyes. "I can't explain it."

"Someone was there," said Winter.

"What?" Now Sandler sought Winter's eyes. "What did you say?"

"There was someone under the ground, Jonas. Did you know that?"

"What? I don't understand . . ."

"Did you know that there was someone in that grave, Jonas? When you went out there?"

"Grave? It was a grave?"

"There was a woman buried there, Jonas. Where you started to dig. About a foot down in the dirt."

"Pa-Paula? Was it Paula?"

"No, not Paula," Winter answered.

"Who was it, then?"

Winter didn't answer.

"Who was it?" the boy asked again.

"Her mother."

Winter and Ringmar were sitting in Winter's office. Winter had a slight headache that might get worse. He had taken ibuprofen and was waiting for it to take effect.

Ringmar blew his nose loudly.

"I hope that isn't contagious."

"It's too late for that," said Ringmar.

Winter felt the wind through the window, which was open a few centimeters out onto the park. He had opened it as soon as they'd come into the office.

"The boy must have seen someone there in the grove," said Ringmar. "Or outside it."

"Why doesn't he say so, then?"

"We haven't asked him often enough," said Ringmar.

"You're welcome to go in there and continue," Winter said.

"I don't think it'll help right now, Erik."

"Why not?"

"He's in some sort of shock."

"It's almost like I am, too," said Winter.

"What's actually up with this list from Revy?" Ringmar said, grabbing the paper that was on Winter's desk.

"Well, the name Christer Börge isn't on it, anyway."

"What was his name, your desk clerk? Saldo? Salko? In any case, didn't he say that it wasn't complete?"

Winter didn't answer.

"And Börge hasn't gotten the question from us, has he?" Ringmar said. "Whether he worked there?"

"No, he has," Winter said. "I remember it. Not whether he worked there, but when I met him in connection with Ellen going missing, he said he'd never heard of the place. Of Revy."

"Really," Ringmar said.

"Why say something like that?" said Winter.

"He probably didn't want you to know."

"But he knew we could check."

"And we have checked," Ringmar said, waving the list, which he was still holding in his hand. "But it hasn't helped, has it?"

"What a fucking mess," Winter said, getting up and walking over to the window in order to close it.

"Have you talked to that desk clerk since all of this?" Ringmar asked. "What was his name?"

"Salko, Richard Salko. No, I haven't talked to him. He's not answering at home."

"The hotel, then?"

"The hotel closed. For good, thank God."

The phone on Winter's desk jangled. Ringmar stretched out his hand and picked it up. Winter was over by the window.

"Yes? Yes, hi. No, this is Bertil. Oh? Really? Mm-hmm. Mm-hmm. Oh, shit. Yes. Yes. Okay, bye."

In the black mirror of his computer monitor, Winter could see Ringmar bang the receiver on the desk.

"That was Öberg," said Ringmar.

"Well? Well?" Winter felt the draft from the window. It felt like he'd opened it up wide. "What did he say?"

"They've found a little saliva on the rope," Ringmar said. "The rope that hanged Ellen Börge."

"Well?"

"It's a woman's."

"What?"

"Elisabeth Ney's."

"Elisabeth Ney's?" Winter repeated. He felt the familiar shiver on the back of his head. "Elisabeth Ney's?"

"Yes sir. That's all they've found."

"But . . ."

"As long as she hasn't returned from the dead to carry out her deed, she's come into contact with that rope before," said Ringmar.

Three ropes, Winter thought. Identical ropes, blue, creased. Good instruments for murder. Nothing stuck. Except for something that Elisabeth Ney left behind.

Winter had placed the ropes beside one another, but it had mostly felt like a symbolic act. He understood neither the symbolism nor the act.

"I don't think there were meant to be any traces on that rope," said Ringmar.

"Especially not from the Ney family," said Winter.

Mario Ney looked up when Winter stepped into the room. Ney got up slowly. He suddenly looked smaller than before, shorter. It was something about his shoulders. His back had usually been straight, but it wasn't anymore. He was standing bent over himself, as though there was a great pain emanating from his stomach.

Maybe he's prepared, Winter thought.

"What happened?" Ney asked.

"Why do you ask, Mario?"

"You look like something has happened."

"And how does that look?"

"Like you, right now."

"Please sit down," Winter said, preparing himself for questioning.

"I have nothing more to say," Ney said a few minutes into the interview.

"You haven't told me anything yet," said Winter.

"I've told you everything I know."

"Tell me about the apartment on Hisingen."

"I have nothing more to say about it."

"Why did you rent it?"

"I've told you that. Do I have to repeat everything?"

"Did you live there yourself?"

"Never."

"Did you live somewhere else in the area?"

"Why would I have done that?"

Winter didn't say anything. Ney wasn't waiting for an answer. He seemed to be studying something in the distance, beyond the walls.

Suddenly he stared Winter in the eyes.

"While we're sitting in here, a murderer is walking around loose out there," Ney said.

34

Halders stroked his scalp. It looked newly shaven. Winter could see the ceiling lights gleaming on Halders's bald head, as though he'd polished his skull.

"What does Molina say?" Halders said.

"He asked me if there's really reasonable suspicion," Winter answered.

"Well, is there?"

"I can usually get a reading on parts of the interrogation, but Ney is something of a mystery," Winter said.

"Maybe that means something," said Halders.

"The traces of his wife on the rope ought to count as a reason to detain him," Bergenhem said. He had come into the room just after the others.

"Molina won't detain him," Winter said. "We have to have more to give him."

"Like what?"

Winter didn't answer.

"As far as we know, Mario Ney has never been in the vicinity of that rope. Any of the ropes," said Ringmar.

"What has he been in the vicinity of, then?" Djanali asked.

Winter turned to her.

"What did you say?"

She repeated her question.

"He's been in the vicinity of Paula's apartment," Winter said.

"Does he still have a key?" Halders asked.

Ringmar nodded.

"Has he been in the vicinity of Hotel Revy?" Halders asked.

"Have you talked to the desk clerk yet, Erik?" asked Ringmar.

Winter didn't seem to be listening.

"Erik? Do you hear me?"

"Uh . . . what?"

"Have you talked to the desk clerk? Salko? At Revy?"

"No. I still haven't gotten hold of him."

"Has Ney been in the vicinity of that neighborhood on Hisingen?" Djanali asked.

"Are we finished with the door-to-door?" Halders asked.

"There's only one name we haven't caught yet," Ringmar said, picking up the paper that was on the conference table.

"What one is that?" Halders asked.

"Metzer. Anton Metzer."

The horizon was red and gray out over the sea. It was a mixture of colors that happened only in November. Winter could see the sky over the horizon, a hint of what was behind it, like blue smoke. Very soon, he would see what was hiding up there, in a country far south. At the moment, it felt unreal, like another life.

Halders cruised between the houses and parked in front of the door.

The police-line tape blew in the wind that whirled around the grove of trees. There were no people out in the yard; no children were playing on the playground. The wind was strong, as though the buildings were on a beach.

Winter rang the doorbell. The sound whirled around inside as the wind was doing outside, but with a more muted sound. Winter pressed the button again.

"He's been gone for a long time," Halders said.

Winter opened the mail slot with two fingers.

He could see only part of the doormat. There was a pile of newspapers on it. He could see white envelopes, brown envelopes. Halders could see, too.

"The guy didn't stop his mail before he left," he said.

"Maybe he didn't have the chance to," Winter said.

"Are you thinking what I'm thinking?" Halders said.

"Wasn't there a property office at the end of the yard?" Winter said.

The caretaker opened the door without Winter having to call the prosecutor. Everyone in the area was shaken up after the discovery in the grove. The discovery. Winter still hadn't asked Jonas Sandler about the skeleton of the dog in the grave. He hadn't told the boy about it. He wanted to wait, but he wasn't sure why. Maybe the boy knew.

The caretaker stepped aside. He was a man in his thirties. He had a clean uniform and an innocent face. We'll let him hold on to that for a bit longer, Winter thought. He thanked the man and waited until he reluctantly went down the stairs and disappeared from sight.

Halders stared into the dim apartment. A faint light was coming from somewhere at the end of the hall. They had both been in there, separately. For Halders, it was a long time ago. Winter had been standing outside that time. Halders had gone in. Winter never saw Metzer; that came much later. It felt like yesterday. Metzer had a unique look. When he'd sat across from Winter on his sofa, Winter had seen the line—or rather, scar—on his face; it went from one temple down over his cheek. It looked like a scar from a sword. Perhaps Metzer was German nobility, Winter had thought.

I became concerned, Metzer had said to Winter. That was why I called the police.

But this time he hadn't called the police.

They had walked carefully through the hall and into the living room. That was where the light was coming from. They had their weapons out.

They had smelled the odor even outside. It wasn't strong, but it was enough.

The light from the yard outside shone over the body that lay stretched out on the couch. They didn't see any blood anywhere. In another situation, they might have been looking at someone who was asleep.

Winter heard a clock ticking in there. He hadn't heard it the last time he was here. But now it was no longer needed.

Metzer could have died in his sleep. He could have died from a sudden illness.

He could have died at someone else's hand.

Halders was already leaning over the body. He had a handkerchief over his mouth.

"It's not a pretty sight," he said in a voice that sounded like it came from inside a tunnel.

"Do you recognize him?" Winter asked.

"No, but it's been a few years." Halders looked up. "And this latest development doesn't help."

"It's Metzer," said Winter.

"Yes, you were here recently."

"That scar is still there," Winter said.

"You mean the marks on his neck? They look a little suspicious to me."

"No, I mean the scar."

"Sorry?"

"The scar," Winter repeated, pointing at Metzer's scar, which was visible as a white line from temple to throat. It was more sharply out-lined in death than it had been in life.

"He didn't have a scar," Halders said. "He didn't have a scar when I was here."

Halders looked at the body again, studied the face. He approached it, backed up quickly, looked up with a bewildered expression.

"Fuck, that's not Metzer," he said, looking up.

"What do you mean, Fredrik?"

"I'm just saying, that's not the Metzer I talked to."

•   •   •

It was a different medical examiner. Winter had never met him. He was older than Fröberg, much older. He looked like he was about the same age as Metzer, but his face was a natural color. His name was Sverker Berlinger. Must be an old, retired character who had to step in, Winter thought. He looks like he's seen this all before.

"Looks like strangulation," Berlinger said, shaking his head slightly.

He had worked with steady hands. He had sighed audibly as he stepped into the room and saw the body, as though to say that he had actually left this kind of thing behind long ago.

"When?" Winter asked.

Berlinger shrugged.

"Two weeks ago?" Winter asked. "Three?"

Berlinger looked around, as though he were looking for the alarm clock that no one could hear anymore. Winter could see it. Below it he could see Torsten Öberg crouching in front of a bureau.

"It's warm in here," Berlinger said. "Could be."

"When?" Winter repeated. "Last week?"

"Hardly."

"So then it's two weeks," said Winter.

"Yes, it probably is."

Berlinger bent over the body again and studied Anton Metzer's face.

"Well, look at that, a Mensur scar."

"Oh right, that's what it's called," Winter said.

"You recognize the term?" Berlinger asked, looking up.

"I couldn't think of it. But I'm familiar with the concept."

Berlinger looked down at Metzer's face again.

"This is a little too long and a little too thick for him to be really proud of it," he said.

"You look like you wish you had one yourself," said Winter.

"I'm not from the right family, unfortunately," said Berlinger, smiling very slightly. "Incidentally, *mensur* also means the measured distance between duelers."

Winter couldn't hear a German accent. He didn't ask about Berlinger's origins.

"Could he have gotten that scar some other way?" he asked.

"Naturally," said Berlinger.

"How old is it?"

"More than two weeks," said Berlinger.

Winter waited until the humor had dissipated.

"More than fifty years," said Berlinger.

"No rope in the apartment," said Öberg.

"No, I didn't see one, either," said Winter.

"But an identical rope may have been used," said Öberg.

"May have been? Or was?" Halders asked.

"May," Öberg answered. "At least, I can't say more than that right now. If it was a nylon rope, it's almost impossible to say that it was a nylon rope, if you understand what I mean."

"And no white paint," said Winter.

"Not on the body, anyway."

"There was no paint on Ellen Börge's body, either," said Winter. "Only the horrible marks."

He looked out through the window, as though to measure the distance between this apartment and the grove. He could see it, but just barely. A dark cloud had sailed in from the North Sea, and he could already hear the rain against the window.

"Is it connected with this spot?" Halders said. "This place?"

"I don't know what it's connected with," Winter said. "I don't know if it's even connected."

"On the other hand, we know that we have four murders," said Halders. "And as far as I understand, they're connected."

"Metzer, too?"

"Well, he certainly isn't a stranger to this lot," Halders said. "Except for me."

"So you say you talked to someone other than Metzer," Winter said.

"We were looking for him as a witness," Halders said. "He was the one who called in, after all."

Winter didn't say anything. Torsten Öberg had left them in order to work over by the sofa.

"What kind of murder machine is at work here?" Halders said.

Winter didn't answer.

"Wasn't he the one who called in?" Halders asked. "Metzer. About that alleged fight."

"Maybe," Winter said. "But he wasn't the one who opened the door when you came knocking."

"Where the hell was he, then?"

"That's a difficult question in this situation, Fredrik."

"Okay, okay. The person who opens the door isn't Metzer, but he apparently thinks it's simpler to say he's Metzer."

"Mm-hmm."

"You don't agree?"

"No, I do."

"Why does he think it's simpler to be Metzer?"

"Because it's more difficult to be someone else," Winter said.

"Why is it more difficult?"

"Because he doesn't want anyone to know who he really is."

"And who is he, really?"

"Mario Ney," said Winter.

"I don't know, Erik. It was many years ago, and the guy who opened the door had a full beard." Halders threw out his arms. "This will probably cost me my career, or what's left of it. But I can't say whether or not it was Ney who was standing there in that damn door eighteen years ago." Halders looked at Winter. "It could have been him, but I don't know. Let me think for a little bit, and remember.

Maybe it will come if I remember what we said. How our chat went. You know."

Winter nodded.

"Could it have been Börge?" he asked.

"I've only ever caught a fleeting glimpse of that man," said Halders.

"Börge," Winter repeated.

"He's been a part of this whole story," said Halders.

"Ney rented the apartment right across the yard," said Winter.

"He's already confirmed that," said Halders.

"He hasn't confirmed that he was here, at Metzer's place."

"Then I guess it's time we ask him to do so," said Halders. "What did Molina say, by the way?"

"He couldn't say no under the circumstances. But it's not enough to detain him." Winter looked at Öberg and his experts working around the apartment. "We need technical evidence."

"Or a confession," said Halders.

Winter looked at the clock.

"I want you to be there for the interrogation, Fredrik."

"I was never there," said Ney. "Where did you say I was supposed to have been?"

"The apartment is right across the yard," said Winter.

"Never been there."

"How often were you in your own apartment?"

"Never."

"You rented it."

"Not for myself."

Halders was sitting beside him. He didn't say anything. If Ney had met him eighteen years ago, he didn't show it. It could be him, Halders thought. But it could also be someone else. It's impossible to say I recognize him. That might be because it wasn't him.

"Where were you, then?" Winter asked.

"I don't understand the question."

"Where did you live at that time?"

"At home, of course."

"And where was home?"

"In our apartment. In Tynnered."

"Did you live alone?"

"I lived with Elisabeth, of course. And Paula."

"Wasn't Paula living with her mother?"

"Just that time. Just for that short time."

"We haven't found anything that proves your paternity," said Winter.

Ney didn't answer.

"You're not registered anywhere," Winter continued.

"Paula is mine," Ney answered.

"What do you mean by that?"

"Just that she was mine."

"For you to do whatever you wanted with?"

"What are you saying?"

"That you thought you could do whatever you wanted with her, Mario?"

"You just don't get it," said Ney.

"What don't we get?" said Winter.

"Look around."

"What are we supposed to see?"

Ney didn't answer.

"Should we keep trying to find out why you can't explain what you were doing during the times in question?"

Ney didn't say anything. He seemed to be looking at the sky out there, at space. It was as though he disappeared into it sometimes, and then returned, and was gone again. As though his feelings came and went. What kind of feelings were they? What memories did he have? What things had he done?

He came back to where he was and turned his eyes to Winter.

"I want to go home," he said.

•   •   •

Elsa was climbing on him as if he were a tree with a large crown. He held his arms out like branches. She was on her way up his right shoulder.

"Be careful so you don't get dizzy," he said.

"I never get dizzy!" she shouted, as though she were shouting to everyone way down on the ground.

"You just wait," he said, standing on tiptoe. He felt Lilly starting to lose her balance as she clung to his right leg. She had been howling even before then. She wanted to climb, too.

"What are you doing?!" Angela called from the living room. "Can't you hear that Lilly's crying, Erik?"

"I only have two branches," he called back. Elsa was on her way over to the other shoulder now. She scraped his neck. Lilly caught her breath for a second.

"What?" Angela called.

"I only have two branches."

Angela showed up in the doorway. Lilly started in again after two seconds of silence. She could be heard for miles. Winter lifted his leg; she hung on.

"I've always thought you were a little wooden," said Angela.

Winter tried to hop on one leg. Elsa held tight to his neck. Lilly screamed again, but now it was from laughter. He hopped another step. The weight around his neck was like a millstone. His right knee began to lock up. His shoulders ached. I'm not really all that young anymore, he thought. He lowered his leg and tried to release Lilly. He bent forward until Elsa could reach the ground with her feet. He was standing in a strange position. Elsa wouldn't let go.

"Watch your back," said Angela.

"Help me," he said. "Please."

The storm had moved off toward the south. The sensation of being very small under the sky remained. He sometimes felt that way after big storms. When the winds roared, everyone had to bow their backs.

"How's your back?" Angela looked at him with a faint smile. He tried to bend backward in the same way as he had bent forward before. "Take it easy, now."

"I don't understand it," he said.

"You should probably start to work out a little, Erik."

"I'm a policeman," he answered. "Working out is obligatory for us."

"So when was the last time you worked out?"

"I work out," he said.

"What kind of answer is that?" she asked.

"Do you want a glass of wine?" he answered.

Elsa had fallen asleep in the middle of the story about the meanest witch in the whole world. Winter made things up as he went along. He never managed to make the witch mean enough.

"She's too nice!" Elsa had shouted. This was not the first time she'd thought the witch was too nice.

"But the witch ate up the little boy," Winter had said.

"She should have eaten up the little girl, too!"

He reached for the bottle of wine. Angela was sitting directly across from him at the kitchen table. She had made scampi au gratin. Winter could smell the herbs and the garlic and the butter.

"Elsa won't settle for doing things halfway," he said. "This time the witch was supposed to chow down all the prisoners." He poured some wine. "All of them children, of course."

"Don't forget that you're the one who tells the story," said Angela, lifting half a scampi over to him.

"What does that mean, if I may ask?"

"They're your stories."

"No, no, they're hers." He lifted the glass. "Cheers."

She lifted hers. They drank.

"She doesn't want me to tell any at all," Angela said, putting down her glass. "She says that no one is mean when I try to tell them."

"You should be happy about that, Angela."

"Well, if that's the case, what does it say about you, Erik?"

"I just want to be nice," he said, smiling. "I just do as she tells me."

"Pour me a glass, please."

"They're only stories, Angela." He poured her another glass. It was Friday. He pulled over the pan of scampi. "They're fantasies."

35

He couldn't sleep, nor had he counted on being able to. But a person had to try. No one could last long without sleep. This line of work caused sleeplessness, but he wasn't alone in that. It would have been better to do manual labor along with mental work; then the physical exhaustion might lead to sleep. But manual labor wasn't without danger. Trees could fall on your head. Scaffolding could fall. Tractors could overturn.

Winter sat up in his bed. Angela was snoring cautiously, as though she wanted to test him. Elsa's snoring had stopped miraculously, as though it wanted to play a practical joke on medical science. She no longer needed an operation. Winter thought that the ear-nose-and-throat surgeon had looked disappointed, but that must have been his imagination.

He had seen disappointment in Mario Ney's eyes when he explained that Ney couldn't go home. Explained. He had just said it.

Halders had shaken his head outside the interrogation room.

"We don't know enough about this guy," he'd said.

Winter had looked at the clock.

"And next week you're off to the sunshine," Halders had said, following Winter's gaze to the face of the clock.

"That's not what I was checking."

"Then what was it?"

"I wanted to know what time it was."

Halders had laughed. It sounded strange in the brick corridor, as though it had been somewhere else, a brighter place.

They had met Ringmar up in the department.

"Jonas took off half an hour ago."

Winter had nodded.

"His mother didn't look happy."

"How did he look?"

"Guilty," Ringmar had said.

"Of what?"

Ringmar shrugged.

"I'm going home," Winter had said.

His whiskey glass gleamed in the moonlight. It was the only light in there; a beam that reached farther in than the streetlights down on Vasaplatsen did. It was a clear night. Winter thought of Mario Ney when he saw the stars up there. It was the same space that Ney had appeared to long for. There were more stars than Winter had ever seen before. They covered the sky all the way from the southern archipelago to Angered.

He lifted his glass. He couldn't see the color inside of it now, but he knew that it was amber. There were no colors at night, if you didn't count black. And white. Winter could see the white light cutting through the darkness in the room. White. He thought of the white hand. He thought of the color white as a symbol. He thought of it as paint. He thought of the can it had once been in. He thought of a wall that has been painted white. Why had Paula Ney's hand been white? Why had Elisabeth Ney's finger been painted white? Paula's white hand. It meant something. It was a message. White paint. The can of paint. A white wall. Painted white. Painted recently. Where did the can of paint come from? They didn't know. Had they asked . . . the painters? The painters in Paula's apartment. The walls there. Half-finished. Almost finished. Unfinished. What is it that we're not seeing? Halders had said. Winter had thought it himself. Think back. Think.

A white, half-finished apartment.

Think!

Nothing strange about a wall that looks like it's been torn down and rebuilt.

But.

A message.

The wall is a message.

Behind the wall. The white wall.

Some careless brushstrokes over it.

Someday it will be finished.

The white will be finished.

He set his glass down on the table. He had been holding it in his hand without noticing for the last minute, and he hadn't noticed until his hand had begun to tremble. He still hadn't taken a drink.

He got up and went back into the bedroom and picked his clothes up off the chair.

"What is it, Erik?"

Angela moved in the bed. The moonlight reached the bedroom, too. The sheets were very white. It looked like a painting in there.

"I have to check something," he said.

"Now?" She sat up. "What time is it?"

"I'll be back soon," he said.

Winter's thoughts moved more quickly than the elevator did on the way down to the garage.

Why was Jonas Sandler digging at that particular spot in the dirt? At that particular time? He was digging for Paula. Was she a symbol? A symbol of what? Childhood? Lost childhood? Love? Or did he really believe Paula was down there? Did he know that his dog was down there? No. Yes. No. Had he seen Börge out there? Seen him digging in the grove of his youth, in the grove of his adultdom? Was that what it was called? Adultdom? Doomed to become an adult.

Winter hit the remote and his car blinked at him.

He dialed Anne Sandler's number.

She answered after the third ring. He identified himself and asked about Jonas.

"I don't know where he is right now," she said.

Her voice sounded distant and muffled. It wasn't only because he was calling from underground.

"I was going to call you," she said.

"Oh?"

He opened the car door. The light came on inside. He smelled the familiar scent of leather. It never went away; it was like a reassurance.

"I thought I recognized a face out here from before," she said. "Recently."

"Who was it?"

"I don't know. A face. Someone . . . who lived here then. When Jonas was little. Or, maybe not lived . . . it was someone I saw a few times."

"And who you remember this much later?"

"Yes . . . isn't it strange?" Winter thought he could see her face in his mind. Her confusion. "Maybe I was mistaken."

"Why did you want to tell me about this?"

"I don't know . . . I told Jonas. That I had seen him again out here, that man. Recently. I . . . don't know why I said anything."

Sometimes the subconscious doesn't tell us why we say something, Winter thought. Not right away. Sometimes it comes out later.

"What did Jonas say?"

"He didn't say anything . . ."

Winter waited for her to continue.

". . . but I could tell that he was affected by it."

"Affected? In what way was he affected?"

"I don't know. He was . . . affected. I've tried to ask him, but he won't say anything. But he seemed to react to the fact that I'd seen that man."

Winter didn't say anything.

"And shortly after that . . . well, you found him out there in the grove of trees."

Winter drove south, up Aschebergsgatan, past Vasa Hospital, where he'd had a summer job in a long-term care ward during a time in his life when he never thought he'd grow old.

He passed Chalmers University of Technology, turned left in the

roundabout at Wavrinskys Plats, passed Guldhedens School, turned
right in the roundabout at Doktor Fries Torg, and crossed the streetcar tracks in order to continue on one of the stree—

The woman came running down the path that led out of the wooded
area.

Her hair floated after her in the wind, the headwind.

She ran with arms waving wildly.

Maybe she saw him; maybe she didn't.

Winter had slammed on the brakes, in the middle of the track.

He heard a sudden clatter and saw the hill to the left light up with
a bright light. The light turned into headlights that were on the front
of a streetcar that was on its way over the hill, headed for him. The
light caught the woman, who was still running toward him. Winter
saw the shelter and thought, Oh Christ, the streetcar has got to stop!
There's a stop there! But it kept coming. No one was waiting at the
stop. No one was getting off there. Winter heard the horrible roar of
the streetcar, the clatter, the warning signal.

The woman was only a few steps away from him. He wrenched the
wheel to the right, put the car in gear, stepped on the gas pedal, and
lifted the Mercedes from the tracks like a fighter pilot taking off from
an aircraft carrier.

36

Her eyes were large, like the surface of the moon above them. She stared at him through the windshield, but her gaze was simultaneously empty and filled with fear.

She lay on the hood and breathed as if she were doing it for the last time.

Winter quickly folded himself out of the car, took the few steps to the hood, and tried to lift her up. She was about to slide down onto the ground. She weighed a ton, like a streetcar.

The streetcar had braked with sparks and smoke fifty meters down the hill. Winter could see it blinking all its lights in confusion; they were shining on the facade of Guldhedens School.

He held her in his arms. She didn't weigh very much now; she braced her feet on the asphalt and her legs seemed to hold her, but just barely.

"Come here," he said, and he half carried, half supported her around the hood to the passenger side, opened the door, helped her into the seat, closed the door, walked around to the other side, and sat down in the driver's seat. The streetcar was still standing still. Maybe the driver was communicating with the police over his radio.

"Are you okay, Nina?"

She tried to say something, but she had begun to shake violently. He extended his right arm and pulled her close to alleviate her shaking. It worked after half a minute. During that time, he saw the streetcar start to glide away slowly. It had a timetable to follow.

"What happened, Nina?"

She lifted her head and looked out through the window, toward the vanishing lights of the streetcar. Winter released his grip.

"What happened?"

"He . . . he got right in front of me. On the path."

"Who?"

She didn't answer. It looked as though she was going to start shaking again. Winter lifted his arm, but she waved it away.

"The man who's been st-stalking me," she said.

"Who is it, Nina?"

"I think it's . . . him."

"Him? Do you mean Jonas?"

At first she didn't seem to recognize the name. She looked out through the window again, as though to see whether he was still out there.

"Jonas? Jonas Sandler? Paula's friend?"

She nodded.

"Was it Jonas?" Winter repeated.

"I think so," she said.

"Did he say anything?"

She shook her head.

"Did he do anything?"

"I . . . I ran. All of a sudden he was standing there, and I . . . I started to run."

"Why do you think it was Jonas?"

"I saw . . . it looked like him."

"In what way?"

"His height . . . I don't know. It looked like him."

Winter looked out through the windshield. No one had come out through the trees. Nor had he expected anyone to. But maybe he was still out there. If he acted fast, maybe he could catch him.

He suddenly heard sirens to the north. He recognized that sound. It wasn't an ambulance. He could see the blue lights over there now, on the way down into the hollow where the streetcar had been standing. They lit up the facade of the school ten times better than the streetcar had.

The siren died as the patrol car skidded in beside Winter's

Mercedes. The blue lights were still going. Lorrinder stared out at all the blue and white as though it implied a new danger. The shadows came and went on her face.

Winter saw one of the uniforms step out of the car and say something into the radio microphone. The other uniform stepped out. Winter didn't recognize their faces in the nervous light. But he saw that they were two male police officers, maybe from Lorensberg.

He opened the car door and stepped out.

"Take it easy there!" called the policeman closest to him.

"It's me, Erik Winter," Winter called. "Winter from homicide."

He took a step away from the car.

"Stand still!" the other policeman shouted. It looked like he was reaching for his Sig Sauer.

Good God, Winter thought. I don't need this, too.

He threw a glance down at Lorrinder, but she was sitting still, thank God. His colleague on that side might draw his weapon. A sudden movement over here and Winter might end up in the middle of another murder.

He saw a gleam from the weapon on that side.

"Put away your weapon, you damn fool!" Winter yelled. "This is Chief Inspector Erik Winter on an official duty. Who the hell are you two?"

He saw the policeman closest to him turn around toward the other one.

"I think it's him," he said. "I recognize that Benz." He turned back to Winter again. "Is that you, Winter?"

"May I step forward?" Winter called.

"Hands over your head!" yelled the policeman with the weapon. Winter couldn't see the weapon anymore.

"No, no," said the closest policeman. "It's Winter from homicide."

Winter started to walk.

"We got a call from the streetcar," said the policeman. "He thought that someone was trying to drive into him on purpose." He smiled, or at least that's how Winter interpreted it. "We thought maybe it was someone escaping?"

"Escaping from what?"

The policeman shrugged. Winter pulled out his ID and held it high over his head. He passed the first policeman, walked around the car, stood in front of the second one, made sure he had put away his Sig Sauer, and landed one lightly on his solar plexus.

The policeman was bent over in front of him, as though taking a deep bow.

"Were you planning to shoot us to death?"

"Take it easy, Winter," said his colleague.

Winter looked up.

"What did you say?"

"I said take it easy."

"Easy? Who is it that should take it easy here?" Winter looked down at the bowing man. He had begun to straighten up, and he was simultaneously shuffling away to safety.

Winter pointed at the Mercedes.

"There's a woman in the car who has just been the victim of an attack in the woods behind us. In the woods is the person who attacked her. It might even be a murderer who is guilty of four murders so far. Whom I have been hunting all fall. Whom I might have been able to catch if you two hadn't come. I seriously doubt he's still there now."

"How the hell could we have known all of that, Winter?" said the older policeman.

"And furthermore, I was about to follow up on an idea," said Winter. "I was in a hurry."

The policeman shook his head. That could mean several things. For example, it could mean that he and his colleague had done most things correctly. That they had played it safe. That Winter ought to know that policemen today drew their weapons more quickly than they had in the past. It was more dangerous than in the past.

"Should we go into the woods and look for the perpetrator?" the policeman asked.

Winter looked over at his car. Lorrinder's silhouette was sharp against the car window, as though it had been cut from stiff cardboard.

"Yes. But first we need to take care of that woman over there. Take her wherever she wants to go."

He stood at the mouth of the path and watched the back lights of the patrol car as it drove up toward Wavrinskys Plats.

Lorrinder couldn't tell them anything more.

She was finally on her way to her friend. She didn't want to go anywhere else.

A patrol was on its way here, but Winter doubted that they would find anything, or anyone. He had asked the younger policeman how he felt. He answered that he felt tip-top. If you want to report me, go ahead, Winter said. I thought you wanted to report me, the policeman had said. Look me up when I'm back from my leave of absence, Winter had said. After June first.

He walked back to his car. No one else had been seen since this drama started when he crossed the tracks. It was as though they had been alone on a stage. But the show was over, and it was as empty here now as it had been before.

Winter got into his car and dialed a number on his cell phone and waited.

He listened to the voice mail message until the beep:

"Jonas, this is Erik Winter. I want you to call me as soon as you hear this. In case you've forgotten the number, here it is."

He recited the number. He also said the time. The night was on its way into the hour of the wolf.

"I also want you to turn yourself in to the nearest police station. Or to police headquarters. I hope you're listening to what I'm saying. I hope you understand, Jonas. I want to help you. I know what happened tonight up in Guldheden. You can stay where you are and call the police. Or call me. It's over now, Jonas."

He didn't know whether that last bit was true, but it sounded good. It sounded like he knew about everything.

Winter put the car in reverse and backed over the tracks again.

He put it in first gear and the car roared away. He started for where he had been heading.

The building was one of five that had been built at the same time and in the same style. This one was second from the left, and it was in the shadows outside the streetlights. It was the darkest of all the buildings. The moon didn't seem to reach it.

Winter had parked in the narrow parking lot and walked across the small yard. There were no swings here, no playground equipment at all. Maybe they were on the other side. He hadn't actually seen any playground here. Maybe there were no children here anymore.

He unlocked the door with the key they'd been using since the murder.

The hall was dark at first, but it quickly became lighter to his eyes. It still smelled like paint and wallpaper paste in there. It was a harmless smell, as though it couldn't hurt anyone. It stood for the future, or at least for change. It lingered for a long time. Winter had repainted his whole apartment in stages, and the smells were like a calendar. Memory was bound up with scents.

He walked slowly through the whole apartment, turning on all the lights.

The electric light might have given a false sense of daytime, but for Winter it only intensified the night.

He wasn't tired.

He felt the excitement, or the first hint of it. Maybe it meant something.

He stood in Paula's bedroom. The gray wall behind the bed was like a half-timbered pattern of wide white strokes, painted with a brush. There were remnants of spackle. The primer coat wasn't finished. Winter wondered what pattern would have been on the wallpaper that never made it onto the walls. He suddenly wanted to know.

37

Winter left the bedroom, passed the hall, and walked into the living room. Three of its four walls were painted white. The color stung his eyes in the bright electric light. The surface of the three walls was smooth. There was still a sheet of plastic on the floor, gray like the sea.

He felt the surface of the wall. It was smooth as sand. It was like touching skin, naked skin. He drew back his hand. The plastic made a dry sound as he stepped on it. It was quiet in there. It was always quiet in Paula's apartment.

He looked at the walls again, slowly turning around in the room. He looked at the plastic. The door out to the hall. The window, which was a hole out into the night. And the hall, which had received the same base treatment as the bedroom.

Winter went back to the bedroom. The bed stood half a meter away from the wall. The painters must have pulled it out. Winter observed the walls here in the same way he had observed the walls in the other room. The brushstrokes of primer back and forth. The uneven surface. The irregularities were visible, but there were so many of them that they formed their own sort of pattern, which stretched from floor to ceiling.

He walked back to the door and systematically began to feel along the short wall between the door and the window with his hands.

He continued along the long wall, passing the window, continuing on the other side. The irregularities slipped past his hands like pebbles on a beach. There was a beach like that about twenty kilometers from here. It was his. There was a similar one about twenty kilometers west of Marbella. He would consider it his in a week.

The rain began to strike the windowpane. The black clouds had looked like they would give way to the clear sky as he stepped into the building, but now they had come back.

He took his hands from the wall and smelled them. They smelled like oil, solvent, paint thinner. It could be an intoxicating odor. Winter lowered his hands and walked across the room to the bed, walked around it, and started to feel along the wall behind the bed, from right to left. The base work seemed to be particularly careful here, or unusually sloppy. Sometimes it was hard to tell the difference. The light from the high ceiling lamp in the middle of the room didn't help.

He felt something at the level of the headboard. It was a meter from the floor. He moved his hands as though around a frame. Yes. There was something under the crosshatched layers of paint. A square. Five by five, maybe. He moved his fingers around the equilateral surface. He carefully pressed his hand against the surface and it gave a few millimeters.

He looked around for something to cut with. He thought about his keys, but they were too thick.

Out in a kitchen drawer he found a small, narrow knife. He took a pair of gloves out of his jacket pocket and pulled them on.

Back in the bedroom, he carefully made a small cut at the upper right corner of the square. He saw a piece of plastic and pulled carefully on the corner, which was now sticking out. It came away. He could see more plastic, and something white inside the plastic coating. A protective cover. Winter carefully cut out the square on two sides and was able to pull out the object.

It was a flat packet encased in thick plastic, the same plastic that covered the floor. That would protect everything in there. Winter carefully unwound the plastic. It was wrapped in several layers around its contents. The contents were a photograph and two sheets of thin paper. He could see writing on the paper. It was handwriting, script. Blue ballpoint, pale text. It looked like letters. He moved his eyes to the photograph. It was black-and-white. Two small children, each on a swing. The swing set was on a playground he recognized. The children were looking at each other. It looked like they were laughing. It was a boy and a girl. Winter recognized the boy, who was in half profile. About fifteen meters beyond the swings was the grove of trees. The branches were hanging straight down, as though all the wind had died the day the photograph was taken. There was a man halfway between the grove of trees and the playground. He was watching the children. The picture was sharp enough and the distance was short enough for Winter to recognize his face. Christer Börge. Winter saw the photograph tremble. It was as though the branches of the trees had moved. He saw Christer Börge's face; that was all he could see right now. Börge's eyes were aimed straight ahead, as though there were no camera, no photographer. Who took this picture? Winter thought. Was it Anton Metzer? He noticed that he was also holding the two sheets of paper in his left hand. He began to read the writing on the top one. He kept going; it went quickly. There were ten lines. He recognized the handwriting. Winter had read these lines before. The paper began to tremble, too, as the photograph had done ten seconds ago. He changed hands, like that would help. He read the writing on the other paper. It was a bit longer, maybe fifteen lines. He didn't count them. Before he had finished reading, he felt tears fill his eyes.

The rain fell as though the world would soon become a landless sea. When Winter had gotten the car door open and closed it behind him, he was as wet as if he had swum from the house to his parking space. He used the arm of his coat to dry his face. He could taste salt on his lips. It wasn't just water.

The rain sluiced over the windshield as if it were coming from a fire hose. He closed his eyes for three seconds, opened them, tried to blink away what was in his eyes, and started the car.

His cell phone rang as he was driving down toward Linnéplatsen.

There was no traffic on the streets. Sahlgrenska looked dark, as if all the power lines had snapped under the masses of water. Another storm was here, along with the new day. Technically, it was a new day.

His phone. He couldn't get the damn phone out of his coat pocket! His wet fingers slipped on the zipper of his inner pocket. Why had he zipped it? It must have happened when he'd lost consciousness for a few seconds. As he left the house. He couldn't remember how he'd left. Whether he'd gone down the stairs. The cell phone gave a chirp in his pocket. At least they had left a message. He turned up toward Konstepidemin, parked outside the Institute of Psychology, finally got the zipper open, and read the screen.

He called voice mail service: You have one new message. It was received . . . and so on. He knew when it had been received.

A voice as though out of a great roar:

"Winter! Is this Winter? If you hear this, call me."

A pause. Winter heard the roaring in the background, or rather in the foreground. It must be the rain. It seemed to be falling against something hard, like a hammer on an anvil.

"Winter! I've go—"

And the connection was broken. It must have been the storm. A slave transmitter gone to hell. But he had recognized the voice.

It was Richard Salko, the desk clerk at Hotel Revy.

Salko had given Winter a list of employees. Christer Börge's name hadn't been on it. That could mean anything. Winter hadn't had time to check all the employees through the years himself.

Salko had sounded agitated.

There was no number to call. The call had come from a private line. But Winter had Salko's home number in the phone list on his phone. He dialed it, waited, listened to the lonely signals on the other end until he disconnected and threw the phone on the seat beside him. He ran a red light onto Övre Husargatan. There was no one to crash into. The traffic lights must have gotten hung up in the storm.

• • •

His phone rang as he turned onto Vasagatan. It glowed on the leather seat as though it had caught fire. Winter grabbed it without looking away from the street.

"Yes?"

"Erik. Where are you? What's going on?"

"I'm on Vasagatan," he said.

"Great."

"I'm just going to check something first."

"On Vasagatan?"

"Yes."

"What?"

"Christer Börge. I'm on my way to his place."

"Now? Can't it wait a few hours?"

"No."

"Don't do anything stupid," said Angela. "And above all, don't do it alone."

"I won't do anything stupid," he answered.

Maybe it was stupid to pick Börge's lock. But no one answered the doorbell. Winter had given him a reasonable amount of time. He could hear the bell faintly inside. The storm outside swallowed every sound.

He slowly opened the door. There was no mail on the doormat. No papers. It was too early for the daily paper, but Winter doubted that any paper carrier would venture out this morning.

He walked through the hall without turning on the lights. He felt his pistol against his hip. The hall was weakly lit by the streetlights outside, but the lights were swinging so violently in the wind that the light streaked around the apartment in a circle that he couldn't follow. It was like a discotheque in the seventies. The trees outside the window appeared to be dancing.

There were no shoes in the hall this time either.

Winter had been in Börge's hall, and in the living room, but no-where else in the apartment. He had planned to come here with a war-rant, but since he was already inside, he no longer needed permission.

The light was good enough in the living room for him to approach the glass case and discover that the three photographs were gone.

He turned around.

There was a closed door at the far end of the room.

Winter drew his weapon, checked it, walked across the room, passed the white sofa, pressed himself up against the wall beside the door, pushed down the handle, and opened the door with the tip of his pistol. He waited a few seconds and cast a quick glance into the room. He saw a bed, a table, a chair, a wall. He pulled back his head, waited, looked again. If there had been anyone in here, he would have known it by now. There was no one there. A narrow door was ajar be-hind and next to the bed. Winter walked across the room and pushed open the door. He saw something flash on the floor. He used his hand to feel for a light switch inside the door, and he found it. The light was weaker than he had expected.

There were shoes on the floor. It looked like hundreds of shoes. Like a gray exodus, a colony of rats. Winter suddenly felt vaguely sick to his stomach, as though he was about to lose his balance. He had seen some of those damn shoes once, many years ago. They were im-possible to wear out. Somewhere down there in that pile they would still be able to find a pair that matched the print on the floor at Cen-tral Station.

He pulled the closet door closed, walked out into the hall, saw how it turned the corner. He followed the bend and saw the door at the end of the strangely built hall. It reminded him of the hotel corri-dor at Revy. The door down there reminded him of Revy. Everything was starting to remind him of Revy. Winter walked carefully through the corridor. He didn't need more light than what leaked in from the rest of the apartment behind him.

The number 10 was painted in white paint on the door. There was some distance between the digits, as though they didn't really belong together.

The door was locked. He put his shoulder into it, but it didn't open. He took his mark and kicked the bolt with his heel. The door flew open and he tried to avoid falling into it while simultaneously holding his pistol in front of him.

There was only darkness inside. The room had no windows. He could see contours, but that was all. This room must be as big as the bedroom. Who built a room without windows? Had Börge built it himself?

He took a step inside and the stench became even stronger than when he had kicked open the door. The sick feeling inside him welled up without warning. He turned away from the door and breathed heavily. Sweat broke out on his forehead. Jesus God.

He forced himself up, fumbled for the light switch, blinked as the light exploded from somewhere inside. He blinked again, looked, blinked, looked.

The ropes hung in neat loops along the nearest wall. They gleamed with the same steel-blue color as the shoes in the closet.

The workbench below was full of objects. All of them were white. The bench seemed to be made of steel. The objects were reflected in the bench, as though they were resting on water. All of them were human body parts. Arms, legs, heads, a miniature torso. It looked like the reconstruction of a Greek temple, three thousand years after a visit from vandals. Nothing was whole any longer. Winter could see strange molds of wood and metal, as though they had been built from memory, from invisible instructions. But the results looked real. He had seen it before. Now he'd had the opportunity to visit the work-shop.

But plaster doesn't smell. These looked like body parts, but they didn't exude any bodily secretions, or any stench. Winter thought the smell had lessened in the few minutes he'd been standing there, but it was still like standing in a room that had been sprayed with ammonia.

He took a step forward, and one to the side.

The metal eyebolts on the wall gleamed dully like the steel work-bench and the ropes. The wall, too, seemed to be made of plaster. Remnants of rope were still hanging from the large eyebolts. The ropes were frayed at the ends, as though someone had tried to chew them off.

There was a large stain on the floor. It spread out like a deep shadow. It still looked damp.

This was where he held her prisoner, Winter thought. Ellen. She came home in the end.

He felt the sick feeling well up again, like the storm.

38

Winter stood on the sidewalk and tried to get all the air he could swallow. The rain had stopped, but the storm was tearing at the lindens as though it were out for some kind of revenge. Maybe it was a hurricane. Winter held his face to the sky to get as much water inside him as he could. The taste in his mouth from his recent vomiting was still chokingly strong. His stomach still felt like fire.

Winter had seen Paula's suitcase to the right of the large stain up there. He hadn't opened it.

His cell phone rang while he was still standing with his face turned up toward the black sky. He was surprised that he could hear it ringing over the roar of the wind.

"Yes?" he shouted into the handset as he backed into the front door for shelter.

He heard a voice but no words.

"I can't hear you," he shouted.

Suddenly he heard, in the middle of a sentence. The line became clear, as though it had ended up in some part of the eye of the storm.

"Say that again."

"It wasn't to scare her!"

"Jonas!"

He got no answer.

"Where are you?"

"I'm . . ."

The words disappeared out into the night again. Or the morning. The morning was coming closer now. Maybe there would be light on this day, too.

"Listen to me, Jonas! Can you hear me?"

Winter heard mumbling, but he didn't know whether Jonas could hear him. They were like two people standing there talking to themselves on the same telephone line.

Suddenly he heard Sandler's voice, strong and clear:

"I wanted to warn her about him! About Börge! I tried to do it before! I wasn't brave enough."

"I'm standing outside his house," Winter said. "I was in there."

The storm took off with their conversation again. Winter thought he heard the name Börge mentioned again, but he wasn't sure. The voice became weaker, as though the person on the other end were being lifted by the storm and swept away. Winter himself could feel it tearing at his clothes. For a few seconds, it felt as though he would lose his balance.

"Jonas?" he shouted. *"Jonas?"*

No answer now.

What should he say? Could Sandler hear him? Did he understand that he was in danger? Should he ask him to stay where he was? But Winter didn't know where he was. It sounded like he was outside. That was dangerous. But it might also be dangerous for him to be inside. The phone beeped in Winter's ear. The call had definitely been dropped. Winter stared at his car. It was still withstanding the wind. He turned around and saw the black windows of Börge's apartment. Perhaps he could see the light that was still on in the innermost room, but only because he knew it was there. He thought of his conversation with Sandler. It had been cut off, just like his conversation with Richard Salko. Salko had never tried to get hold of him unless it was important, life or death. Winter knew that. He kept the phone in his hand and dialed Salko's home number. No one answered this time, either.

There was one place Salko could be. It was the only place Winter could think of now. It was the place where it all began.

Hotel Revy looked as if it were swaying in the wind. The narrow streets in the neighborhood around the building seemed to have disappeared. But they were there; Winter had driven on one of them until he couldn't get any farther because of two downed birch trees. There were more trees in this city than anyone had realized. Downtown looked like a jungle, like a sudden northern wilderness. That couldn't be on purpose.

He stood on the stairs that led up to the closed, dark hotel. The sign was still there; in the storm it looked even more like a giant spider on its way up the wall. The early dawn colored the sky behind the cracked facade with black and with a dull shade of red that began to rise up out of nowhere. Winter could see the window that belonged to room number ten. He walked up the stairs and pressed down on the large brass door handle. It swung open without a sound. Winter illuminated the lock with the flashlight he'd taken out of the glove compartment of his Mercedes. He didn't see any damage to the lock. But the brass was just as ancient as everything else belonging to the hotel, and its even surface could just as easily be made up of ten thousand scrape marks.

The lobby was cold and raw. It felt colder in there than it did outside. When the heat had been turned off, the cold must have come creeping in, as though it finally had the chance to take over.

The stairs creaked with every step he took. The thick walls kept out most of the noise from the storm.

"Hello?" he called. *"Hello?"*

He stopped on the stair second to the top and listened.

It was quiet in there, as though the silence had taken over for good, like the cold.

"Salko? Are you here?"

He stood up there in the hall and let his flashlight light up all the corners it could reach.

The corridor that led to room number ten was to his right. Winter turned his head and saw the farthest door. He aimed his flashlight in that direction, but the beam of light didn't quite reach it.

As he walked closer, he saw that the door was half-open. The light from outside seemed to be wavering back and forth in there, like the beam of his flashlight had just done. Back and forth. He took a few more steps.

He saw the body swinging in the fiery glow.

He saw a back, a neck. The rope. It was black now, but he knew what color it would be in daylight. The body swung slowly toward him. Winter was two steps from the room. He suddenly heard a cell phone ringing; it must be his. He felt the vibrations across his chest, but they could just as easily have come from his heart.

He stepped over the threshold and saw the shadow of the blow before it hit him across the throat.

Djanali heard the ringing from deep within a dream that she would forget when she woke.

She woke up and reached across Halders, who always slept the sleep of the innocent, for the phone. It normally took more than a telephone to wake him up. The room was completely black; it was night. She fumbled for the receiver for a few seconds.

"Yes, hello? This is Aneta."

"I'm sorry I'm calling so late . . . or early . . . this is Angela . . . Angela Hoffman. Erik Winter's partn—"

"Angela," Djanali interrupted her. She had heard the deep concern in Angela's voice. "What's going on?"

"I . . . don't know. Erik took off . . . tonight. He was just going to check something, he said. And then he called. And . . . and he hasn't called again since."

"When did he last call?"

"It was probably . . . about an hour ago. Maybe a bit less. I tried to reach him a little while ago, but he didn't answer his phone."

"Where was he calling from?" Djanali asked.

"Vasagatan. It's right nearby. I'm so worried. I didn't know what I—"

"What was he going to do?" Djanali interrupted her.

She heard Halders sit up in bed behind her.

"What was he going to do there?" she repeated.

Halders leaned close to her so he could hear.

"He said he was on his way to . . . that . . . Börge guy's place," Angela said. "Christer Börge."

"I'll go," Halders said, flying out of bed. "I'll call people in." He reached for the cell phone on the bedside table.

"What a fucking idiot," he mumbled as he pulled on his pants.

Something scraped against Winter's cheek, but he hoped it was just part of a dream. I don't want to wake up from this dream, he thought.

He woke up. He didn't know what he had dreamed, or whether he had already been awake.

He was lying in a semiprone position. He tried to move his arms, but they were tied behind his back. His feet were tied together tightly.

He felt a horrible pain across his throat, and now he could hear that he was breathing as though his windpipe had been broken in two.

A pair of feet came toward him across the floor. That was his perspective, the floor. A pair of shoes stopped right next to his face. Winter recognized the brand.

His face was lifted up. It was difficult to fix his gaze.

"You finally came, after all," said Börge.

Winter could see Börge's face. It was a face he'd never forgotten, and which he would remember as long as he lived. It might be the last thing he would see. Yes. No. Yes. That depended on what Börge had to say. How long he would take. I've got the car two blocks from here. Soon everyone will be here.

"I don't have much to say," Börge said, smiling. "I'm not much for explaining."

Winter opened his mouth and tried to say what he'd planned to say, but no sound came out. He could hear the hiss through his throat, but it had been there long before he'd opened his mouth.

"I think your voice has had a shock," Börge said, standing up. He grabbed Winter's collar and started to pull him up, against the wall. It felt as though Winter's throat were breaking in two again.

The back of his neck was at a strange angle against the wall. His tendons were already starting to ache.

"But I can say this much: I didn't like it that she left me," Börge said.

He was still standing in the spot where he had stood up.

"Didn't like it at all." Börge appeared to lean forward. "I saw her, you know. Actually, I've seen her several times, but right now I mean that time, at the station." Börge gestured with his hand, as though he was pointing in the direction of the station. It wasn't far away. Nothing is far from here, Winter thought. You can almost reach out your hand and touch everything. But he couldn't move his hand.

"She was going to help the girl leave," Börge continued. "They were both going to leave." He nodded twice. "She was going to leave again." He nodded again. "But it was too late for that this time. I couldn't let them do that. Not this time. Not for good."

Börge crouched down, but he was still several meters from Winter.

"Well, of course you saw her, too. Or the traces of her, you could say. I presume you've been to my place." He smiled again. It was a smile Winter had seen only a few times during his career. "She . . . well, she was sorry. But it was a bit late by then." Börge gestured with his arm, some sort of circling motion. "And now they've left us, all of them. There you go. Call it revenge, call it whatever you want. She did bad things. It's bad to do bad things. She lied. She did much worse things." His eyes suddenly became small.

"They all lied! And who thought of me, huh? Who out of *all* of them thought of me?" Börge shifted position but remained crouching. "They didn't deserve to be able to keep lying. I wanted them to beg for forgiveness for what they did to me. And in the end, they did. They all begged me for forgiveness. Maybe then they weren't guilty anymore. Maybe the white paint helped them with that, too. And led you here at the same time." He changed position again. "But I don't care anymore, and I don't think you do either, right now, do you?"

He smiled again. Winter tried to move his head, but it was stuck where Börge had placed it. He felt as though his throat were about to burst, as though he were being strangled.

They didn't beg you for forgiveness, he thought. Paula didn't beg you for forgiveness, you bastard. She begged for some kind of hope that you couldn't give her. She begged for all the lies to disappear.

"And of course you're going to follow them, Erik Winter. You're going to go away, too, like they did. Call it . . . logic. It will be a one-way trip this time."

Börge got up again and took a few steps closer to Winter.

"Are you uncomfortable? Shall I help you?" He leaned over him and tried to drag his upper body up again, pressing Winter's head to the side at the same time. "Is that better?"

I have to say something, Winter thought. I have to try to say something.

He saw Salko's hanging figure. It was still now. Börge must have set it in motion before Winter stepped in.

Börge followed his gaze.

"You're wondering about that old bellhop?" He looked down at Winter again. "There's nothing to wonder about. He just got scared. He knew a thing or two, and apparently he didn't tell you. Maybe he should have. Maybe he tried, what do I know? But he wanted to see me, and this was the best place, wasn't it? There's peace and quiet here." Börge turned his head again and looked up at Salko. "He wanted some money, but I had no desire to give him any. He thought I had something for him, but it wasn't what he thought it was."

Börge looked down at Winter again. "That's actually how it started. Salko wanted something. You could say that he put some-thing in motion. Maybe you're wondering why it took so long for me to . . . react. Well . . ." Börge shrugged. "It was like the old joker out on Hisingen, Metzer. You've met him, too. Maybe he didn't want money, but he didn't want to keep his mouth shut either. He didn't think it was fun anymore. It was like he only wanted to have fun." Börge's eyes became small again. His voice became that of another. "But everything isn't fun, is it? And when it's not fun, maybe a person should think carefully. Not threaten to rush off and talk to just anyone. He wanted to talk to you, for example. About me! He threatened to do it."

Börge's eyes became larger, and they seemed to turn to another direction, another time. "And in one way he already had. Do you remember the Martinsson couple?" Börge smiled. "Of course you remember them! You and your colleague went out to that place on Hisingen when someone called about a fight." Börge smiled again. "It was Metzer who called, but you know that. And I was the one who was fighting! Although it wasn't really me. I was only in that apartment because it was close to Ellen's. I had gotten to know the Martinssons. But that idiot Martinsson thought I was interested in his ugly wife." Börge wasn't smiling now. He looked wronged, misunderstood. "How could he think that? How could he think I was interested in anyone but Ellen? She lived out there then, Ellen and her fucking bastard child. I kept an eye on them. It was my right. Martinsson didn't get that. Not just anyone would get that." He nodded at Winter. "People like you, for example. Just anyone. You are just anyone, aren't you?"

Börge smiled. He looked as though he was going to say something else, but his gaze moved away from Winter's face.

"But that's enough talking," he said after a few seconds.

I have to say something, Winter thought. It's life or death.

Abruptly Börge walked over to a plastic bag that was behind the door. Winter could see it out of the corner of his right eye. Börge bent over the bag and stuck in one arm. He suddenly looked up.

"There's something special about this room, isn't there? This was where Ellen ran the first night, but you know that!"

I have to say something, have to say something, have to say something, say something, say . . .

"Jo . . . Jon . . . Jo," he said, and it sounded like he was trying to whistle.

Börge gave a start. His arm was still in the bag.

When he lifts up that arm, it's all over, Winter. Then it will be a one-way trip.

"Jon . . . Jon . . ." he whistled again.

Börge lifted his arm. His hand was empty.

"What? Are you trying to say something, Winter?"

Winter couldn't answer. He felt exhausted by his attempts to speak. But the horrible pain in his throat began to abate. It was as if his throat was starting to heal. And thoughts were starting to move in his head again, as though they too had been temporarily strangled by the blow.

The blue lights swept over Vasagatan. The wind tore at them, making them rotate irregularly, like a broken carousel. There were two patrol cars outside the front door of Börge's building. Halders had left his car door open behind him as he ran to the door.

There were already people inside the apartment.

"The door was wide open," said the police inspector outside.

"Is he in there?" Halders asked.

"It seems empty."

Halders walked into the hall. It bent strangely, and he followed the bend. He saw the open door at the far end. He could see a uniform moving in there. He saw a face turn to him. He saw the expression on it.

"What is it?" he shouted, starting to run.

While he was still in motion, he saw the ropes, the metal eyebolts, the workbench, the body parts, the molds. A large stain on the floor, shining in the naked light.

The female inspector was holding her chin, her mouth, her nose. Halders could see only her eyes.

There was nothing alive in this room. Erik has been here, Halders thought. He must have seen this. He must have understood. Did he understand where he would go from here?

There was a can of paint on the floor next to the wall on the right side. There was a paintbrush on the floor. The white paint had spattered in the shape of a fan when the brush had been thrown. There was writing on the wall. The writing was snow white against the grayish-white plaster of the wall:

MURDERER

The word was painted with letters that were half a meter high. It covered the whole wall. The paint had run down the wall and out onto the floor and had become part of the fan.

"Someone was here after Erik," said Halders.

Börge walked across the room and leaned over him. He leaned closer, placed his ear near Winter's mouth.

"Maybe it will work better if you whisper?"

"Jon . . ."

"Jon? Jon? What are you saying? Jon?"

"Jon . . . Jona . . ."

"Jonas? Aha! Jonas! You're asking about Jonas?!"

Winter blinked. That meant yes.

"My God, Winter, don't tell me we have more old friends in common! You saw the photo at Paula's house, didn't you?" Börge's eyes were large now, as though he were the happiest person on earth. "Sweet boy, that one. Like the girl. They were both so sweet." Börge appeared to lose himself in memories for a few seconds. "He got a little worked up by my little joke when he was little, Jonas did. I was just joking around a bit with that hand he saw." Börge smiled, but it was a different smile than before, a warm smile. "That was a hobby of mine even back then. A person has to work a little with his hands, don't you think? Old Metzer didn't think it was funny, but I didn't care all that much what he said."

"He . . . he . . ."

"What are you saying, Winter? Hee-hee? You're right, it is funny."

Winter gathered all the lung capacity and muscles he had to be able to squeeze out a few more words.

"He . . . he saw you."

Winter breathed heavily after his exertion.

"Saw me? Saw me?" Börge grabbed Winter's shoulder and shook it. "Saw me when? When I was here? Hardly. When I was there? Hardly then, either. Here or there, doesn't matter. He came snooping around when I stole the rope from Paula's apartment, but I was already out by then. Those two poor souls clung to each other somehow."

Börge let go of Winter's shoulder.

"He's dependent on me, that boy. Just like she was dependent on me. You read the letter, I assume?" Börge nodded, as though at his own words.

Winter had read it. Paula had written it to Börge. Winter hadn't understood at first. How can you understand something like that? She had written about her life, about the right to her life. She had wanted her freedom. She had demanded it. Maybe she thought that all the secrets would stop then, all the lies. That something else would come after all the silence, something better. She had also demanded Jonas's freedom.

"The fact is, I invited the boy here," said Börge. "He's welcome to come at any time now. He's dependent on me, as I said. I did say that, right? Has he told you anything, for example? About anything? The answer is no."

Winter's cell phone rang. He had forgotten that he owned one. It belonged to another world, another life. Börge reacted to the sound, but only for a second. It didn't matter, not for him, not for Winter.

Here I lie. Or sit, or whatever the hell it is. I sat here myself. I set myself in all of this. I was yanked along. I stopped thinking. No, I thought, but in the wrong way. I was alone. Who did I talk to last? It was Jonas. Was it Jonas? What did I say? I don't remember. I heard hardly anything he said. Too much happened in a short time. The night was too short. I talked to Nina, too. I told her that I was going to Paula's apartment. I did do that, didn't I? But that doesn't help. I wanted to do everything. Solve everything. A complete solution. I wanted it done before I got on the plane. Now nothing will come of any of it. I shouldn't have hit that young policeman. I didn't even ask his name. That was Angela on the phone, I could feel that it was Angela. Jesus! Elsa, Lilly. I should have married Angela. She wanted to. I love you all and I will always love you all no matter what happens. Paula knew. She wrote about forgiveness when she was allowed to write what she wanted. Her murderer wasn't dictating. She wrote what she wanted when she knew she was going to die. She took the blame upon herself. I understand it now. All the chaos that happened in her life was because she was an unplanned child, maybe unwanted. She must have seen, understood, discovered. What did Börge say to her in this room? Did he have to say very much when she already knew? She wanted to ease the sadness for those who survived her. God in heaven. Help me now, now that I understand, now that I know. If my legs had been free, I would have kicked this bastard to death. Now he's getting up. He's walking over to the bag. I have to prepare myself for this. He's pulling something out. Yes, yes, it's a rope; he has enough rope to reach around the world. Can I head-butt him? He has to come close enough to put the noose around my neck and if I can reach, then . . .

Börge approached with the rope. The noose was already made. He suddenly disappeared behind Winter's back. Winter was half lying with his side against the wall. He had started to slide down to the floor again. He couldn't see Börge at all. He heard him moving behind. It was pointless. He was helpless. The only thing he could see was the window, and there was no help to be had from there. Winter didn't know how much time had passed since he had stepped in here; it could be hours, days, but life out there was of no help to him. He couldn't even tell whether it was day or night outside the window.

He felt the noose around his neck. Börge pulled on it. The air began to disappear, what little was left in his airways. Börge shoved him, maybe so that he would slide more easily across the floor.

Winter suddenly heard a sound somewhere outside, like metal

against metal. There it was again. He saw something flap at the edge of his field of vision. He didn't know when he actually realized that the wild shadows outside the window didn't belong to nature, the sky. Maybe not until the glass broke. When Börge shouted. Maybe when the black figure flew in through the window, like a strange, wild bird. Winter's air was about to run out. He had no thoughts left. The last thing he thought was that Jonas Sandler must have climbed up the scaffolding.

39

He heard the children laughing out in the hall. He saw the open suitcases on the polished pine floor. He could see their reflections. Tomorrow they would be off, early tomorrow. It had taken longer than they'd counted on at first, but the clinic in Marbella had been understanding.

John Coltrane was blowing hard and loud from *A Love Supreme*.

Winter got up and went out into the hall and caught Lilly up in the middle of a step.

"Time for bed, darling."

Later that evening he had a short conversation with Halders.

"Don't fucking call me unless it's for completely private reasons," Halders said.

Winter laughed.

"I'm not kidding, Erik."

"I'm not going to take anything away from you, Fredrik."

"There's not much left to take," said Halders.

"How are things with Börge?"

"Forget it."

"I'm trying."

"He says he did everything he had to do," said Halders.

"Not really," said Winter.

"*Do you want* me to remind him? That he didn't get rid of you? And the boy? He did have plans for the boy, too."

"He got rid of me," Winter said.

"If he had, we wouldn't be having this conversation now," said Halders.

"He's no boy," Winter said. "He's not a boy any longer."

"I agree with you there," said Halders.

"I called him this morning," Winter said. "He's a lonely man. Paula had become something special for him."

Halders didn't say anything.

"It's not over for him, Fredrik."

"No. And I'm not planning to forget about him."

"I know."

"And Mario isn't, either."

"I know that, too."

Winter heard the faucet running in the kitchen. After ten seconds, Angela came into the room and sat down on the sofa. She had her morning robe on, and that was just as it should be. Morning wasn't that far off.

"Börge found a way to get to her through the two children," Winter said into the phone.

"Mm-hmm."

"Paula was . . . the center. She was the proof that everyone had betrayed him."

"Yes."

"But it wasn't just that."

"No."

"Talk to you soon, Fredrik."

"Take care of yourself now, Erik, and the family."

Later that evening, Winter was still thinking about what he had been thinking when he was lying on the floor in room number ten. He didn't want to think about it, but he would come back to it again and again during the coming months.

"There's a Swedish church in Fuengirola," he said.

Angela looked up. They hadn't gone to bed yet. Maybe they would keep sitting here until it was time to leave for the airport.

"Do you want to get married there?" he asked.

"To whom?" she asked.

"I was thinking to me."

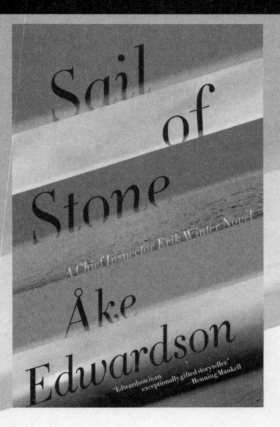